THE DANGEROUS KINGDOM OF LOVE

Neil Blackmore is the author of four novels. After attending university at Leeds and in London, he published his first novels in his twenties. His work has been acclaimed for its radical redrawing of the historical fiction form and the parameters of queer historical fiction. His third novel, *The Intoxicating Mr Lavelle*, was shortlisted for the Polari Prize for LGBTQ+ Fiction. *The Dangerous Kingdom of Love*, his most recent title, was memorably described as 'Hilary Mantel on acid' and chosen as one of *The Times'* Best Historical Fiction Novels. He lives in London.

Also by Neil Blackmore

Soho Blues
Split My Heart
The Intoxicating Mr Lavelle

THE
DANGEROUS
KINGDOM
OF LOVE

NEIL BLACKMORE

PENGUIN BOOKS

PENGUIN BOOKS

UK | USA | Canada | Ireland | Australia
India | New Zealand | South Africa

Penguin Books is part of the Penguin Random House group of companies
whose addresses can be found at global.penguinrandomhouse.com

First published by Hutchinson in 2021
Published in Penguin Books 2022
001

Typeset in 11/15 pt Sabon LT Std
by Integra Software Services Pvt. Ltd, Pondicherry

Printed and bound in Great Britain by Clays Ltd, Elcograf S.p.A.

The authorised representative in the EEA is Penguin Random House Ireland,
Morrison Chambers, 32 Nassau Street, Dublin D02 YH68

A CIP catalogue record for this book is available from the British Library

ISBN: 978-1-529-15743-7

www.greenpenguin.co.uk

Penguin Random House is committed to a
sustainable future for our business, our readers
and our planet. This book is made from Forest
Stewardship Council® certified paper.

With special thanks to Stephen Kolawole, Veronique Baxter, Anna Argenio, Adi Bloom and Zahid Mukhtar. Thank you to the members of the North London Writers Group.

'[...] There is no danger. It is merely a disturbance.'
    'What did he say?'[...]
[...] 'Just the same words – Remember you must die – nothing more.'
    'He must be a maniac,' said Godfrey.

Muriel Spark, *Memento Mori*

AUTHOR'S NOTE

This is a true story. All significant, named characters were real people. Most of the major events – from one angry woman shooting at her unfaithful husband's dog to the eventual, tragic outcomes – are inspired by historical fact.

Some sequences of time have been altered for narrative effect, and some linguistic choices are intentionally modern.

Oh, and Francis Bacon changed the world. And he changed *your* life.

Dramatis Personae

Francis Bacon – politician, philosopher, novelist, creator
of the modern world
George Villiers – the future
King James I & VI – a sodomite & a failed intellectual
Anne of Denmark – a sodomite's wife & Bacon's friend
Robert Carr – a pretty whore
Frances Carr – a lively lady murderer
Mrs Turner – a witch!
Lady Grace Mildmay – a scientist & Bacon's friend
Ben Jonson – a playwright & Bacon's friend
William Shakespeare – another playwright
The Earl of Suffolk – an aristocrat
The Earl of Southampton – another aristocrat
Edward Coke – a terrible person
Sir Thomas Overbury – a dead body (soon...)

ENGLAND

SPRING 1613

ON THE SUBJECT OF HYPOCRISY, SODOMY & ALL-ROUND TOMFOOLERY

$\mathscr{E}$veryone says I am the cleverest man in England. *Everyone*. But in this country, it's a worthless thing to be clever. Which books you've read, which poets you can quote, matter nothing. In fact, such fripperies disgust my fellow Englishmen. (Or, at best, they do not see the point.) Knowledge revolts people, its application enrages them. Because in England, in our times at least, only two things matter: the nobility of one's lineage and the exquisiteness of a boy's face. *That's not fair*, you bluestockings protest. But this is England, where life is not fair, where life does not give a shit what you think, unless you are an earl – or a pretty boy with a tight hole, lolling in the bed of our good King James. This, I'm afraid you will have to accept, is the truth.

And what of me, you ask? Francis Bacon? Polymath, politician, philosopher, all-round know-it-all. (I am being ironic.) I am long past forty years of age, and in those years I have published books on what people call a bewildering

5

range of subjects (then how easily are people bewildered!). Frankly, hardly anyone has read them. I have no title, no great position. I have been a Member of Parliament, a legal advisor to the Crown, even risen to the post of Solicitor-General, but still I spend more money than I earn (I even went once – briefly – to debtors' prison). I am not Baron This or the Earl of That. I have no children, and no likelihood of ever acquiring any. My family, despite its intellectual and reformist connections, was not aristocratic. I was raised by a father who loyally served old Queen Elizabeth as the Lord Keeper of the Great Seal and died with nothing, and a mother who was in contact with some of the greatest minds of the age, but could not feed her servants. After years of hard work at court, *years* of doing first the old Queen's and now the current King's bidding, why do I still have so little to show? I deserve success, but deserving things and getting them are distinct propositions.

When I was still a very young man, I published my first great work, *The Essays*. It was then that men first called me a genius who had invented the essay, but of course, those men have not read Montaigne or Castiglione. If you have not either, just nod and look *as if* you have. (That's England, right there, in that knowing nod.) Then, in my *Advancement of Learning*, I suggested that philosophy might be separated from theology, that human beings might have things in their lives that are not explained by God. (They could have burned me at the stake for that suggestion.) Continental scholars said that I was going to transform the approach to knowledge, create a new empiricism, a rational approach to life in which scientific evidence might actually matter. A new and modern world. I was going to be the great philosopher of our age, those scholars said. All of which stands to prove one thing: *people talk the most awful shit.*

After all this time, I have no money, and not enough power. I remain an outsider. But suddenly, something has changed. King James called me to Theobalds, his favourite palace. And so that was how, one pale, misty morning, I rode the two hours north from London. What had changed was that the King was going to make me Attorney-General of England, the kingdom's most senior lawyer, one of his closest advisors, and – I was sure – I was in with a chance of finally being rich. *Oh,* you say. *Philosophers must not care about such things.* Well, philosophers love the same things as most fellows: money, position, parties, cock. It's just that they make their name pretending that they do not.

On the open fields before the palace were arranged the most august bodies in the land: the King himself, his court and advisors, and the noblemen of England, feathered hats on heads, muskets in hands. It was a shooting day; the air shivered with the sound of guns just discharged. Smoke sifted, birds had fallen from the air and dogs were running off into woodland scrub, snuffling for avian corpses. Away from the shoot, the ladies with their starched ruff collars and high bejewelled wigs had gathered to watch the game. Some wore gloves and carried small, pearl-handled pistols. Others glugged down wine though it was not yet eleven o'clock; this is the way of the court. Around this coterie, the court dwarves sat patiently and buffoons performed, all of them waiting for the inevitable pinches – and punches – that would come as their mistresses became soused.

An ice-pick voice rose on my approach, clear and aristocratic. The Earl of Southampton: the most avowed of all my enemies. He is a glamorous fellow, clever in some ways, one of the first to invest in America, a distinguished and tasteful patron. But he sees no advantage in the intelligence of others, or the possibility that a man could – or should – rise in life. So he hates me. (There are other reasons he hates me, but more of that later.) Know this, though: My Lord of Southampton, he would kill me if he could.

'Look, fellow noblemen, here comes *Mister* Bacon!' he spat, the insult being that I was knighted by the old Queen, but such an honour means nothing to someone of his background. He turned to the Earl of Suffolk, member of the Howard dynasty, which regards itself as a true whiff of England, several notches above our *Scottish* royal family. These two men – very seriously – are my enemies. When their eyes met, Southampton's handsome face glimmered with malice, and then he looked back at me. I bowed to him, most decorous, but then I immediately turned from them. The whole while, he and Suffolk glared at me.

As I turned, I saw the King: James I of England, VI of Scotland, uniter of our island. With his accession back in 1603, for the first time in history, England, Scotland, Wales and Ireland had a single ruler. So now it was ten years since he arrived from Edinburgh following the death of the old Queen, who was his cousin. She had kept him hanging on so long that, when she finally died, standing on her feet to almost the last moment – which should tell you everything that was marvellous and infuriating about her – he almost did not believe that his ship had finally come in. He had waited since he had ascended the Scottish throne at ten months old, the king of nowhere, to become the king of *somewhere*: England. He left for London and never went back.

8

He was not alone in his flight south. About half the kingdom of Scotland followed him to this land of (relative) milk and honey, bollock-eyed and open-mouthed at all they were about to gorge themselves upon. Yet the true prize was not the green pastures of England but the scabby, heartless riches of London. At the time, Londoners had complained about all these Scots coming down here and taking over, but I knew which side the future was on. So I wrote my *Discourse on the Union*, which put forward the idea of a single 'British' state. The King had loved it, and I thought his favour was secured. But quickly, I was reminded of the truths of this country. Under the King, as it had been under the old Queen, the pretty face rises quickly, and the aristocratic title never falls. Everyone else just bobs around, sometimes inching upwards, sometimes plummeting down. But now I was finally getting my reward.

The King was sprawled on a makeshift gold-painted wooden throne, watching other, fitter men shoot birds, a huge tankard of wine slopping in one hand. Physically, he was unremarkable in every possible way – not tall but not short, his body wrought by high living and laziness, but in the way that any man who lives on meat and wine would be. His red hair was frizzy and unattractive and gone brown-grey with age; his tongue was too large for his mouth so that he spat at you as he spoke in his intense yet uninteresting manner; his lips were stained purple with so much claret.

Every day he drinks from waking until he collapses into bed at night, and he eats only meat and candied sweets. No wonder his health is bad. He is not alone: people at court refuse to eat fruits and vegetables, believing they are bad for the constitution. It's chicken and venison, pastry and pies, all washed down with bottle after bottle of wine. How he lives has now, in middle age, begun to take its toll on his body. His gout is so bad, and his feet and legs so covered with ulcers, he can no longer stand long enough to shoot birds. (No doubt, there will eventually be a science of food and health that will explain very many errors of belief and behaviour.)

On that makeshift throne, and on the royal lap, something – *someone* – was writhing and giggling. It was his lover, Robert Carr: vicious, beautiful Robert Carr – as pretty as a bauble, with a heart as black as jet. The King was slobbering red-wine kisses all over the boy's neck, while the boy – who was really a man – squirmed and laughed and sometimes accepted them. The whole court stood around, pretending not to notice.

In case you are one of those types that hears 'sodomite' and thinks 'pederast', let me make clear that Carr was not so much of a boy any more. He was nearing thirty, but it was important that the world continued to see him as a boy. That way, it could pretend that this was some elegant Platonic ideal of the older man leading the youth to adulthood. Carr had been the King's favourite for six or seven years by then, a long time in the firmament of these things. At the King's request, revoltingly, he calls him 'Daddy', for then we can all pretend that they are the paradigm of that thing called father and son. But we all of us know that this is not what is going on; we all of us know into which slot the royal favour truly goes. What the King does to Robert Carr, I am pretty sure fathers should not do to their sons.

All of Europe knew about the King's desires, yet there are some who point to various dreadful (I mean, insightful!) works the King has written to attest he cannot be a sodomite. Oh, yes, the King is a scholar too: a fucking dreadful one. In his *Daemonologie*, for example, he railed nonsensically about how to catch witches. (When he asks if I believe in them, I say, 'I have never seen one, sire, flying across the moon, have you?' and he laughs.) Meanwhile, in his terrible book on kingship, *Basilikon Doron*, he denounced swearing, drinking and sodomy. But here he was, on a spring afternoon, pretty much doing all three. People believe whatever they need to. They shut their eyes to the obvious truth, and find it very easy to lie to themselves. This is how scholars make terrible fools of themselves.

'*Beicon*, there ye fucking are!' the King yelled, turning his mouth from Robert Carr's. He has never truly mastered the English language, speaking instead some hybrid half-Scots. I bowed deeply. He rose forward on his throne, Carr half-tipping, half-slipping from his lap as he did so.

'Sire,' I said, 'you summoned me.'

'Ach, aye!' he hooted. 'That I fucking *did*!'

There is one other thing you should know about Robert Carr. For the last few months, he has been blackmailing me, saying he wants a thousand pounds from me to convince the King that it was a good idea to appoint me as Attorney-General of England. If I didn't pay, he would speak against me, so that the King would not consider me for further promotion. A thousand pounds! He might as well have asked me for my soul. But I paid it. I had to mortgage my country house at Gorhambury, inherited from my father out near St Albans. I had to borrow even more again, and here we all were.

Boom, boom, boom! A musket fired into the air. A dove thumped to the ground, smashed to bloodied bits but still – just about – alive. Its mess of guts and dislocated wings heaved around, its beak arched open, its head thrashing. I looked away, thinking I could puke, and at once saw Carr staring at me, the hint of a smirk on his face. But that face was beautiful like no other at the English court, and therein lies his dominance. That court is a world of diamond-hard lineages into which ordinary people could not break. But fate had handed young men like Carr a specific opportunity: intense physical attractiveness at the specific time that a monarch reigned who openly craved such things. Beauty was their skill, as much as working stone was a sculptor's. And power, in its many forms, was their prize. They want access to power in its simplest, most aggressive sense: riches, titles, control over men and the affairs of the world. Sometimes, they just want the power that comes with the authority of another's age, or access to a cultured man's knowledge and understanding of the world. They want the power that comes with being young and beautiful and desired and they want it from those that are none of those things. This, then, is a story about power. *Nothing else.*

The King has had several favourites here in England, and more famously in Scotland, where among the thin-mouthed northern Puritans, his preferences got him into trouble. But no one has ruled him so absolutely as Carr does. He came here with that half-kingdom of hungry

Scots who drifted south after the old Queen died. At some point between Edinburgh and London, he was befriended by one Sir Thomas Overbury, who is every bit as awful as Carr. Overbury has the meanest mouth at court, and they say that he saw in the then-innocent Carr his opportunity to make a fortune for them both. It is said that it was he who trained Carr to be a favourite, crimped his hair, cleared up his spots and shaved his arse, and taught him how to ensnare the King; that it was he who set up their first meeting, which ended in Carr breaking his leg at a tournament, and the King rushing to scoop up the broken, beautiful boy who had entranced him that day... and every day since. No two Scots were hungrier than Carr and Overbury, and no two have done better among all those who came south.

Now Carr rules the King not with kindness, not even with sex (despite what my spy in the Royal Bedchamber reports about their twice-a-day activities). It's the blowing through of terrible moods that gives Carr such mastery over the King: lightning sulks, ferocious tantrums, sparkling gales of laughter, seemingly earnest declarations – and then sudden withdrawals – of love. The King grew up entirely without love – abandoned by his mother, that flame-haired fool Mary Stuart, queen of idiots; gobbled up by the sharp beaks of his vulture-aristocrats. In Carr, love came not as salvation but as tropical hurricane, as icy North Sea storm. (Note to self: I shall write something on some future science of the mind, in which its practitioners will be able to understand what makes men behave the way they do. If I ever live to see this mind-science, I shall recommend they study first the love of our own King James for Robert Carr.)

His eyes still on me a moment longer, Carr sauntered off towards his best friend, Overbury. The King watched his lover's smooth, egg-domed buttocks sashaying away in perfectly pert silk britches, his furry red tongue moving over his cracked purple lips, growling to himself, transfixed. All these years and nothing has abated his desire for Carr; nothing has even come close to threatening it. Only when his lover was gone did the King's eyes flick to me. He grinned and said, utterly without warning: 'I know that ye tried to fuck my Rabbie once, you know, *Beicon*.'

So here is another thing you should know about Robert Carr. I had indeed tried to fuck him once – years before – and he'd turned me down. He told me I was too poor, too low-born, for him to consider. I did not realise then that he had his eyes on a much, much bigger prize than me. Still now, a rigid fright went through me, hearing the King say those words. 'Majesty,' I said with alarm. 'I... I do not know what you mean—'

Understand this, before we proceed: power is a game. A deadly game. A game of enormous losses and enormous rewards. And in the game of power, you must always be alert to the threat in its moment. When a king says something like this, what does he want? To warn you? To humiliate you? To give notice that trouble is coming? Or just to gloat?

'Sire...' I began to gabble, pressure at my temples, a pulsing against my throat. 'What you refer to was many years ago, before you and Rabbie... I mean, Robert... And nothing happened!'

The King began to laugh. '*Beicon!* I am just teasing ye, man. Do not worry, I am not sending ye to the fucking Tower yet, y'know!' His laughter rained around me, hard and heartless. 'These pretty boys, they're all the same. They think with their pussies as much as their noggins, *eh*?!' He rapped the side of his head with his knuckles, to imply an empty skull, when his was the emptiest of all. I bowed and smiled, and felt my fear recede – for now. But fear is in the nature of proximity to kings.

Sighing happily, the King took a greedy gulp of wine from his tankard. Then he declared, 'Us two, *Beicon*, we are the *real* fucking intellectuals. I want to talk to ye about *intellectual* things!' Then he belched so loudly that a bird in a tree above us took fright and flew off, and some random earl fired a musket at it, missing.

Oh, God, I thought. *Why? Why do people see me and want to talk about 'intellectual' things?* The King is the worst type of idiot: one who thinks himself intelligent. But I bowed; what else could I do? He is the King, the sun around which the rest of us orbit (according to Mister Galilei, at least). He did not blink but gazed at me, through his alcoholic haze.

'Tell me, *Beicon*, what are ye scribbling these days? Some fucking *conundrum*, I should not wonder!'

How I did not want to talk about this. 'I am working on a critique of Aristotle, sire.'

'*Aristotle?*' he cried. Wine spittle splattered on my face. I smiled. I did not dare wipe it away. 'A fucking critique of Aristotle? What is there bad to say about Aristotle? Every cunt loves Aristotle!'

Well, indeed. *Every cunt loves Aristotle*. That's the problem, a problem that has ruined European civilisation. All of Christian thinking in Europe is founded on the work of Aristotle. He created a methodology for knowledge – specifically, scientific discovery – which has been the cornerstone of all correct thinking for hundreds of years. The foundation of his method is the pronouncement of existing, accepted ideas which the scientist or philosopher is then instructed to prove, from which they can *deduce* the facts.

Except *I* have realised it is wrong. And so, I, Francis Bacon, disagree with Aristotle. I believe that rather than starting with the premise and using the data at all costs to prove it, the scientist should start with the data and work up from that, to outcomes that are unknown, ever-openingly unknown. My idea is that the scientist should not assume he knows answers before he searches for evidence. If they looked for evidence and then *induced* answers, that, I believe, could transform knowledge, create the foundations of a modern, *scientific* world.

Science could become a kind of revolution, a tool for the betterment of all people's lives that could revolutionise medicine, technology, industry, everything. This change, I believe, could be the foundation of a new, modern world of ever-expanding knowledge.

I explained all this news to the King and he just hooted: 'What nonsense ye will pick at, *Beicon*! Thank goodness you're clever for you're nae kind of looker, are ye! Maybe that's why Rabbie never gave ye a second glance!'

I smiled at the insult, for what else can one do? (I did not reply that Carr's objection to me was his precise attraction to the King: I had no money, and precious little power, whereas the King had plenty of both. I am too nice to point out such things, you know!) He rolled his eyes around in his head like marbles knocking together. He tried and failed to let out a small burp. The King's attention had moved on; the child was growing bored. 'So, let me tell ye my good news.'

I held my breath. 'News, sire?'

'I have decided to offer ye the post of Attorney-General, *Beicon*. What do ye say to *that*?'

What did I say to that? What did I say? I felt every knotted year of tension in my shoulders release, I felt every waking night worrying that I might have to go back to the debtors' prison vanish. I looked over at Southampton and Suffolk who were watching me with the King, like two bulldogs that had just been lapping bowls of sour verjuice. I felt my enemies' hands around my throat... letting go.

'Thank you, sire,' I said, bowing deeply. 'Thank you, I am honoured.'

'Ha!' went the King. 'Of course ye fucking are!' Then he lifted his tankard up high and called for more wine. 'Wine for me! Aye, and wine for the...' He waggled his bushy eyebrows. '*Attur*-ney-General!'

With me marvelling at my new fortune (minus the thousand pounds I had given Carr), we turned to watch the shooting. The numbers on the field increased. Queen Anne had arrived with her ladies, but to little fanfare. A Danish princess by birth, she was very tall, towering over most of the bow-legged men of her husband's court, with a great fizz of blonde hair on her head and pale blue eyes that could intensely peer at one and yet reveal nothing, something that people mistook for emptiness. She was speaking to her ladies – and then to her dogs – in her loud, deep Scandinavian voice. Most people say that the Queen is an idiot. Or perhaps not an idiot: a nincompoop, a cipher, a tomfool, a goose-egg, a void. Most people say those things about the Queen – but they are wrong. I always liked the Queen and she me.

She was accompanied by her only surviving son, the young Prince Charles. Of the Queen's seven children, only he and his sister, the Electress Elizabeth, were still alive but the sixteen-year-old girl had recently left for Germany to live with her new husband, the Elector Palatine of the Rhine. We would likely never see her again. The Queen's eldest son, Prince Henry, had died a year before. Intelligent and energetic, the Prince had been the hope of these nations, but then one day, a strapping lad of eighteen, he had gone swimming with friends, caught a fever and just died. He had slipped away so fast, everyone was stunned: the court, the country, *everyone*. Each day for four weeks after his death, Londoners queued, a thousand deep, to see his body at Westminster Abbey. Even the old Queen hadn't got such a send-off. The King and Queen had, like most parents, lost other children, infants and babies, but the Prince's death, on the cusp of manhood, was shattering. It was especially hard for the Queen, however. Only now had she reached even the most fragile level of stability. But do not misunderstand: she was tough. Her life – so very privileged and so very neglected – had made her tough.

Just as the shooters, the Queen included, took up their positions, a tiny spaniel ran up to me, yapping at my heels. Carr had given the dog to the King as a gift, and so it was much prized – thoroughly spoiled, in fact. 'Ritchie, *stop*!' the King cried. 'Fucking dog! Ach, I do love him... Ritchie, stop!' The dog did not stop; its teeth were so close to my ankles that I could feel the air whip against my stockings. 'Ritchie, fucking stop it!' the King kept on yelling. Still the dog did not stop. *Do not bite me, you little mutt*, I thought. '*Ritchie, fucking stop it!*'

A musket went off. The dog scampered away in the direction of Carr. There was a moment of silence then loud laughter. I looked up and there were Carr and Overbury, bent over guffawing, each of them a few feet either side of the Queen, who was holding her still-smoking musket. Only then did I notice on the ground the still, dead body of a bird. It was a crow. The Queen must have shot it by mistake. I did not understand, for she was an excellent markswoman. Had something been said to make her miss?

Then came Overbury's unpleasant squawk: 'Oh, madam, all you brought down was a crow, a bird hardly fit for eating. Madam, have you not read Leviticus? The raven is not an eating bird! It is an *unclean* bird! Do they not teach that in Denmark? Or is it the Swedes who scoff down crows?'

Laughter everywhere! Even the Earl of Suffolk was laughing. I did not understand. Suffolk, proud English Howard, despised Carr, common Scottish whore. Something was afoot, I could sense, but I did not know what. But more than that, I thought of the Queen, now just emerging from the horror of her grief. She deserved better than their cruelty.

'Sire,' I began to say to the King, 'I think perhaps the Queen is unhappy.'

The King slurped some wine then licked his lips. 'Ach, no,' he said, 'she's as happy as a fucking *clam, Beicon*!'

I saw her raise her musket and point it directly at the dog, Ritchie, sitting at Carr's feet. *Oh, shit*, I thought. *She is going to shoot the ugly little mutt*. 'Majesty!' I cried, meaning to call to the Queen, not the King. *Boom!* A puff of dirt. The dog yelped. I caught my breath. Then the King, realising what had happened, started to scream. '*Ritchie!* No! Ritchie, Ritchie!' The whole court – all those cruel laughers – fell silent. Carr started howling; Overbury's face was white with shock; the Queen had struck back. The puff of dirt cleared; there was the dog, whimpering, cowering on the ground, not dead. Carr was shrieking like a fox caught in a trap. The King staggered to his gouty feet, yelling at everyone to *calm the fuck down.* His yelling calmed no one. Then, miraculously, as cool as an icicle, the Queen looked directly at me and smiled.

'Oh, Bacon!' she called to me, without a care in the world. 'What a pleasure to see you!' I walked towards her, bowing a little. Meanwhile Carr was running towards the King, still screaming his head off. 'How did you like the shooting?' the Queen asked as I came up to her.

'I thought it extraordinary, madam.'

'The crow or the dog?' she asked with a small smirk.

'Neither, madam. I was thinking more of Robert Carr.'

Behind us, there was bedlam. 'Bacon, you are as sly as a snake,' the Queen said, majestically ignoring the din.

I bowed. 'You insult me, madam?'

'No, I compliment you. I like snakes. Snakes catch rats.'

Finally, without a single flicker of worry, she looked back at the commotion. Carr was crying hot, enraged tears; the King was pleading with him to calm down; the dog was whining; and Overbury looked like he had crapped in his own britches. Momentarily there was a cool smile on her lips, then it passed and she looked back at me and said, 'Did you pay Carr his bribe, Bacon?'

'Yes.'

'*Ha!*' the Queen cried, turning to leave. 'Good day, Bacon. Let me know if you ever want to catch a rat for me.' She gazed at me very directly, and then looked away, returning to her ladies, who gathered around her to whisper and giggle at what their mistress had just achieved.

*

For me at least, the afternoon continued not with shooting and drinking, but with work. Always, for me, there is work – endless, absorbing, exhausting work. I had been constantly overburdened in my role as Solicitor-General. Now that I was Attorney-General, I knew this would only increase exponentially. I found a small, quiet room in a remote part of Theobalds, away from the commotion of the court. There were a few hours of paperwork, then I held meetings with plaintiffs bringing cases at the highest level. The King had already told me that he needed to raise money to cover his vast and glittering mountain of debts. One of my first tasks would be to summon a Parliament to help the country secure some funds to (even begin to) pay them.

After a short while, my loyal court secretary, Meautys, appeared and handed me a note. Meautys is a still, quiet sort of man, who expresses few judgements and thinks carefully and deeply; exactly the sort of person one needs at one's side when playing the game of power. Often he stayed at Theobalds when I was in town, or remained in town when I was called to Theobalds. On the front of the note was a string of letters:

AAAAB BABAA ABABB ABABB

*

The art of the cipher is very important in spy work. Knowledge of it is a great skill, but ciphers are sometimes broken, as the King's own unfortunate mother found out at her trial for plotting against her protector and cousin, the old Queen. I have invented a new cipher language to use in secret communications. This code is simple yet unbreakable. These letters were a name, the writer of the letter. The name read in the cipher, BULL, but even that is not the man's real name, rather the name of the inn where I first met with him; another layer of code.

Some years before, I placed this spy in the Royal Bedchamber. As I have said, he is witness to the most private moments of the King, including that twice-a-day relationship with Carr. Bull is not a good spy, but he is a faithful one and at least spots things that are worth reporting. The letter, also in code, although poorly misspelled either way round, read: THERE IS DRAMA A-FOOT WITH THE REAL QUENE – the real 'quene' being Carr. I looked up at Meautys, and I at once sensed trouble. 'Come on,' I said to him, springing to my feet.

We hurried across the palace to the royal apartment. As I neared it, people seemed glued to the closed door, listening intently – ears to the wood – to the furious shouting inside. My instinct for trouble was never wrong. A voice railed in caustic Scots: *'Ye fucking dog! Ye filthy fucking cunt! Ye lying boaby! Ye duplicitous, revoltin' scunner! Ye said ye loved me, but ye nae love, ye nae love anyone, your heart is plain deid!'*

Do you think the voice belonged to the King? It did not. Entering the apartment, pushing past bodies of courtiers lined up, watching but saying nothing, I saw the mayhem within. Robert Carr was entirely prostrate on the marble floor, slamming his hands and feet against it, screaming exactly as a child might when refused an extra scoop of cream pudding. The King, in full state dress, his voluminous padded silk doublet festooned with diamond-encrusted brooches, chains of office and purple sash, was standing red-faced with upset, bending forwards and begging loudly: 'What can I *doooo*? Rabbie, ach, tell me what I, your daddy, can *doooo*?'

Carr took the longest, rawest in-breath I have ever heard, and every second of it was charged with a hate-filled sob: 'You can *stop* being such an *evil* fucking piece of *horseshit to me*, that's what you can *fucking do*, you whore-eyed son of a fucking *bitch*!'

The whole court held its breath. (Some of us actually remembered the days of the whore/bitch in question, Mary Stuart, even if the King himself did not. Now, *she* was hard work!) And still we held our breaths, for at court, one must look at all times, but *one must not see*. To *look* at the body of the King is respectful, but to *see* what a foolish man he is would amount to impertinence.

I turned and looked to my right. There was the Earl of Derby. 'Ah, Bacon,' he said to me, with a cheerful roll of the eyes. 'Another day, another tantrum.'

'What's going on, my Lord?'

Derby dropped his voice conspiratorially low. 'The King has found out about Frances Howard.' This was the Earl of Suffolk's pretty and adored daughter, a true Howard princess. Famously, she was seeking to divorce her husband, the Earl of Essex, who had never consummated their marriage, contracted when they were fourteen and thirteen respectively. Thus far, she had got nowhere with her petition, for in England, usually, only kings may divorce their wives. But Frances Howard was a girl with determination. And she was a Howard, of course, so even flat royal refusals had not yet discouraged her. As her father, my Lord of Suffolk knew, the Stuarts are nothing but upstarts compared to the Howards.

'What about her?' I asked.

Derby gave me a quizzical look. 'Didn't you, of all people, know, Bacon?' he asked with genuine surprise. 'Carr is fucking her, Bacon! Has been for months, and right under her father's nose!' He laughed. No sooner were the words out of Derby's mouth than Carr began slamming that beautiful face against the marble floor so hard as to draw blood. The King started weeping openly, pleading: 'Ach, Rabbie, my ain heart! Will ye nae take care? I cannae see ye breaking your beautiful *heid*!'

'Fuck you!'

'Will you nae stop, my sweet son?'

'FUCK YOU!'

Then Carr came to a rest, closed his eyes and lay stock-still, as if he were quite dead. The King was hopping around still, his face puffy and wet with tears. The court breathed in as one. Did some of us wonder – *perhaps* – that Robert Carr had smashed out his own brains? (Oh, happy day.) But then he opened his eyes, looked straight at me and a small, malicious smile formed on his lips.

*

That night, I had to return to London; Meautys had already left and gone ahead. By the time I was leaving, the lovers were reconciled, canoodling in front of the seeing-unseeing court. By now, predictably, Carr was sulky but receptive, his 'daddy' indulgent and mollifying of his 'pretty son'. They would not want me interrupting this part of the game (and it was a game) so I did not bid farewell to the King. Leaving discreetly, I walked out of the palace into the night air. It was cold but I did not mind. It had been a turbulent day, filled with surprising events, and I was glad to have a restful moment alone.

In the blackness of the palace forecourt, the horses of those riding back to town tonight were snuffling, the dark patterned with brief plumes of white breath. I walked towards my steed, being held ready by a squire aged about thirty. He was broad-shouldered, square-jawed, not especially handsome but with a certain rough sensuality, exactly the sort of man I prefer. Seeing me, his wide mouth broke into a knowing grin. I stopped to look at him: had I fucked him before? There have been many such men, so many dark places, where faces are hardly visible and names never exchanged. Can I be expected to remember them all? No. But before I could remember, I heard a voice behind me hiss: 'Bacon!' I turned.

On cue, the clouds broke. Silver moonlight streamed down and revealed a devilish vision: Carr. I murmured his name, 'Robert.'

He pretended to look offended. 'Do you not call me by my title, Bacon?' The year before, the King had made him the Viscount Rochester, so I should have called him 'my Lord of Rochester'. But to me, however, he was still the young man who would offer his arse to anyone who could afford it. Carr glanced icily at the squire, then spat, 'He won't *fuck you* after he's spoken to me, so why don't you piss off over there somewhere?'

The squire's eyes widened with shock. Bewildered, he bowed and scurried off into the night, leaving me to catch my horse's reins as I looked at Carr.

'Charming,' I said. 'Once, you refused to let me fuck you, Robert, and now you stop me fucking others.'

He bowed his head, sarcastically. 'I block cocks wherever I can, Bacon.' He grinned. 'But especially yours.'

I held a perfectly beatific smile. 'Was there something you wished to discuss with me?'

'I have asked Frances Howard to marry me,' he said.

I almost choked. 'But she is already married!'

He knitted his brow. 'She pursues a divorce. Her marriage was never consummated.'

Then I realised what this meant. 'And I suppose the King has promised you he will push the divorce through the Lords, this divorce she has been pursuing for years without any trace of progress.'

Carr bowed to me satirically then added a bolt of surprise to his face. 'Oh! He wishes to make us the Earl and Countess of Somerset too!'

I said nothing, rather just grinned idiotically as he glimmered in the moonlight, majestic in his victory. I nodded briefly and turned towards my horse. The squire returned, but now I had other fish proverbially to fry. Now I could understand why Suffolk had laughed at the Queen earlier that day. Carr hated the Queen, and she him. He and Overbury liked to flex their power at court by being cruel to her, even now in the wake of her son's death. The King hardly ever intervened to stop them, and even when he did, all Carr had to do was pout or begin to scream. Suffolk bore the Queen no particular liking, but before, he would have been more revolted by such impertinence: the Scottish *parvenu* mocking his natural superior, the daughter of one king and wife of another.

But here was the trick and, my word, it was a clever one. Carr offered Suffolk an opportunity. His precious daughter was miserably married, unlikely ever to be a mother and thus fulfil her dynastic role. Carr's seduction of, or by, her might have been an outrage but it presented a magical solution: a man who very much wished to fuck Lady Frances, wanted to marry her; and to sweeten the deal, she could stay an English countess too. All that was left was the divorce, but now the King would drop any objections to that.

Suffolk laughed at the Queen because it communicated to the world of the court that power was shifting. He and Carr were friends now – and family soon. Suffolk had not laughed at the Queen that day because he hated her. He wanted the world to see him do it and to understand something: that he was now powerful enough to do so, without care because this new alliance had been formed. The game had moved on. Pity the poor fuckers who were left behind.

I felt only horror: I was precisely one of those poor fuckers left behind. Now Carr was to become son-in-law to Suffolk, Southampton's best friend. My three great enemies were suddenly allies, united in common purpose. They all hated me, and I was no use to them, because I was an honest man in a dishonest game. So where, precisely, does that leave me? Haven't you worked it out?

It leaves me dead in a ditch.

ON THE SUBJECT OF POWER
AND A PORKCHOP

*T*here is a myth that power destroys people, that it makes them unhappy. This is a lie. This lie is told by poets and philosophers, priests and preachers, who do not want *you* to have power but want to have it for themselves. But these poets, philosophers, priests and preachers know that they will never obtain power, and so they sit, curdled with bitterness and failure, making pronouncements such as this.

Wait a moment, Bacon, you might say, *you are a philosopher, and maybe a kind of poet, perhaps not a priest but, in a funny kind of way, a preacher. You are trying to deceive me!* But I am not, for I am going to tell you the truth. Power does not make people unhappy – not one tiny bit. Think about it. If power made people unhappy, they would flee from it in horror and pain. But do they? *Do they?*

Exactly. Power makes men happier than anything else: more than love, than God, than their children. They do not admit this, but what men – and women – admit about their ambitions is worth nothing. People lie all the time, especially to themselves. What power does is put them in control, of their own lives and of others'. That is what makes them happy. That, beyond money, and palaces, and fancy friends, is why they want power in the first place.

*

Leaving Theobalds, I looked up at the same moon that had illuminated the cruel, exquisite beauty of Robert Carr. Now black clouds were rolling across it, the darkness opening and closing, revealing the moon as a white rose in midnight blue. North of London, apart from the odd tiny village like Islington or Hampstead, the landscape is still all woodland or heath. At night, it is perilous to ride out there. There are thieves and bandits everywhere in the English countryside, so known for its violence. Keep your head down, ride fast, and look like you have nothing worth stealing. That night, I covered my head in my customary dun-brown hat and wrapped my body in a huge black felt shawl; my clothes are modest even if my ambitions are not. My horse flew past the dark, wooded outskirts of Enfield Palace, the empty pastures of Tottenham, their shepherds long since in their beds, up and down the Stamford Hill and on through the open marshes of Hackney, where the bodies of the robbed-and-murdered litter the swamps that drain before the city starts.

As I rode, I was consumed by thoughts of how I had started the day in such hopes – of my glorious advancement – and ended it in the bitter reality of the turning of the game. Now I saw not my advantages but those of the new Howard–Carr alliance: of the unlikely son- and father-in-law, Carr and Suffolk, and Carr's lover, the King, and Suffolk's friend, Southampton. Where did I get a look in there? The King trusted me and liked my work, but these things are easily changed. Words whispered in that drunkard's ear, week after week, month after month, will easily sway his mind. The King is a fool, a child, and he is in love – the worst possible combination.

So, the next year would play out like this: first the alliance forms, then it closes around the King, whispering in his ear of my plots, disloyalties and corruptions, and when he says, 'What? Good old Bacon?' they whisper yes, and yes, and yes again, until he starts to believe their lies. After that, it is only a matter of time until the King *wants* to believe the worst of me. Oh, the universe likes a joke – and the best ones are at my expense!

Out in the countryside, I hardly saw a soul. Where the pastures and enclosed farms of Clerkenwell start to break up into hamlets, the city truly begins. I heard my horse's hooves echoing on the cobbled lanes so narrow that neighbours on either side could open their windows and catch hands. I only stopped at my longtime lodgings at Grays Inn just to stable my horse, wash my face and change my sweat-damp shirt. I had arranged to meet my friend, the playwright Ben Jonson, and his friend, Shakespeare, another playwright, to drink and talk. Grays Inn is at the very edge of London, at its north-eastern fringe, but Jonson and Shakespeare always want to meet in Southwark. They never want to drink in London, because the true fun lies south of the river.

Southwark is a temptation that Londoners can never resist. People talk of London as one city but in fact, it is three. Yes, three cities splay out from the river, quite separate in history and identity, and never touching. London, the old Roman city, is where trade – the most important thing in England, the foundation of its power – is conducted. A country road leads the mile or two down to Westminster, the medieval village of palaces, where the only business done is government. Open water cuts off both from Southwark, the only part on the south side of the Thames. There, other kinds of business are conducted: drinking, gambling, whoring, fighting. And the theatre. Southwark, then, is the city of pleasure, or more specifically, sin. So I *had* to go on to the George Inn, where the two playwrights would be greeted as great heroes, and people would applaud their appearance. The people there would not notice mine.

But before getting there, you have to cross the thicket of bodies on the Bridge. The carriage I took got stuck in the throng of other carriages and stalls and people pushing this way and that, in and out the shops and houses along the Bridge. Waiting for the traffic to move, I looked out downriver, the water burnished with lamps on barges, illuminating the Tower beyond. I always shiver a little when I see it, this place of torture and death where the King joked he was not sending me – *yet*. Every courtier fears that one day he will end up there, and that fear is justified. Spies, Catholics, suspected Catholics, royal cousins, royal wives, Irish princes, Guy Fawkes and all his friends, even the Earl of Southampton (more on that presently) have all languished there. On that very night, Sir Walter Raleigh himself had already been there ten years. Huge, black and impregnable, entering the Tower means there is *always* the chance you will never leave it again. And so it is a fourth city: the city of destruction. The carriage started to move, and my dark thoughts shifted. There was Southwark – and its fun – ahead.

Arriving at the George, inside the fires were roaring. Too many bodies had been sitting for too long, afraid of the cold night, so you could cut the hot, stale air as you entered. Even worse, everyone likes to smoke tobacco these days. A thick cloudy fug filled the space, and the sound of coughing. A grey tinge on the tongue. Everyone says how good tobacco is for them, that it 'openeth up all the pores and passageways', and that the American peoples all live to a great age as a result. But if I was to apply my rudimentary science, I would ask you: *Then why the hell are you coughing?* Above the din, I heard Jonson's voice calling to me: 'Well, if it isn't Old Porkchop, back from all his fancy friends!' He beckoned me over.

I cannot tell you how much I love Ben Jonson. He is the funniest person I know and the most honest. We met when he was poor, so much poorer than me that I gave him money. Imagine! Me, giving someone else money, that's how poor he was! He started calling me 'Porkchop' on the second day of our acquaintance, and never called me Bacon ever again. I would miss it, if he stopped calling me it now. Sometimes, I think Jonson is the only person in the world who truly likes me. I mean, there are those who find my company – or my ideas – interesting or entertaining. And there are even those who might think of me as very 'useful' to know, but I think Jonson alone is truly my friend. I do not mind, I tell myself, but know that if I do not, why, then, do I cherish this one friendship so?

Jonson was over in his favourite spot, a cubby-hole next to the back door, where he could hide from, or regale, his admirers as he preferred. Next to him, I saw the shiny top of Shakespeare's bald head. Even though I knew he was going to be there, still I groaned inside. I shall tell you this plainly: I do not like Shakespeare. He has that revolting aspect of the successful writer who asks you – with a genuine, wide-eyed curiosity – why not try to be successful? 'Why not try *earning* some money, Bacon? You know, *for a nice change.*' He says things he wants you to believe are pleasant, when in fact they are noxious. (I suspect that he knows you know that, too.)

As I arrived at my seat, I could see they had been drinking a while. Their eyes were woozily, happily pink. 'Ale!' Jonson yelled to the bar. 'Ale for our mighty friend from court.'

I shushed him. 'People will think I am rich if you keep saying that, and they'll rob me when I leave.'

'Ha!' Jonson croaked. 'No one will think *you* rich, Porkchop. Not with that fucking hat.' He laughed and I bowed ironically, removing said hat from my head.

'How was court?' Shakespeare asked.

'I saw your patron, Southampton, there,' I said.

'Did he enquire after me?' he asked greedily. So I smiled at him, with the edge of curdled cream. Seeing that, his tone changed, into its natural meanness. 'I am sure he did not ask after *you.*'

At last, I shall explain why Southampton hates me. Our enmity – or rather, his for me – is old now, having begun almost fifteen years ago, before the King came down from Scotland. The Earl of Essex – the last Earl, the father of Frances Howard's unpenetrating husband – was the old Queen's final favourite. At that time, I went into great disfavour with the old girl, over a minor matter of law.

(She was one of those bosses never more furious than over minor matters.) To try to find my way back in – for a person in politics cannot prosper without royal favour – I befriended Essex. The Queen, who was in love with him, was persuaded to admit my presence again. Then disaster struck. Essex had been sent by Queen Elizabeth to quell a revolt in Ireland but made a godawful mess of the whole thing and came back in disgrace. Among his best friends was none other than the Earl of Southampton, then very young and even more of a hothead than today. There was talk that Essex, outraged by his entirely deserved disgrace, was going to launch a revolt against the Queen. Essex gave me assurances of his loyalty, and I told her the same. A week later, he launched a coup, which failed. Essex and Southampton were both arrested.

In that kind of mental game of which she was so fond, the old Queen forced me to write the official report of events, in which I was to damn Essex. But she found my analysis too fair and angrily rewrote the report herself. It condemned her former favourite, although he had already gone to the block; it was more of a massaging of history than anything else. Southampton was sentenced to life in the Tower. It was widely whispered that I had betrayed my friends to curry favour with the old Queen. This absolutely was not true. I am guilty of many toadying things, but I was not guilty of destroying Essex. But people get over things at court – you have to – or, at least, I thought they had.

Then the game did its trick and turned again. When the King came from Scotland, he freed Southampton, who at once told anyone who would listen what a traitor I was, what a worm of a man, what a crook, what a jumped-up *parvenu* snitch. The destruction of my reputation was an easy task: I was the outsider and they were the earls. In fact, if you asked half the people at court who hate me why they do so, they would respond: 'He betrayed Essex.' But I betrayed no one. The other half would be more honest and admit: 'We do not like outsiders.' Anyway, the truth means nothing. What men *say* is the truth is all that matters.

Jonson sat back and groaned. 'Why do you go there, Porkchop? Why do it to yourself? Why do you not just write and earn a living that way? Give up all the politics, give up your machinations, and *write.*'

I knew what was coming. Jonson and Shakespeare would lecture me about why was I not writing, why was I not trying to live as a writer? And I would say, it's all right for you, you write plays for paying audiences, when has philosophy made anyone rich? And then they would hold their noses like I had just belched in their faces!

'Because, my old friend,' I replied instead, 'my parents forgot to plant an orchard of money trees at Gorhambury.'

'You be careful,' Jonson said. 'I do not want you getting yourself poisoned or sent to the Tower.'

I saw that his words were genuine, but I just laughed and raised my ale. 'Bacon lives to plot another day!' This is one of my favourite sayings: it has helped me shut down all kinds of pertinent questions about my failures.

But Shakespeare was not done. He gave a snippy little 'Hmm!' then continued, 'I do not understand your motivation, Bacon, doing all this skulking around. You can do what you like. It's not like you have a family to support.' It was that moment when an idiot says something idiotic, but does not yet understand what an idiot they are. I looked at Jonson. His throat clucked with shock and then he gave a great, laughing groan as if that might make things all right. He knew Shakespeare had said the wrong thing, a cruel thing. But did Shakespeare know, or was he just too stupidly pleased with himself? Do *you* see the meanness of the question, the hostility and arrogance? I have no children, so how can I have motivation? What is the point of me continuing my existence, a faggot like me? I flew across the table and made a grab at Shakespeare's throat but he sat back too quickly for me to catch him.

'Fuck your family, Shakespeare!'

Instantly, he looked simultaneously shocked and aggrieved. 'What?'

'Fuck your wife and fuck your children, Shakespeare!' I yelled. 'You say that I have nothing to live for—'

Shakespeare raised his hands. 'No, I did not say that. I asked, what do you have to lose?'

Did he think that made it better, the cunt? '*Fuck you, Shakespeare!*' I spat with such force, it shocked even me. But Shakespeare – who had left his wife to rot in her country hole for twenty years, not paid her a moment's thought since, who would sell his children to Barbary pirates if it meant writing a play as good as the ones he wrote ten years before – kept raising his hands.

'I did not mean that,' he began to say. 'You've misunderstood me.'

I had not – not one bit. 'Then what did you mean?'

'Nothing, Bacon! I apologise! I apologise!'

'Come on now, fellows,' Jonson began to say, to soothe tempers. I turned my face to one side. I felt such anger, and I do not like to show anger; it is a weakness for a man like me.

People say things like this all the time. Shakespeare had meant to shame me: the hot currency of the 'Normal Man'. When the Normal Man says to the sodomite, 'But you do not have a family,' what he truly wants to say is: 'You know that you are worth nothing, do you not?' What Shakespeare did not like was not the fact he said it, but the fact I reacted. If I had sat quietly, my cheeks burning with sodomitical shame, he would have thought himself as wise as fucking Solomon. He did not yet give up, because who wants to confront the fact that they are a mean-mouthed piece of shit? 'I just meant you do not have to live this life, if it pains you so,' he whined. Oh, that was *not* what he meant.

Now he refused my gaze. 'I play the game because I want to, Shakespeare, and why shouldn't I? No, I do not need to have a son who died not even knowing what my face looked like to have permission to take that which you could not even imagine was not yours to take.'

At this, Shakespeare reared up as if to throw a punch, but I knew he would not do it. He was not that sort of man. I confess I said something cruel, in talking of his dead son Hamnet (cheapening myself in the process), and that I knew Shakespeare was punching no one. Jonson slammed the table. 'Enough!' My anger relented, because now I was the one in the wrong.

'Gentlemen …' Jonson repeated. 'Enough…'

I lifted my ale to my lips. 'Let's talk of other things,' I said.

The three of us bristled a few moments. 'So, Porkchop,' Jonson asked eventually. '*Are* you writing?'

'Just legal reports and articles of government,' I joked, in a forced way given the atmosphere. Jonson tapped his ale jug on the table in fake annoyance. 'All right!' I cried. 'Yes, I have an idea for a book.'

Jonson looked at me, suddenly hopeful. 'Your *Novum Organum*?'

The *Novum Organum* was the name of the book which I had been planning for years, where I would collect my ideas about why Aristotle was wrong, how he had affected our civilisation's thinking, and how it could be corrected – the culmination of the ideas I had (not really) discussed with the King that same day. This book, when published, I was sure, would create the modern world I was dreaming of, and would make people remember my name long after my death. But the *Novum Organum* would be a huge amount of hard work. I was thinking of something far easier, far sillier.

'I want to write a fiction,' I said. 'A storybook.'

Now Shakespeare looked quite affronted. 'A *story*? A fictional thing?' This was his terrain.

'Yes,' I said. 'Why not?'

'I did not have *you* down as a storyteller,' he said.

Jonson rapped the table with his knuckles to stop any resumption of bickering. 'Come on, then, Porkchop, tell us what it is.'

I drew in a breath. I did not know why I felt so nervous.

'A utopia.'

'What?' Shakespeare sneered. 'Just like Sir Thomas More? Huh,' he went. 'Look what happened to him.'

I ignored the little sneak. 'I have conceived the story of explorers who visit a world – a utopia – which they realise to be a new Atlantis. As they travel around this land, its rulers fear their presence and what they bring with them from our corrupted world. The rulers of this utopia are philosophers and their regime is fair and wise and generous. There is no slavery. Torture is seen as ineffectively coercive and is banned for being unscientific. Women are considered the same as men in matters of wisdom and intelligence. Husbands do not own their wives but ask them for their advice and take their views into account. There is no corruption and no excess.' I was feeling very modern and moral, saying all this. 'But most of all, the whole society revolves around rationality, and the expansion of knowledge is the goal and responsibility of the state.'

When I had finished speaking, the two of them were staring at me, their faces completely still. For a moment, I thought perhaps they were about to applaud. Then Shakespeare spoke.

'That's a terrible fucking idea.'

'What?' I said.

He shook his head and actually started to laugh. 'What, some people sail off to the other side of the world, find out some boring stuff, and sail home? Where's the story in that?'

I glanced at Jonson.

'Honestly, Porkchop, your idea is dreadful. It is just you mashing your liberal ideas into a row. That is not a story anyone wants to hear.'

I was shocked. I was sure this book, my first ever fiction, which I thought I might name *New Atlantis*, would be another arrow in my quiver.

'All right,' I protested, half in jest – and half not. 'Then what should I write, you geniuses?'

'You should write a love story,' Shakespeare said.

This made Jonson laugh. 'What does Porkchop know about love?' He laughed and laughed. 'Porkchop does not love anyone or anything!'

I raised myself up in my seat. 'I do not love.'

'I do not believe that!' Shakespeare said. 'Everybody loves!'

'Not our Porkchop,' Jonson said. 'He is not a subject of the kingdom of love!'

I laughed too, because it was true. 'There is no reward in the kingdom of love,' I said, 'only punishment. The kingdom of love is a frightening place. A dangerous place. What kind of fool wants to live there?'

Shakespeare looked like he was about to burst into tears. 'Oh, no, it is a *wonderful* place,' he cooed, like one of his libidinous heroines. Jonson and I glanced at each other and burst out laughing, both spraying ale into the air. But even as I laughed, I felt it: the sadness in my heart.

*

So, it is true: I do not love. I learned young that love is not for men like me. How can it be? The old King Henry had changed the law and made buggery a capital offence, and then the Protestants took over, and suddenly things had become even worse for men of my kind. Now, in England, the state kills sodomites, and then takes all your stuff too. Things are not as bad here as on the Continent – where religious authorities round up my kind in great numbers, break open their skulls and mouths with mechanical devices, tear out their fingernails, burn them alive in market squares, asking them right up to the end, 'Do you love God?' – but an accusation is still a career-ending disaster. And for someone like me, with so many enemies, an allegation is all that's needed. I would not survive it.

But before love develops, however, there is desire. And I have plenty of that. Past midnight, I went off into the night, leaving Jonson and Shakespeare drooling in the cups. I did not feel terrible, yet I was quite drunk. I like the night air after alcohol: it burns off the worst of the excesses, and when you work as hard as me, that is no bad thing. I crossed London Bridge, which, even so late, was its usual riot: the earlier flow of carriages had ebbed, replaced with a new traffic, of bodies, hawkers pushing carts, banging into shoppers stopping at stalls to choose a pair of kid-leather gloves or a Papist corn-dolly, diners shoving through the oily lamplight, their arms folded against strangers' backs, warm pies cradled in their hands, or spatchcocks on sticks, grease running down their faces as they ate, then bumping into someone else, their food falling to the ground.

The Bridge at night was always this endless slow stampede. Everywhere there was music and noise, men with bright parrots from the New World, or dogs in Puritan bonnets made to stand on hind legs and dance, or pigs dressed up as children, trained to smoke a tobacco pipe. Mothers and fathers strolled with their children, who in turn squealed, driven mad by candied sweets or already falling asleep lolled on fathers' shoulders, and me, half-drunk, trying to get through it. Why did I not catch a carriage back to town? Why? Well, there *is* a reason.

Once I reached the north side, I started to drift along the wharves on Thames Street. This is not my quickest way back to Grays Inn, but then again, no one comes to

Thames Street this late at night looking for a quick route homeward. Down here, in the darkness, there is a different sort of business to be plied, away from the blazing lamplight of London Bridge. Men come here when they have that itch that is their Devil's mark, the stain they cannot shift. Here, in the unlit black pitch of night, bodies move in orbit, eyes linger on eyes moving past them.

I kept walking on down. Out of the shadow of one of the pulleys used to lift cargo from barges appeared the willowy form of a boy, no more than eighteen years old. 'All right there, sir? You looking for an *entrepôt*?' A clever kind of pun: a port for entry, at a price. I laughed out loud but did not linger. These are not the sorts of men to whom I am attracted: pederastic fantasies of peach-skinned boys straight out of ancient Athens. What I want is a man, with a wide smile, a pair of rough hands – a man like the squire Robert Carr had scared off. At the river's edge, men milled about in greater number. People lived only a street or two away, and perhaps knew what went on down here, but no one came near. The sodomite lives in a parallel world to the Normal Man, and his sinful secrets confer an air of mystery on the most prosaic of places.

'Evening.' I heard the deep, rich voice before I saw the man. I turned. It took me a moment to make out his form in the gloom. He was broad-shouldered and hard-bodied. His black hair was short but the front fell in a thick, roughly cut wave that swept across his just-as-dark eyes. As he was looking at me, his hand ran over his fringe to push it away from his face. This action, by any man, has always provoked me, and it did so now. He asked me if I had money. I lied and said no; he replied that it did not matter. We walked together in silence down the wharves until we found our way onto a covered barge, empty of goods, tied to the docks. I understood at once it was not his boat. As we climbed aboard, he turned and said: 'Are you drunk?'

'A little.'

This man gave me a brisk nod, then his wondrous smile again. 'Because I like to get fucked. I do not want to fuck.'

I shrugged and grinned. 'Suits me.'

We lay in the rough sacking piled at the end of the barge. He pulled his britches right down to his knees, and we were kissing. He reached down to grab my cock. Then, feeling it only half-erect, he drew back from me.

'Is it hard enough?' he asked. Well, isn't that a question for the ages?

'Sort of,' I said. 'I think I can push it in.'

At this, the man's face changed. 'What does "sort of" mean? Is it hard enough or not? Are you too drunk?'

'No,' I said, but I did not actually know if that was true.

Lying beneath me, he lifted his legs, curled them around my back.

'I want you to fuck me,' he whispered; bang, my cock was hard. These are truly the moments of a man's dignity. I spat in my hand, wet the end of my cock and eased it inside him. At first he winced, but then his groan turned into a sigh of pleasure. I began to move and each time I did, he let out a low, intense moan. *Who needs love?* I thought as I fucked him. *I do not love. It's easier that way. This is easier. Safer. Fuck Shakespeare,* I was thinking. *And fuck Robert Carr. I do not need their love. I do not need whatever love brings a man.*

I am better off without love. Love is a threat to me, in the way that it is not to you – you, with your loving spouse, and your houseful of children, your certain hopes for the future. My thoughts moved on as all the time I was inside this man whose name I did not know. I have so many enemies, and they are looking for reasons to attack me. I know the risks. Truly, I do. I do not love because I cannot be loved. It is not allowed. I do not love because I am afraid that one day you – or someone like you – will kill me for it. Do you arch an eyebrow and say, uninterested, 'How dull'? Or do you clutch your Erasmus letters and say, 'Oh no, not me'? I do not know from where the accusation will come, from whom. From you or someone exactly like you? Tolerance, even that of the liberal, comes with no guarantee.

'Oi!' I felt a punch on my shoulder, bringing my thoughts back to the present moment. The man I was *still* inside was looking at me angrily. 'Are you fucking me, or not?' The man pushed me backwards, spitting his irritation, forcing me out of his body. 'Yeah, well. There's no end of men out there who would only be too happy to stick it in me.'

He was getting up, pulling up his britches. 'Fucking idiot...' he mumbled as he clambered along the barge, and off into the night.

I fell back against the sacking and turned my head, gazing out at the starlight on the river. How ridiculous, and how lubricious, men are. Even in the depths of fear and despair, they will come and do things like this. And why? Half to make themselves feel better, and half to feel nothing at all. Men like to feel nothing: it's much safer to have no feelings, only sensations. When men fuck,

45

they can grind their feelings down to zero and replace them with sensation. That nameless man called me an idiot. In moments like these, could I honestly say that he was wrong?

*

Two days later, I was in the Palace of Whitehall, down in Westminster, the city of government. It was a morning of meetings with the King. The whisper was that he was in a very industrious and determined mood. That seemed unlikely. Usually, he is lolling around with red-wine lips by luncheon-time. There was Privy Council in the morning, in which the King's closest advisors and leading aristocrats – including the Earl of Suffolk – gathered around a long table in the meeting room. Carr was present too – a Privy Councillor now, for God's sake. That morning, the Council discussed the election of a new Tsar in Russia, a man named Romanov, and the news of an American settler who had sent a packet of tobacco to the King, saying he had the means to begin growing the crop in full production and ship it to England. The King, famed for his objection to smoking, now wanted to discuss the revenue-raising implications of such a development. Suddenly, he seemed to have no objections to tobacco at all.

As Privy Council ended, the King asked me to stay behind. Suffolk remained too, as did Carr. This was not at all unusual and, whilst sometimes tedious, not unwelcome: it was good that the King wanted me there, confirming my new standing. Wine was brought and cups filled, and the King immediately took a deep gulp and belched loudly, as was his pleasure. It was not quite noon, meaning the workday was coming to its end – for the King at least. I, for one, would be working many more hours than this. Then in came the man that I hate beyond all reason: Edward Coke.

Yes, yes, I know I seem to have a lot of enemies, but let me tell you this: there are different flavours to an enemy. Some people you hate but you admire, and some you like but must attack. (A reality of power, I'm afraid.) But Coke is the most perfect enemy. I feel both loathing and contempt for him; he repulses me, he has an ugly soul *and* he is bad at what he does. What could be more perfect in an enemy?

We have known each other years: both lawyers, both scrabblers, both hard workers and harder plotters. Our careers have circled one another, up and down in the fortunes of government. Over time, through the days of the old Queen and into those of the present King, we have grown to despise each other; yes, he despises me every bit as much as I him. In fact, perhaps he despises me more for at least I am good at what I do. Not a man alive can say I am a bad lawyer. But Coke has grubbed and lied and abused his way up through his career. He brings the law into disrepute, something I cannot forgive. He is known to rail at defendants in court cases, screaming at women accused of witchcraft that they are Satan's whore, fucked by demons in every hole, all in front of their fathers or children, until they are in tears, confessing real or imaginary sins. When he tried the conspirators of the Gunpowder Plot, he refused the men legal representation and told the accused that he would make sure they died terrifying deaths – in the middle of the trial! But I am an excellent lawyer – careful, honourable, knowledgeable, able to bring the results that I want and do it elegantly and within the rules – and so he hates me.

But do you know what secures his hatred of me all the more? He is a churchy prig, a self-declared moralist, someone who likes to lecture the condemned on the love of Jesus Christ as he puts a wooden collar around the necks of the innocent (but expedient to kill) and has them marched to the scaffold. And he knows I watch him, and see him, as both that lawyer and that man, and that I do not need to do those things, and that I know precisely that he does. But none of this has stopped his rise.

Coke has a hideous double charm: he is absolutely convinced he is always morally and legally right, and if you disagree with him, he is equally convinced that you are evil itself. But there is one more thing. The mob loves Edward Coke, because he gives them exactly what they want: sanctioned barbarity. And isn't that depressing? What the modern man, the liberal man wants, the mob does not.

'Now,' the King began, gazing adoringly at Carr, 'my Lord Rochester here, my ain sweet darling Rabbie, is about to get married.'

He had a happy look on his face. As long as it did not affect him directly, the King was not a jealous person. He himself had been married off at a young age, for political advantage, so why shouldn't his favourite enjoy the same privilege? As long as Carr's arse remained tilted in the air, everything would be fine. He wanted his beloved to be happy, so now he was happy. There was a weird, low ripple around the room. Everyone glanced quickly at everyone else. The Earl of Suffolk coughed and looked very determinedly at the tabletop. Instantly, Edward Coke was bubbling.

'To whom?' he cried, as if the King's semen went in one end and then out the other, right into the fundament of some poor girl. *Now, this*, I thought, *this, I am going to enjoy.*

Suffolk writhed in his seat, coughed again and then answered, 'My daughter, Frances.'

Coke's grey beard almost curled up with shock. 'But, my Lord, your daughter is *already* a married woman!'

This was my opportunity to get ahead of the trick. 'Coke,' I said, 'you know that Lady Frances seeks a divorce.'

All of England knew it, and right up until that moment, all of England did not care one fig. 'On what basis?' Coke growled.

I breathed out long and light, looking at Suffolk, who looked briefly back at me and then down at the ground. 'Non-consummation,' I said... helpfully.

'What evidence is there?'

'Well, the girl says that the Earl of Essex cannot get it up! I would think if anyone knows what's been inside her, it would be Lady Frances.'

Suffolk went to growl with outrage, but the King roared with laughter. 'Ach, *Beicon*! Ye know when to hit the nail on the fucking *heid*!' He took a good glug of wine then lifted his glass as if in a toast. 'What say ye, *Beicon*, eh? Can ye give us a divorce to free up the poor wee lass for my ain Rabbie?'

So here it was: my dilemma. The King wanted me to be the lawyer to arrange the divorce to allow the marriage that sealed the alliance that one day would plot my demise. I was Attorney-General, the most senior law-yer in the land. The King would not tolerate my refusal, so how could I refuse? If I did, my enemies would have a clear signal to move against me. All their ancient resent-ments towards me could be indulged by my destruction. If I helped, I would be the midwife at the birth of my own execution. Now you might 'cleverly' say, why not look like you're helping but make sure Coke is the one who lets the divorce fail, because then you will appear to have done your bit but still outfoxed your enemies? And if you said that, I would know that you have not spent much time in the company of kings. Kings want what they want *to happen*. They are not interested in your noble failures. Noble failures, to kings, are exactly the same as tart refusals. So my choice was this: if I accepted the challenge, I might be destroyed ultimately; but if I went against the King's wish, that Carr married Frances, I would be destroyed now. It was like he was asking me, Bacon, what would you prefer, the hemlock or the mercury? '*But ye have to choose one fucker, mind!*' There was no third choice. This way at least, I can live to plot another day.

'We can try,' I replied. 'There are no guarantees.'

Suffolk flashed his eyes to the King. 'I think there *should* be some guarantees, sire.'

The King nodded enthusiastically. 'Oh, aye, I'd prefer some fucking guarantees, *Beicon*!'

Oh, yes, everyone murmured, apart from Coke and I, who actually had to pull the whole thing off. I tried to think of what to say, to keep the ship sailing. 'Well, I think it is wonderful news, Robert,' I said. 'Congratulations to you and to my Lord of Suffolk.'

Carr's eyes lay on me for a moment. He was smiling very sweetly, and his face looked so angelic with its pretty blue eyes. Nothing fills me with greater dread than when Robert Carr is trying to look agreeable. 'Truly, Bacon, are you happy for me?'

'Of course,' I lied.

But then something in him shifted. His smile, the prettiness of his eyes, all disappeared. 'Perhaps then you would like to pay for the wedding, Attorney-General Bacon, as an act of your love for me...' he raised his hand towards the King '... and for your love of His Majesty, too!'

Mistake this not: for one man to pay for another's wedding is no old tradition, no well-worn act of faux-aristocratic friendship. Carr was staring at me, the most delicious certainty in his expression. I could not protest: he had invoked my love of my king. But then to seal the deal with a hammer blow, he turned to his lover: 'Wouldn't you say that would be a kind thing for the *new* Attorney-General to do, to show his happiness for me and his love for you?'

The addition of 'new' was particularly brilliant – I almost admired it – for it reminded everyone that I had only got the post because I'd paid Carr his bribe. Now, publicly, he was saying: I will shake this shit down a second time, too.

The King clapped loudly. 'Oh, aye, *Beicon*! Why not show the world how much ye love me and how happy ye say ye are! Oh, aye! It's *decided*! Bacon will pay for *everything*!'

As an act of sheer malice, having already had my thousand pounds, Carr was now squeezing for more. Not because he needed it, but simply because he could – he wanted to humiliate me. Truly, what had I done to him that was deserving of so much vengefulness? Suffolk's scowl had turned into a wide, malevolent grin. 'Then huzzah for Francis Bacon, who shall host *my* daughter's wedding!'

Oh, yes, indeed, I thought: *huzzah for fucking me. Drink the hemlock, Bacon! Drink down the mercury! And now you can pay for the pleasure too!*

*

In the justice system of England, of course, a judge is also the prosecutor. He hears the case but he also prosecutes it; his job is thus to seek to prove your guilt, in law, and then to decide whether or not he has succeeded. It is a miracle that judges ever find in favour of a defendant, but they do, all the time. And why? Because the case is not strong enough and most judges are men of honour who love the law, as I do. Only bad judges like Edward Coke never find against themselves! A judge applies the law's principles and standards not against the defendant, but against the evidence presented by *the investigator*, a different person altogether. An acquittal is not the failure of the judge: it is the failure of the investigator. It is the investigator who puts the case together, who gathers and chooses between evidence to give to the judge.

And so it was agreed that Coke would prosecute and judge the divorce case, and I would investigate it beforehand. I knew if I let Coke manage the investigation, in no time he would have people on the rack confessing to whatever he liked. I also knew that if Coke was to prosecute and judge the evidence, he would almost certainly not find against himself. He did not have such a morality. His morality was strictly dogmatic. So, do you see how my thinking links up? I will collect the evidence and present it how I wish. I can control the case, produce the findings I want Coke to make. Then the answer will naturally emerge, a ruling Coke will be directed *evidentially* into making. But Coke told me he wanted one thing to reassure him: to know that the girl was a virgin still.

In English law, a girl who sues for non-consummation must prove that she has not been fucked not only by her husband but by *any* man. She must be a virgin. Whatever the logical nonsense of that, the law is what the law is. But we know – and if Derby knew, likely half the English court was whispering – that Frances had been fucking Carr. My job would therefore be to convince Coke that this was not the case. To do that, I had to begin work not on Coke, not on Carr, not even on the limp-dicked Earl of Essex. The person I had to work on was the young woman herself.

*

I arranged to meet Lady Frances at Suffolk's palace on the Strand one afternoon not long after. I was told not to come before noon, as she did not rise early. The Strand runs east to west, connecting the cities of London and Westminster. When I was a child, it was little more than a country road along which the odd city mansion was built. Now little clumps of servants' cottages have grown up amid the meadows that run up from the river's edge. Anyone can see now, after so many centuries, the different cities are beginning to merge into one, vast London.

I grew up down here at York House, which my father had been given when he was Lord Keeper to the old Queen, in the distant days when she was still the young Queen. York House is still there, dilapidated now, unloved by recent occupants. I pass it every time I travel to Westminster. Sometimes I stop and reminisce on the past, my late parents and my beloved brother, Anthony, who died some years ago. I love the place still. It is a symbol of my childhood, now forgotten by everyone but me – because I am the only one left of my family to remember. That day, on my way to the Strand, I stopped a moment and searched for signs of life inside. The windows were broken. Ivy had covered whole walls. Tiles were coming loose. I wondered who occupied it now; it would have usually been given to an officer of state. Perhaps it had reverted to the Crown; I could check.

I sighed and walked on to the Howards' palace, where I found Lady Frances waiting for me on the front steps. I was surprised: she must have been keen to speak to me. She came down towards me and extended her hand for me to kiss, as I bowed deeply. She was barely twenty years old, pretty, fashionable, smart, and she knew that men like me should bow and kiss a hand like hers. She was dressed – by her exquisite standards – quite simply in a pale blue dress, with a matching jacket, all discreetly expensive silk. She had decided not to wear the starched ruff collar, dyed saffron-yellow, so popularised by her fashionable friend, Mrs Turner. Everyone in London wore Mrs Turner's collar these days – I had seen Frances wearing them spectacularly vast, showily ruffled, deeply saffron-golden. But today, Frances just wore a diaphanous white silk collar. I understood why immediately: she was trying to show me what a sweet, simple thing she was. I was not sure she was. I rose out of my bow and let go of her hand. 'Lady Frances.'

'Oh, Bacon!' she cried. She spoke as if we were old friends, with all the sunny confidence of one of her lineage. She did not curtsey. 'To where should we go? Is it somewhere private where you can...' her eyes, large and lovely and blue, glowed with mischief '... *examine* me?'

I bowed again and laughed politely. 'No examinations today, Lady Frances,' I said. She grinned broadly. Her eyes held mine suggestively, intriguingly.

'I am teasing you, Bacon!' Here she was, a girl of twenty, playing with me, the man much more than twice her age.

'I know, Lady Frances,' I replied, in case her father had led her to believe that I might be some kind of fool.

We decided to walk up as far as the open orchards at Covent Garden. It was not warm that day, but late-spring sunshine bathed the wet ground. As we walked, her pale cheeks gained a rosy colour. She was telling me a great deal about a book she was reading. It was about magic, a subject which deeply interested her, she said.

'Is it a demonology?'

'Oh, no, Bacon,' she cried. 'It is a book of spells.'

'Spells, Lady Frances? You need to be careful. If the book is proscribed, you may get into trouble.'

The King was obsessed with witches. Back in Scotland, he greedily burned their bodies at the stake, the Scottish way. In England, though, we hang them. Only the year before, there was a great, stupid killing of women at Pendle in Lancashire. Europeans did not always burn witches – only Englishmen hang them – it is a new thing, a moral craze sweeping the Continent, one country after another. Some say it is due to the anxiety of our age, with its wars and religious manias, but perhaps men just like burning people to death. Remember Occam's Razor!

But Frances looked quite confused: she was the Howard princess, there was no way she would swing for witchcraft, from any gibbet. Her confusion passed; her privilege shooed it away. Clapping her hands together with unrepentant delight, she cried: 'Oh, Mrs Turner, you know, is a great one for spells. And love potions, and all sorts.'

'Love potions?' I asked, arching an eyebrow. Had she used one to bewitch Robert Carr? Of course not: don't you remember? I do not believe in witches.

We entered a little pear orchard. As we walked under the gnarled trees, still just about white with blossom, I told her what I knew and what the King and her father had asked me to do. I asked her about her love for Carr. She spoke giddily and freely about him, how wonderful he was, how attentive and kind. (I thought of Carr slamming his head against the marble floor at Theobalds, screaming that the King was a cunt and a scunner.) Did she not deserve to be loved? she asked. *Don't ask me,* I thought. *I am the last person you should ask.*

The pear orchard was very lovely. Strands of sunlight fell through the pale green trees. Around and about one could see the ruins of the old convent, which gave Covent Garden its name. We were standing in what had been the convent garden itself, until old King Henry had dissolved the religious houses. The pear trees had once been their domain, but they were now, like the nuns, long since abandoned to their fate.

'I have to speak to you now, Lady Frances,' I began, as she was snipping the very last of the pear blossoms from a gnarled branch, using only her fingernails. She turned to look at me and lifted a sprig to her nose to draw in the flowers' scent. All I could see were her huge eyes watching me over the white blooms. 'About something very delicate,' I added. She blinked and began to twirl the twig of blossoms, letting the petals brush her lips. 'I want to help you with your divorce, but Chief Justice Coke is not so minded.'

The flowers stopped moving. 'I *hate* him,' she spat.

Well, I did not say, *don't we all?* 'He will want to perform a test on you.' I paused for decency's sake. 'Do you understand?'

'A test?' she asked, pouting, amused. 'Like a Latin grammar? I am terrible at Latin grammar.'

She was playing with me, of course. It was only slightly annoying at first.

'No, Frances,' I said firmly. 'He will want someone to inspect you. To test your virginity.' Those huge eyes revealed nothing; her amused pout remained. 'By putting a finger inside you... down there.' At this, she straightened a little. I felt sorry but I wanted her to see me as her friend, the person who would help get her what she wanted. (I was not her friend, of course.) 'He will find a nurse – a very experienced nurse, a midwife perhaps – who will come and put her fingers inside your private places...' She started twirling the pear blossoms again. '... And she will make a judgement on whether a man has ever penetrated you.' I watched her thinking about what I might ask next. '*Has* a man ever penetrated you, Frances?' She continued twirling the pear blossoms. 'Put the flowers down, Frances,' I said, at last irritated. (Had that been her design?) She did not move. 'Put them down!' I commanded. The eyes widened, she watched me, then she dropped the blossoms to the ground. 'Are you a virgin, Frances?'

'No,' she whispered.

I paused, let her breathe her nerves. 'Have you known Robert Carr intimately?'

'Yes.'

I know that you must be thinking how cruel I must be to pry so forcefully, but if you do think that, I say this: *grow up*. There are men far crueller than me, and power is our game. This young woman is no exception. *Grow up: you are in the convent no longer!* I can help her; some, like Coke, given the chance, would stamp her down to dust.

'I am going to help you, Frances,' I said. 'No one must know you are not a virgin. No matter what anyone says, you must never admit that you are not. Do you understand? Not even to your father. Not even to your lady mother. Not even to your priest at confession.' (*Especially not him*, I did not say.)

'There has only been Robert,' she said.

I was smiling at her. 'All right,' I said, avuncular now. 'Do you have any maids who are about the same height as you, the same sort of figure?' She nodded. 'Good,' I said. 'I want you to get someone – Mrs Turner perhaps, someone you trust absolutely – to question the maids who look most like you and find one whom she is absolutely sure is a virgin. The girl just has to be your size and shape. If possible, the same hair colour as you, for the hair on her private parts must be identifiable as yours.' Frances's cheeks darkened a little. 'Don't be ashamed,' I said to her. 'Be brave. You will still get what you want if you do as I say.' She nodded and smiled a little in relief. 'But what is essential is that Mrs Turner must believe, with absolute conviction, that the girl is a virgin.'

Frances spoke very quietly, now respectfully. 'And what then?'

This was the cleverest part. 'You will make no complaint about the virginity test at all until the day it is to be performed. You will be in another room, with the maid. You will start to cry. Not shout. Not scream. Not accuse. Just cry. Mrs Turner will come out and say that you are mortally humiliated, to have to be fingered in public like a horse for sale. I will have prepared a set of notes saying it is permitted that you may cover your face during the examination. The nurse, having read my notes, will naturally make the suggestion. You will then cover the maid's face and send her in to be examined, the midwife will not realise it is not you, the girl's hymen will pierce, there will be blood on the midwife's fingers, everyone will be happy.' *Apart*, I thought, *from the maid*, and so I added: 'Pay the girl five guineas for her trouble.' For a maid's hymen, five guineas was probably a good price.

'Five guineas?' she exclaimed, as if a serving girl could not be worth that much.

I smiled at her, hiding my distaste for her patrician miserliness. 'Lady Frances, what this girl will give you will be worth far more to you than five measly guineas.'

A beautiful, suddenly conspiratorial smile spread across Frances's face. 'Oh, Bacon,' she cried happily. 'You are a genius!'

Yes, I thought, *so everyone keeps saying*. I walked the girl back to her family's house on the Strand. Arriving at its door, we found the Earl of Suffolk waiting. Frances half-skipped towards her father, with the light steps of a high-born girl used to getting her way and getting it now. At once, Suffolk began striding towards me, leaving Frances on the steps.

'Your daughter is very intelligent, my Lord,' I started saying. 'I think, with the right counsel—'

Then I saw the knife clutched in his hand. My God, was he going to stab me? I stepped back. He ran at me and put the blade to my throat with one hand, whilst grabbing my wrist with the other. Terror – horror – washed through me, a great, rushing tide. I felt the tip of the knife, sharp against my skin. *My God*, I thought again, *he is going to kill me here, in the street*.

'I do not know what I find more disgusting about you, Bacon,' Suffolk spat, 'the fact that you are such a snivelling upstart or that you are such a filthy *faggot*.'

I pulled away from him again as he spat the last word, but he did not resist and let me go sharply, so that I stumbled backwards. The knife remained fast in his hand.

'You better not fuck this up, *faggot*!' he roared, loud enough for any person on the street to hear. I turned around, ashamed, to see if anyone was within earshot. There, in the palace gardens, I could see the Howard staff pretending not to notice. My shame deepened. 'Oh, and none of your tricks!' he yelled. 'If you send one of your fucking spies against us, I will slit his damned throat too!'

Then Suffolk stalked off. I was left, my heart thumping in my chest. What if Bacon does *not* live to plot another day? I staggered out onto the Strand, and only then, the sweat of humiliation and panic pouring down my face, did I feel the terror fully. I turned back to look at the Howard palace, Suffolk and Frances standing at the door, watching me. I watched them watching me, in all their unassailability, at their palace door, and me left gasping for air, with the scrape of a knife's blade still tingling on my skin.

ON THE SUBJECT OF...
QUEENS

$\mathcal{L}$ ife continues – even with that scrape of a knife along one's throat. What Suffolk did had frightened me, of course, but it also served as a reminder: time is short, Francis Bacon. But time had no compassion for me, for that year was filled with work. There was absolutely no writing. The *Novum Organum* did not take a single step nearer completion. My *New Atlantis* utopia remained nothing more than a bad idea in my tired head. Even worse, I saw no way to break the advancing threat. I had to continue the strategy I had devised: to survive today, in hopes that I would have time to find a way forward.

During that summer of 1613, a curious affair broke at court. Among everyone who chortled and raised eyebrows – but said nothing – about the new Howard–Carr alliance, Carr's odious and disliked friend Overbury stuck out like the proverbial sore thumb. He did not welcome the shift in power one tiny bit. It was an open secret that Overbury despised Frances Howard. Perhaps he was frightened of

someone else whispering in Carr's ear, someone else direct-
ing his best friend's career, when it was his vision, the
beautiful one's rise to power, which had made him rich
and influential. Where, in Carr's new world, would the
friend who hated the wife live?

Stupid Overbury never knew when to keep his mouth
shut: that was how the Queen had ended up shooting the
King's dog that day of the hunt. So, as news spread of
Frances's divorce proceedings, scurrilous poems appeared
as pamphlets on London's streets, openly saying she was
already Carr's lover. A rumour began that Overbury was
the author, and Overbury did little to deny it. He was all
too happy that Frances was humiliated. But I understood
the *real* risk that Overbury posed to her. He almost certainly
knew that she and Carr were already fucking. And while
lots of other people might know, they also knew it better
to keep their mouths shut. That's how you please a king.
(Well, Carr knew another way, of course.) If Overbury
foolishly chose to reveal the truth out of his hatred for
Frances, Coke could challenge the legal basis for the divorce.

To try and get rid of Overbury – at least until everything
was sorted out – Suffolk came up with the idea that he
be given some ambassadorship somewhere. I do not know
who suggested, of all godforsaken places, Russia. Why do
these people always think of the worst solution instead of
the best (say, a few fun years in Paris or Rome)? Overbury
rejected the post out of hand. The King took offence and
ordered that Overbury be arrested. There was little legal
basis to do so, but as no official charges were brought, I
did not get involved in the case. Besides, I was still pushing through Frances's divorce. There would be a conflict
of interest if I suddenly popped up punishing her enemies.

I explained this to the King early on, and he nodded, 'Ach, very wise, *Beicon*!' And so Overbury disappeared into the black tunnels of the Tower, where he died soon after of a sudden fever in September. He was entirely unregretted – even by Robert Carr, apparently. But I will confess that it brought a shiver on my spine. Who at court would regret my fall, if and when my turn came?

One day, in early autumn, with the divorce still unresolved, Frances asked me to come and meet her at a house on Cheapside. This is the very lowest part of London, save for the filth of the east end that stops at Whitechapel. The streets around Cheapside, like Honey Lane, Bread Street and Milk Lane, are day and night filled with traders and hawkers yelling of their eponymous wares. Children stand black-footed on the end of Gutter Lane waiting for a passing man to whisper words to. I wondered why she had chosen to meet me here. Ladies like Frances Howard shouldn't even know about places like this. The house was unprepossessing but tidy enough, with glass windows and a heavy door. I knocked on it. The door pulled back, and a wizened old servant peered around. I gave my name.

'Oh,' he wheezed, evidently unimpressed, 'you'd better come in, the ladies are expecting you.'

'*Ladies?*' I asked, signifying the plural, but the servant did not care to answer. I was shown, not upstairs to the receiving room but, to my surprise, out into a tiny back garden. Most houses in London have something like this, where ordinary folk grow vegetables for their winter stockpot. The door out from the house was so rough that its bottom scraped loudly on the cobbles outside as the servant pushed it open, helping it along with a small kick. The garden was a shabby square of green, lush with pots of herbs and towers of small fruits ripening in promise of autumn. And there, in its centre, stood Frances, luminous, inspecting the plants. Hearing the scrape of the door, she turned towards it and immediately – almost nervously – laughed when I appeared.

'What are you doing out here, Lady Frances?' I asked.

'I am most interested in horticulture, Bacon!'

I walked towards her and bowed. She extended her hand for me to kiss, as she had when we had met at her father's palace. But now we were in a mean little house on Cheapside and, since then, her father had put a knife to my throat. The game plays on, I suppose. I held her hand and merely lifted its fingers to my closed lips.

'Does it surprise you that I am interested in such things?' she asked, not in any way reacting to my changed manner. (She was too clever for that, I suspected.)

'Very little surprises me now, Lady Frances,' I replied, though in fact it did surprise me. 'People are rarely as they appear. Life has taught me that.'

She giggled again a little. 'I find they are *exactly* as they appear.' She held my gaze. Was she testing me, mocking me, or was she just a girl of twenty trying to appear clever before someone she knew *actually* to be clever? She looked up briefly. Sunlight fell against her eyes. Then she looked back at me and smiled. 'Mrs Turner will call us presently,' she said.

'What a thrill,' I replied.

Mrs Turner was a famously mysterious person. She was from Cambridgeshire, of a very modest background, had married and then been widowed by a doctor. This in itself was an achievement for a simple country person like her, but then, after her husband's death, she appeared in London society. There were rumours that she was a witch and had used her powers to beguile some of the greatest ladies of the court. The few known facts about Mrs Turner were stranger than the rumours. Somehow – no one could find out how – she had obtained the monopoly of starch dyed with saffron powder. The world of monopolies – the system of obtaining exclusive control over a trade in a given service or commodity, and charging a fee on every single transaction it produces – is a competitive one. The granting of a monopoly on a major trade – Madeira wine, French lace, African slaves – gave the holder a cut on each sale and so could make a person fabulously wealthy. But no one had ever hungered for the monopoly on saffron-dyed starch. What purpose did it even have? Mysterious – and resourceful – Mrs Turner found one.

She started to dye her ruff collars – which had been white for the fifty years they had been in style – a bright, gold-hued saffron-yellow. It was a sensation. Within weeks, every woman of fashion in London had a maid with bright yellow hands and a full set of bright yellow collars. London could not buy enough saffron-dyed starch. Its price doubled, quadrupled, raced away. Overnight, Mrs Turner, through sheer ingenuity, made herself rich enough to take part in the expensive world in which she found herself. Those same women of fashion queued up to befriend the strange, stylish Mrs Turner. At the front of the queue had been Frances Howard. The exquisite aristocratic princess and the elegant country doctor's widow became the very embodiment of fashionable London.

For a moment, Frances looked down at a huge pot of mint, brushing her fingertips over the top of the leaves, then lifting them to her nose to smell the scent. 'Bacon, may I ask you a question?'

'Of course.'

She paused; her timing was astonishingly, naturally good. 'What do you know about sodomites?'

'Beg pardon, Lady Frances?' I croaked.

Her eyes moved directly to me; astonishing again. 'If they will not accept non-consummation, I am wondering if I might be able to petition for divorce on the grounds that my husband is a sodomite. I have heard rumours that London is full of sodomites. Can you imagine such a thing?' Her eyes lay on me meaningfully. She was entirely Suffolk's daughter, but possibly cleverer than a brute like him. I remembered how she had watched from the steps of their Strand palace, as her father pulled a knife on me. How cool she had been watching her own father do such a thing. No screams of protest, and no shame about it now. But you must realise what this truly was: merely the determination and native brutality of her patrician contempt for someone like me.

'I do not believe in imagining things,' I said coolly. 'I prefer evidence.' *Preferably not any which can be used against me*, I thought to myself.

She paused again. 'You know what men say about you, Bacon.' I resisted any temptation to enquire: *Oh, what do they say?* 'I do not judge, Bacon. A man must find happiness where he finds it.' Then she took a little breath, as though she were sipping the air. 'May a woman not too?'

I was trying to think of what to say next, something that would not provoke her and harm me, when the garden door scraped open again. The two of us swung round, like secret lovers caught in the act. The old servant appeared, indicating upstairs with his thumb. 'She's ready,' he barked.

Lady Frances let out a little hoot of pleasure. 'How thrilling!' She breezed away from me, her question unanswered, her threat lacquered on me.

We were led upstairs to a sparsely decorated room. There was a table and on it were a lit candle, a pot with some herbs inside, a small mirror. Sitting at the table was Mrs Turner. We had never spoken before. She wore a black dress, exquisitely stitched, expensive but not showy, and her ruff collar and long cuffs were her trademark saffron, dyed expertly. The effect was of sunlight miraculously appearing at night.

Watching me as I entered, her eyes were liquid with intelligence and her mouth pursed with amusement, though what amused her was not clear. Me, perhaps?

'Mister Bacon, welcome,' she said. Her accent was Cambridgeshire through and through, that soft Anglian burr, but her manner was as stately as that of a French duchess. 'Please sit, will you?' She held my eyes as I sat, and I held hers. I am not afraid of such things. I am an investigator, after all.

When the three of us were seated, Mrs Turner took a long breath as one does after a cleansing thought.

'Ladies, are we here for a spell-casting?'

'Mrs Turner is the very, very best, Bacon,' Frances gushed.

'Do you object, Mister Bacon, to spell work?' Mrs Turner asked.

In fact, I do not. I am a scientist, so I am prepared to see any phenomena at work. Who knows what works and what does not until it is tested? 'I would be very interested to see it, Mrs Turner,' I said noncommittally.

She nodded just as coolly. 'This, then, is a vanishing spell. It is called the Banishing Mirror.'

'Oh, excellent!' Frances cried, turning to me. 'Whom do you wish to banish, Bacon?'

'Shh!' Mrs Turner raised a finger in warning. 'You must not say the name. You must write it down.' There were scraps of paper and pieces of charcoal on the table too. 'Write it down, fold the paper up and give it to me, and later, I will burn the paper on the candle, so no one will know. The person whom you despise will vanish from your life, and will no longer oppose your plans, whatever it is you wish.'

Frances picked up her charcoal and at once wrote down a name, covering her work with her hand like a schoolchild. But I could see that she had written five letters and, even though I could not read it, it was not hard to guess whom she named: E-S-S-E-X, her fuckless husband. I did not have to think whom I wanted to vanish, but I also knew I could not write it down so plainly. I wrote quickly, determinedly.

Mrs Turner raised the mirror. 'Now, each in turn, you must pick some mugwort from the pot. Then place your folded paper on the table with the mugwort on top, and put the mirror face down over it. Finally, repeat these words: *Now you cannot see me, no longer do you hear me, no more will you want me, so finally set me free.*' She chanted the words so solemnly, I had to suppress a laugh. 'And then I shall take the paper and burn it in the candle. I will read the name you wrote down, but not speak it. Silence will make the spell stronger – if someone is banished, they must never be heard from again.'

We did as instructed, and began to chant the spell. I stumbled over the words, but Frances breezed through it – evidently not her first time. She handed Mrs Turner her slip; her friend read the name, nodding. But when I gave Mrs Turner mine, she looked confused. What the hell did AAABB – AAAAA – BAAAB – BAAAB mean? If you knew my cipher, you'd be able to read what I'd intended: 'Carr'. But Mrs Turner wrinkled up her nose, squinted her eyes, and still it made no sense. Her eyes lifted to mine briefly, annoyed. She burned the paper slips, and we all took a breath. It was over.

When the spell work was done, Mrs Turner's manner changed at once into that of cheerful London host. She asked if we would take some sweet cakes or drink some sack-wine with her. The wine came in elegant little crystal glasses – the very, very latest thing, very expensive too – and we sat and chatted, mainly about court gossip and the talk of who was rising and who was falling, with neither my name nor Robert Carr's mentioned. I kept my conversation very careful whilst laughing happily at theirs. I play a game, and it is not one for fools. After half an hour or so, I decided that there was nothing more of value and that it was time to go.

I got to my feet: 'Ladies, thank you for inviting me here, but I truly have to be on my way.' I raised my hands in a weary shrug. 'Meetings. I have so many meetings!'

'Oh, no!' Frances cried half-heartedly, remaining seated.

Mrs Turner stood up and said that she would show me out, revealing her lack of breeding. It would never have occurred to Frances to show anyone out: that's what servants are for. Mrs Turner held her large, hooped dress to squeeze down the narrow stairs. When we'd reached the bottom, she said to me, quite cheerfully, 'I suspect, Mister Bacon, you do not hold with country ways.'

She opened the front door and I stepped outside.

'Country ways, Mrs Turner?' I asked, pretending I hadn't grasped her meaning.

She looked at me, amusement grazing her lips. 'Frances,' she used her first name, a very great privilege, 'she is a great believer in my spells. They have helped her very much. Hopefully, this will work too.'

'Hopefully,' I said neutrally. 'To be honest, I am not sure why she wanted me to come.'

'Aren't you?' she asked, then paused. There was a moment of heavy silence. 'I could not read the name on your paper,' she continued, still watching me intently.

'It was written in code.'

She tilted her chin, peering at me. 'I see. But not telling me the name won't help the spell.'

'I'll take my chances, Mrs Turner.' I bowed. 'After all, the name Lady Frances wrote was plain to me, so I do not think there was much confidentiality.' Mrs Turner frowned. 'Five letters,' I said. 'It's not hard to work out who she meant.'

'Who?' she asked, with an arched brow.

'Well, Essex, the man she wants to divorce.'

Mrs Turner seemed amused. 'Mister Bacon, everyone says how clever you are. But suddenly, you seem quite, forgive me, *naive*.' The mood had changed. 'There are other people with five-letter names.'

Our eyes were locked together. 'James?' I murmured. 'She wants the King to vanish.' So she would have Carr to herself.

Mrs Turner pursed her lips as if to say, *Gosh, aren't you stupid?* (Me, of all people!) 'Who else has a five-letter name, Mister *Bacon*?'

'I do,' I replied, with the soft, revelatory hush that her emphasis had craved. 'I have a five-letter name. She wants me to vanish?'

Mrs Turner laughed and started to shut her front door. 'Good day, Mister Bacon. I hope we meet again!' *IF*

– *YOU – DO – NOT – VANISH – FIRST*. I put my hand up to stop her closing the door.

'You are an intriguing creature, Mrs Turner.' I rarely feel the weight of someone else's intelligence, but I did hers, not least because it was so different to mine. She was uneducated, unlike me, and yet she was now rich (yes, also unlike me). She had no birth to her at all, and yet the entire world was fascinated by Mrs Turner and clamoured to be her friend. All I had was Jonson – and, at a push, Meautys. 'I would like to meet you again one day,' I said. 'I feel we could be friends. We are both outsiders.'

Her eyes widened with mischievous delight. 'Oh, Mister Bacon, how funny you are!' she cried. 'You are no outsider. With your education, your career, and your access to the King, and your country house, and your ever-so-decent mother and father – the Lord Keeper, no less! How can you possibly think you are an outsider? Ha! I am an actual outsider, a country girl from Cambridgeshire made good. You, Mister Bacon, you do not even begin to know what being an outsider is! Oh, men's *vaaan-ity*!' she cried, satirically emphasising her own accent. 'It's never-fucking-ending!'

Laughing, she made to shut her door. I put my hand up again, to stop her once more, and now she looked annoyed. 'I do not want to be your friend, Mister Bacon!' she spat. 'I have friends, and much better ones than you!' Then she slammed the door in my face, making me step back. In a second, I heard it bolting from inside.

*

Autumn came and went. Coke accepted the outcome of the virginity test, heard the legal arguments about the

73

Essex marriage and, in due course, ruled in favour of the divorce. The news was received with rapture by the King, who said, at last, his darling sweetheart Rabbie was going to be a grown-up man and husband, and the wedding was scheduled for Christmas. Everything had gone superlatively well. Overbury was all but forgotten. Coke, to my irritation, was promoted to Chief Justice for *his* success in the matter, as presiding judge. (I was just the investigator. Do you *see* how it works?) Then, one day, in front of half the court, Carr loudly remembered how, at Privy Council, I had 'offered' to pay for the wedding. 'Oh, aye,' said the King, 'and ye better put on a good show, *Beicon*! This cannae be no half-*baked* affair!' I gave His Majesty my best rictus grin. 'Of course, sire,' I drawled. It felt like there was a knife stuck in my throat.

The cost of the wedding would wipe out just about every penny I had earned that whole year – dwarfing Carr's bribe. I reckoned it would cost me two thousand pounds, a staggering sum. Suffolk sarcastically offered to buy my house at Gorhambury from me if I was 'short'. Now you must think I felt very aggrieved about all this, and I did, but my paying for the wedding bought me more time. It was actually a misstep caused by Carr's base spitefulness. Well, that's what you'd think if you were looking on the bright side...

I had imagined the King would prefer the wedding to be held at Theobalds, away from London's nosey, resentful eyes – but alas, it was to be at Whitehall, in the Chapel Royal itself. That would drive up both the expense and the attention. But the King was quite sure that London would want to celebrate 'our good news'. In reality, outraged pamphlets flew around the city's streets, and Puritan preachers railed about fornicating whores stepping where our saintliest queens once stepped. The preachers were bungled off to prison and had their tongues torn out. Guess who bloodily oversaw their cases? Edward Coke.

The days got colder and shorter, kissing boughs of mistletoe were hung to celebrate Christmas, and the day of the wedding arrived. The Chapel Royal was covered in white and yellow flowers – and I had intimate knowledge of precisely how much every single bloom cost, much to my disgust. Now and then lone petals fell from the displays and I would count how much of my life's savings was falling gently to the ground: fractions of shillings, halves of pennies, the full unfettered cost of my humiliation. I was not alone in that humiliation. The King was ecstatic, somewhere between a not-so-proud father and the bride herself. I thought of him up there, in white veil and virginal blush. He would never have been happier than to slip Robert Carr's ring on his finger. The King invested the happy couple as Earl and Countess of Somerset, just as Carr had told me he would that first night outside Theobalds.

The wedding reception took place in the fine new Banqueting House adjoining the Chapel. At the top table sat the main party – the King and Carr, Carr's new wife, her parents, their faces half-thrilled, half-ashamed, Mrs Turner (who avoided my gaze), the Earl of Southampton, and such. I had to sit among the rank-and-file guests, and at a wedding *for which I was paying*! With every dish that was brought to me, the poor dead animal at its centre seemed to turn its blank head to me and whisper: 'Bacon, don't you know, you're going to get your head chopped off?' A quarter of stag, preserved in Breton salt, Indian peppercorns and Sumatran cloves: 'Not today, Master Bacon, sir, but *soon*!'

A chicken stuffed with a pheasant and decorated with gilded plums: 'You'll be off to the Tower, Bacon, and like Overbury, you'll die of the damp! *Cluck, cluck, cluck!*'

To everyone's surprise, the Queen had a wedding gift for the new couple: an intricate masque. The King had the cheek to say it was a reflection of the happiness of their own marriage! You might think it unexpected that she should offer such a thing, and that was precisely why it was so intriguing.

Everyone loves a masque. But people ask, what is a masque? Is it a play? No, people like to respond, but there is a set design. Musicians play pieces especially written by the country's finest composers, but it is not a concert. Those on stage are not actors but courtiers. Although, of course, courtiers are always actors. (Oh, stop it, Bacon, you're embarrassing yourself.) A fanfare sounded and a team of royal buglers led the way, followed by more musicians, already playing lutes and viols and drums. The music, soothing at first, abruptly became louder and faster, transforming into a pounding, approaching battalion. When the din rose so loud that some people put their fingers in their ears, in rushed the dancers: five women led by the Queen herself, and five men. But the women were not dressed prettily or demurely – they were dressed as warriors, brandishing stagecraft swords and fake gold chestplates. The fury in their eyes was real: they were the Amazons of ancient myth.

The drums and viols thumped and screeched. The warrior-women ran to the front of the court, brilliant and attacking. People nearest them jumped back and gasped. A kind of war dance was taking place: women against men. Despite their effeminacy, the men rushed like giants against their opponents. The women – who seemed more masculine than the men – raised their swords high, bared their teeth. A tidal drama of swordplay played out back and forth until the men seemed on the verge of conceding defeat. But then, unexpectedly, the women relented. Pushed back against a wall, they seemed trapped, about to be killed. The music fell silent, and one of the women began to sing in a pure, sweet, sad voice. Hearing the beauty and emotion of her melody, her opponents stopped to listen, entranced.

It was a trick. Suddenly, the drums became a cavalcade of noise. The Amazons rushed forwards, hacking with their play-swords, the men falling to their knees, ostentatiously but silently screaming. They drew their swords to the men's necks and dramatically slit their throats. The music stopped and the Queen stood among her Amazons, breathing hard and proud, the victor. Her eyes passed over the crowd, which was too drunk or distracted or immediately dismissive of her that it hardly seemed to respond. Did it not see what I had seen?

The Queen had come to her enemy's wedding – her husband's male lover, no less – and danced for him a war of the sexes, in which women triumphed. I looked at the King, unsure if he would burst out laughing or roar with rage. But then I saw the sight of him, repeatedly pecking the new Earl of Somerset on the mouth, at the latter's own wedding feast, whilst the bride and her parents sat alongside, furious smiles plastered on their faces. I turned to the Queen, who blinked once then called her ladies to withdraw. Did she feel defeat? The court should have thrown garlands.

I felt a tap on my elbow, a discreet place where people in a crowd might not notice. I turned; it was my faithful court secretary, Meautys. He whispered that he had news. I looked away, so as not to draw attention to us. 'From Mister

Bull.' My Bedchamber spy, my mediocre writer of ciphers. Meautys turned, wordless, walking out of the main hall of the Banqueting House into a corridor beyond. I followed him, glancing around carefully to see if anyone was watching. We walked in train down to a little stairwell, so far away from the din that the sound of the wedding faded, and only then did we acknowledge that we had to speak. Just as I was about to say something, Meautys raised a finger to quieten me. He looked up the stairwell for several seconds, just to check no one was near, waiting, listening, unseen.

'What do you have?' I asked as he turned back to me.

'The last three nights at Theobalds, my Lord of Somerset did not come to the Royal Bedchamber.'

I shrugged. 'So?'

Meautys, who was artful with discretion always, looked at me meaningfully. 'He said he is married now and he can *never* return to the King's bed.'

'Never?' I was surprised. 'But Carr sits on the King's lap right now, with the royal tongue almost in his mouth.'

Meautys rarely spoke frankly. 'Do you trust appearances, Bacon, or what your spies tell you is the truth?'

A flicker of excitement ran through me. It had to mean *something*, Carr leaving the King's bed. I know nothing about love, but I know a lot about fucking. I was amazed. How could Carr be so stupid? Did the Howards know that this had happened? It was madness. Their new alliance rested on the King's obsession with Carr. At the moment of their triumph, they were giving up the very thing that afforded them victory.

At that precise moment, there was some small commotion further down in the corridor, and I heard the Queen's voice. I turned towards it. It was like her loud, curved

Danish vowels were summoning me. *Over here, Bacon. The real plan is over here.* Because suddenly – brilliantly – I put together everything I knew about the King, and Carr, and the Queen, and sex and the world, and power, and I understood what I had to do. Magically, marvellously, just like that: I knew what I had to do.

I began to walk down the corridor, but it felt like I was running, waving my arms, I was so excited. 'Majesty,' I called out, now fearless. The Queen had been telling her ladies to go back to the revelries and dance, but now the group, as one, looked at me.

'Bacon...' the Queen said. 'What are you doing here?'

'Oh,' I said, turning back, as if that offered some explanation. Meautys had already vanished into some corner. 'I just wanted... some air... for a moment. It is very hot in the Banqueting House with so many people. In fact, I was thinking I might go home...' I paused and tried to act the innocent you know full well I am not. 'Are you leaving, Majesty?' I asked, to change the subject. 'Would you like some company if you are walking somewhere?' I had dropped my voice to a whisper. Her pale eyes rested on mine. I could see her trying to read my intentions. 'I think there are rats about.'

'Rats?' she asked, forgetting what she had said to me all those months before.

I nodded. 'Maybe I could catch some for you.'

Then something in her face changed: the smallest possible smile, perhaps.

'I am going to Somerset House,' she said – a palace she had bought and was renovating on the Strand. She was famous for her love of building and liked nothing more than to spend a day with her architects. 'Would you walk me there?' *Of course I would.*

The night is always very quiet in Westminster, and one feels very far from London. Few people live outside the palace. As we walked, with her guards hanging twenty yards behind, I told the Queen everything I knew about developments in the Royal Bedchamber. I was not evasive with her about the details: we both knew the reality of her husband's life with Carr. So I told her I had a spy who had revealed that Carr had ended his sexual relationship with the King. She did not blink, hearing that. I told her of my fears, that the Howards and Carr would seek to destroy me and humiliate her. I said I thought I had a year, two at best, before they came for me. Paying for the wedding had bought me a bit more time. I thought she might tell me that I was worrying unnecessarily. She did not. Queens know the score as well as any person on Earth.

'So, what is your proposal, Bacon?'

I turned around to look at her guards, who were holding their distance. I took a step closer to her.

'Do you want Robert Carr gone, madam?' Her face twitched a little. 'Do you want the Howards knocked down a peg or two? The Earl of Suffolk laughed in your face that day at Theobalds. Do you think he will treat you any better now that he and his crew control the court?'

She was too clever just to say no. 'You still haven't told me your proposal, Bacon.'

I paused and breathed in the December night. It is miraculous how the *strategic* mind works; how suddenly, mysteriously, a plan can just come together; a plan that was there, possible, all along, but up until that moment, you simply had not seen it; and then, just like that, you saw it.

'We will find our own boy, madam. A young man as beautiful, or more beautiful, than Carr. I will search the whole kingdom if I need to. A young man who is created by us, and us alone. We will find our own beautiful boy and we will put him in the King's bed. We will train him how to love the King, and make the King feel loved. I will find him, prepare him, and you will introduce him to His Majesty. It would be too obvious for me to do it. We will train the boy to love us, and no one else. We will control him – he will be ours. Carr will fall, and the Howards will realise they have tied their fate to the wrong star. The right one will belong to us. *We* will win.'

A breeze moved up from the east, along the river valley. Suddenly, an ice-wind cut straight through us. The Queen, born in Scandinavia, did not flinch. She was used to the cold. She laughed brightly, confident and with an air of long-awaited relief.

'I knew it, Bacon,' she said.

'What, madam?'

'I knew that you would help me catch these *rats*.'

*

What is the best part of the game of power? Is it the money, or the fear you inspire in others? Is it the sex you can get, or the access to decisions, feeling the blood-pulse of influence, or the invitation to sit and sup with kings and queens? Is it titles, estates, high-born friends, eager artists seeking patrons and willing – perhaps – to trade a blowjob for the pleasure? *No.*

The best part is making plans that you know will change everything, that you know will transform the game itself, and then – hopefully – watching those plans become reality.

ON THE SUBJECT OF
A PLAN

A plan! How ingenious! How wonderful, a solution! And *all* I had to do now was comb every London street, every English village, and find the perfect boy-who-was-not-a-boy to supplant Carr. But who was this boy to be? What did I want from him? The Queen had agreed to my plan, and then immediately shooed me off to achieve it. She would expect me to return and to have succeeded, but she never once provided me with a list of her requirements as she did her architects. She had just said: 'Yes, find a boy and I will support you.' The rest would be down to me. That, I did not mind. I am happy with a plan, sitting alone, with a quill and scroll of paper to write on. This has suited me well so far; sometimes I feel like my brain is all I have, my truest friend. But now I must imagine a creature for love. And at this moment, my brain froze, stuck. What do I know of what makes men fall in love? (Well, nothing.)

I formed the first scraps in my head. He must be like Carr and then unlike Carr. *Easy!* He must be beautiful – as beautiful as Carr – but he must also be sweet, pliable, manageable. *Simple!* He had to be intelligent, but someone who would listen to me. *Okay...* I had to find someone who would trust me and, more importantly, keep trusting me, and not flounce off at the first opportunity. I had to make him hate the Howards, and yet he should be someone who was not driven by hate. I wrote some words down on a sheet of paper:

OBEDIENT
COMPLIANT
TRUSTING
PATIENT
LOYAL

But this was not a person. These are the qualities of a good dog. Then it struck me that the boy *did* have to have some of the qualities of Carr. My dislike of him could not blind me: the empiricist in me – the scientist! – had to think about what the world, or more specifically, the King, liked in Carr: the intensity of their relationship, and maybe, with my mind-science hat on, he liked the turbulence too. There had to be something of that in the boy: something mysterious or unknowable, something you felt might... slip away. Not the mean-spiritedness, the tantrums, the spite: no, the mystery. I wrote down more words:

HANDSOME (*No.*) BEAUTIFUL
FUN
OR FUNNY?
CHARMING
BEGUILING

84

What a wonderful thing, to beguile. I wonder what it must be like to be so. Who doesn't want to be beguiling?

And then, at the end, I added another word:

PERFECTION

(Oh, *that*, you say. Just *that*.)

*

In the New Year of 1614, only weeks after the wedding, I began to send spies out to search for boys. I tried to describe what these boys needed to be, but I had to obscure the reason. (You never know when spies will suddenly turn moralist – or, indeed, sell you to the other side.) When Meautys deadpanned that the boy had to be 'beguiling', the spies, who usually had a wife with cook's handprints on her pinafore, pretty daughters at a kitchen table, swinging their legs, reading Philip Sidney with moving lips, asked him, 'What does *that* mean?' *I wish I knew*, I said to Meautys. *Good-looking*. No, more than that. *Funny*. Perhaps. *Sweet*. 'Sweet?' Meautys asked. 'How do these men know what a sodomite finds sweet?' I looked him up and down. 'With their intelligence?' I replied, which made him shrug and me laugh.

But there was a complication. I was Attorney-General now, and there was so much work to do, endless cases to hear and review, work the King wanted me to catch up with. He began summoning me to Theobalds from London three, four, even five, times a week, on any given whim, to talk about politics, to draft policy, or to chat inanely about some book he wanted to read, or one that he wanted to ban. I raced between London and Theobalds endlessly, towers of papers waiting at either side, to be read, amended, commented upon, discussed. So there was so little time that the plan proceeded very slowly. And yet its culmination was my best hope. Do you see the bind? I had to achieve the plan but had no time in which to achieve it.

To make things more complicated, as that plan ground on, Carr did not fall, did not even budge from his position. But neither did he return to the King's bed, and neither did he leave the royal side. There was no hint that the King's affections towards his Rabbie had changed. Was it possible that I was wrong, that Carr could quit the King's cock and remain in place? The Queen said she was nervous. If it was true that the King no longer fucked Carr, why was he still favoured, why was he not just cast aside? *Hearts are persistent, damaged things*, I said. *We have to be patient.* I decided not to show her my worry. Worry is infectious, and infections turn into plagues.

I had good cause to worry, too. At the end of May, the King was to go on his Royal Progress, an annual tradition whereby the King set off to see his subjects, and he'd be gone for two or three months. He never got much further than the great country houses of England, where he would be fed and wined until he was fit to burst. But this year, significantly, I was not asked to go with him. This truly was something about which to worry. The King should have wanted me with him, but *someone* had managed to persuade him not to invite me.

As days passed, and the invitation still did not come, I would spend hours pondering this, wondering at its meaning. And with every day the King did not mention it, the lack of invite grew in significance. But I knew what it meant. For the other interesting thing about this particular Progress was that almost every house at which the King was staying belonged to either a Howard or one of their creatures. Only a handful did not. The Howard–Carr alliance was tightening its grip on power. The divorce was done; the Somersets were married; I was being pushed out. Suddenly, I could hear the clock that ran up to my downfall ticking very loudly.

Finally, by that time of year when the fields around Gorhambury are sharply, freshly green and the air hums with new life, warmed through by the return of sunlight to England, Meautys came back to me with a list of young men. There were in total eight candidates. They were all aged between eighteen and twenty-four, so not boys at all. You see, like I say, these are not boys: they are men. These are word-games that those in power like to play. They think them clever classical allusions. But they're not.

The first boy was from a family of courtiers, the Monson family, with whom I was well acquainted without ever being friends. Sir Thomas Monson was a lawyer like me, largely a self-made man, whom the King had knighted. I knew Sir Thomas professionally more than personally, and though I would never describe him as anti-Howard, he was ambitious. And when it came to whoring out his children, frankly, the man had form. Have you blanched at those words? Know this: this is the court. It is a brutal game, knives out, with no room for your anxieties about good parenting. Earls marry off their thirteen-year-old daughters without a second's doubt, expect consummation within the year, put it in the damned marriage contract too. (Go ask the Earl of Suffolk about his once-unfucked daughter.)

Sir Thomas egregiously misunderstood what the King wanted from a lover, assumed that some bilge he had read in Plato meant that he wanted to fuck little boys. (Them classical allusions again!) Sir Thomas started to parade one of his sons, an eleven-year-old named John, around under the King's nose, in varying degrees of powder and rouge, until the King himself had to command him to stop. 'Get your vile spawn away from me and be a good *fether*, and get that fucking slop off his *face*!' The King, to his credit, was never one to hold a grudge and, fucking slop removed, all had been forgotten. But I never forgot the very amorality of Monson's ambition. It's the most useful kind of ambition there is.

The boy was eighteen now. I had seen him several times on the fringes of court life. He was a handsome boy, with a quality that was both masculine and feminine, graceful movements, very clear skin and luminous eyes – all attributes the King liked. On the brief exchanges I'd had with him, he seemed sweet, if a little dense. I asked Monson if he would meet me 'out of town', and when he asked me what about, I replied I could not say. I knew that ambition of his would be piqued by that. I suggested a rural tavern in Clerkenwell, where the only people one might bump into were absolutely minding their own business. Or their master's sheep.

So, one evening, we were sat in a discreet corner of a country tavern, staring at each other as those who know they are not there for pleasantries do. Being Englishmen, we then exchanged those pleasantries. I asked about his wife, a simple but good woman; she was fine. I asked him in turn about his three younger sons, rising from youngest to next oldest in turn; yes, they were all fine too. Finally, I asked: 'And how goes John these days?'

'He is studying law,' Sir Thomas replied.

'Law?' I cried, unable to hide my surprise. 'I did not think that...' I stopped myself from saying that I did not think he was bright enough.

'Pfft,' Sir Thomas went. 'There's no brains in studying law, Bacon, you know that. Any idiot can become a lawyer, the law is full of fools. That's why men like you and I do so well, because we are not.'

'Fools?' I drawled in disbelief.

Monson winked at me. 'Precisely...'

I grinned, to show that I understood him, but now I felt only dread. A pretty royal favourite who was also a trained lawyer – how could there be *any* problems in that, hmm? Is there anything less 'beguiling' than a pretty face full of half-informed (or worse, well-informed) opinions?

Monson was looking at me, waggling his eyebrows. 'So, Bacon,' he said, 'what brings you here? About what mysterious thing do you wish to speak?'

'Who says I want to talk about anything at all?'

Monson's brow furrowed. 'Then why arrange to come here? I should have thought you wanted to discuss matters at court.'

It was I who now feigned confusion. 'What matters could I want to discuss?'

'The fall of Robert Carr,' Monson replied. I said nothing. 'Do you think you are the only one awaiting it? Or if not awaiting it, expecting it?' I remained silent. 'What do you think, Bacon? Or have you not heard? Carr is no longer letting the King fuck him.'

Gosh, some people are stupid. It is like they *want* to get hanged. To whom else might he and his lawyerly son be talking? I knew then that I did not want to say anything more to him. Already the risk was too large, the boy sounding less and less tempting all the while, the father blabbing to whomever the hell I was about the fall of Carr. (Carr had not fallen – that was precisely the fucking problem!)

'You should beware, Sir Thomas,' I began sharply, 'with your free talk of who you allege the King might or might not fuck. There are spies everywhere in England. I hope you do not accuse the King of being a sodomite.'

'What, Bacon?'

'I hope you do not conspire about the King's good friend, and beloved son, my Lord of Rochester, I mean, Somerset. Just saying these words could surely get your tongue cut out.'

Panic. His, not mine. 'No, of course, we have to be careful!'

'Careful?' I said. 'Why, I should go find my Lord of Somerset right now, and report what you have said.' Now the man truly was panicking, getting to his feet, and saying I had misunderstood. But if he panics for me, he will for someone else too. Coke would have whisked him to the Tower and chopped him up like mince. And if the father panics, what are the chances the son won't? He offered me a bribe, which I refused as unnecessary. 'Watch your step, Monson,' I warned, also getting to my feet. 'I shall not speak against you.' I paused. 'Not this time.' The poor fellow had turned seasick green and thanked me for helping him. Of course, I had not helped him one bit.

*

For the second boy, I travelled to Bedford the next day, fifty miles north from London, and from there to a village nearby named Biddenham. Here, one of my spies said that he had found a 'very holy' family with a son whose beauty was famous in the district. The spy had heard a rumour about the boy that suggested he was not quite as 'holy' as the rest of them. From whom did he hear that? I wondered whether that spy with the wholesome wife and industrious daughters had allowed himself a bit of this sodomitical apple. (Oh, don't blush and fie! People are every kind of fucked up, and they love to quench their desires whilst condemning yours.)

At Biddenham, I was directed to a little manor quite in disrepair. The family must have once been quite notable, but it was very plain that this was a family who no longer could afford to keep what it owned. I had written in advance to tell them that I, Attorney-General, had been looking for young men to enter the King's service. I needed amanuenses and scribes and I had heard very good things about their son – I had to look down at my notes – 'Will'. The truth of the matter is this: when you pay someone a compliment, they rarely seek to examine your motives. People's greed is only exceeded by their vanity.

So when I arrived, there was much hushed excitement that Francis Bacon – 'Of course we know who you are, sir' – was at their door. I was ushered by the bent little father through spartan rooms – I did not know whether because of faith or finances – until we came into one of the old-style manor halls. Inside lined up were his portly, cheery-looking wife, and a whole gaggle of flaxen-haired children, all of them startlingly beautiful, quite the opposite of the parents. If I believed in hocus-pocus, I would have thought that faeries had brought and swapped their pudgy, plain babes for these changelings.

The tallest and oldest child was Will, the one I had come to see. As I walked along the line of family, I could not help but stop to look at him. He was the most extraordinarily ethereal person I had ever seen. Tall and slim, even just standing there, his body had a peculiar kind of floating grace. His skin had a creamy quality. His face and hands were flawlessly clear. His eyes were a soft violet colour, his hair blond to the point of white. He bowed his head in greeting and there was something innocently moving about his strange loveliness. I am not attracted to these boyish men, but Will was beautiful in the most other-worldly way. I knew at once that, in a physical sense, he was that thing we were seeking.

'You think I might make an amanuensis for the King's service, sir?' he said simply.

I nodded. 'How is your education?'

'Scripture, sir. Some mathematics.'

'No French? No Latin?'

'A little French, sir, but no Latin.'

At this the father interjected: 'Latin is the Devil's language, sir.'

I found this genuinely funny in its Puritan stupidity. 'I did not know Cicero was the Devil,' I said almost with a wink.

'Oh!' went the man. 'He certainly is, that... Siss Rowe!'

I dined with the family. They asked me to talk about my work, and I did – about science and reason, about the acquisition of knowledge, about how governments might not just rule people but also improve their lives. Now and then, they asked disturbed questions like, 'Where is theology in all this rationality, sir?' I did not answer. The answer I had would not have pleased them. 'I have separated philosophy as a force for knowledge and human good, away from the interiority of theology!' I could have said, and my God, they would have stoned me to death in their own back garden.

I asked finally if it was possible to spend some time alone with the boy, to question him on the possibilities of his bright future. 'Oh, yes,' the holy parents went, licking their ambition off their lips.

We were shown up to the boy's chamber on the first floor, a room so bare as to be almost punitive, which he shared with his younger brothers. It had that smell of boys: sweat and dirt and crumpled sheets. I asked the father to leave us until I called. I warned him I had many questions to ask and it might take a while. 'Oh,' the father said, fully trusting, 'do you want the key to the room? That way, you can lock the door from inside in case my other sons forget and rush up here.' I looked at the man, in his stupefying innocence: yes, please do let me lock myself in this bedchamber with your ravishing son!

For about twenty minutes or so, I questioned Will. I could hardly believe that he was twenty-two. In his guilelessness, he could have been thirteen, and that was no good thing. Power is a nest of open, greedy beaks ready to snaffle up innocents. I asked him what his ambitions were and he could hardly conceal that he had none. It had never occurred to him that he might have any, clearly. When I was twenty-two, I was already in Parliament, conniving to get into court. Would he like to live a different life to his parents? He said he had never thought about it. Well, I said a little irritably, think about it now. Would he like to be at court? Would he like to have nice clothes and money? Would he like to be powerful? To all of these questions, he replied: 'I do not mind, sir.' Would he like to meet the King? This question seemed to stump him utterly; he could not even find an answer. And then I said to him, would he like to fuck girls? The boy's colourless, flawless cheeks, reddened in angry blotches. 'No, sir,' he whispered. 'I would like to get married and honour my wife.' *Yes, well, so did Robert Carr.*

I wondered at the spy who said he had 'heard a rumour' about Will. I realised I had to bring this to a conclusion, one way or the other.

'In a moment, Will,' I said – a speech I had already practised, knowing how crucial it was to what followed – 'I am going to do something. You are free to react however you wish. If you are happy with what I do, I will take you into my employ and seek to give you many opportunities at court. If what I do offends you, you can stop at any moment. I will not in any way react to it or damage you. In fact, I shall give you ten pounds this very day – enough for you to live half a year in London, I should add. You will never hear from me again and, as long as you do nothing to harm me, I shall do nothing to harm you or block your way if you seek another path into court. Do you understand?'

Will looked rather confused.

'If you do not understand,' I said, 'I shall go no further. It is nothing terrible. It is just a small thing but it is crucial for me to see how you react. It is important you understand and want me to continue. There is not a scrap of harm in saying no.'

Something lit in the boy's eyes; some desire to see. 'I understand, sir,' he said.

'Do you accept my terms about not doing any harm, in either direction?'

'Yes.'

I stepped forwards, took his face lightly in my hands, and put my lips to his. For a moment, he drew away – but I knew at once that it was in surprise more than disgust. In faltering jerks, he drew his mouth back close to mine, his eyes flickering upwards nervously. I kissed him again, quite chastely. Momentarily I parted my lips and Will did the same. He opened his mouth quite widely. I felt his tongue flicker out for mine. So he certainly knew what kissing was; this was not his first kiss from a man, perhaps.

I drew away. No more was necessary. This was enough. I stepped back and smiled at the boy, who had his eyes closed and his mouth still open, waiting for the kiss to continue. I glanced down at his britches. His hard cock was clearly visible.

'Thank you, Will,' I said. 'I shall not do that again. It was a form of test.' I nodded to him. 'Are you all right?'

Immediately, there was a haze of panic in his eyes. 'Please, sir, please, Mister Bacon, do not tell my father what has happened. He will say I will go to hell. I do not want to go to hell. I do not want him to say that. I do not mind if you do not take me to court, I do not truly want to go, but please, do not tell my father.' I was so confused by this, I was silent a moment, and this only served to upset the boy even more. 'Oh, sir! I beg you! Please say nothing!'

It was sad. Will was so beautiful, in an unreal way, but his shame was too great. I knew it at once. He would never be able to trot off to court and fling his legs up in the air, for all the world to know what he was, and his parents back here, writhing in pain over his soul as they counted the gold he sent them from beastly, glittering London.

Shame is the river in which the sodomite is drowned. His parents drag his body from the water and hold it up towards the sky, and ask a vengeful God: 'Why has this happened?' But here is the truth: it was the parents who drowned their son. Like two Abrahams and an Isaac, they were the ones who obeyed that God and led their son to the river, and held his face under the water until it was still, the last bubbles escaping from his mouth. And as the sodomite son they helped murder lies cold and dead in their arms, they cry to God: 'Why did this happen to *us*?'

All of which was to say that this was not the boy. I had written the words 'Fun – or Funny?' – and how was he either of these? I went back to that word 'beguiling'. Poor Will was closer to depressing. I smiled at him, and patted him gently on the chest. 'Do not worry, Will,' I said, 'I won't say a word to anybody.' I told the father I would write to him if Will was chosen, but I had other boys to see. They were not to take offence if they never heard from me again. The father looked very cheery – it did not seem to occur to him that I was, in fact, telling him he would not. I confess I even forgot to leave the ten pounds. But now I was two boys down and nowhere near perfection. I was starting to feel a little bleak. (Never fear: bleakness can so quickly turn to despair!)

*

From Bedford, I rode south-west to Buckingham, where I met a young man who screamed blue murder when I attempted to kiss him. It was all I could do to convince him that he had misunderstood. Then I went westward to Worcester where the boy I was sent to see had bucked teeth, crossed eyes and knock knees – all in one scoop – and I realised that my spy must have got him mixed up with another. I was left in the awkward situation of asking in some awful country town if anyone knew where I could find a beautiful boy. People looked at me with such horror that I was lucky they did not hang me from the church spire.

The angelic young man I went to see in Wantage – a full day's ride south – was perfect physically, but was so incalculably boring that I did not even get as far as the kiss. When I told the boy in Leominster – riding back north again – that I wanted him to work for the King, he became irate, protesting that Scots were as evil as foxes. They were entering England in such number these days, and someone ought to stop it, he said. I stared at him as he ranted. *Are these people mad?* Then I received a letter from my spy at Northampton who told me that the boy there had died of plague. Nothing was going my way. (Or the dead boy's, for that matter...)

*

The last boy on my list was at a place named Stow-on-the-Wold. Here, I had been told of the son of a local physician, a boy of the most startling beauty. He was twenty-one, bright but not clever, which was ideal. When I was asking for directions to their house, a complete stranger said the boy had a 'lively spirit'. Well, that did not sound too bad. The family hoped he would become a physician too, my spy reported, and doctors always have a good mix of intelligence and bone-thick stupidity.

I went to meet him in the morning, having slept at a tavern in the little town. His name was Ambrose. He was potently attractive, not like Carr at all: lusty, muscular, short and dark, with something intensely sensual about him. Ambrose's cock was hard, banging into my thigh, all through the French-kiss test. I told him not to be embarrassed. He replied – with determined eyes – that he was not. I looked at him and his eyes were shining with the knowledge of sex, the desire for it. I could have – if I'd wished, if I'd been a different, simpler kind of man – led him to the bed and fucked him. The boy would have let me – that was abundantly clear. But it would have been a lie, a suggestion that I would take him where he wanted to go: court, London, the King.

Here I was at the end of my search. Ambrose was the eighth boy – the last. He was far closer to what I needed – attractive, fun, shameless, hungry – than anyone I had seen so far. But would I truly be prepared to go back to the Queen with this perfectly lusty, hearty, sexual lad, and say: *behold, madam, the most entrancing creature in England*? The truth was you could find an Ambrose in any village, and very fine that is too. But he was not the perfection I was seeking, or the exquisite trick on which to hang our plan. That was the moment I felt despair kick in. The plan was not working out. And all the while, the edge of Suffolk's knife was brushing my throat.

Just then, there was a tap at the door. Ambrose was standing with an obvious erection in his britches. 'Cover yourself up,' I hissed. A hand on rattled the lock. I went to stop the servant from coming into the room. The servant, surprised to find me only inches from the door, stammered: 'Oh, s-s-sir, there is a letter, come from...' The voice hesitated. 'Thee-old-bolds.'

I ripped the letter open. It was from Meautys, written in cipher.

BULL'S BODY WAS FOUND IN THE NEW RIVER. HIS HANDS WERE TIED AND HIS THROAT CUT. SHOULD YOU GO THERE? KING AT APETHORPE FOR SEVERAL DAYS.

ALSO, NEWS FROM WHITEHALL. THE QUEEN COMPLAINS THAT COUNTESS OF SOMERSET ASKS TO BE NEW LADY OF THE BEDCHAMBER. THE QUEEN OPPOSES BUT KING IS MINDED TO AGREE. SHOULD YOU SEE THE QUEEN?

'Shit!' I hissed. 'Shit! *Shit!*'

The game was now fatal. My spy in the Royal Bedchamber was dead, murdered. Frances Carr was conspiring to infiltrate the Queen's household.

'Is everything to your liking, sir?' Ambrose asked. I turned to look at him.

'How far is it to Apethorpe from here?'

ON THE SUBJECT OF
THE MOST BEAUTIFUL 'BOY'
IN THE WORLD

I rode fast the seventy-odd miles north to Apethorpe Palace. It was owned by Sir Anthony Mildmay, one of the few neutral hosts the King was staying with on the Progress. Over hours, I crossed the meadows and fields of England, the corn and lavender fields, through crumbling little villages, until at last Apethorpe was in sight. It was a beautiful house, all new, elegant restraint in sandstone. By the time I arrived, it was glowing golden in the late afternoon. Tethering my horse near the entrance, I found a number of courtiers, beautifully dressed, sitting in drunken clumps around the steps. Some nodded, some smirked – funny old Bacon, come to toady and work. *How boring!*

Inside the house, servants were buzzing everywhere, fetching plates of food, removing others. The grand foyer was thick with yet more aristocratic bodies, turned out in spectacular court dress, sniffing contemptuously at the endless this and that of their own lives. A group of violists were playing Italian music – very stylish. Dwarves danced along, making much display. Their nervous glances betrayed their true worries about the long day of drinking ahead. Somewhere a man was reciting Virgil in bad Latin, knowing no better. Up the very wide, very grand staircase, someone was picking prettily on a lute, running counter to the ensemble below. A man played with a small monkey, teasing it with a honey-sweet. I could see the monkey was growing irritable. It was only a matter of time until it bit the fool.

'Bacon!' a woman's voice cried ahead of me. 'Oh, how dear to see you!'

It was Lady Grace Mildmay, Sir Anthony's wife. She is a most excellent person, a very remarkable one too, having published her own very detailed and thoroughly researched book on medical treatments. I had read it and found it very inspiring. She had created a sort of encyclopaedia of medicines, speaking to doctors, midwives and cunning-folk. It had been for her own interest but had turned out a spectacular and well-deserved success.

I bowed. 'Lady Grace.'

She curtseyed to me, although we were old friends. 'Bacon, I have a proposal for you, for the country.' She took my arm to lead me around her busy foyer. 'I have been practising something on my own estates – to create my medicines in huge quantities, so that remedies can be applied immediately as needed, an intervention sure to stop illness faster. Thus the people will always have cures and medicines to hand, do you see?'

I did see. It was very clever, resourceful. 'Now, if someone is injured in the field or driving a carriage or cart, we will not need to make up the medicine. We'll have it ready to hand; we'd only need to send for the made-up medicine and treat the person in no time. Even a non-medical person could administer it. Isn't it wonderful?'

In truth, my head was awash with Bull: the threat, the plan, the fact of his murder. Who killed Bull? What next in the game, as it turned more brutal?

'Potentially a great saving of life and time.' I smiled at her. 'But what is your proposal, Lady Grace?'

'Oh,' she went, as if that had been self-evident all along. 'That the King proposes to Parliament a whole national network of the same. The country, each city, each town, could build up a stock of medicines and treatments. Where one area was lacking, the government could send supplies, or marshal them in times of great sickness. Medicines everywhere, in every town, in every village, ready to be used at any moment, a national service. What do you think?'

It was a marvellous, creative idea, and I told her so, but also a good example of why creative people are poorly placed to run countries. Where was the money for such a scheme? I had just spent months getting Parliament to release money to let the King buy jewels for Robert Carr and his cronies. Not a single Member of Parliament (save perhaps me) was going to pay to stop injured peasants dying of blood poisoning.

I told her I sought the King now. She directed me up to the Great Hall. There, servants were lighting the candelabra, standing on step-ladders, with burning tapers flickering perilously above their heads. I saw a maidservant standing on tiptoe, on a step-ladder, which began to wobble a little as she reached higher to light the lights. I rushed over and steadied the ladder to stop the girl from falling.

She looked down at me as I did it and in so doing dropped the taper, which fluttered to the floor and snuffed out. 'Watch it!' she cried reflexively; then, seeing it was not another servant she was speaking to, sort of bobbed respectfully in mid-air, and almost toppled over again.

'Do not curtsey, girl!' I exclaimed. 'You'll fall and crack your head.'

'Ooh, yes, sir!' she replied too enthusiastically, wobbling again.

'Be careful!' I cried, holding up my hands to catch her if she went over.

Behind me I heard laughter. It was loud and unrestrained: the King. '*Beicon!* Look at ye, saving the common folk from their ain *stupid* selves! Let the bint fall on her arse if she has nae *sense*!' The girl clambered down the ladder and scurried off, bobbing and afraid. The King kept laughing. He raised his wine-glass in the air: 'My *ain Beicon*! Why are ye here?'

I did not have a reason why. 'I have brought papers for you to sign,' I improvised.

'Where are they?' he said, inspecting my empty arms.

I hadn't thought of that. 'Downstairs, sire.' I changed the subject. 'How goes the Progress, Majesty?'

'Ach, excellent. I have been very well received wherever I've been. And the common folk – ach, they truly fucking *love* me!'

I bowed, to beg the question: *and how could they not?* But the truth is that the King was not unpopular. Everyone was glad when the belligerent old Queen died, and the endless wars she fought against the Irish and the Spanish were wound down. Taxes were lowered (at first, before the King started spending) and people were so relieved that a dancing bear could have sat on the throne and no one would have minded. And the King, to be fair, is a little brighter than a dancing bear. But hear his delusion. He had been a king for as long as he could remember – almost from birth in Scotland. This was his life. Kings cannot see the truth of the world. How can we expect them to, when the golden spoon is all they ever eat from?

'I hear strange news of the Queen,' I said, improvising again.

'Truly? What news of my precious lassie, *Beicon*?'

There was not a trace of irony in him calling the adult daughter of Christian IV of Denmark and Norway either a 'lassie' or precious to him, when patently she was neither.

'I hear that she is unhappy. Someone has tried to change the structure of her household.'

'*Ach, I did!*' the King cried, loud enough to make people turn. I knew this was a risk but sometimes you just have to whack the mole on the head. 'Did she complain of that?'

'Oh, no,' I said. 'The Queen often talks of what a kind husband you are.' Of course, she never breathed any such words. 'But, sire.' I dropped my voice. 'It is not even two years since the death of Prince Henry.'

He put his grubby fingers to his wine-stained lips. 'My sweet ain bairn!'

Quite. 'I do not think that the Queen wants much change at the moment. I think she is happy with the company of her established ladies. And my Lady of Somerset is very high-spirited.'

'Ach, aye, she likes a drink methinks!' he said, with sharp moral concern. Given how drunk he was all day long, I could have laughed, had I been more foolish.

'I meant more that she was very lively. Perhaps the Queen needs quieter company these days. Sober company. After the death of Prince Henry, I mean, sire.'

The King's own eyes misted a moment. 'Oh, aye, true enough, true enough.'

Listen, I know how manipulative I was being. You do not have to furrow your brow. The dead son... The unhappy, bereaved mother just wanting a bit of peace... My enemies blocked from the Queen's apartments... Did I not tell you? Did I not say? This is a cruel game.

'I think a new household will unsettle and upset her,' I continued, 'and of course, Prince Charles is so sensitive to his mother's grief.' I pretended to let myself get carried away, then I stopped, looked the King dead in the eye, and asked: 'But what do *you* think, sire? What do *you* think is the best thing to do?'

At once, the King began to fluster and flounce. 'Oh, my sweet lassie!' he cried. Then he squared up to me, as if it was me trying to upset her. 'I will let nae man harm her, d'ye hear me? D'ye see? She is the most important person in the world to me. D'ye hear me? D'ye hear?' (In truth, I would be surprised if she cracked the top ten, but whatever.) I nodded to the King to remind him that I agreed, that it was me who had brought it up. He turned around and began yelling. 'Nae changes to the Queen's household!' the King cried. 'Nae changes! Stop them at once!' He had already forgotten that the proposal had been his. I bowed and said very good. At that exact moment, with lightning speed, my Lord of Suffolk was with us.

'Bacon,' he growled.

You know I like to laugh, but seeing Suffolk like that – suddenly behind me – made me flinch with fear. But I bowed to him too, very calmly. Never let them see you fear them, even while you shit your britches.

'My Lord.' I turned back to the King. 'Shall I memorialise that in a written ruling, sire?'

'Oh, aye! Fucking memorialise it, *Beicon*!'

Music struck up on the other side of the room, a lively little jig of some northern, maybe Scottish, dance melody played on a honking harmonium and a bowed rebec. The King raced off, waving his arms in the air.

Suffolk was staring at me intently. 'What's this? Why are you here? What is the *King* –' he had to gulp the word down '– memorialising?'

'His decision that no changes are to be made to the Queen's household.'

Now Suffolk's eyes narrowed. 'Well played, Bacon,' he spat. A moment of silence passed, and then a menacing grin made its way slowly over his face. 'Sad news about your friend, Bacon.'

'My friend?' I asked, not understanding.

'Mister Cratchett.'

Still I remained in the dark. 'Cratchett?' Then I remembered: Cratchett was Bull's real name. Suffolk would have no cause to know that I had ever met the man; I had been very careful never to reveal our connection. I shuddered; did he see me shudder? He kept looking at me, searching for the signals of my fear. Did Suffolk kill Bull, or did he just know who had?

'I know no Cratchett, my Lord,' I responded calmly, smiling, and I bowed a last time. But as my head lowered, I felt the most awful dread. As I lifted out of the bow, Suffolk was gone. Like the Devil, he had vanished into thin air.

Lady Grace had already had a bed made up for me. She took me aside and apologised that it was only a simple room, but the earls had all insisted on the best ones. Of course they had. I told her I did not mind at all; I would happily sleep on a log. After dinner, there was to be a masque and we were all to watch it. The masque would run late into the night and I did not cherish the idea, having ridden at speed halfway across the country that day. And as ever in these situations, part of me was thinking: *I could be in London, working, or at Gorhambury, writing.* But it was better I had come. The note about the Queen's household had already been drawn up and signed and sent back post-haste to London. That would secure things for a while. But still so much still stood ahead of me. So little had gone right since that night of the wedding at Whitehall, when the Queen and I thought we had found our answer.

We sat down to dinner in very long rows of tables that ran, like a toothcomb, away from the table at the head where Sir Anthony, Lady Grace, the King, the Somersets and Lord and Lady Suffolk sat. Carr talked loudly the whole while in the moments before service began. Despite the din of chatter filling the room, his voice cut through the noise. I could not quite hear what he was saying – more its loudness and effect – and felt its confidence and my imperilment. Now and then I thought I saw him looking down at me, but I think I was mistaken.

For my part, I was sat between people who were very much in the Howard circle: Lady Knollys, Suffolk's sister; her husband, the Earl of Banbury; and Lord Rutland, another fellow traveller. I do not think this was deliberate – the *placement* was down to Lady Grace – it was more a delicious universal reminder, a memento mori. *Bacon!* the universe was shouting. *Bacon! Remember you must die!*

Each of my dining companions asked me polite questions, and each question I scanned for possible deeper meaning. One can never relax entirely, and beyond that, these people were my enemies' friends. I could never quite shake the feeling that Carr was watching me, but any time I looked at the top table, all I saw was the King, rather cross-eyed with drink, gazing on and his favourite chattering gaily about himself. I am normally a gregarious fellow but now, sullen before the soup course, I retreated into despairing silence. My companions stopped asking me questions and I did not touch my wine. I sank into an interior place of worry, my life swirling around my head. How had I got to this point? How might I get away from it?

More than anything, I thought of my failure to find our 'beautiful boy'. It was now several months on from my proposal to the Queen. The Howards were secure – I was literally sitting among them and their creatures – and Robert Carr was safely within their orbit. The King no longer had his 'lover' in his bed, but the 'favourite' had not even vaguely fallen. It should have been easy! Just find another boy with a pretty face and an accommodating arse – for the right price. Surely that's every third chap in England! But I had been across half the kingdom in search of my 'boy' and come up with nothing. It all felt so disastrous: a trap of which I was partly the builder and partly the prey.

The soup was starting to come out of the kitchen. Absentmindedly I watched the servants move through the maze of tables, as careful and choreographed as dancers in any masque. These lads – the youngest sixteen, the oldest in their middle-twenties – were not ordinary servants. They were boys from good gentry families, all around, no one fancy but courtly enough, and each of them with the dewy grace that comes with being young and alive. Some of them made mistakes – I smiled softly when they bumped into each other, or when bread rolls were knocked out of baskets – and some of them made none. They were like Robert Carr had once been, what felt a thousand years ago: that army of rough Scots boys – just about gentry class – who came to London, of whom Carr was now the catamite-King. They were expected to converse with the diners in a mannered, modest way. Perhaps one or other might give them a job, even whisk them away to court, or failing that, at least to London and away from their 'dreadful' provincial fate. All around me was empty high-born complaint.

'Truly, I do not know what else they expect from a marriage portion. We have negotiated the financial aspects of the dowry and now they want to talk about liens on property!'

'Well, I said to the grubby little fellow, it is your business to earn the money and mine to spend it!'

'Can you imagine, a *carpenter*? The fellow was a carpenter and he spoke to me like that!'

'What did you do, my Lord?'

'Oh, I had him arrested, of course.'

'Quite right too! Did they hang him?'

'Oh, *I expect so*.'

They spoke of men as if they were nothing more than dust to sweep from a sill. Minor infractions, perceived insults, were enough to crush those whose souls were every bit as eternal as theirs. I was thinking of my mind-science and what it might say about the aristocrat, who poses so grand and impenetrable and yet finds anxious offence at the merest thing. They rail and opine, and declare things good, bad or *ridiculous*, but if someone dares to do the same, about them, they whine and scream how things have gone *too far*!

Something in the rafters of the hall attracted my attention. I looked up and saw that a tiny sparrow had found its way into the house, through some open door or window. It hopped among the rafters, quite happy and free, not yet aware that it had imprisoned itself. It's always the same. They hop around cheerily for a while, flit from perch to perch, until they realise they cannot find the way that they came in and they are trapped. *Once you're inside, it's not so easy to find your way back out.* A servant tries to chase them and they panic. A house cat, bored of catching mice, finally has a far greater puzzle of a prey: airborne and aerial. Then one day you find the bird's dead body, having slammed into a window, or a door suddenly opening and crushing it flat. I watched the sparrow. For a moment, I thought its small black eyes were watching me too. *What little mystery are you?* I wondered. *You're watching us, seeing us, thinking us foolish, all sitting here in our long lines, waiting for something to happen when all we might expect is nothing.* The bird flicked out its brown tail and took a tiny white shit, which landed – SPLAT! – on top of Lady Suffolk's bright auburn wig.

No one seemed to notice, including the venerable Countess. It was all I could do not to burst out laughing.

I pressed my lips closed, avoiding looking at my dining companions, one or two of whom cast curious eyes in my direction. *What is Bacon smirking at, hmm? What's his game?* I lifted my eyes back up into the rafters, searching for my new, revolutionary hero, but the sparrow was gone. I let my eyes drop and move across the room. And then I saw him.

He was probably twenty-one or -two years old. He had fairish, red-brown hair that rose in great, curly waves from his head, so that his face, pale, heart-shaped, masculine yet pretty, was perfectly framed. His complexion, a pure lily white, gleaming with his youth, was so clear it made me catch my breath; his smile was both shy and knowing. There was something sensual about him, a hazy sexual nature, full-lipped, dewy, yet adult. He was not virginal, but rather a halfway between the unworldly Will and the lusty, lustful Ambrose of my search. He had been talking to a woman he was serving, but my stare alerted him. He looked up and at me.

His eyes were large and direct, a colour somewhere between green and hazel, discernible even from a distance. His eyes held mine for a few seconds, in the way that men's eyes do, on the street, so to say: *I know you are looking at me, and I am letting you look.* I saw something flash across them: searching, intelligent, and then he smiled at me sweetly, without guile. Physically, at least, he was perfection.

The person to whom he was speaking asked a question, so he turned and spoke to her attentively, laughing with charm. There was a soft blush on his cheeks as he spoke, his pale skin becoming alluringly pink – a shyness that was unexpected, delightfully so. He seemed both confident and vulnerable, beautiful yet suggestive of some sensitivity – a kind of rawness – beneath. The woman must have said something humorous, for he broke into a wide grin, revealing a lovely, open smile and pearly teeth. We live in a world of broken teeth – grey ones, yellow ones, rotten ones – but his were quite perfect. Briefly, he turned back to me – those same hazel-green eyes falling on me directly, with a hint of flirtation. That look that men like me understand.

Someone behind called to him, giving orders. He turned to walk off, and I knew I had to speak to him. I started to stand up; I could not let him get away. *Hey, you!* I almost shouted. *You, the future! Look back, the future! Look at me!*

Another of the servants near him, carrying two full bowls of soup, tried to squeeze past down the long toothcomb of tables. Someone sitting down reached back to talk to a friend, and knocked the servant with the soups. Bowls went flying, soup splattered all over the boy, all over the guests. A woman was yelling in cut-glass tones: 'There is soup all over my husband and he is seventy-*four*!'

Lady Grace's eyes shifted towards the commotion. Society hostess to the bone, as much as medical scientist, she was on her feet at once, commanding that everyone get up so that they could have their clothes sponged off. 'It's only soup!' she cried. 'It's not wine! It won't stain! Let's be rational!' *In England?* Fuck that. People were screaming. Some were laughing. 'Oh, look, *do* look!' 'I am covered! *Covered!*' A swirl of bodies overwhelmed the moment, the soup-stained being ushered away, the spilled soup on the floor being cleaned up. And in that commotion, I lost sight of him.

I had to find him. I felt panic, nausea. No, I could not let him slip away. How did I know he was who I had been looking for? Perhaps I did not, perhaps I have mis-remembered now, perhaps I did not know. But I do remember the rush, the elation, and again, panic, in that moment. Had fate finally smiled? Or had she smirked and lifted her middle finger? It all had to mean *something*. I was up on my feet and pushing my way through the bod-ies of servants. Stopping a serving boy, I asked where I should go to have soup cleaned off my jacket.

'But you have no soup on you, sir,' the boy reasoned. '*Where?*'

The boy pointed to a small door that opened to a set of stairs, filled with people coming and going. I pushed down through them, like a leaf in the tides of a fast stream, spinning and bobbing.

Suddenly I tumbled out into the vast, hot kitchens. On tabletops, people were stuffing tiny violet woodcocks in huge number. Someone hauled a roasted half-carcass of beef up onto a counter, attacking it with knives and saws. Everywhere pots were simmering and steaming on fires. Children were fetching water or scrubbing pans. I was turning and turning but could not see him. I could feel my panic; I had had my chance and let it get away. Then suddenly there he was, in the corner of the room, dabbing at his soup-splattered suit with a wet cloth.

I walked fast, straight towards him. I wouldn't let him out of my sight again. He glanced up at me as one who is not sure if an angel or a demon was swooping down on him. We were looking each other directly in the eye – but he did not flinch, and gazed at me warmly and openly. 'Sir?' he said.

He was a few inches shorter than me, and in that moment, we assumed the effect of me towering above him, although I was only slightly taller. 'Do you know who I am?' I asked.

'Yes, sir,' he whispered. 'You are Francis Bacon.' He knew my name. That was good, it meant he was not ignorant. His eyes were alive, and I saw it again more clearly: his intelligence. Close up, he was every bit as beautiful.

'What is your name?' I asked. His eyes were like still ponds in summertime – if you closed your own, you could feel the warm air, hear the birds calling in the trees, the dragonflies buzzing over the water.

'George Villiers, sir.'

'I need to speak to you.'

He looked around, in confusion. There must have been no end of kitchen eyes trained upon us. 'Sir, I do not understand. Do you need some help with something? Do you need something fetching?'

'I just need to speak to you. I have a proposal for you.'

His brow twitched. 'A proposal, sir?' Then a small smile, his lips pert without parting. 'What kind of proposal can sir have for someone like me?' There was something knowing in it, something that understood what this might be – that was good too, very good. Somewhere in the distance, I could hear Lady Grace telling everyone to calm down, it was not like the roof was on fire. His mood changed. 'Sir, I'll have to go,' he said, looking around nervously. 'They'll need me back.'

'When can I see you again?' I asked.

'Sir?' I could see that he did not understand.

'*When?*'

His eyes ran over mine and suddenly became quite calm. 'Tomorrow, sir.'

I shook my head. 'I have to leave tomorrow.'

'I am serving table at the breakfast, sir. I can see you then, sir.'

'When can I see you on your own?'

Now some alert passed through him. He paused, searching my question for meanings. 'I will be able to meet you in the gardens, by the little pond, by eleven. Will that suffice?'

'All right,' I said. 'Eleven.'

And with that, he nodded, he walked away. I watched him go, and then at the last moment before he went back upstairs, he turned and grinned at me.

I felt it then. This *had* to be him.

*

Before I went to bed that night, I wrote down the words again.

BEAUTIFUL
FUN
OR FUNNY
CHARMING
BEGUILING
PERFECTION

*

I looked up out of the small window of my attic room. The stars formed an arc over the woods beyond the

Apethorpe gardens. I got into the bed in my humble little room, and lay there, smiling broadly to myself, in the dark.

*

By ten-thirty the next morning, I was already out in Apethorpe's lovely gardens, waiting for him. I found a little walled area near the pond. Bees buzzed around in the air. I went to sit on a stone bench, closed my eyes and just waited. It was very quiet but one could just about hear a breeze fluttering. I let the sounds of the location's near-silence calm me. With my eyes closed, I could smell the sharp freshness of the grass, mown regularly now because of the presence of the King. It was a smell that was familiar, soothing. It took me a moment to place it. It reminded me of the little garden at the back of York House, where a lush, wet patch of green ran down to the Thames, and where, when young, I had splashed around in the edges of the river. 'Mister Bacon, sir?'

I opened my eyes. He was standing only a few feet from me, his hair brushed neatly, wearing just a simple wool suit, cut tight to his athletic form, no ruff, no silk. I had not misremembered and I had not exaggerated in my memories. If anything, here, in daylight, his beauty had even more of an extraordinarily luminous, magnetic quality. It was hard not to stare at him, like he had stepped out of some exquisite painting.

'You wanted to speak to me, sir?' he said.

'Yes. I wanted to question you a little, if I may.'

He looked uncertain. 'Question me?' He smiled his wide, pearly smile. 'What could sir have to ask someone like me?'

He had asked me the same question the night before, and I had not answered. I tried to trace through his question and its repetition. Was it clever or sincere, modest or maybe even manipulative? I had to be strategic. I had to think what I wanted from him just then. 'Have you met my Lord of Suffolk since you've been here?'

He seemed confused by the abrupt change of question. (Any interrogator knows that surprise questions are good and useful. They interrupt what the person is anticipating, which compels them to answer frankly.) 'No, sir.'

I nodded. 'My Lord of Somerset?'

'I served him wine one evening.'

I nodded. 'And how did you find him?'

He paused a moment. 'He was quite sharp with me, sir.'

'Sharp how?'

He did not want to say something that might harm him, I could see that. 'I would say that sir is trying to test me, but I do not know what the answer is, what's right and what's wrong.'

I liked that he said this. 'Maybe there are no right or wrong answers,' I said.

He shook his head. 'Sir, that is something a tutor says when trying to get you to speak up. But there are always right answers – and wrong ones.' Again, I admired his directness. I was a powerful person, he knew that. I wanted something from, or of him, he could see that. I was the mystery in this moment – not him – and I liked that he wanted to take something of the mystery back. 'What do you want to ask me about, sir?'

'My friends call me Bacon,' I said.

I could see how this confused him. 'But I am not your friend, sir.'

I laughed. It was a fearless kind of answer, and I appreciated his ability to appear fearless even if he felt afraid. 'Men want to be my friend,' I said. (Yes, I know that that's not *strictly* true.)

'I am happy to make a friend,' he said. 'But friends speak frankly to each other, don't they, sir? I still do not know what sir wants from me.'

The sunshine was on him and I let my eyes drift down to the elegant, angular fold of his cheekbone and jaw. On his neck, long muscles stood out against the ruffless collar he wore. Then I looked up at his beautiful face again; he was staring straight at me. I could not work this boy out. He had the most astonishing physical beauty and yet he was sensitive in a way that the beautiful rarely are. 'Shall we take a walk?' I asked.

'As you wish, sir.'

'Bacon,' I said.

We moved around the pattern of lawns, our shoes crunching on the gravel paths. I asked him to tell me about his background. He was twenty-one, he said. I had been more or less right about that. His family was good gentry, but his father died when he was a child and left them nothing. His mother had struggled to keep a roof over their heads but somehow had managed to educate him. He had spent some small time in France, learned the basic gentlemanly things. Did he speak French? *Not really*. Had he made good friends in France? *Not particularly*.

As he spoke, I felt his presence next to mine, felt it on my skin. His body in his suit, his shoulders broad, his waist narrow, his limbs long and loose. He walked elegantly, not in a courtly way, but as one comfortable in his own shape and form. He smiled frequently, turning to smile directly at you, whether he was confident or unsure. Sometimes, charmingly, he seemed to be both simultaneously. He laughed when you made jokes and listened attentively when you were serious.

We talked on; the conversation was easy. He was open; rather sweet, in fact. He spoke respectfully of his lady mother and laughed about his brothers, calling them 'stupid' in that fond way that brothers do.

'Do you hope to go to court?' I asked him, trying to direct the conversation. He pondered this, pushing out his lower lip.

'I have no connections,' he said. 'With whom could I go?'

I arched an eyebrow to test him, as if to say, 'Are you kidding me?' but he revealed nothing.

'What did you want for your life before today, Villiers?' I asked.

He wrinkled his brow. 'Before today, sir?'

'Bacon. Yes, before you met me.'

He looked at me for a few seconds without answering. Perhaps he was thinking of his answer – or more correctly, of what that little phrase 'before you met me' implied. I had planned it, used it, quite carefully.

Before he spoke, he took a short, hesitant breath. 'I do not know. I wanted to support my family, my lady mother, who has struggled so hard since my father's death. And I suppose I wanted an interesting life.'

'Did you think that would happen here?'

He broke into that beautiful, knowing smile and laughed softly. 'No, sir.'

'Bacon.' For a moment, he looked confused so I said it again: 'My name is Bacon, not sir.'

He grinned very sweetly, the faintest blush on his cheeks. 'Bacon.'

'Are you ambitious?'

'Ambitious?' he repeated, his eyes on me.

I saw him trying to think of answers. 'Don't repeat things back to me,' I said, 'don't do that. If you do not understand, just say.'

He paused, looked down at the path, then back up at me, his eyes full of light. 'I *could* be ambitious,' he said. 'Yes, I think I could.'

We had come to a path between two adjoining lawns, but one had to pass through a gate in a little wall. The brick wall was heavy with thick, dark ivy shading the spot from view. He was looking at me, then cocked his head to one side, and – just briefly – screwed up one eye. Then he smiled, revealing his white teeth.

'Do you know the nature of the relationship between the King and my Lord of Somerset?' I asked.

He hesitated a moment. 'Yes.'

I nodded once. 'Describe it to me.'

He looked around. Just because everyone knows something does not mean there is not a risk in saying that truth aloud. 'You can speak,' I said. 'We are quite alone.'

He thought for a second. 'I understand, sir, that my Lord of Somerset is the King's… catamite.'

'Can you speak more plainly? Lots of people have heard that word without knowing its full meaning.'

He straightened his back and gazed directly at me.

'The King fucks my Lord of Somerset in the arse.' Then suddenly, unexpectedly, that lovely smile again, the smile accentuating the angle of his cheek, a slight tilt of the head revealing his long neck; it was all so perfect. He was laughing, gorgeously, intelligently, but without malice. 'Is that plain enough?' I began to laugh too. He was funny. You never expect beautiful people to be funny.

Our laughter faded and instinctually we continued walking. 'You know about men who fuck other men?' He gave a curious little hiccup of a giggle. 'And what do you think of that? Of men like that?'

'I do not judge any of them.'

That was an interesting answer.

'Would you like to be rich?' I asked.

The change of subject again made him pause. 'Yes.'

'Would you like to be powerful?'

His eyes widened. 'I did not know it was possible for me.'

'You said you do not judge those men.' (Can you see how I use the trick now?) 'Most people would.'

He shrugged, without meaning any deep affect. 'Then I am not like most people, sir.'

'Bacon.'

A grin. 'Bacon.'

'Are you a virgin?' Many men of his age still are.

'No, sir,' he said, without shame.

I felt encouraged. 'You have lain with girls?'

'Yes, sir.'

'Bacon.'

'Sorry. Bacon.'

'Have you offered to marry any of them?'

He giggled nervously, a little scandalised. 'No.'

That was good. We did not need some merry wench turning up in a few months with a bump and a promise of a marriage contract.

'And boys?' I asked carefully.

Something playful skittered across his face. 'Have I offered to marry any boys, Bacon?'

He said my name certainly, with a glint in his eye, and his reply was knowing, winking, but careful. Only later did it occur to me that he was being as strategic as me, using 'sir' to throw *me* off *my* path. I had thought I was being so clever with my unexpected questions, but maybe *he* was wrong-footing *me*...

We were standing close to the wall, beside a doorway into the next garden, staring directly at one another. I was itching to move things forwards, feeling the deal could be closed.

'In a moment, Villiers,' I said, beginning my script, 'I am going to do something. You are free to react however you wish. Knowing what you know about the King and the sort of person he prefers – a catamite, as you say – you may wish me to continue. If you do, I will take you into my employ and seek to give you many opportunities at court. If what I do offends you, you can stop at any moment. I will not in any way react to it or damage you. In fact, I shall give you ten pounds this very day – enough for you to live well half a year in London, I should say. You will never hear from me again and, as long as you do nothing to harm me, I shall do nothing to harm you or block your way if you seek another path into court. Do you understand?'

His eyes were on me. Whatever nerves he had had before now seemed long gone. 'Yes.'

'And do you accept my terms?'

'Yes,' he said without hesitation, without doubt.

I stepped forwards and kissed him on the mouth. At once, he moved into the kiss, and as I was about to pull away, as I had before – quickly, the test complete – he opened his mouth, and his breath, sweet and warm, entered mine. I found it heady, narcotic, much more than I expected. His lips were soft and briefly they parted, and his breath was in my mouth. He moved his body into mine. At once I felt his erection. It was a moment of such tenderness, but desirous too; that first, sweet moment of something. But at once, my good sense crashed in. I did not like young men, anyway. He was not for me; he was for the King. It would be madness to begin something now; a far greater game was being played. I stepped away from him. The moment was gone. He moved back too, lifting his hand to his mouth. He laughed in a sweetly embarrassed way, to show that all this was so unexpected, then swept his hand over his forehead, pushing back his hair, and glancing up at me with his shy, deep eyes. The laughter continued but faded. But I could see some concern – or perhaps it was nervousness – in his eyes, too.

Suddenly – before we had a chance to speak, for me to tell him this was a test – over the little wall we could hear female voices deep in conversation. We both moved in a fidgety rush, as those about to be uncovered do. The door in the wall opened, and through it walked not only Lady Grace but also my erstwhile friend, Lady Frances Howard, now Carr, Countess of Somerset. She immediately looked angrily red-cheeked to see me. Lady Grace, who held a basket overflowing with herbs – rosemary, lavender, mint – looked utterly confused to find the two of us there: 'Georgie? Mister Bacon? Why, what on earth are you doing here?'

Villiers bowed to her, too quick, too antsy. Suddenly he was a country boy again, a humble lad, in the presence of his employer, catching him in the act – of *something*.

'Lady Grace,' I said. 'I have just offered George here a post in my household. I think he will do very well at court, do you not?'

Out of the corner of my eye, I saw Villiers turn to look at me. Lady Grace clapped her hands. 'Oh, excellent,' she said. 'Oh, Georgie, how marvellous!'

I then bowed to Frances, who stared suspiciously at me. 'What are you two ladies doing here at this early hour?' I asked, to throw the conversation in a new direction. It was now well past eleven, and while it was not early for Lady Grace, it certainly was for Frances, who was not used to anything resembling a morning.

'Lady Somerset is very interested in potions,' Lady Grace said. 'She asked me if I could show her some of my medicinal garden.'

Frances gave me a small, defensive smile. 'Lady Grace has been very kind to show me the gardens, but now I must get back to my husband.' She nodded at me. 'Mister Bacon.' Then she pulled away and left me standing with Villiers and Lady Grace.

'Georgie,' Lady Grace said, 'you should run along back to the house. There is a great luncheon today. You will be needed. I am sure Mister Bacon can let you go for a day or two here until the King's visit is over, then I will send you by coach to Gorhambury.'

Villiers looked at me from under his brows, his mouth slightly crooked in a charming, playful way. He smiled a little, his eyes on me very directly. Finally, he turned and slowly walked away, vanishing into the garden's great yellow light.

And so I rode home to Gorhambury at full speed and, arriving at nightfall, told Meautys to dismiss any servants in the house that we could not trust. I explained to him that a young man would arrive at the house, and we must keep his presence as secret as we could. He was to go to London and tell people that I was sick with a fever and would be absent from town for at least two weeks. People must understand that I was not dying – I did not want anyone to think this was their chance to act against me. He nodded and said he would depart straight away. With Meautys gone, I sat down by candlelight and wrote to the Queen in cipher:

MADAM, I HAVE FOUND THE BOY.
AND HE IS PERFECTION.

ON THE SUBJECT OF A
~~PHILOSOPHICAL~~ POLITICAL
EDUCATION

$\mathcal{S}$uddenly, I felt hope again. Perhaps all would go according to our plan after all. The note went off to the Queen on bat wings that night in hopes that she would go to bed knowing the good news. 'I have found the boy, and he is perfection,' I had written. The words felt like a spell. Mrs Turner could have created some alchemist flash, a puff of golden smoke, a bird pulled from a hat, and I would have been no less a believer. It was strange and intense, and it surprised me. I am Bacon, the coolest of the cool, and here I was, like a child quivering with relief at not being found out in some caper. I thought of Will and Ambrose – sweet boys, after a fashion, but both wrong – too ashamed, too amenable, too boring, too bold – and now here was this Villiers, who was just *right*. The whole plan had fallen into place, through sheer good luck. I was not supposed to have been at Apethorpe that day. It was all just luck. Or, if you prefer, fate.

Two days after my return to Gorhambury, a second note arrived post-haste from Apethorpe. It was from Lady Grace. The King had left, moving on to the next house on the Progress and George Villiers was free to come to me. She would send him the next day. Now a whirlwind of preparation took over. Servants scurried to clean and air suites of rooms. I wrote down notes about those subjects which had to comprise his political and philosophical education. I sent to London by return of horse-post for clean silk and cotton shirts, for a suit of clothes and a good hat that could fit his head. I had to guess his height and waist, and his inner thigh. Was a French tutor necessary? No, not yet. A dancing master? Perhaps. Or maybe I could not risk it yet. Tutors talk. I did not yet want anyone to have cause to whisper in town: 'Bacon has a boy...' 'Did you hear Bacon has a boy...' 'A boy?' 'But for what purpose...?'

The room I was giving him was not some servant's garret high up in the attic, but a large and comfortable chamber, with a good view of the gardens. It was freshly painted in a sunny yellow, and I had it furnished with a large *chaise longue* and a chair for reading. (Was he someone who read? Should I have asked that question before? There would be reading enough for him to do in the next weeks.) I did not want him to feel like my servant; I wanted him to feel like my friend, to like and trust me. But I also did not want there to be any mistakes. Mistakes are costly, in money, time – and in other ways. I wrote to the Queen and said that the boy was en route, and then to my spies on the Royal Progress, asking them to alert me to any sudden changes of itinerary. I knew that the

King was due back in London in several weeks. We had that long, and no more. We had to be ready.

*

Mid afternoon on the third day after I left Apethorpe, I was in the library at Gorhambury, attending to paperwork Meautys had sent up from London, when I heard carriage wheels on the gravel drive out front. I knew immediately that it was him. I got up from my seat and walked towards the window that looks down the lane leading up to the house. It was a beautiful, sunny day. A huge cabbage white butterfly fluttered up against the windowpane. It bobbed on the air, carried by invisible forces, dashed against the glass, trying to get in, before flying off, swallowed by the light. I looked back out to see a small black coach-with-four pulling up. On its side were the arms of the Mildmay family. It was him.

Menservants – the trustworthy ones we had retained – flew out to meet the coach. They had been told by Meautys before he went back to town to expect a guest and to cater to that guest's every whim. They stood at the doors either side of the carriage and pulled them open, bowing. A wavy mop of red-brown hair appeared from out of one door, standing on the lip of the coach runner, and then a whole shape followed, hanging off the side of the carriage. I felt a flicker of excitement, seeing him. He jumped down with a boyish thump onto the gravel. Happily, he greeted the servants one by one who, rather confused, bowed their heads and muttered good day, sir, good day. It was an odd moment, a dissonance between who he was now and who he was going to become.

He looked up and around at the house. I stepped back only slightly, from the window, to watch him in those first moments. He walked away from the coach, turning in a full circle, gazing over the wide fields around the house and then back up at Gorhambury itself. He was wearing a simple country suit in a pale blue colour, his head was bare – he did not even carry a hat with him. The breeze over Gorhambury's flat fields whipped his thick hair about his head. Absentminded fingers tried to catch it from going into his eyes, to push it away, neatly, as he had at Apethorpe. His ruff collar was high and white, in the old fashion, from the days before Mrs Turner. He was, if described one way, nothing at all, truly: an ordinary English youth, tall and lithe and full of life. And yet he was nothing like an ordinary boy: thrilling in the immediacy of his beauty, his youthful joy, his mix of knowingness and the innocent, intelligence and the unformed. I said that you could find a boy like Ambrose in any English village. There was something about Villiers, though, that both hinted at the everyday, and yet, at the same time, seemed so remarkable. The intensity of the afternoon light radiated on him. How mesmerising he was, as a *physical* object, in that sunlit moment. There was something of the painting in him, as though he had stepped out of the canvas – this ordinary English Apollo – and deigned to turn and smile at us, his observers.

For a moment, 'Apollo' was watching something above his head. He looked up and smiled broadly, then he turned to the right, his eyes following whatever it was. Only at the last moment did I realise it was the white butterfly. It had flown from me to him. My fingers fell against the windowpane at the exact spot where the butterfly had fluttered. Then he turned around suddenly and noticed me standing at the window. I stepped back swiftly but it was too late. He raised his hand high above his head and gave a great, gushing wave, grinning joyfully. I took a step forward so as not to hide from him, and yet I felt exposed, hot, ashamed. Did he think that I had been spying on him? Well, hadn't I been? I raised my fingers in a sheepish half-wave. He turned around, galloping off to help my servants with his trunks. Briefly, my servants wrestled with him to take hold of his luggage until at last Villiers relented and let them carry them. He looked up at me again, and shrugged boyishly, as if it were all so stupid – and amusing.

Minutes later, we were seated together in one of the receiving rooms my lady mother had kept. They were hardly used these days. The only people I received at Gorhambury were secretaries and spies, not earls and philosophers. That was why it was so perfect to keep him there. We would be alone, and I could start to shape him without prying eyes watching.

'How was your journey?'

He was looking at me up from under his eyebrows. That hazy mystery again. What was he thinking? I would ask myself that many times in the months – years, perhaps – to come.

'It was very comfortable, thank you,' he said.

'And how were the last few days at Apethorpe? Busy, I expect.'

He nodded. 'Lady Grace said it will take her a month to get over it.'

I laughed. 'Lady Grace will be fine by tomorrow, off brewing her potions, making up poultices.'

He nodded. 'I expect so.'

'She is an excellent person. I wish there were more like her.'

He grinned. 'She speaks very highly of you, sir.'

Those were pleasantries, and I wanted to move on from them. 'Are you hungry?' He said he was not. He refused a glass of wine – which any cultured Englishman should accept when offered.

'Do you not drink?' I asked, fearing that now he might reveal he was in fact a Puritan. He may well accept kisses from unknown gentlemen with mysterious offers, but if he did not drink, that would be disastrous with the King. In England, they cannot bear people who do not drink. It's half the reason they round up Puritans.

'No, I drink,' he said. 'I do not want to drink right now, is all.'

He gazed at me until I felt I had to say something. Usually, I say whatever I wish – or assiduously wait until I have something to say. But now I spoke.

'Do you want to see your room?' I asked.

We went upstairs and as we walked, I told him how the house had been rebuilt by my father just before my birth, using the brick rubble from the old Benedictine Abbey down at St Albans, which old King Henry had dissolved. As we got to his room, the sun had turned slightly so that the chamber was no longer in dazzling sunshine but instead had long shadows falling distorted at a sharp angle. It yellowed the room even further. 'It's not much, but it is comfortable,' I said.

Villiers seemed amazed. 'It is the nicest room I have ever had for myself.' He walked around it, looking at the bits of old furniture, the hangings on the wall, the big bed, letting his fingers drag over the top of the writing desk, then gazing out of the window. He seemed genuinely delighted, and I was happy to see him that way. He turned back to me. 'Or do I share it with other lads?'

I laughed a little. Did he truly think that he would be bunking with some new pals? Did he *truly* not understand what any of this was?

'No, it is your room, Georgie. You can use any room in the house you wish. This is your home now. Have you had to share your room with many lads?'

'Oh, yes.' His eyes ran briefly over mine. What did they communicate? 'In England, at home in Leicestershire. All my brothers. When I went to France. At Apethorpe. Lots of them.' More specifically, what did his eyes *seek* to communicate? That is the more important question. The only thing was, I did not know the answer.

'Villiers, do you know what I want from you?'

Quickly he looked towards the door in case servants might burst in and catch us *in flagrante delicto*. 'You kissed me.'

His words buzzed around me. I wanted to crick my neck but instead I nodded. 'But that was a kind of a test. You are not for me. Do you know for whom I want you to be?'

He blinked. For a moment, he looked confused. I had not had a chance to tell him the same at Apethorpe because Lady Grace and Lady Frances had interrupted us.

'*Bacon*,' he said my name awkwardly, like he was having to remind himself not to say sir, 'I would prefer it if you told me straight.'

I smiled. 'That is reasonable enough. I do not live in a world where straight talk is always appreciated, but I am going to speak directly now. You remember at Apethorpe when I asked you about the Earl of Somerset, Robert Carr?'

He nodded, and so I told him what I thought he should know at this stage. I told him that the relationship between Carr and the King was over, and that I wanted to find another young man to take the role of favourite. I did not explain the ins and outs of court politics but only that I thought he was perfect for the role, and I wanted to form an alliance with such a young man, promote him, change his life, become his friend. His eyes were focused on me throughout my explanation, but most fiercely when I used that word 'friend'. That was why I had kissed him in that stilted, rehearsed way, I added. It was a test, to see if he would accept a kiss from a powerful man.

'A *powerful* man?' he repeated softly. 'Oh, I see. It was just a test.' His eyes looked away from mine to the window. The daylight was still bright. He seemed to be considering what I had just said. I felt his physical presence very strongly again, his luminous, sensual quality. Did he understand that he had a power too? Of course he did, I said to myself. People who look like this always do. How can they not? We are a world entranced by beauty. Someone who possesses it must know, as much as someone like me – or you, perhaps – knows that we do not. What is less easy to understand is the effect of beauty on its possessors. Is it a good thing to be beautiful, or exhausting?

Villiers was thinking, working it out. 'You wish me to be a new Earl of Somerset?'

I laughed. 'God, no. The last thing I want is a second Robert Carr. I want someone different to him.' Now I took a real leap of faith. 'I am in alliance with the Queen, and we propose to replace Carr with another young man, just as beautiful, but with better qualities. The King remains in love with Carr but it cannot last. The King wants love in return. He expresses love through, well...' My eyes drifted to the bed, and Villiers nodded, a little round-eyed, understanding my point.

'If you understand anything about the King, Villiers, it is that he craves love. I want someone to give him a different kind of love to the sort that Carr gives him. I think with a bit of preparation, Villiers, you will absolutely beguile the King. The Queen and I can get rid of Robert Carr, and you can change your life forever, become rich, powerful, get a title. Your lady mother, and your siblings, will never have to worry for money ever again. They will have more money than they could ever have dreamt of, and you will have secured it for them. But this is not just a play for money and connections. I mean, you will get those things, but money and titles do not exist on their own. They derive from *having* power. You asked me if we were friends and I said we were. But you must know this, for it is crucially important. There are no friends in this deadly game of power. Only allies. No duke truly likes another, no earl another, no king, no bishop. So to be friends – true friends – two people who truly care and look out for one another – is a trump card beyond all others. That is what I want for us, Villiers,' I said. 'I want us to be friends in power, and that way, I believe we can be invincible.'

He nodded as if remembering a memory from long ago. 'There are no friends in power,' he repeated back to me slowly. This irritated me slightly. I could not tell if he was being tricky.

'*Do you* understand?' I asked, firmly.

'Who shall have the friend, you or me?'

'We shall be each other's friends, always. It shall be an equal friendship.'

'How can it be equal? You know so much more than me.'

Now I felt he was definitely being tricky. I did not like it. 'It will be equal in that we will trust each other absolutely. You have your skills, and I mine.' He seemed content with the explanation.

'You said it was a deadly game. What did you mean?'

When I told him what had befallen Bull and about Suffolk pulling a knife on me, his eyes grew wide with shock. I explained that it was unusual for such things to happen, but they did and he needed to understand that. I thought of my long-dead friend, Kit Marlowe, whom I had recruited as a spy. They say he died in a drunken fight over some boy, but I heard otherwise, that he got his throat slit for what he knew.

'That frightens me,' he said with alarm. 'I don't want to be murdered.'

I let my fingers touch his arm in consolation. His eyes glanced down to my touch. 'If you trust me, you will be safe. I won't let any harm come to you.'

'But what about your friend?'

'My friend?' I asked, confused.

'This fellow, Bull. Do you grieve for him? It must have been very painful for you, to know that your friend died such a horrible death, and that you were in some way implicated.'

'*Me?*' I cried. 'It was Suffolk who killed him.'

'Oh, yes, but Bull was working at your bidding, was he not? Did you feel no guilt at his death?'

I gave a loud, sarcastic laugh. (Yes, of course it was defensive.) 'Villiers, understand this. We are not responsible for the sins of others. We are only responsible for our own actions. We only have to answer for those.'

'To God?' he asked.

'No, to posterity.'

This seemed to amuse him. 'I do not care about posterity!'

I caught his hand. As I did so, his fingers moved lightly so that they just briefly stroked mine. 'You should,' I said. 'Only posterity will mark a man's true success. Children will not. Love will not. Not even money will.' I laughed to myself, pleased with my joke. 'You must want posterity – or you might as well go back to Leicestershire. Do you want to go back to Leicestershire?'

'No, sir,' he murmured, more chastised than I'd intended. I let his hand go. It fell to his side. 'I do not want to go back to Leicestershire.'

'Do not call me "sir". I already told you that. My friends call me Bacon.'

His eyes had grown very wide, almost childlike. Was he playing with me now? 'May I call you Francis?'

'Only my family ever called me Francis, and they are all dead.'

'Then that's good,' he said, not missing a beat. 'Then I shall call you Francis, too. And I shall be as close to you as your family.'

He smiled at me very sweetly. Much to my surprise, I was touched that he should have said it.

My priority was readying Villiers to be introduced to the King. The process had to take weeks not years – as most educations do. By the time the King got back to London from the Royal Progress, we had to be ready. I told Villiers something of my own worldview – liberal, reformist, that of the outsider in an insiders' world – but that was not yet the education he needed. He not only understood, but also was able to ask pertinent questions and sometimes offer interesting views on subjects to which I had only just introduced him. He had this ability to perceive truths about things, to speak the truth too, and do it without being hurtful; that was quite unique. I thought of how it might affect the King, this king of ours who, like all monarchs, privately – very deeply, almost secretly, indeed – wanted someone who could just *know* him. I thought of how Carr had used terror and tantrums and reconciliation to dominate the King, who had crumpled under the brute force of such 'love'. What could Villiers offer that would be different? His compassion. His understanding. His gentle good humour. Well, that was what I hoped.

I asked a local fencing master to come and give him some lessons – but Villiers quickly beat the man. I watched them fighting; how easy and fluid Villiers' movements were. In this, there was a double perfection. He had qualities that were both feminine – a gentleness, a modesty and his own sylph-like physicality – and masculine – a man good at sports, shooting and japes, though he did not like hunting much. This ambiguity was good for the court, which valued both, but also good for the King, who precisely wanted a man who was not too much of a man, but still a man nevertheless.

No matter how incompetently, the King loved to talk philosophy, and of this, Villiers knew nothing. He knew nothing of Aristotle, let alone Anaxagoras. I tried to give him a basic education, but he found it hard. He did not have the right sort of mind for it: he might himself have a mystery, an elusiveness, but he did not like to think of the intangible. He saw that the world could be modern, that science could be organised to help mankind, that the state should not needlessly kill and torture, whatever it was I suggested to him. But when presented with philosophy, he could only see it as ephemeral, solipsistic nonsense – or worse.

Once, I gave him a short accompaniment to St Augustine. Several days later, we were discussing his thoughts on the City of God.

'I cannot decide whether St Augustine was a very stupid person, or a very unhappy one, but either way, I cannot help but think he is the most evil person in the history of Europe.'

'*What?*' I cried, half mock-offended, half actually shocked.

'Francis, do you believe that an unbaptised infant deserves to burn in hell for eternity?'

'No, of course I do not.'

'But according to St Augustine, any baby that dies at birth, before a priest can get there, or dies in the womb, is damned to hell for ever. Does that make sense to you? A baby burns in hell because fate – God – gave it no chance to live?' I went to speak but he continued. 'But thanks to St Augustine, almost every woman in Europe in the last thousand years has believed that, and almost every one has had a baby that has not survived to baptism. And so almost every woman has had an awful, paralysing grief and guilt inside her, that she has somehow condemned her poor, dead baby to burn in hell for eternity. But I do not think she has. I think St Augustine made up such nonsense, because he diligently pursued some philosophical dead end. And the result? Millions of women live their lives in misery, thinking their dead babies burn in hell. What good is philosophy if all it does is hurt – and lie to – people?' This was a very good question. But more than anything, I wondered at his compassion for grief-stricken women mourning their dead children. And so I thought also of the Queen.

Once, he asked me the difference between Socrates, Plato and Aristotle. I sighed that we were at this stage, that he wanted these levels of explanation, but I decided to treat it as a game for myself. How do you explain the deeply ephemeral to those uninterested in ephemera? Socrates, I said, asked questions, and he believed people should ask themselves questions about their own life and its meaning, their own actions and behaviours. 'The unexamined life is not worth living.'

'Can I read one of his books?' he asked.

I said no. 'He did not write any.'

'Then how do we know he truly said what he said?' This was a surprisingly astute question, because it brought me on to Plato, who, I suspect, was an inveterate liar.

'Plato told us what Socrates said. He developed his ideas into his plans for a perfect government and society named The Republic. Socrates taught Plato, and Plato taught Aristotle.' I nodded. 'And Aristotle educated Alexander the Great.'

He looked surprised at this information, then added, thinking himself clever: 'Then Aristotle educated all of us.' *Well*, I thought, *maybe. Let's see.*

I explained to him that Plato's idealised society consisted of a republic ruled by a class of educated gentlemen, who would use their erudition and knowledge for the betterment of all society. At this, he openly sniggered. 'Like those aristocrats at Apethorpe do?' I laughed too – he knew how to engage in satire. I explained how Plato believed that an austere regimen was necessary for this class: no fish, no sauces or sweets, no meat unless roasted. By following this diet, these men would have no need for doctors. At this, he fully burst out laughing.

'If Plato knew so little about healthy diets and medicine, how dare he write such rubbish about it?'

I thought about other things Plato had said, suddenly hopeful of more derision. Now I *wanted him* to say these things. I wanted him to say that Plato was a fool and those who deified him morons. 'He said that all children – aristocratic children – are to be taken away from their parents at birth, and raised collectively, not knowing who their father is. Infanticide was compulsory to any child born to a woman younger than twenty or older than forty, and any deformed children were to be abandoned in some mysterious place. People should have no choice in whom they married and should not feel any emotion about their spouse.'

'Oh, my goodness, Bacon! These philosophers are idiots! They say the most ridiculous things and everyone accepts it as if it is the wisest thing, when it is nonsense. Why, merely because they call themselves philosophers? What fools intellectuals are! What stupid idiots!'

'I am a philosopher! I am an intellectual!' I cried happily. We were laughing with such gusto that we quite forgot what we had been saying. 'You have broken philosophy,' I said, and he shook his head charmingly.

'It broke itself,' he said. 'By being so stupid.'

*

So philosophy was a bit of a disaster. But more important than philosophy (a line with which I am sure he would have agreed), Villiers needed a political education. It was essential that he understood the machinations of the court. I told him of the divorce case, every part of it: the background, the relationship between Carr and Frances, Coke's view, how we faked the virginity test, even down to giving the maid five guineas for her trouble, and how she had gone off happily to her new life.

'How did you know the maid was happy?'

'She was a servant who could leave her job with five guineas. Believe me, she was happy as a clam.'

'A clam with a stranger's fingers inside her,' he deadpanned – and I laughed. He did a little, too, though with a strange, chilly air. I felt uncomfortable.

Such machinations truly served only one purpose, I told him: to gain access to power, which always – *always* – ultimately derived from the confidence of the King. He who controls the King controls England. That is the truest secret of power: control.

'Is that what makes men happy about power?' he asked, and I thought it an insightful question.

'Perhaps.' He seemed to grasp my meaning immediately, which was good. People, in my experience, have a natural feeling for power; they understand it natively. 'Some people are born into power,' I said. 'Kings, queens, earls. It is their fate on the basis of their birth. Other people seek it. I truly do not think that anyone understands what a trap power is before they access it. Once you are on the treadmill of power, it is impossible to get off – you seek power, and so you make enemies; if you lose power, your enemies will get you, so you seek more power, and gain more enemies, on and on – until the loss of power ultimately results in a loss of life.'

'So you must never lose power?'

'Precisely,' I said.

'And what if you do?'

'Then you fight with everything you have in order to survive.'

'What happens to friendship then?'

It was a good question.

'You have to want power,' I said. 'You have to want it and fight for it. Do you understand?' He nodded but I saw a little fear in his eyes. I could have shouted at him, I suppose, but instead I caught his hand. 'It's going to be all right. We are friends, and we want this together.'

He nodded again, but this time, I could see his relief and trust in me. I was glad of this too.

*

Usually there is no sex at Gorhambury. Absolutely none. I am fond with my servants – pay them well, do not whip or punch them as most men do at the slightest whim – but I do not fuck them. But one night, when the household had long taken to bed and, alone by candlelight, I scratched a quill-nib on government papers, I felt the old itch come on me. I could have pleasured myself, but I wanted more than quick relief. I wanted to touch skin. I wanted to hear someone else's soft moan as I pushed inside.

I rode – close to midnight by now – down to St Albans. It is just like any other market town in southern England: wattle and daub, thatched roofs, pretty lanes in springtime with the hawthorn out, humped little bridges that loop above trickling, trout-filled rivers. It should not be large enough, with only three thousand souls, to reliably find sex with men, but St Albans has a trick up its sodomitical sleeve. Here, most travellers break the night at a coaching house before entering London the next, or more likely, bypassing the capital to head to the English Channel. And so in the scraps of woodland that fringe the town, you can often find, late at night, men who are bored and lonely and far from home. Sex: it gilds itself with the poetical meanings of love and marriage, but is just as brilliantly a function of loneliness and tedium.

There is a stretch of low trees – walnuts and apple – that putter away from the old town down to the Ver River, which runs back up towards Gorhambury. Here, over years, I have come to know that at night the 'hunting' is good. I tied my horse in a discreet place, but where, as the town clock struck twelve, two other horses were also mysteriously tied. That meant I was not alone. Taking a risky breath, I plunged into the blackness of the trees. I circled a while between dense, ripping woodland and brief open copses. The night was star-bright, so in the open areas, every shape and surface – every blade of grass, every branch on every tree – was painted a purplish silver.

146

A breeze ran through leaves, and I could hear frogs croaking, an owl hooting. Otherwise everything was silent. I was alone. Suddenly, from nowhere, a male body appeared, melting straight out of the dark. I moved nearer to him and him to me, staring at me directly, hungrily. As he got closer, his form was revealed – young, slim, boyish.

'You all right there?' he said, his eyes twinkling through the darkness.

'Very good, thank you.' I brushed past him as he reached out to catch my hand. But I do not want boys. I went to turn away. He watched me going and hissed under his breath.

'You're old anyway.'

It almost made me laugh. 'I know,' I said back to him. 'You're not telling me anything I don't already know.' He glared at me, with all the arrogant uncertainty of youth, before turning and striding off.

I moved into a larger body of trees. Here, it was darker again, with less starlight penetrating the cover. The night remained quiet. Sometimes down here, it could be thick – writhing, even – with bodies in the dark, but not that night. I began to wonder if I had chosen badly, if I would not have been better spending five minutes masturbating and falling asleep in my bed. I thought about going back to my horse, riding home and doing just that. Then I became aware of someone walking behind me. I turned. It was so dark, it was hard to see. But the shape of a man was definitely following me. I stopped and his outline became clearer: tall and broad, a shock of dark hair. I turned more fully towards him. He walked up to me. It was exciting. I felt the blood move in my body (you know where).

'All right?' the man said, as he came closer, in some northern accent – a traveller, I guessed. When he was very close, I saw that he was maybe in his thirties, masculine, roughly handsome – just what I liked. But then he walked past me, not looking back. Had I misunderstood, seen things through the wrong lens, the one that desires more than it thinks? Just as he was being swallowed up by the shadows from which he had appeared, the man turned back and grinned. I knew I was to follow.

We began to move through the trees, the two of us. Now and then he turned back to look at me, with a handsome, masculine grin. His hand ran down his body, over his hip, momentarily touching his buttock. As it did so, my cock started to harden. I looked at his hand on his body, then saw it fall away, as he was turning around to face me more fully. Soon the two of us would stop, and who knows what then? Maybe we would kiss. Maybe my hands now would touch his lean and muscular body. Maybe he would whisper, 'Fuck me,' and we would go off into the bushes and disrobe just as much as we needed. I would spit in my hand. He would pull down his britches and...

The man spoke. 'Give me your fucking money,' he growled. The shock of the moment made me freeze.

'What?'

'Give me your money, or I will slit your throat, faggot.' He grinned again, but now the grin was different, filled with hatred. 'Would you like that, huh, faggot, for your friends to find your body down here, where everyone knows filth like you goes? Would you like that, you disgusting pervert, for your lady mother to know that you take men's cocks up your arse and that you died for it?'

Something flashed in the dim light under the trees. I understood at once it was a knife.

'No!' I cried, instinctively, an impulse of fear.

'Then give me your fucking money, faggot, and I'll let you run squealing like a forest piggy.'

He raised the knife higher into a shard of light from above. Suddenly the blade was shining as brightly as the moon. That moment with Suffolk returned to me, but more intensely than before. Suffolk probably never meant to kill me. Could I say the same now, there, in the wooded darkness? I had a bag of gold tied at my belt. I pulled it away, panicking, not wanting my shame revealed in death, more even than not wanting to die. My shame, my horror, was screaming at me. *I do not want to die this way, with my secrets all on display.* The rope tying the bag snapped, the bag opened, and coins flew everywhere.

'You tricky cunt!' the robber yelled and barged straight at me. The knife was in his hand and, for a moment, I was sure he would stab me, but then his arm lifted and he punched me hard in the side of the face. I fell backwards onto the ground, feeling only the shocking, dazing force of his blow and where the brambles of the thicket floor had ripped at the skin of my hands. The robber scrabbled for the gold, and then, having gathered what he could, landed a hard kick in my side and was off. I lay there, in the darkness, rolling around in pain. I was afraid that the robber might come back, just for the mad-man's spite of killing me. Finally, I scrambled to my feet and ran, breathless, through the blackness of the wood.

I somehow found my way back through the woodland to my horse. Untying the reins, I grabbed at my side, fearing my ribs had been broken. I touched my face, wondering if my eye would blacken. Slowly, I rode home to Gorhambury and, with every minute, my shame engulfed me. Look what the Normal Man does to us. He does it without *any* shame. He does it because it is his right to kill a sodomite. And then I heard my own impotent whining, and that only *deepened* my sense of shame. Impotence was the last of my problems. That was what almost got me stabbed.

Arriving home, I let the horse loose in the stable, which I closed myself. I alerted none of my servants. It was better that they did not know – or guess – what had happened. When I got myself to bed, I was so relieved to be home – to be alive – that I fell asleep almost instantly, exhausted by the vestiges of my fear.

*

In the morning, I could see even in the round, green-hued mirror in my room that my eye was indeed black. Thankfully, the bruise was not big, just a smudge of purple-black in the well of the socket. I wondered how I might disguise it, but what was I to do, lead my face white like the old Queen? I touched my ribs and felt sure that they were not seriously damaged, thank goodness. The last thing I needed in the next few weeks was broken ribs.

I went down to my parlour and asked for breakfast to be served. The girls who came to table, with bread and cheese and malt, said nothing, but I saw them look at my eye. Did they guess at what had happened? They were young things – bright, but innocent – and maybe they knew nothing of what – who – I had been the night before. Eventually, Villiers appeared, tumbling into the parlour in good humour. 'Oh, I am ravenous,' he was saying, as he came through the door, but the moment he saw me, he stopped in his tracks.

'Francis, what happened to your eye?'

I affected a great confidence, a cheery countenance. 'Isn't it obvious? I struck it.'

'With what?' He pulled a chair close to mine and, physician-like, inspected it closely. 'An iron bar?'

I was going to make a joke but something in his proximity prevented me. He was so close, I could feel the warmth of his body next to mine, and innately, I wanted to be honest with him. 'Someone struck me.'

He sat back. 'But *why*?'

'I went out last night, late, and they robbed me.'

'Robbed you? Who would rob you?' He started to get to his feet. 'I shall send for the sheriff from St Albans. Your assailant must be caught—'

His words – his obviously sincere care – touched me, but I pulled at his sleeve to calm him. 'Do not do that!' My alarm stilled – and alerted – him. 'Do not,' I said more quietly. He was watching me.

'Why not, Francis?'

I paused. The truth was on me then, a treacherous interrogator, desperate for me to reveal my secrets.

'I am a sodomite,' I said. I watched his face for signs of disgust but found none. 'Last night, I went to a place where sodomites go. You understand why they go there?' He nodded slowly. 'I have been there before, but last night, I met a man who designed to rob me. He just stole a little gold—'

'And gave you a black eye,' he said, with bright outrage for my sake. I was his friend. I understood it then, that this friendship might be real. But I needed him to be calm, to recognise what mattered in the situation.

'And if we tell anyone, I might be burned alive in St Albans market square. Or worse, the gossip might get back to London.'

He came close to me. He leaned forwards and, tenderly, put his hand on the back of my head. I could feel his fingers through my hair. It was just a small act of consolation, for one who has had the rough end of things, and yet in that moment, it genuinely moved me. 'We should call for some mint,' he said.

'Mint?'

'Yes. We will get some mint cut from the garden, and have it pulped in the kitchen. I will spread it on the bruise. It will cool and heal it.'

I laughed. 'How do you know how to heal, Georgie Villiers?' He just shrugged and grinned, and let his eyes settle on mine, those marvellous strange hazel-green pools.

As the next hour unfolded, handfuls of mint were cut and ground down in a pestle and mortar. Villiers brought it up with some vinegar and water and mixed it to a paste. Then, with such care that I thought it might have been something Lady Grace had taught him, he knelt down between my legs, as I was seated, and painted my skin with the astringent, green balm. At first, it stung slightly, and I wriggled and groaned. He laughed and called me a baby, told me to stop making a fuss. But then we became quieter, the two of us, as his fingertips gently rubbed the mint paste into my skin. I watched him working, our faces close.

When he was done, to my amazement, there were tears in his eyes. 'What's wrong?' I asked, hearing the surprise in my own voice.

'No one should have done this to you, Francis.' His emotion – its vulnerability – startled me.

'Hey,' I said, touching his cheek, those remarkable eyes sparkling and intense as they watched me. 'I live to plot another day.'

I said it to make him laugh, but he just gazed at me with the utmost seriousness. Our faces were very close, our mouths only inches apart. I felt the most extraordinary – not desire – but connection to him in that moment. It was something I had never experienced with a man in my loveless life.

I felt so breathless. He had just been this boy – yes, exquisite, yes, charming and funny – but now he was no longer just that physical object, that glittering pawn to be played in the game. He had become *something else*.

ON THE SUBJECT OF
A MADNESS

$\mathcal{W}$e tipped fully into summer in those weeks, and our friendship – our intimacy – deepened. The bruise under my eye faded, but now, in the revelation of the truth, something seemed forged between us. These were small changes, but tangible. We began to speak in whispers when others were near. I had always found him amusing but now we laughed more and more when we were alone.

The two of us began to go out for long walks in the countryside around Gorhambury. Over two or three hours, we would discuss politics or law, the machinations of the court, the endless tide of the King's whims and weaknesses – and how Carr manipulated them. It was during those peaceful times together that our closeness became evident. I felt certain of our new intimacy. I had once said to him, quite glibly I see now, that there are no friends in power. Had I reckoned on what it would mean, to be his friend, truly?

Meautys wrote to me every day with court work to be done, reports from spies on the Royal Progress, whispers about the Howards and the Carrs. He started to send me notes asking why I had not dealt with all the correspondence I had been sent; it was not like me, I knew, to fall behind on my duties. He couched his requests for that work to be done in polite enquiries about my wellbeing. Was there a problem? Was I unwell? Was something distracting me? I stayed up late at night, to catch up with what was late being sent back to London, working through the hours of darkness, sometimes falling asleep at my desk. As hard as I work, I don't think I had ever done that before. But in the morning, I would want to be up in time to greet Villiers at breakfast and to listen happily as he chattered away about this thing or another. I knew it was a pleasure to be in his company, but I had not especially expected how much I would rearrange my days to spend my time with him.

Gorhambury seemed to fill with his presence. Every day, more packets of correspondence came from Meautys, and many other letters – some written in cipher – arrived. But more and more, I gave my time to Villiers. We were, quite simply, having too much fun, long after a man expects fun to be what he wants in life. I began to dream about him, which, on the one hand, was quite natural: of whom else should I dream? But I was also aware of *how much* I thought of him too. I wondered, sometimes, if I was ever not thinking of him. And yet it never occurred to my – conscious – mind that I desired him. I could observe his beauty as one might an exquisite jewel belonging to a friend, which one thinks astonishing but does not plan to hide in one's own pocket when the friend is not looking.

*

One afternoon, we agreed to go on one of our walks down towards the Ver River. It had become one of our favourite places during lessons. It is very quiet there; if you do not walk towards St Albans, but stay in the woodlands further upstream, you hardly see a soul. The area around Gorhambury is generally flat and open, all fields and pasture, but there the altitude tips downwards. Feet hurtle down slopes, towards the level of the river. Thick ferns and nettles grow, sycamores and beeches form dense screens, so that you can walk quietly, unseen by the shepherds and drovers passing by.

As we walked, he asked me about the proposal I had made to form a union of the crowns of England and Scotland. When I published my *Discourse* back in 1604, the year after the King had come to the throne, proposing a formal union of the kingdoms – a united kingdom – I had been accused of toadying, I told him.

'Were you?' he asked with such a winking sort of mischief that I could not help but grin.

'Of course,' I said. 'The person who pretends they are not toadying in the presence of a king is a liar. It is half of what our lives are. I wanted to get ahead, I wanted to impress the new King. I am an outsider. Those who accused me, with their lands and titles, were not. They did not know how precarious my life had been under the old Queen, especially after the Essex debacle. I wanted to prosper. I am not ashamed of that.'

'No,' he said, 'you should not be.'

I smiled at him. 'Nor should you. Those people will try their best to make you feel small, but only you can actually feel it.'

'Oh...' he whispered, as if that was the first honest thing anyone had ever told him. Suddenly he bent forwards and pointed. On a rock in the small tumbling river, a heron stood, watching for fish. The bird was long and elegant, a sweep of nothing but fine pale-grey lines, as if painted into existence. It was beautiful. Watching it, and watching Villiers, I saw his boyish wonder, his wide eyes, the quieting finger at his mouth. Was he silencing me or himself? He stood there, rapt, like some kind of naturalist, in search of New World specimens. A full minute passed, with Villiers and the heron each in perfect, elegant still-ness. Eventually, I gently tapped his shoulder and whispered that we should walk on. My voice, no matter how hushed, alerted the heron, and it took to the air, with slow flaps of its great, silvery wings. There was in him then both great joy at the marvellous sight and a sadness too that the magical moment was over.

We dawdled on, and the trees grew cool and shadowy around us. 'What was it like,' he asked eventually, 'when the King ascended the throne?'

It seemed so long ago, I had to think. 'The old Queen died in the spring, the early part. It was still cold. The moment the breath was out of her body, a rider was sent to Edinburgh to offer the current King her throne. There had been secret discussions for *years* because the old Queen refused to name an heir.' I groaned. 'She really *was* a pain in the arse sometimes.' His eyes lit up to hear me speaking so irreverently, for most people still spoke of her in hushed Gloriana tones. 'It would take a few months for him to arrive, for Scotland is a wild country, not at all like England, much given to rebellions and plots. His own mother lost her throne in one. He has himself faced many rebellions there. People mock the King for his drunkenness and silliness but somehow he managed to bring his Scottish people peace and has thus far avoided war much here, whilst the old Queen revelled in military things. It is not glamorous to avoid war, but it is a sign of greatness.'

He furrowed his brow too ironically. 'Do you mean the King is a great man?'

'Ha! Let's not get carried away.'

We were smiling at each other. There was something else in the smile too: his beauty, its intensity. Suddenly my head seemed abuzz, like when one wakes after drinking too much. It confused me but I pressed on. I told him what the King had been like, arriving in London, how amazed he had been by the new wealth he had inherited, dressed more like a country doctor than a European prince, but how soon that would change. I sighed. 'He discovered the joy of having more money than you can spend, and accepted the challenge.' I looked at Villiers and shook my head. 'Power is not a spendthrift's place. You need to enjoy money, but know its value too.'

'Value?' he asked, looking at me very directly, satirically. 'How can one misunderstand the value of money?'

'I do not mean guineas and farthings. I mean that money is a form of power. It helps you accumulate power, it helps you demonstrate power, helps you acquire it. You will gain money soon, but it is important that you respect it and spend it freely, to show your power, but not so freely that you are out of control.'

I thought of paying Carr the thousand pounds and then paying for his wedding. I still had not recovered financially. Now here I was, doling out financial advice. Clever old Bacon, eh?

'What about love?' he asked, lightly, sincerely.

I turned to look at him as we walked, but he did not look at me, preferring to keep his gaze in front. 'Love?'

Still his eyes did not meet mine. 'Aren't we also saying that love is power?' I thought this very clever: love was absolutely a currency – a very great one. His thinking took him further: 'And you say power makes men happy, but what about love?'

Somewhere above us a songbird sang a line or two. He still did not look at me.

'What we are doing is nothing to do with love,' I said. 'It is the mimesis of love.'

'Mimesis?' *Still* he was not looking at me.

'An imitation,' I replied, aware that he knew no Greek. Then he turned to look at me with his extraordinary eyes. I felt something in my chest catch, the suddenness, the alertness of the movement.

'I do not believe in imitations,' he said mysteriously, a pink blush on his cheeks. All my pretensions – Greek words, proclamations about power – fell away. The song-bird's voice vanished as we resumed walking under the trees. 'But what about love?' he asked again. 'What role does that have?'

My thoughts drifted again, but towards what? After-wards, it might all seem clear, but then in our moments together, I could not imagine what was to follow between us. But some unease – the unease that knows it must not be expressed – settled on me. I shrugged awkwardly, to show I neither knew nor cared. 'I know nothing about love. I am not someone who loves.'

'What do you mean, Francis?'

The question felt awkward, pressing. I did not want to answer it. That flicker of desire was still in me. It disturbed me. I did not want it. 'Love is not for someone like me. I turned away from it, a long time ago.'

'I still do not understand what you mean.'

Suddenly, I felt bothered. I did not know how to explain myself – I, who can explain anything – and truly, I did not even want to. 'Love is too much of a risk for someone like me.'

'You mean a sodomite?' His directness was bold, almost challenging.

'Yes.'

His brow furrowed. 'Do you expect the sodomite to live without love?'

'I don't expect anyone to do anything. We each of us make our own choices. I've made mine.'

'And have they made you happy, Francis?'

There was something too bold in his question; it felt like a trick. I did not answer him and then, perhaps sensing my resistance, he walked on, saying nothing, leaving me standing on the river trail. He did not look back, and so I followed him. We walked in silence for a long time. I started to feel bilious, actually dazed. I did not want to upset him in any way; had I upset him? I wanted that happy, curious boy to return to me, but he remained resolutely silent. Here and there, wood pigeons softly cooed. Somewhere in the distance, I heard a cuckoo calling. As we went deeper into the trees, further and further away from the order of the fields higher up, the mild, green cool of the river began to sink into me.

'If you had money, what would you do with it?' he asked me suddenly, absolutely apropos of nothing.

'Money?' I asked, confused. 'Why do you ask me that?'

'Shouldn't we talk about money?' He laughed. 'After all, isn't that one of our priorities in carrying out this plan, to make money?'

I laughed, but it was mostly a grimace. I was not sure why he said that. I was not really sure about what we were talking at all, and why I, Francis Bacon, felt quite so discomfited.

'I think that I would buy my own childhood home, York House, and refurbish it.'

'Where is it?'

'By the river, on the Strand.' He did not know the Strand yet. He did not know London either, but he would. He was so close to me, and I wanted him, and I did not understand why. These 'boys' – I am supposed to be immune to these boys. 'What would *you* do with money?' I asked, in return.

'I would buy beautiful things.'

The mix of innocence and acquisitiveness surprised – perhaps even amused – me.

'What beautiful things?'

'Jewels and paintings. And silks.' His eyes shone. 'And palaces on the...' He faltered in his knowledge of London.

'Strand,' I said.

'The *Strand*.'

It was funny to see him like this, and it was good that I could see his ambition. In seeking power – which was what we were really preparing for – ambition is the one thing you cannot lack. Everything else is negotiable, in some way: intelligence, brutality, beauty. But ambition cannot be missing. The game is too hard without it.

Our conversation had wandered; I wanted to get back to his education.

'What... what have you been reading?' I asked.

'Machiavelli. It has been helpful.'

'Why so?'

'The thing he said about not trying to be a meteor, but to be a star in the firmament, never changing. I understood what you've been telling me about being steady and loving towards the King. What I should offer him is a peaceful kind of love, to allow him to be happy.'

'You are learning *how* to be,' I said.

'Yes.'

'But do you know *who* to be?' I could see that he did not understand. 'Do you have a sense of who you have to be to the King?'

Some light of recognition passed over his face. 'I have to be the Anti-Carr, the opposite of what he provides. Instead of fury and intimidation, I will bring calm and understanding. Instead of harsh demands, I will bring empathy. I will be the mother he never had.'

I stopped walking. Here was this boy, twenty-one years old, with an observation that most people in court could not have come up with. I was thinking about my mind-science, about what such an observation of the effects of parents on children could mean, and of Villiers' perceptiveness, his intelligence, to recognise such a thing.

He turned and looked at me. His mood changed absolutely, for now he laughed in a lightly satirical way. 'You remain surprised that I am not stupid, Francis.'

I shook my head emphatically. 'I never thought you were stupid. That was why I liked you from the very first day we met. Clever people are everywhere. Go to Oxford, go to Cambridge, you will find those cities full of well-read idiots. The better read they are, the more stupid they become, because they delude themselves that academic achievement is the same as intelligence. Usually, it is its reverse.'

He arched an eyebrow. 'And I am just a simple country boy with a little bit of common sense?' His tone was sharply ironic, and he started grinning as soon as he had said it, but I remained serious.

'You have an ability to see people, I think. To see straight through them. Many highly cultured people have nothing of the sort. Their vanity means that they are only looking at themselves.'

We had come close to the river. I had hardly heard the sound of the water until then. It is more of a stream than a river, it has no great volume. It is quite still in stretches, and shaded by thin trees, and fast where the incline gathers. Here, though, the water was very placid and tempting.

'Can you swim?' he asked.

The question surprised me, and viscerally, before I had a chance even to analyse why, I felt wary. That flicker of desire had left me, but even so, a man knows his body. I did not want to go swimming with him; I absolutely did not. 'Do you think it is hot enough?' I asked, by way of dissuasion.

He shrugged. 'How hot does it need to be? It's just us, so as long as it is enough for us to be naked, of course.' He giggled. 'Come on!' His voice was happy.

At once, he began to slip off his jacket and unbutton his shirt. I had not agreed to swim but here we were, Villiers stripping himself of his clothes in front of my eyes.

He was staring straight at me, grinning. Then he started to pull off his shirt. His body did not have a scrap of fat on it, all long limbs and narrow waist, his skin pearly pale over a rippling, supple landscape of muscles and ribs. He was so youthful, so flawless. Of course he was beautiful – I have told you that a hundred times – but until then, as I say with the friend's jewel you may admire but do not actually steal, I had not felt desire towards him. I said that he was like something that had stepped out of a painting, but in truth, we do not want Apollo to come down from his plinth, to slip away from the canvas.

Seeing him like that – happy, half-naked, in his perfection, when the object became real, a person that was wanted, desired – was the moment; the moment that it changed. Suddenly, in all of desire's mystery, I felt overwhelmed by his presence in a new way, in a way I had not seen – or at least understood – before. All the parts of the puzzle that had not fitted together did so now: his beauty, his intelligence, his humour, his strange mood that day, his questioning, our intimacy, what I wanted for him, to care for and to protect him, to bring him full-formed into a world that would give him everything he – and I – wanted; it all just fitted together. Before, I had not understood that these things might interrelate and produce in me that intoxicating, dizzying rush of desire. I do not like young men. He was not for me. It would be a madness to begin anything. All those thoughts had run through my head, and I had accepted them. In that moment, they were dispersed. What I felt then was utterly, impossibly full-formed. I felt my heart thumping in my chest, my mouth dry, and worst of all – oh, the *worst* thing of all – the old self-treachery – my cock began to get hard.

I could feel it in my britches, thickening, lengthening, forever my enemy, getting ready to make a fool of me at the worst possible moment.

'Are you going to take your clothes off?' he asked brightly.

Literally, I could not breathe. 'What...?'

'To go into the water!'

I, who have fucked numberless nameless men, suddenly felt excruciatingly aware of myself in the presence of this boy. 'I do not think—' I began to say. I was unbearably aware of my body – its age, its ugliness, its dumb fucking erections when it was old enough to know better – how it was my enemy far more than it was my friend, in moments like these.

His brow furrowed – he did not understand anything that I was thinking, or at least I thought he did not. Absent-mindedly, he went to kick off his boots. In a moment, he would be naked. Just the thought of it alerted every drop of blood in my body to move in one direction.

'Stop it!' I said much too sharply. His face fell with shock at my severity.

'What's wrong, Francis?'

'Stop it...' Now my voice had crumpled into a whisper.

'Stop what?' he asked, genuinely confused. 'I just wanted to go swimming.'

'I think you are mocking me.' I don't even know why I said it. I didn't especially think that.

'*What?*' he cried. 'How am I mocking you?'

'Here, with your nakedness and knowing what I am. I think you are making fun of me.'

I could see his shock, at my tone and at the turn of events. 'Francis?'

I said nothing. I was embarrassed, ashamed, that I had brought myself to such an idiotic pass. I felt such confusion. From that moment with the mint, his sudden kindness, how I had told him my darkest secret, and he had not judged me, I had not even realised that I had opened myself back to those thoughts that had passed through me during our first, rehearsed kiss at Apethorpe.

'*Francis?*' he repeated. I could say nothing – his eyes were on me very intently now, the sunlight flowing through the branches above coloured them more green than usual.

'It's nothing,' I murmured, shaking my head, trying to smile. 'Can we… can we go? Just… just get dressed.' I had turned from him so that he stood at my side, staring at me. I could hear how hard I was breathing, whilst he seemed entirely still. I could feel his weight almost as if it was a heavy pull on my body, a foundering force dragging me down. And then he said something so forcefully yet so peacefully, it made me turn back to face him.

'Have you changed your mind about me?'

I heard the sharp gasp of panic that was in him then. Again, that sense of breathlessness was back inside me. 'What?'

He blinked slowly. Were his eyes pink? Or was I mistaken? 'Do you no longer see in me what you once saw? Are you about to send me back to Leicestershire?'

'What? No. No, of course not.' I paused. 'Can we just walk?'

I saw him there, and he seemed so vulnerable. My shame burned, and my disappointment at myself. I did not want to be this way. And here is my confession: I realised that I still desired him. The passing of the moment had changed nothing. The realisation that he was a puzzle waiting to come to its finished form could not be pushed away. I had been fooling myself. And who more than I wishes never to be fooled, and certainly to return to that state, of being one?

'But I know you, Francis. You wouldn't tell me if you had. You would play some game, perform some trick and—'

At this, I felt angered, that he should think that of me. 'And what?'

Now his eyes widened with terror. 'Your enemies, they killed that man.'

'Bull?'

'Yes, Bull.'

'Why are you talking about him now?'

He gasped like this were the stupidest of questions. 'They *killed* him, Francis. They *might* kill me.' He blinked once, very heavily, an action filled with sadness. 'And you play the same game as them, Francis. *You* might kill me.'

'Stop it,' I said firmly. 'You are getting carried away. You are saying stupid things.'

'But, Francis—'

I grabbed his shoulders, staring deeply into him. 'Stop it! I would *never* harm you.'

'You are the most extraordinary person I have ever met, Francis.' I watched something move across his face, a memory perhaps. 'Do you remember, at Apethorpe, when you kissed me? And when I came here, you told me it had only been a test?'

'I remember.'

'I did not know what to think when you said that. I accepted what you wanted from me, I think, before. I accepted that you would want to... to seduce me. And then, when you said you did not want to, I was surprised.' He sighed, long and hard. 'May I ask you a question, Francis?' he asked quietly, almost fearfully. I nodded. 'If you are a sodomite, why do you not want me?'

'What?'

I could hear my own dishonesty. His eyes were on me, penetratingly. 'Why do you not want me for yourself?'

Was there some sense in him that something had changed? Did he ask me that now as some kind of trick? These beautiful boys: how does the ugly man know what they understand of the world? What does Apollo *not* know of love, when I know nothing?

'That was not the plan,' I said.

'The plan...' he repeated with a long sigh that buzzed around me, on the air. 'You do not desire me?'

I am the master of spies, the questioner extraordinaire. I knew better than to answer that. 'Come on...' I said, reaching down to pick up his shirt.

'Why do you not love?' he asked. I stood back up, his shirt untouched.

'I told you. Because it is too dangerous.'

'You mean because you love men.'

Of course that's what I meant. Before, simply, we had been teacher and pupil. But now something seemed to have shifted; he seemed to have taken command of the moment. I did not like it and felt threatened by it. 'I have already explained to you. You are playing with me now.'

He sniffed and looked up into the sunlight. His eyes whitened and shone as he did so. He remained very close to me. 'Do you believe that someone *couldn't* love you?'

'You are mocking me again.'

He shook his head sharply. 'No.'

'I do not think about love,' I said. 'I do not look for it. I never wanted it.'

'What, never?'

I whispered: 'No.'

Now I look back and wonder: is that true? Did I *never* dream of it? Or have I just created a persona for whom the idea of it is so ridiculous – and perilous – that I have forgotten some past me who looked at men and thought, would he let me hold him in my arms, just to stay a little longer, to lie like this, overnight or for ever? Villiers seemed to be asking: could another version have suited me just as well? Or even worse: was that other, lovable version inside me all along?

'Enough talk, let's go.'

It was then that he kissed me – for the second time, the first being at Apethorpe. His movement was unexpected, sudden. If I had had time, I might have moved away, refused it, but he was too quick. The touch of his lips against mine was heart-stopping, but I felt only dread. This was not supposed to happen. I pulled free of him – I could still feel the kiss on my lips – it terrified me – what about the plan? Only moments before he was madly asking me if I was going to kill him, and now this?

He was gazing into my eyes. 'This is what you want, isn't it?' I did not reply. I felt his hands catch my arms. 'Isn't it?'

I could hardly breathe. 'Yes,' I said. 'Yes, I want this.'

'Good,' he said. 'Then I'll want it too.'

Shall I tell you how we hurtled into a golden time, two unlikely lovers? Villiers and I were alone, apart from the handful of trusted servants, at Gorhambury. We covered keyholes and cracks in doors, so that spying eyes could not see what was going on inside. Every day letters arrived: from my spies on the Progress, about business in Whitehall or in town, legal cases I had outrageously put on hold, from Jonson asking me when I was coming back because he wanted someone intelligent to talk to. I knew that soon I would have to return to that world. Villiers would go off to his new life, too. I could not resent or deny any of that. But for now, it was a wonderful time between us: two people, two bodies moving together through an experience that neither of us had expected. We had sex a great deal. I shall say it felt like a dream, because it did, but it was one of those dreams from which the sleeper knows they must eventually awaken. But for now, I let myself sleep on for the pleasure of what it was, my eyes shut, hoping that no one would shake me and say sharply: 'Wake up, Francis Bacon, wake up! You are making a fool of yourself!' But still I did not wake up. Still I refused.

Most days, I wrote in cipher to the Queen, telling her that Villiers' development had been rapid, he was intelligent and picked things up quickly. She wrote back to me: 'Is he too intelligent? Is his intelligence a risk?' I understood why she asked, though I thought it sad. Of course, intelligence is a risk, but where are we in the world when we have to ask those questions? I wanted to tell her: he is perfect. I stopped myself, because resolutely, repeatedly, he was not mine and I was not his. Yet just to feel his skin – warm, smooth – under mine felt like I was flickering back into life, like a bud opening in springtime. (Yes, I know full well I sound ridiculous. Yes, *I know*.)

*

We fucked on his bed every night, and after I ejaculated inside him, I would fall against him and he would draw my body into an embrace, on top of his. 'I love to feel your weight on me,' he whispered. I would laugh, 'And my sweat.' He would say yes. *Yes, even your sweat. Even your lips against mine after a kiss, and before another, as you whisper to me.* And our faces close, our eyes as one, in that utterly secret place only lovers share, we would lie together a long time, whispering in the darkness. All this was new to me: small revelations perhaps, but revelations all the same – even if I only see it now, in retrospect.

*

Still there were lessons to carry on with. We continued to go out on our long walks, but now during our discussions, all it took was for one hand to touch the other's – helping the other over a stile or a stream – and our desire would overtake us. In seconds, we would be flying at each other, me pushing his body up against a tree, or onto a rocky muddy patch of ground, kissing deeply, hearing animals rustle in undergrowth, birds calling in trees. It was a long time since I had felt so alive, I, who had lived in the casualness of sex, in the holding away of it, in the pleasures of anonymity. New things appeared to me, things I had not imagined would matter: the studying of another's body, understanding the rhythms of their pleasure, what they needed to hear, what you wanted to say to them to make them happy, the touches they needed to feel, mutual sensuality, the growing sense of safety. I came to see afresh the intense, subversive wonders of sex, not for a stranger but for one you know: how it was possible to want to consume another person a second time, and a third, and sixth, and a twentieth, like a map or a painting you are studying, seeing more detail, more wonders, each time you look. That such a process could bring not tedium but magical compulsion, a perpetually unveiling pleasure, deep satisfaction, was amazing to me. I had lived my whole life without this, without regretting its absence. And now, with Villiers, it was all-consuming, and it felt revelatory.

*

Never once did he make me feel as if I was not as beautiful as he, when of course, I was not – ridiculously, obviously so. When I fucked him in the evening and I murmured to him I was about to ejaculate, he, with his legs looped over my shoulder, without even masturbating, would moan, 'Me too,' and semen would spray from him. I had never known such intensity of desire, shared equally between two people. But what I had truly *never* known was those moments after, when I collapsed on top of him, and let my head fall against the crook between his shoulder and neck, and calmly, he stroked the back of my hair, and lightly kissed my forehead or my cheek with gentle, closed lips. No one had done that since I was a child. Anonymous lovers do not stroke your hair under the cover of night. They do not let you rest against them, listening to their heartbeat, whilst putting their lips' loving pecks on your skin.

*

Once, I fucked him in the window of his bedchamber late at night, in full silvered moonlight, both of us naked, with my foot against the sill so that I could put some force into it. He arched his back slightly, so that his spine became a beautiful, architectural white slope in the moon's glow. He turned his lovely face back to mine, his full lips open, so that my cock grew very hard inside him and I was about to ejaculate, and said, '*Baise-moi, monsieur.*' Both of us burst out laughing, so that we were laughing and laughing. The whole time I was still hard inside him. And it was all wonderful. Nothing of it was anything other than wonderful.

Afterwards we lay on the bare floorboards of his chamber, our bodies covered in sweat, our breaths destroyed. We lay loosely connected – arms and legs touching – but our bodies separate, facing each other. I asked: 'Why are you doing this?'

'Doing what?' he said, not understanding.

'Letting me fuck you.'

His eyes were troubled. 'Because I want to,' he said, looking at me very carefully. 'Isn't it what you want?'

'Yes,' I said. I felt his relief. 'But we have to remember what we are supposed to be doing,' I continued, and I heard the fear in my voice.

'Shh,' he went. 'Shh,' and I was quiet. 'You are unlike anyone I have ever met before, Francis. So clever, so kind to me. I want you to fuck me. Why wouldn't I – shouldn't I – want that?' He breathed out, long and calm.

That night, at great risk, we slept together. I woke in the morning with him nestling against my body, his lips touching the skin of my neck. And I shall confess this: I felt happy. Truly happy. But then I remembered what we should have been thinking about, and it was not this. Yes, this was a madness. And yes, I knew it had to end.

ON THE SUBJECT OF A
TRANSFORMATION

nd then a note arrived. Meautys wrote that the Royal Progress had turned back towards London. The King had declared himself bored of the countryside. He wanted to get back to town. He felt he deserved some *fucking luxury*. The morning I received the letter, I told Villiers we should go for a walk that afternoon so he could ask me for one last lesson before we left. He seemed surprised when I said it, as if somehow I had not been serious that this moment would come. I showed him the letter – he could not read the cipher yet – and told him its contents. 'Oh,' he said, just staring at it. I did not understand what he was feeling. Weren't we supposed to be dreaming of this?

I spent the rest of the morning with government papers. I gave Villiers a few documents to look at, to familiarise himself with the language of the mechanisms of the state. But I did not want him to understand too much. I had seen all too well with Carr the irritations that emerge when the royal lover begins to think himself worthy of sitting on the Privy Council. He needed to know enough only not to make a fool of himself. He had to be able to listen to the King's problems.

The day was hot, the sun was strong. We agreed to meet on the drive outside the house at two o'clock. I sat working all through my luncheon, until at last I heard the churchbells tolling, carried on a breeze up from the Cathedral of St Alban. One, two: I looked up from the desk, my quill in my hand. As I stopped, I heard the soft pop of a bubble in the ink bursting and looked down to see a pool of blue-black on the paper on which I was writing. I cursed under my breath and wiped the ink that had stained my fingers.

Getting up, I went to the window. There on the drive, Villiers was waiting for me. He was talking to Joan, a girl who had worked in Gorhambury's laundry for some years. She was pretty, tall, with raven-black hair that she failed to keep neatly under her maid's cap. Her hands were bright red from scrubbing sheets in lye. I watched them talking for a moment, engaging in a little flirtation – she shyly, aware of status, and he with the eagerness of the young man for the young woman. They were unaware that another's eyes were on them.

Joan has never married. I do not know why. She is not especially religious and she speaks to me quite openly, without the fear of men some country maids have, but now she is nearing thirty, the world must be asking why she does not wed. Oh, I know what you are thinking: *Good God, Bacon, do you not see the irony?* But I am a person of substance and power; Joan is a maid in a Hertfordshire village. Women like her are subject to the worst suspicions by those who have lived down the lane from them all their life. Her lack of a husband will make people whisper of the coven, and one day, some mob will form and drag her to a tree to hang her. In not marrying, Joan lives on the edge of peril. Married people do not understand the unmarried precisely because they are their persecutors.

I watched Villiers speaking to her attentively – the same absorbing attentiveness he had shown to the diner at Apethorpe the very first time I saw him. I would come to recognise how women were drawn to him, the magnetic power of his charm and, of course, his looks. She stood before him, her eyes on the ground not out of girlish modesty but, rather, the force of his presence. They looked like any young man and woman on any street corner in London. Was she smiling? I could not quite tell, but she seemed happy that the mystery man in the house – a subject of some discussion amongst the servants, I had no doubt – was talking to her now. He leaned forward as if to say something, his mouth close to her ear. Joan turned her face towards him and it was as if they might kiss. I caught my breath, to see it. What had he been saying to her? That he would like to kiss her, perhaps. That he would like to take her down to the wood and fuck her, fast and hard, against a tree, whilst she gathered up her skirts and touched herself. I blinked, watching them. *He does not belong to me*, I kept telling myself. *He does not belong to me. He does not belong to me*. And as I thought the words, I felt better. It was like an olden-times plainchant, sung-spoken by monks, weird sacred words to protect yourself. (In the past, before old

King Henry, we were Catholics still, and could just cross ourselves for luck.)

Eventually, I went down to meet him. By then Joan was gone, off on her duties, and Villiers and I were quite alone.

'I want you to take me somewhere and fuck me,' he whispered as I walked towards him. I shook my head, laughing, although I knew if he came close to me, so close our lips might touch, my hand might brush his body, I would be unable to resist. 'Why not?' he asked brightly, as if it was madness not to.

'Today we work.'

He furrowed his brow. 'Work?' He lifted his hands upwards, to indicate the splendour of the weather. 'It is too nice to work. Today we should go to a field somewhere, filled with high wheat, take off all our clothes, and you fuck me there, with the sun on our skin, away from the world.'

He gazed at me as he said it. I cannot deny it. I felt my cock start to swell. 'No,' I said, stepping back from him. 'Today we work. There is always work to be done.'

'For you, perhaps,' he quipped. 'I am going to spend the rest of my life lying on a *chaise*.' He was enjoying his own joke. But I wanted him to know that this would not be his life. The life upon which he was about to embark would bring riches, influence, titles, perhaps, but it was an anxious life, an existence of waiting – for plans to unfold, for plots to go wrong, waiting for the King to die, not knowing what would happen after, for the game to change, for the Tower's gates to slam behind you. At court, as favourite, even decorous lying-on-a-*chaise* was work. It was part of a performance, and performance – day in, day out – was hard. Maybe that was why Robert Carr had resorted to endless yelling. (Oh, wherefore art thou, mind-science?)

Villiers kept gazing at me. What was he thinking? Was he laughing at our shared path, or even at me, in some knowledge I did not yet understand? I felt a curious trepidation. I did not want him to make me feel like that. Soon we would be in London, and we would each have to know what we were doing, and know that the other did too. Still he was gazing, knowingly, intensely. *What are you thinking?* I asked again, in the uncertainty of my own head.

'Shall we go?' I said and he nodded. As I walked past him, he lifted up his fingers, letting his fingertips brush mine. A lightning bolt passed through my body. We could never have caught hands, of course; the people around, my servants included, would have led us down to the pillory in St Albans to be attacked by those who once doffed their caps to us. So I pulled away from him, surprised by the sudden splash of my shame.

We walked north towards the old village at Redbourn, though not quite getting there. We traced the route of the Ver River but I was careful not to go down near the water itself, where he might pull me towards a shaded spot and kiss me. So we stayed up on the open slopes of fields, walking along ancient paths that had been cut – who knew, a thousand years before? In the next weeks, the green wheat fields would turn golden. Swallows were diving in the skies above us. We saw a great black buzzard, floating on the air, looking for rabbits and fieldmice that scurried away from our footsteps.

'So,' I asked eventually, 'was there anything you wanted to discuss about what we have been learning?'

We were walking in parallel at an easy pace. 'Not any-*thing*,' he said, 'an *anyone*.' I asked who. He stopped momentarily, and I stopped with him. There was a hint of a grin on his lips. 'Robert Carr.'

I had spoken of Carr at length: how he ruled the King, his tempers and tantrums, his selfishness, his cruelty. I had told him how he had to be unlike him, to use different strategies in his approach to the King. Villiers had to bring a kinder, quieter love. What else did he want, or need, to know? 'What about him?'

He turned and walked off. I began to follow him. 'He is very good-looking. And you want me to look like him.'

'No,' I said. 'Not like him. But he is a person of fashion, and you must be a person of fashion. I remember him before he was the King's lover, when he was just another rough Scottish boy on the make. It was his friend, Overbury, dead now, who smartened him up, did his hair, bought him jewellery and ruff collars. It was Overbury who understood how to win over the King.'

'What happened to this Overbury?' he asked.

'He died in the Tower.'

Villiers' eyes widened. I knew he was fearful of what could go wrong, that he might end up getting destroyed in the game. The truth was that he might – as anyone who plays the game might – but it was important that he did not let that fear overwhelm him.

'Do not worry,' I said. 'Overbury fell because he was a fool, and you are not a fool. And you have me, whilst Overbury only had Carr, who betrayed him in the end. They were always the same; even years ago, they were mired in their own cruelty, self-interest.'

Then something changed in him: I could see the question appearing in his head. 'So you knew Carr before he was the favourite?'

'Yes,' I said.

'I knew it,' he said, shaking his head, his irritation plain. I did not understand.

'Knew what?'

'I knew there was something personal in your dislike for him.'

'It's not personal.'

'I do not believe you, Francis.'

I sighed and felt an annoyance that made me turn my head on my neck, almost a crick. 'All right,' I said. 'I tried to fuck him once.'

He was at once all alarm. 'You *fucked* him?'

'No, I said I *tried* to. He did not let me.' He began to walk ahead, faster now, in long, angry strides. 'What is it?' He said nothing. 'What?'

He turned around. The breeze that had carried the sound of the churchbells now hit him. His hair fluttered and he went to stop it, pushing it away from his eyes. He was staring at me intently. 'But if he had let you, you would have fucked him.'

'I suppose so,' I said, watching him, wondering just how tame this cat might be. 'Does it matter? It was a long time ago.' He said nothing. Then I realised what this was. 'Are you *jealous*?'

He did not even attempt to deny it. 'Yes! Yes, I am!' His frankness shocked me.

'What about Joan?' I asked.

'Joan?'

'I saw you from the window, flirting with her. I do not mind,' I added quickly, 'but do not pretend that you are my wife, and I your errant husband.'

I had now gained the upper hand in anger. I was gazing at him, all hot cheeks and furrowed brows. The weight of my stare began to bother him. He looked down at the crumbling soil of the path, drying out as the weather got hotter.

'Once you desired Robert Carr,' he said, 'and now you are preparing to destroy him. What if...' he began but his voice faltered. The wind continued to flutter his hair. He had stopped trying to catch it, keep it out of his eyes, and now it blew around wildly. 'What if you turn against me as you have turned against Robert Carr, or how he betrayed this Overbury?'

I took a step closer to him. 'I will not. We will be friends. Real friends.'

'Friends?' he said mysteriously. 'Is that what we are?'

'What else?' I asked, and at once regretted doing so. *Never ask the questions the answers to which frighten you!*

'I wish we could stay here, like this,' he said. 'I wish nothing would change.' I took another step towards him and his head fell forwards, lightly touching my chest. Instinctively I looked around, fearful that we might be seen. 'I wish I *was* your wife,' he said then, with his head still on my body.

'What?' I whispered.

'You said I am not your wife and you are not my husband. Well, I wish we were a country husband and wife, living out our days here at Gorhambury, with nothing to intrude upon us.'

'What—? What do you mean?'

He looked up at me slightly and then away again. I saw the pink embarrassment on his eyes and cheeks. 'Nothing,' he whispered. He left my side and picked up a long, thin branch, fallen from some high tree across the fields, blown here. Walking away, he dragged it along the ground boyishly. He walked a distance ahead of me, and I watched his body moving, his elegant, slim legs and arms, his domed buttocks, and his wide, straight back swaying in soft rhythm to his footsteps. I wanted to know what he meant. I wanted to know what he was thinking. There was something maddening, no, intoxicating about him.

*

When we got back to Gorhambury, a note in cipher was waiting for me from the Queen:

THE KING RETURNS TO LONDON IN TWO DAYS.
BRING THE BOY TO LONDON AT ONCE.

Within an hour, Villiers and I were riding on horseback to London. There was nothing to take with us, everything could be sent on by cart. What was urgent was that our bodies – or rather, Villiers' body – be in town in time for the King's return, and it was less conspicuous for us to travel by horseback. Watchful eyes would notice the Attorney General's coach with a beautiful boy hovering inside its windows. We rode in full daylight, and yet, like that night that had blackened my eye, I felt a sinister, unseen danger.

As we got nearer to the city, one of the horses' shoes started coming away. We therefore broke at Stoke Newington, a tiny village several miles north of London, where a community of Puritans lived in great sobriety and fear of arrest as traitors or heretics. We found a forge, and the smithy said he could fix the shoe within the hour. As we waited, we talked about finding something to eat, but everything seemed joylessly shut. That is Stoke Newington's reputation – a miserably churchy place, made for churchy miseries. There was a safe well, so at least we could quench our thirst. As he drank, I watched Villiers' throat as he gulped down the water, the muscles in his jaw and neck, the bob of his Adam's apple. When he was done, he caught me looking at him, and blushed a little. I quickly averted my gaze.

'I would that I could kiss you, here, now,' he whispered. I looked back up at him, unsmiling.

'We cannot,' I said, 'not here. The Puritans would crush us under stones.'

'I know we cannot!' he cried. He gave a short, confused laugh. 'I was only telling you what I want.' I had been joking, but he seemed upset, annoyed.

Who was this person? Who was he, that he could be so mysterious and then so turbulently open? It felt like he was using honesty – transparency – as a weapon. I am not used to it: I have no defences against the plain confessions that hearts make. I come from a world of lies and schemes. Nothing had prepared me for it.

'The Puritans would burst into flames if they knew our sin,' I joked, my best defence, and he laughed finally.

We walked into the grounds of an old church they said was built by King Athelstan seven hundred years before. I wanted to direct him back to what we needed to think about. 'How do you feel now that the plan is near?' I asked.

'Oh, I do not know. It is exciting to think that I will soon be in the company of a king, I suppose.' He was gazing at me, wearing his intriguing, mysterious smile. I could see the wonder in his eyes. Was it, conceivably, for me? He took a short breath, as one who is about to speak does, but held it – nervously.

'I am in love with you, Francis,' he finally said, quietly, another damned heart's confession. 'I know I was not supposed to, but I have fallen in love with you. And now I am afraid that you will turn against me.'

The words ran out of him so easily. They were so open, and so sincerely meant, and so devastating. I blinked. No one had ever said those words to me. Shall I tell you that it felt like the very first drops of rain, after a long, harsh drought; cool water on desiccated skin, a flash flood over parched soil? Is that what the poet in us wants to hear? Then hear this: I felt terror. I felt fear and horror. Not quite contempt, but the desire to push those words away.

Bacon, you are just afraid to love, you say? *Yes, I know who I fucking am – thanks very much. But*, you say, *it might be nice to be loved, it might be wonderful, it might be more than you ever imagined.* Well, calm down. Stow your enthusiasms. Love can kill men like me. Love gets you dragged from your home in the middle of the night, puts a noose around your neck. Love is something to murder – before it murders you.

'I have shocked you,' he said. He gave me a small, vulnerable smile. 'It's all right if you do not know what to say.

It's all right if you are not ready to say it back. It's enough that I love you. You do not have to love me in return.'

Could that be true? Could it possibly be true that one person does not mind if the other does not reciprocate? Can one person declare love and not mind that the other does not? Does that person shut their eyes, prey to some demon lurking under a country bridge? Love is the demon, love will suck out your soul. Bring this person's love to me, Satan says, so that I can drink it deep. Bring his love to me and let me be the leech that feeds off it.

I am a man who has lived without love, and who has felt that lovelessness has only served him well. Suddenly, Villiers was offering me his hand to come with him, to cross the rickety bridge, promising that we could avoid the demon underneath.

A shout rang out. It was the smithy from the forge. I looked at Villiers for a moment, his hazel-green eyes on mine.

'Come on,' I said. 'It's time to go.'

He gazed at me a moment, then smiled again and said, 'All right.'

*

When we got to Gray's Inn, a second note awaited me. The Queen would meet us that afternoon at Greenwich. Greenwich is on the other side of the river, far from London. We did not travel over the Bridge and through the lawless countryside at Rotherhithe. Instead we took a private barge at St Katharine Dock, the last part of London before the open country begins. Here and there, we saw little factory villages. The barge moved quickly along the Thames, even though we were sailing into a sharp easterly wind. Our eyes wandered over the swirl of the river's tides. Out here, the gulf between the shores was wider and the sailing slowed. I used this time to talk to Villiers of the Queen. I told him that she was a rather lonely person and that her life, for all its luxury, had been hard. He looked at me briefly, with a curious eye, as if to intimate that the same might be said of me. I did not show him that I knew what he was thinking. I told him about the effect of the death of Prince Henry on her, how she seemed to be all right but truly she was not. I spoke a little of how much hope there had been in the intelligent young prince, at court, throughout the machinery of government, and from his mother, and how shattering his sudden death had been.

'Be respectful to her,' I said. 'Be kind. She has not always known a good deal of kindness.'

'Do you think I have learned nothing, Francis?' he laughed.

'Bacon,' I said.

A mist of confusion was on him. 'What?'

'You should call me Bacon now, I think. It will sound better now that we are in London. It will seem like we are less connected.'

He went to speak but his voice failed, a desperate cluck in his throat. 'I – I do not understand.' I shook my head and smiled, and mumbled at him that he was not to worry. That made him only more confused. 'I was not worried,' he said, but he did not add: *But I am now*. 'What I said...' he began, but seemed to think better of it. I stood before him. If I had been a braver man, or a man more experienced in the ways of love, I might have known how to be frank with him, there and then. Instead, I looked at him and allowed him his silence.

Time passed. The mood brightened between us because we let the uncertainty hang, unresolved. The barge picked its way along the unpopulated Isle of Dogs, a famously poisonous place where not much could grow. A century before, a catastrophic flood had reduced the land here to a soft, dead marsh. The waters had never receded, and the area had been abandoned. They say that the marsh's muddy channels are still thick with the skeletons of those long drowned. Here and there, we saw shepherds walking ragged flocks along the saltmarsh that had formed in the flood's wake. Otherwise there was not a soul in sight. Then the barge turned, and we crossed the river to the south bank's open country until we came to the jetty landing at Greenwich.

There is nothing now of its ancient palace of Placentia. The Tudor kings had loved this place and in its day, there were houses all around for people who serviced the royal court of Henry VIII, whose daughters were born there and whose only son died there. But under the old Queen, the palace of Placentia had fallen into disuse. It stood there now, in accelerating ruin, unloved, almost forgotten. Villiers and I walked the short distance from the river to the old palace. The wind hardly abated at all, loudly fluttering over the open green pastures dotted with rotten, ruined cottages. As ever, Villiers struggled with his hair, but he laughed as he tried to push it behind his ears, to keep it out of his eyes. He was laughing to amuse me. It should have been the happiest thing. But I strode ahead, telling myself to concentrate on my – our – no, *my* – plan.

In front of the old palace, a vast complex of mismatched halls and towers and stables, stood the Queen, with her architect, Inigo Jones. They were poring over large, unfolding architectural drawings. I could hear the Queen before I could hear Jones: her loud Danish voice booming out, 'Excellent, excellent! This is excellent work!' They were alone save her ladies and the men of her royal guard, who stood in two separate groups at some distance. They were a curious sight together, she tall and elegant, with her great puff of blonde hair, and Jones, half her height, his head a riot of brown curls under a close black cap.

The Queen looked up. 'Bacon! You are come!' She seemed in high spirits but did not even look at Villiers. I understood immediately she meant that there be no introductions in front of Inigo Jones. 'Come, see what Mister Jones plans for me.'

She talked me through it all. They were going to build a new house, not a palace like Placentia, but a modern, white-painted house, fashionably restrained in every way, in the new Italian style of Palladio. Jones's drawings looked glorious but the house would seem incongruous next to the old, rambling Tudor palace.

'Will you take down the old palace, madam?' I asked. I spoke in my light manner but so sharply aware that Villiers was there, in some unknown mood, silent, waiting for whatever was next for him.

The Queen spied me hard, with a mischievous wink. 'I might ask you one day to speak to the King about it. I will need money.'

She handed her plan to Inigo Jones and said that that would be all, that the progress was wonderful. Inigo Jones took that as his cue to leave. We watched him go until we were alone, ladies and guards at a safe, unhearing distance. Then the Queen turned sharply; the brocaded silk of her dress rustled loudly.

'So, this is our boy?'

'Your Majesty, this is George Villiers.' He bowed but said nothing. I laughed. 'I have told him not to speak too much, madam, so now he does not even say: "Good day, Your Majesty."'

Just for the briefest moment – so quickly, in a way that only a lover could detect – Villiers flicked his eyes towards me. Then he bowed again to her.

'I'm sorry. Good day, Your Majesty.'

She turned and looked at him, smiling kindly. 'Georgie.' That was what Lady Grace called him; I never had. What was it in these two intelligent women to immediately confer on him a child's name? Was it just his beauty that compelled them, I wondered, or some other quality in him that made people speak to him that way? The Queen smiled then stretched out her hand, indicating that he should leave us. 'Will you go over to the royal guard and then my ladies, Georgie, and tell them that I will be ready to leave in a few minutes?' She laughed to herself. 'My ladies will be very happy in such handsome company.'

He smiled beautifully, gloriously revealing his white teeth. The pink blush appeared on his cheeks. I noted how the Queen smiled back, instinctually, reflexively; this was his effect. When he was gone, I said: 'Well, madam, what do you think?'

She took a step towards me, so that we were close enough to whisper in the wind, although there was no one there to hear. 'You were right. He is perfection. Very beautiful. You have chosen well. I think the King will like him. More than like him.' I felt pleased that perhaps our plan would work. She put out her hand, fumbling for mine. 'I am afraid, Bacon.'

'Of what, madam?'

'I am afraid that we shall create a monster, one as bad, or perhaps worse, than Robert Carr. I am afraid that he will betray us and we will live to regret this plan.'

'No, madam,' I said urgently. 'He could not be more dissimilar to Carr. He is sweet and placid. He is funny and smart, but he wants to do the right thing. He wants to succeed and I have taught him about the mistakes Carr has made, and as such – forgive me, it does not serve us to prevaricate – I am encouraging him to trust in you and treat you as a friend. I cannot recommend him highly enough. He is a wonderful boy. I feel most hopeful about the future, madam, about all our futures—'

I saw the Queen's face: a mix of surprise and amused irony. I was gabbling, making a fool of myself. I had to stop. I felt embarrassed in front of her, a woman of my own age, as I rhapsodised this *boy*, like some silly old fool. I gulped. 'Forgive me, madam,' I said. I bowed to recover a little dignity. 'Madam, there is nothing to worry about. I assure you. We can trust Villiers.'

Suddenly we could hear bright laughter on the air. I turned and saw him with the Queen's ladies, charming – dazzling – them as he had Joan that day outside Gorhambury. Soon he would be everywhere. Everyone would be whispering his name. Let them. It will be the realisation of all our dreams. He and I had to hold on to that. We could not be weak. Or foolish. Or plain stupid. We could not get distracted by – by what? – by love?

'All right,' the Queen was saying, loud enough for her companions to hear. They started to get to their feet. 'We shall go.' Just then the Queen turned back to me. 'Oh, Bacon, the King returns to London tomorrow. He is *alone*.' The Queen spoke in a way that was for the benefit of her ladies and the guard, who were coming into earshot. Who knew who was a spy among them? (Truly, one never *knows*.) 'I understand,' the Queen said in a clear voice, 'that the Earl of Somerset is not coming back to London yet. I understand that he and the Countess have gone to spend a month at Sherborne Castle.' She looked at me meaningfully and privately. 'Very nice, Sherborne.'

This was a delicious whiplash irony. The King, years before, to please the Spanish, had imprisoned Sir Walter Raleigh, who had ever since lingered in the Tower, a shadow of a man. The King had seized Raleigh's home, Sherborne, and given it to his lover. The 'very nice' castle was a double symbol of the vagaries of success: the newness of Carr's and the transience of Raleigh's. If Raleigh could fall, so could Carr, and then someone else – Villiers, perhaps, or even I – might own Sherborne next. The game plays on. Fortunes turn. Men fall.

The Queen bade us good day, and her group moved away. Villiers and I watched them go. When they had finally vanished out of sight, and it was just us alone in the unbuilt or derelict loneliness of Greenwich palace sites, I turned to him.

'You need to be careful,' I said.

'Of what?'

'Flirting with girls. Or boys. It is not your task to flirt.' He laughed playfully. 'We need to be beyond reproach.

There can be no flirtation, no suggestion of disloyalty. You said yourself you have to be the Anti-Carr. You have to be more than him: if he is the personification of all that's wrong and turbulent about love, then you have to be all that's good and safe. That means no flirtation, no other interests at all. Do you understand?'

My voice had risen. He was looking at me, utterly absorbed by how I was hurting him.

'Why are you being like this?' Suddenly he grinned magnificently. I wanted to get away from him then, from his magic spell. 'Are you the jealous one now?' He laughed, hoping perhaps that he was right. 'You know that I am in love with you,' he said, and again the fear rushed at me – utterly merciless.

'Then don't be!' I yelled, so furious I could see his shock. 'Don't be!' I repeated, because what else was there to do, when you have behaved so cruelly, but to repeat the damage, to say the hurt all over again? The moment turned instantly frigid. Those same magnificent eyes grew icy and wide.

'What is going on, Francis?'

And faced with his distress, what did I do? Why, I heated the moment up. 'Bacon! Call me Bacon! There can be no you and me any more, at least not in the way there was at Gorhambury. No more talk about love. No talk about...' I felt the choke in my throat. His eyes instantly glazed with tears. 'No more you and me.'

I stopped speaking, him watching me. 'I am in love with you,' he said quietly, and it felt as though he had just stuck a knife in my stomach. He blinked slowly. A tear ran down his cheek. 'What about in the future?' he asked, and I heard his desperation.

I shook my head. 'There can be no future. We cannot think about any future. The King might live twenty years.'

'I would wait twenty years for you!'

I gave a bitter, knowing laugh. 'You are twenty-one years old. You have no idea what twenty years means when you are twenty-one. When you are forty, you will probably not even remember me at all.'

'That's not true!'

I hardened myself. 'Then maybe it should be.'

What was the worst thing he could have said to me then? That I was old, and he had only ever been playing at love? That I was not the good person I claimed, but cruel, hard-hearted, manipulative, a hypocrite? That he would ride back to Leicestershire right now and I could fuck my idiotic plans? The wind was fluttering up the slope from the river. He was looking eastwards, away to an invisible sea, blinking as the breeze bothered his eyes. Then he turned around, looked up at me and said the worst thing he could have said: 'Will you take me somewhere and fuck me?'

'What?' I muttered.

His eyes were on me very hard. 'Will you take me somewhere and fuck me? Even if it's for the last time.'

I blinked, went to say something but failed. He started to walk back towards the ruined palace, and I – wordless – followed. We found a window on the ground floor that opened into a once grand parlour room, now rotted by the elements. Rain had brought Flemish wall hangings crashing to the ground. Pigeons had nested on the top ledges of the panelled walls; their shit had discoloured and eaten into the wood. Villiers walked towards a bay window with a table in front of it, removed his boots and britches, and saying nothing, spread himself across the top, revealing himself to me. I knelt down and put my tongue against him, as I had many times now. But this time, he did not groan with pleasure. His fingers gripped the table until the knuckles went white with hatred, and as I began to fuck him, he remained resolutely silent. Usually, during sex, he masturbated as I fucked him, as men who get fucked should, but now he did not. His knuckles just gripped the table, whiter and whiter with rage. When it was over, I waited for him to ask me to kiss him, but he did not. After a minute, he pushed me off him, an act of disgust, and rolled to one side across the table, pulling up his britches.

There was no denying it. It was over. It was now truly over. The schemer in me should have felt nothing but certainty that the plan had been restored. Instead, an intense sadness threw its shroud over me. Never again would I hear him say, *kiss me*. He did not look at me, only cleared his throat and sighed, straightened his clothes and walked out towards the sunlight. Then at the last moment he turned around and looked at me.

'You know, Francis Bacon... You say that power makes men happy, because it gives them control. But I think it just gives you control, and not much happiness. Are you happy, Francis? *Are you?*' Then, appallingly, he started to weep. He raised the back of his hand to wipe the tears from his face, like a child might. I felt disgusted with myself, with my own cruelty, and the need for it, because of our plan. 'I think sometimes you are the best person there is,' he said. 'And then sometimes, I think you are the worst.'

He had bested me. I had no answer to that. No answer to the truth: what a thing for a philosopher to admit. He turned and walked down the grassy slope towards the river. It reminded me of that first day at Apethorpe, in the garden, when he had vanished, a mystery, into the daylight. I called his name, but he did not turn around. I called his name again, and still he did not turn.

*

That evening, the Queen sent a note ordering us to arrive at Whitehall by nine the following morning. She added, in cipher, so written by her lady, that she did not know what time the King might arrive but she wanted us to be ready.

Villiers' mood was high the next day. Nothing was said of all the emotion the day before. It was like he had forgotten all about it, now that a gorgeous plate of sweet and golden things was before him. We took a carriage from Gray's Inn down to Whitehall, a long walk for Londoners. It had rained overnight – heavy summer rain – and the streets were thickly wet with mud and carriage marks. As we rode, I reminded him that this was still a delicate time. We needed the Queen to trust him, so he should remain discreet. Push nothing. Speak only if spoken to. Did he understand? He looked at me as if I were being ridiculous. He wanted me to feel his contempt, I knew; I did not fight it.

We arrived at Whitehall exactly at nine and were shown up to the Queen's private apartments. As we walked through the palace corridors, we stayed silent. All I could hear was the clack of our shoes' high heels on the newly laid marble floor. How much did he hate me now? I wondered. (It did not occur to me that, in fact, he loved me, or that love survives the injuries it inflicts.) When we got to the Queen's apartments, she was with a French tailor. Her ladies sat away from them, half-listening in their way. The receiving room in her apartment had several pieces of suits, shirts and shoes, all in sparkling saffrons, primroses and golds – the most fashionable colours. I had not quite expected this. She meant to dress him as a solar faerie prince, composed of yellow light. I looked around at all the fabrics.

'Madam, do you think this is too much?'

The tailor seemed brightly offended. 'Too much, *monsieur*? This is the very height of fashion in Paris. This is the very *zénith* of taste.' He sniffed, looked me up and down. 'This word, in English?'

'Zenith,' I deadpanned, turning my back to the man.

'Madam, his beauty lies in its naturalness. If the King wants to dress him up—'

'Bacon!' the Queen chided, indicating the tailor. 'This man is very knowledgeable. He knows better than you how to dress someone. What you think about how to present the boy—' She cast her hand towards me, my black jacket, brown britches, dun-brown hat. 'Forgive me, Bacon, but you are *not* a person of fashion!'

The Queen walked towards one suit, in particularly spectacular brocade, picked it up and took its jacket to hold against Villiers' body. Its golden colour was so deep, it shone against the paleness of his skin. She turned him towards a standing mirror at their side, and the two of them gazed at his reflection in the glass. It was like he was sunlit by the gold jacket. 'What do you think?' the Queen asked.

'It's so beautiful,' Villiers whispered, in genuine awe, looking at it then at her. The Queen's eyes warmed to his.

'Good, Georgie. I am glad you like it.'

He smiled at her. 'I just want you to be happy, madam,' he said softly. I thought nothing of it at first, but then he added: 'You have had so much unhappiness, and all I hope is that I can help soothe some of it.'

A moment of unease filled the room. The Queen's ladies looked up. They knew as well as I that he was talking about the late Prince Henry, her son. I felt my cheeks grow hot. This was *precisely* what I had told him not to do. Did he dare disobey me already? Here he was, twenty-one years old, daring to console a woman in middle age, a queen, about the death of her adult child. But then she – with sudden tears in her eyes – held out her hand to him. He caught it and curled his fingers comfortingly around hers. He was touching the Queen in a way so casual, so intimate, that the attendants in the room just stared and stared.

'My Henry,' the Queen murmured. 'He was like you. Natural in his kindness.' I saw her squeeze his fingers. The ladies-in-waiting exchanged glances. If any one of them looked at me, I did not see them; I was also just staring. 'Thank you, Georgie, for reminding me of what a good boy he was. And now I am happy, for I see him in you.'

I would never forget that moment. I understood then that he was like liquid, pouring into any vessel that needed filling. I see that now.

An equerry appeared with news: the King was at Camden Town. He would be at Whitehall within the hour. Now everything moved into a different pace and determination. The tailor and the coiffeur began to fuss around Villiers. The ladies were sent out, and the Queen followed. With only men remaining, Villiers took off his clothes, until he was naked before the tailor and me. The tailor's eyes widened with desire but he gathered himself and began to pick out clothes. Villiers stood there in his nakedness, never once looking at me.

The tailor dressed him. Ivory-yellow silk stockings were rolled up his leg. He stepped into full, gold-silk pantaloons, over which went the gold brocade jacket he had so loved, and one of Mrs Turner's fashionable saffron-coloured ruff collars added last. The Queen returned to the room, and her ladies took over now, in the art of the *toilette*. Venetian whitening powder was patted over his face and a pinch of red added to his cheeks and lips. His hair was brushed and brushed until it fell – almost naturally – into steady reddish waves, and then fragrant oils of musk and ambergris were added to make those waves ride back over his head. Finally, a necklace of garnets was hung around his shoulders and chest, a chain of little red hearts. When all was finished, the Queen clapped her hands and cried, 'How wonderful you look, Georgie! How fashionable!' She extended her hand and led him back to the standing mirror. 'Do you see how beautiful you are now, Georgie?' she asked.

I watched him looking into the glass. How hungry he was for his own reflection. He laughed at first nervously, and then pridefully, to see the gorgeous, gilded image of himself returned to him. He turned to me and softly, happily said, with wide, intimate eyes: 'Look!' Then at once his eyes grew cold, scared; he had remembered. Love was dead.

*

The arrival of the court is like a great tide coming in. In the distance, with windows open through the palace to air it after weeks of idleness, we could hear trumpets sounding followed by the far-away rumble of cart wheels, horses' hooves, the excited chatter of hundreds of people, getting nearer. An army of servants rushed around in the great courtyard, girls swept gravel, men heaved back the gates to the palace, standing at attention, ready to bow to their returning master. And then finally, the royal carriage turned into Whitehall, pulled by four piebald horses, followed by endless horsemen and smaller carriages. In the end, it is not so much a tide as a flotilla, an armada, even.

At a high window, above the courtyard, the Queen and I watched, Villiers behind us, being fussed over one last time by the household ladies. Outside, people began to dismount; the earls of England stretching their legs and rubbing their sore arses. Among them, I could see relatively few Howards. There was Lady Knollys and I saw the Countess of Suffolk – Frances's mother – but not the Earl. Maybe they had drifted away as the Royal Progress passed their own estates. We were having very good luck so far.

'It's time,' the Queen said.

The three of us walked out to the palace's central staircase. Young Prince Charles and other members of the Queen's household followed, as we all began to descend. The Queen moved to the front of the group and readied herself to accept her husband back into her life. But this time, she had a trick up her sleeve. All of us assembled behind the doors to the palace building, the Queen, Georgie and me in the centre of the hallway. There was silence. At the very last moment, I heard the Queen whisper: 'Come a little closer, Georgie. Stand next to me.' She opened a hand and beckoned to him, maternally. Again, I felt a knot loosen between the two of us.

The great doors of the palace creaked open. Outside, it was starting to rain. Silver-grey light fell against our faces. People began hurrying in, crouching over so that they did not get too wet in the last few steps inside. Menservants held their coats over the crooked, bloated body of our King. 'Ach!' he cried. 'Fucking London! Ye are away two months and the fucking minute ye cam back, the fucker belts it *doon*!' I glanced at Villiers, looking at the prospect of his future. His eyes were ablaze with certainty, there in his gold brocade suit, yellow collar, garnets and pearls. There was no fear in him at all. What new version of him was this? And then I realised: it was the one I had created.

ON THE SUBJECT OF A...

FIRE!

Who is this boy? all of London began to whisper. *Who is this extraordinary boy?*

His rise was immediate. As we had expected, the King was instantly, overwhelmingly enraptured, by his beauty, by his sweetness, his lack of demands, his kind and funny company. By the time Carr raced up from Sherborne and the Howards to court from their nests, it was too late. The King was in love. He was happy, he was fucking again, and the boy he was fucking was all he could think or speak of. He immediately invested him with estates and riches, and when I – of all people – told him that there was no money to be so lavish, the King raged at me that the boy deserved everything. *Everything.* 'You dunnae understand,' the King yelled, 'what it is like to love, *Beicon*! You dunnae understand!' But as he yelled, I was happy too. My plan had worked. I had been right.

There is a however... however. Now, I was not expecting Carr to disappear in a puff of smoke – or be thrown into the innards of the Tower – overnight. The King was not a vengeful person. He was the sort of person who treated old favourites well. But there was something persistent in Carr's presence in court that worried me. The rise of a new favourite did not displace the old. The placid good nature of Villiers was a different thing to Carr's whirling storm. So one time, while the King was fawning over Villiers drunkenly in exactly the same way as once he had over him, Carr had a full-blown tantrum in front of the entire court. He kept screaming, 'My ain daddy has deserted me! My ain daddy has killed me!' The tantrum reached such an intensity that Carr began striking himself in the forehead with a silver cup, so hard it broke his skin and dented the cup. It felt like a crucial moment, over-played, too much. The King rushed to pick up his Rabbie and dab at his wound with bloodied royal fingers and protest, 'No, no, no! Ye are always mine, Rabbie!' But Carr did not say the thing he should have said: 'Take me to bed, Daddy.' Instead, he said: 'I hate you. I've always hated you. This is why I dunnae come to you nae more, Daddy, because ye have drowned me in your hate.' And there is the most fascinating part of the puzzle. The worse that Carr behaved, the stronger the King reacted. I had wanted Villiers to bring a different sort of love, but it was so different that they were two completely separate things, unrelated in the King's eyes.

Villiers voiced his alarm to me that Carr was not fall-ing. I told him to be calm, not to be worried, but I cannot say that I was not; I was. As the King reeled from Carr's latest onslaught, Villiers remained patient and kind. When the King gave him sumptuous gifts, Villiers said sweetly, 'You do not have to give me things, Daddy,' then paused as the King's eyes widened, 'but thank you – they're lovely.'

The King would rage at Villiers sometimes, just because he was spoiled, and Villiers would simply smile and say, 'Daddy, you do not have to snap at me. You only have to tell me what you want, and I will do it.' This seemed to amaze the King, and control him too. But still Carr did not fall.

Sometimes the King was so consumed with Villiers' apparent goodness that he would burst into tears and clutch his wee boy to him. 'What father could want more in a son?' he would declare nauseatingly. Villiers might glance at me at these moments, in a curious mix of triumph and embarrassment and – maybe – of what might have been. And then sometimes, he did not. He would give himself up to wet, drunken kisses, giggling as one who desired nothing more than that swollen, purple tongue, reeking of wine, investigating his mouth. But this was his job now, and he did it brilliantly. I looked on and tried to feel nothing: no jealousy, no regret. Over time, an uneasy peace settled between us. We were friends, we told each other, in the knowledge that that was not all we were. There was the acknowledgement that we were on the same side, we wanted the same thing, and that we should trust each other, but there was never a suggestion that our love affair should resume.

Meanwhile, I told Meautys to find a new Bedchamber spy to replace the murdered Bull. Notes began to come in cipher, and Meautys showed them to me.

VILLIERS IS SWEET WITH THE KING AND
WITH THE QUEEN.

or

EVERY MORNING AND EVERY NIGHT, WE HEAR THE
KING WHISPERING NOTHINGS AND THEN GRUNTING
ONCE VERY LOUD FROM BEHIND THE BED CURTAINS

or

VILLIERS NEVER ONCE SPEAKS AGAINST OUR FRIEND

I was 'our friend'. Meautys asked if we should let Villiers
know that there was a spy, and I said absolutely not.
Meautys looked a little surprised, for I had told him that
Villiers was our firm ally. But you have to watch your
allies too, Meautys should have known. Regardless, he
came with the same daily reports from the Bedchamber
spy: that every night, two, three times during, they awoke
to the sound of the King's loud grunts, the boy sighing
and giggling, the shuddering, bedhead-knocking climax,
and finally the words: 'Kiss me, Daddy.' Jealousy? Regret?
Now Villiers asked for the King's kisses – not mine. I
shook myself. This was what I had wanted, these were
the symbols of our success. Meautys was gazing at me as
he read it out. 'Do we truly need to know this?' he asked.
'Yes,' I said. Yes, I needed to know, needed to hear these
things. If I had written up my mind-science, what things
would it have to say about that?

Sometimes weeks would pass when I would not see
Villiers alone, grabbing scraps of conversation in a corridor. I tried to reassure him, but the more I reassured
him, the more anxious he became. Sometimes I saw the
worry on his face, but he had stopped admitting his fears
to me. Did he think I was growing impatient with him?
I was not.

And *still* Carr did not fall. The Howards remained grand forces at court, even as they hissed and pouted about Villiers' dazzling rise. The Queen, who was not well much of that year, also began to feel vexed by it. She could not understand how we had played everything so well but had not conclusively won. Yet through it all, I shared the concern that Carr was as yet unvanquished. It was not that I thought he would come back, but I did not yet understand the full consequences of him remaining in our lives.

*

I had been working very hard; of course I had. Eventually, Jonson insisted that I accompany him to the theatre one night. We were going to the Globe, the theatre Shakespeare had built more than a decade before in Southwark, to see a performance of his new play *Henry VIII*. Someone – not Shakespeare, of course, who would never have admitted such a thing – had told Jonson it was mainly written by John Fletcher, and that as a result the play was bad. When we met on Eastcheap, Jonson pulled me into a great bear hug, claiming he had forgotten what I looked like. I laughed, but I confess, I felt very moved. It was nice to be touched by another human being, even just a friend. A year before, it would never have occurred to me to think that: that body can grow to miss touch.

We ate at a chophouse on the north side of the river and then pushed through the crowds on the Bridge to get into Southwark. The Globe was a magnificent building, three storeys high, rising from a dirt-floor pit in front of the stage, where people could enter for a penny, up into the fancier seats above. I had heard that Shakespeare was very clever with property, that it made him rich.

Jonson and I would have our own private box, away from the chatter and clamour of the pit. Up there in the heavens, the wood was painted beautifully – English white cloud burst out of Italian blue skies, angels and gods flirted and frowned. We ordered ale, then Shakespeare came and sat with us for a short while before the performance began. He himself was playing the King. His eyes flashed at mine quickly, and in his unpleasant little way he asked: 'How goes your writing, Bacon? Getting much done, or are you still *grubbing around* at court?'

I made a low bow, even though I was seated. 'Still grubbing around. Doing grown-ups' work. How go your *little* plays? I hear Mister Fletcher has been very busy.'

At this, Shakespeare bristled. 'Some of us are writers and some are not, Bacon. Maybe you are not.'

I bowed again. 'Well, at least you are churning them out. Everyone knows the value of a writer who churns things out.'

Shakespeare is a fool. He never knows what to say. Sculpting words over months and months is fine for him, but he never has a comeback in the flesh. His eyes went round, so I went for the kill. 'Maybe you should go back to your little play, Shakespeare, before Mister Fletcher comes and claims the credit for *Macbeth* and *Lear* and all those others you wrote years and years ago.'

Shakespeare huffily made to leave, saying goodnight only to Jonson. When he was gone, Jonson smirked at me: 'Porkchop, you are the biggest bitch there is.' I nodded elegantly in thanks, and Jonson laughed. 'The *biggest* bitch.'

The play began, but we did not watch it much. It was as bad as people said. Besides, Jonson wanted gossip from court. He did not know my connection to Villiers, but I told him that we were friends. 'Friends?' he asked me with a wink. 'I hear he is as beautiful as Apollo.' The ordinary English Apollo: I had forgotten I had thought of him that way the first day at Gorhambury. I laughed in order to say nothing, and Jonson did not seem to twig. 'Besides, Porkchop, you like a whole other kind of fellow. I hear you like the rough sort.'

'Oh, is that true?' I asked archly.

'So, what is he like, this Villiers boy?'

Everyone wanted to call him a boy. That was what they wanted to believe: that he was a boy. But he was not (I knew). He was an adult (I saw it). 'He is funny,' was all I said, 'in a sweet way.'

Jonson drew back. 'Funny? Then you should put him on that stage. What is he *truly* like?' He came closer to me, in a fake-flirtatious way. 'Come on, tell all.'

I spoke carefully. I did not want to get carried away and embarrass myself as I had the first time I introduced him to the Queen. 'He has this open spirit. It's very beguiling. He is sweet-natured and a little mysterious. When you think you know what he is, he does or says something that catches you by surprise.'

'And you decided to bring him to court?'

I laughed, but it felt so hollow in my throat. 'I think he is probably quite tough. On some level, these boys always are. Look at Robert Carr.'

'You compare him to Robert Carr?'

'God, no! No, they could not be more different.'

I was smiling to myself. I could feel it. Jonson's eyes were glinting with mischief. 'Are you in love with him?' he asked, meaning it solely as a joke. 'Like you were with Carr?'

I laughed too quickly. 'What?' I dissembled. 'I was never in love with Robert Carr.'

'Yes, maybe love is not *exactly* what that was.' Then he paused. 'So?'

'So what?'

'Do *you* like this boy?' Jonson was looking at me. I said nothing; I did not know what to say; I, the investigator, the questioner, silenced by a writer's stupid question. What kind of numbskull gets outfoxed by writers? (Me, I guess, another writer.) Suddenly his stare was no longer satirical. I understood then – too late – that he had been joking and it was my reaction that had exposed the truth. (Did I know nothing of my own game?) 'Oh, fuck, you're in love with this boy, aren't you?'

'*What?* Stop it!'

'Jesus Christ! What kind of game are you playing?'

'I am not in love with anyone.'

He winked at me. He was joking after all. 'Not even just a little bit?'

'Stop it,' I barked, relieved that he was not serious. 'We are friends. Nothing more.' Jonson was smirking. '*Nothing more!*'

There was a brief, awkward silence. 'Watch out for yourself, Porkchop,' Jonson said. 'You don't get to play with the King's tinkle.'

I squirmed in my seat. 'Fuck off,' I snapped, with the purr of a laugh that exists only between close friends.

He changed the subject. 'So how goes court? How goes *the game*?'

I raised my tankard as if in a toast. 'I live to plot another day.' Jonson laughed and raised his tankard to chink with mine.

'You have too many enemies, Porkchop,' he said. 'If you only had fewer...'

'But I do not, do I?' I said. 'The Howards and all their creatures hate me so. Now, if they were able to get at me, my knees would be knocking.'

'But they're not?'

I shook my head. 'Not now. I am safe.'

'For now.'

'For ever.'

He took a sip of his ale and sighed. 'You have too many enemies,' he said again, shaking his head.

We were drawn back into the play, into a scene in which Catherine of Aragon was shouting at Cardinal Wolsey, in front of Henry VIII. The unfortunate queen, of course, was played by a young lad, for women may not appear on the London stage. (Something about their reputations. Or London's, I can't remember.) The boy was probably fourteen and so looked nothing like a woman of fifty being driven to distraction by her faithless husband. I thought of *our* Queen. If only Catherine of Aragon had been smart enough to put Anne Boleyn in Henry's bed herself. Those two ladies had more brains together than every other member of the Tudor family combined, save the old Queen, of course. They would have made an excellent team.

'What about *her*?' Jonson asked, pointing at the boy Queen Catherine, emphasising the pronoun. 'Would you fuck *her*?'

Jonson liked this game. Normal Men who acknowledge the existence of sodomites always like this game. It flatters them to be so liberal, at no cost to themselves.

'I would fuck every one of them,' I drawled as if it was all too tedious. 'I'll fuck you too, Jonson, if you have

213

enough cash.' Jonson snorted awkwardly but he really wanted to play his game, not mine, in which the Normal Man's hole is as negotiable as anyone else's.

'Would you fuck a man who was wearing a dress?' he teased.

'*Would you?*' I groaned. He sniggered as if it was not out of the question, though I knew Jonson's tastes were for hearty, funny girls.

'Oh, go on, Porkchop, I want to know what it's like.'

He did not, truly. He was being provocative.

I turned and looked at him. 'Well, then, why don't *you* go backstage and offer the Queen a shilling if you're so fascinated?' I relented to amuse him. 'And hope he keeps his headdress on while he bends over a banister and lets *you* pump him from behind?'

I expected Jonson to laugh but he was staring very seriously across the theatre at a box on the other side. 'Look,' he said, 'over there. Your friend is in. He is looking at you like he would slit your throat if he had the chance.'

'Who?' I asked, glancing across the gloom of the back of the theatre.

A stage cannon, an effect used in the play to blast out a fake bomb, was lit. Sparks shot out of its end, as brightly as a firework. The whole theatre was illuminated for a moment. Shocked, gilded faces gasped at the spectacle. But for me, there, in that second of illumination, was the long, lean Earl of Southampton glaring at me, with the eyes of one who would train the cannon straight at me if he could.

'He's never forgiven you, has he?' Jonson said. 'For your writing that report about Essex's rebellion.' He sniffed. 'Well, Essex did die, I suppose, and Southampton did go to the Tower.'

I do not know why I became so aerated. I probably would not have with anyone but Jonson. 'Has everyone forgotten what the old Queen was like? She was a nightmare. Do people think it should have been me who died instead of Essex, when it was he who rebelled and I just wrote a damned report?' And then I realised, yes, that was precisely what people thought, and I was being defensive *because* that was what people thought. My innocence had become irrelevant. Like the actors on the stage, it is reputation, not fact, that matters – and mine stank.

I noticed Southampton's companion then. It was – of all people – Mrs Turner. Here she was, the spell-caster for money, a Cambridgeshire country widow made good, a woman of fashion and business intelligence, chattering easily with earls and countesses of the sneeriest sort, the sort who should normally feel revulsion at her type. How high she had risen; how unfathomably high. And without a husband, too. It was against all the rules of English society. She had despised me when we'd met, but I still found her fascinating: a riotous wild herb in a garden of manicured roses. What influence did she have? Was it really only because she had once – admittedly, brilliantly – figured out how to turn saffron starch into a fortune?

Watching them, I became aware of a faint smell of smoke. Darkness had returned to the theatre space, but there was enough light to see Southampton's face again. This time, it was not looking at me but up at the eaves of the theatre. The Earl leapt out of his seat – as if to throw a punch at me. I shuddered in horror at the prospect of violence, but Southampton was pointing up at the Globe's gabled roof, shouting at the top of his lungs: '*Fire!*'

As one, the audience looked about – there was a second of confused silence – then screaming, rising until it was deafening. The roof of the theatre was in flames. The trick cannon had been too realistic; it had set fire to the thatch! People were clattering down stairs, as all around us huge, bright cinders hissed on our clothes and hair. The whole place became a blazing whirlwind of panic. And yet by all accounts, no one was killed and no one was even hurt, save someone whose britches caught fire, the flames put out with a jug of ale. You laugh? Do not laugh. Many Londoners lost their livelihoods that night, and some their fortunes. Dreams turned to ash so quickly in fate's cruel riot. Jonson and I found Shakespeare crying like a baby, his theatre reduced to red-black charcoal embers in what felt like minutes, saying he would leave London, go back to wherever it was he was from, he had had enough of trying.

I went, like many others, to the river's edge to wash my soot-black face in the water of the Thames. People of fashion stood in great number, with the river's waves rippling over the tips of their shoes as they leant forwards and wiped their faces with the hems of their dresses and the cuffs of their sleeves. Some were coughing and crying, and others laughing with that rush that comes from disaster narrowly avoided. Rising, I saw the tall, elegant figure of a woman. She wore a huge, yellow ruff collar and was gazing straight at me. I bowed.

'Mrs Turner.'

She smiled at me meaningfully, then nodded without going so far as into a curtsey. 'Good evening, Mister Bacon.'

'You look very well in the circumstances.'

She laughed in her bright, sharp way. 'Mister Bacon, to-night we were almost burned at the stake. If my cheeks are red, it is from near suffocation not rouge and pinching.'

I gave an appreciative laugh. 'Where are your friends?' I asked.

Her brow furrowed. 'Friends?' But she must have known who I meant.

'My Lord of Southampton and his circle.'

She kept her eyes on me. 'Mister Bacon, even here, amid scenes of hell, you politick.'

I gazed at her a moment, tried to look amused.

'You keep very fine company these days, Mrs Turner. I'm impressed.'

'Oh, outsider,' she drawled, 'you must think me very low that you are impressed by my rise.'

She mocked me again! 'This is England, Mrs Turner, so I am impressed. I mean no insult.'

'No,' she said airily, 'I do not think you do mean it. I do not think you even understand what the insult might be. But then you and I have very different memories of Cambridge, I am sure, Mister Bacon, you in your dream-ing spires, me scrubbing a floor.'

'Dreaming spires is Oxford, Mrs Turner,' I said, thinking I was ahead of this game of wits. But she twinkled with a mysterious smile, blinking once, heavily, with the satis-faction of the trap clapping shut.

'Thank you for correcting me, Mister Bacon. I hope it made you feel better to put me down so, knowing what you know and what you *think* I might not.'

She had tricked me into patronising her, so that she could grin with her winning hand. I remembered when I told Villiers that scholars were stupid. Had she just proved my own point with me as the evidence? *I am not the person you make out*, I wanted to yell at her.

'I am very interested in what you might know, Mrs Turner. When last we met, at your house on Cheapside, you pretended to know a good deal about me.'

'Pretended?' she cried, mock-outraged, but then smiled broadly. Her eyes were flickering with a dark pleasure. 'I see things. I know things. I sense things.'

'You are magical?'

She let out a cluck of laughter filled with sarcasm. 'The universe is magical, Mister Bacon. And full of mystery. Do you not believe in mystery?' Me, empirical. Me, rational. Me, scientific. I let her question hang, unanswered. There was no benefit in answering it. 'I have had a dream about you, Mister Bacon. I have had it several times, just lately.'

I arched an eyebrow. 'A dream about me, Mrs Turner? How convenient that you dream of me when we have not seen each other for months, yet now here we are.'

She smiled and nodded. 'The universe was telling me that we would meet again, and passing on a warning for me to give to you. Do you not believe in predictions, Mister Bacon?'

'I do not believe in games, Mrs Turner.'

'Ha,' she went; we both knew that was not true. 'I would have thought you of all people believe in games, Mister Bacon.' She made to turn without saying goodbye. What compelled me to reach out for her, catch her arm, so that she turned back, smiling? Her eyes glowed with knowing mischief. 'You want to know what I dreamt? You do, in fact, believe in the mysterious and the magical, do you not, Mister Bacon?' She laughed gaily. 'I dreamt you were in danger.'

'From your friends?'

She bit her lips. Her eyes kept glowing, so brightly they were in competition with the flame-licked moon that night. 'No, you think that those people pose danger, but that is a mistake, Mister Bacon. The danger to you comes from quite another place.'

'I think, Mrs Turner, that people like you – necromancers and cunning-folk and superstitious soothsayers – throw out these warnings, vague enough that they mean everything and nothing.'

She shrugged. 'They mean what they mean, Mister Bacon. I have dreams. It is not for me to live them.'

'Everyone wants to live their dreams,' I said.

This seemed to amuse her. She leaned forwards and whispered: 'You do not need to tell me that, Mister Bacon. I *do* live in a dream. I dreamt the life I wanted and I made it happen for myself.'

'So, from whom does the danger to me come?'

She shrugged again to suggest she did not know, and drew back. 'That is the mystery, Mister Bacon.' She walked away laughing, turning to me only once. 'That *is* the mystery.'

That night, I crossed the Bridge back to London and went down to the wharves on the north bank of the river. There, in the darkness, around the boats and barges, bodies slunk about, eyes blazed, shapes slipped into the darkness. I went there because I wanted to fuck, but in the end, I dawdled away. I did not find anyone I liked. It is not because of Villiers, I said to myself. It is not. But it was. I knew it was. I had been fooling myself all along.

I was in love with Villiers, but it was too late. I had let him get away.

ON THE SUBJECT OF
A MURDER

And so, without love, work continued. Always, work continues.

Come the end of autumn, the dark nights getting longer and colder, I was at Gorhambury with Meautys for a few days. We left London to get through all the reports and accounts that needed signing off and the other paperwork outstanding. Still, more work arrived every day from London: legal cases, bribes in great number, gossip from spies, requests for money from the King, notes from Villiers speaking of his anxieties about Robert Carr. On and on, the two of us worked through the mounds of paper, with Meautys helping me by sorting out what needed to be signed, what needed an answer. I would say, cancel this, return this, ask for this information, yes, this is fine. At the time, I was doing a good number of legal cases that had come back on appeal from lower jurisdictions. Meautys showed me letters that had come with gifts, or rather bribes.

Listen. Ours is a world of bribes. I am a judge, and when a case comes before me, the plaintiff will send me

221

a letter defending himself which inside contains a small bag of gold. The defendant, receiving his writ, will write up his reply and, guessing gold has been received, send it alongside a small bag of diamonds and pearls. Nothing too fancy, but enough – so he believes – to sway me. Most lawyers in this land will accept the bribe and take the side of whoever pays the most. *I do not.* I am a rare breed: a lawyer who loves the law. Yes, I love the plotting and the trickery too, for that is my nature. But the layers, the history, the intellectual arguments, how they can be constructed and reconstructed for a later case – that's what I adore the most about the legal world. So I make the judgements I think best and truest to the law. If the law fails, morality fails. If I fail the law, I fail morality. But...

Gosh, isn't there always a 'but'? If I were to say, *no, thank you*, to the first bag of gold, the defendant would protest loudly, *Francis Bacon is biased! Francis Bacon has refused the gold!* And if I said, *but I do not take bribes*, they would both say: *how can we prepare a case not knowing the outcome? How can we trust a judge who is so wildly out of touch with all that's reasonable? We demand a different judge!* And so it goes. Do you see the logic? (Do you? If so, can you explain it to me?) But listen: of every man practising law in England – *any* man – none has been more honest than me. You take the bribe, you do not reject it, and you square your morality – whether you are swayed by it or not – whichever way you wish.

When it seemed the work was done, Meautys brought a last letter. It was from an agent in the Low Countries, he said. 'You should read it,' he added. 'I am not sure if it matters.' Then he paused and looked at me very intently. 'But I think you should read it.'

So I read the letter, which claimed that an Englishman had died of the plague as he passed through Brussels. Before perishing, he had made a fearful confession of his sins, realising his time on Earth was at its end and his soul was in need of saving. He claimed to have once been an apothecary's boy in London where, in the service of his master, he fetched poisons to a woman of high fashion. These poisons, he said, were the sort that could be used to kill someone. The dying man had admitted that he knew for certain that this poison had been used to murder a man whose name he believed was Overbury. My blood seemed to quicken around my body, and I read on, my eyes focusing, somehow knowing what was next. The name of the woman of fashion, he'd said, was Turner.

'Good God!' I looked up at Meautys, who gazed back at me in his unknowable way. 'Is it possible...?' I began to ask, but did not complete my question.

'Everything is possible, Bacon,' was all Meautys said.

In the next days, we sent spies out to London's murder business. Oh, yes, you read that right: murder is a business in this town. There are those who deal in finer forms of poison: apothecaries. Then there are those who will find a blacker kind of phial, not for what does ail a man, but for what might. My spies' black wings fluttered all over London, to every known purveyor. Eventually, out in the village of Kensington, an apothecary was found whom ladies of fashion liked to visit when their husbands were off fucking their mistresses. He was at pains to say that he had never done business with Mrs Turner but had heard rumours of her scouring London. *For what?* Arsenic, blister-beetle sweat, mercury sublimate powder. One could add these to food or a drink, and slowly poison someone to death. He had heard that Mrs Turner said she was coming on the part of someone 'terribly high up in court, as high as a body can go'.

'*Good God!*' I said again.

More information came out when my spies got inside the Tower. The elderly Countess of Shrewsbury – who had been in and out of the Tower for years on account of her entirely benign support for her niece, Arbella, the King's cousin and rival for the throne – had made some complaints. She claimed that there had been, inside the Tower, an allegation that Overbury, an otherwise young, healthy man, had very quickly become sick: grey and vomitous in the nature of poisons. Strange cakes and jellies had been sent in terrific number to Overbury, who consumed them greedily and ostentatiously. Even in the throes of death, he longed to make others feel bad. How very Overbury...

The Countess, who gave up everything for her sense of justice, had filed typically robust complaints with the governor, Gervase Elwes, but absolutely nothing had been done. Apparently, Elwes refused to even discuss the complaints. (With someone as formidable and august as the Countess of Shrewsbury?) So the rumour had grown: Elwes and the principal gaoler, a man named Weston, had allowed poison to reach the prisoner, who in time had died. More specifically, Overbury had boasted the gifts were from Frances Carr. And so the puzzle fit together. Mrs Turner had obtained the poisons; Frances had delivered them in cakes and jellies to her enemy, Overbury. But the crucial question was: what had Robert Carr known?

I arranged to meet Edward Coke at the Old Bailey. It was one of the first days of snow that year. I waited in a small chamber up in the high parts of the ancient courthouse, where there would be fewer ears to listen through a keyhole, or to press against a gap in the plaster. I looked out at the city rooftops just dusted with white. Ten minutes later, I heard rough fellows crying out in the street: 'God be with you, Judge Coke!' 'How well met, Mister Coke, sir!' I groaned inside. How the mob loves torturers, especially of the weak. A minute later, the door slammed open – Coke never knocked – and in he flew, all heavy, flapping black hair, long, grey Methuselah beard and eyes round and dark with native, permanent fury.

'What is this about, Bacon? What tomfoolery are you up to that you have to meet me here, not at Whitehall?'

I explained to him what I knew about the allegations around Overbury's death. He did not understand the significance of what I was telling him. The governor of the Tower and his gaoler had covered up the poisoning of a fallen courtier at the possible behest of a louche lady of fashion, Mrs Turner, of whom he claimed not to have heard.

'Oh!' he cried. 'All this tittle-tattle is only interesting for your *fancy* sort, Bacon.'

'Fancy' meant effeminacy – or perhaps, more correctly, degeneracy. The Normal Man insults then pretends you misunderstood if you react. So I stayed as cool as ice.

'Coke, let me try again. Mrs Turner, an intimate of the Countess of Somerset, furnished poison to kill Overbury, an intimate of the Earl of Somerset. The complication is this. The Countess and Overbury hated each other. The Earl, and no doubt his soon-to-be father-in-law, my Lord of Suffolk, feared that Overbury had information that could stop the marriage, information that would ruin the divorce case: that Frances had been fucking Robert Carr for months.'

Coke gasped. 'But she convinced me that she was a virgin!'

I, the architect of that deceit, smiled sweetly. He was bubbling with annoyance.

'What is the evidence like against the Carrs?'

Truth was, it was circumstantial at best. From another view: plainly thin. 'We can get Turner and the functionaries at the Tower without problem.'

'And you want me to try what?' he asked.

'The initial trials. Hopefully, the others, if we get that far. I will handle the investigation.'

He regarded me with open contempt. 'Why don't *you* prosecute the case?'

I assumed the question was a play-act. 'You know why.'

'Because you do not want the political motivations of the trial to be revealed. You do not want your grubby fingers all over the undoing of Carr when you want everyone to admire your *fairness*.'

Oh, everyone knew that I hated Carr and he me. Everyone knew I would be happy to see the Howards badly damaged. But aristocratic families, like garden weeds, always return eventually. What I truly wanted was, as with the divorce, to let Coke be the face of the trial while I held the puppet strings. It was better for everyone.

'What does the King say?' he asked.

'The King sent me here,' I lied. (The lie was necessary.) 'Will you do it, Coke? The King needs a yes or a no.'

That afternoon, I asked to see Villiers privately. He suggested we meet in a small room high above the Great

Courtyard at Whitehall. When I found it, it was barely furnished, just a few chairs and nothing on the walls – so different from the splendour of the rest of the palace. He was already waiting, leaning against a window ledge. The veil of snow had melted; it never stays in London. A soft, pale river light laurelled his saffron-yellow ruff and his bright-blue silk suit. He smiled gently when he saw me. I remembered his kindness to me that day after I was robbed. There was the same tender quality in him then. We had not been alone for some while. And now we were, I felt nervous – reckless, perhaps. I felt my chest pound with the weight of the love I had let slip away.

'How are you?' he asked as I entered.

I turned and shut the door behind me. 'I am well. I have been working hard.'

'Of course you have. All you do is work.'

He smiled softly, mocking me gently.

'I have news,' I said. He let his head fall backwards so that it rested against the windowpane, looking at me with a hazy smile. His eyes were focused on me; I felt desire for him. I cleared my throat and began to tell him everything. I saw his manner change. He grew alert, his head left the glass.

'What does this mean?' he asked.

'It means that we can get rid of the Carrs, hopefully.'

At this, his demeanour changed from awkwardness to a strange excitement. He stood up properly. 'What do you mean, get rid of them? Convict them of something?'

I shrugged. 'I don't know. Why are you so antic?'

'*Don't know?*' he cried. 'Antic? I want them to be gone! I want him...' He took a raw breath. 'Gone. So convict them.'

'I do not know that we need to convict them. I think we can give it a go—'

'What do you mean we don't need to convict them, Bacon?'

His use of my surname like that irked me, even though I had told him to use it.

'Well, the scandal will be enough to force the Carrs into retirement. The King can send them from his presence. A trial is a risk. We might not win.'

'So you do not think you *can* convict them?'

'The people who did the killing: definitely. The Carrs: *possibly.*'

'Who cares about the people who did the killing? It's the Carrs we want.'

At this, I turned the legal moralist. 'A man *is* dead.' He shot me a look that could have turned milk. 'I need to speak to the King,' I said. 'I need to get him on side.'

His attitude changed; he nodded in agreement. 'We are going to Windsor tonight. Tell him there, early in the morning. Do not come with us. Arrive early and out of breath, even if you stay in a tavern in the town overnight. Make it seem like you have pelted from London with news of murder.'

I laughed a little. 'You are quite the plotter.'

He grinned. 'You taught me well.'

Suddenly we could hear footsteps outside. I saw him take fright.

'I cannot be caught here with you. People will talk,' he said and made to leave.

At the last moment, I said to him: 'Do not tell the King. Let me do it – urgently, apparently without a plan. Let it be a shock.'

Turning, his eyes studied mine. He had a look I could not read. What was he thinking? He nodded briefly and left, and as he walked out into the corridor, I heard a servant gasp: 'Sorry, sir.' Villiers began to speak to him, with good humour to relieve the man's worry. I heard his voice receding asking for some help on another floor, saying the servant should come with him, arranging my escape.

*

The old Queen loved Windsor. The high, impenetrable walls made her feel safe. Like King James, hers was a childhood of loss and danger. Now the King rarely went out there, finding it cold and gloomy, its dark towers and bare stone walls too reminiscent of the freezing Scottish castles of his unhappy childhood. The castle was too small; the aristocrats always argued over rooms. But its smallness also meant he could come without the court, to indulge in drinking and hunting, and sometimes new love. A lack of glamour can have its advantages. (Yes, of course: *I* would say that.)

Before dawn, I travelled upriver by barge, the safest route. The water was covered in a white mist as the light came up. Boats appeared out of thin air, mere feet from us, and vanished again. As we travelled westwards away from London, the banks of the river gave way to woodland. Here and there, country people watched the barge from the shore, like ancestral ghosts. It is not unknown for them to rush barges, to raid and steal, but that morning, they simply stood and watched us floating past.

At Windsor, the castle seemed quiet. Entering without fanfare, I was taken to the Royal Apartment and asked to wait. I was told meaningfully that the King was still not at *levée*. I insisted that what I had to say could not wait, and so was admitted and found the King and Villiers both in nightgowns still. The King was seated, having his ulcerated foot bound, while Villiers remained lying in bed. The room smelled fetid, traces of sex lingering in the air. Villiers' thick hair was ruffled from pressing into a pillow. I shuddered, confronted with the cold reality of what they were. I felt a rawness in my chest that surprised me. I imagined the King on top of Villiers, his wine breath, his slobbering mouth, drink-extended belly, his raw, ulcerous foot, and I felt sorry. Villiers had been so happy with me in Gorhambury, such a pure happiness. But to my surprise, what I also felt was rage; in a way I had not felt before.

'Ah, *Beicon*!' the King cried. I bowed and said nothing. Villiers shifted on the bed, but I did not dare look at him again, his body in the nightgown, his beauty under a veil that might reveal its form to me, who no longer could bear to see it.

I asked the King to dismiss the Bedchamber servants – if I had a spy here, so could anyone else. When it was just the King, Villiers and me, I told him *almost* everything I knew. After a while, the King raised his hand for me to stop, and for a moment, I was unsure whether he was going to tell me to say no more, that he did not want to know. 'I will nae hear it of my Rabbie!' The King's eyes flickered around to Villiers.

'Georgie has explained everything already.'

Amazed, I looked at Villiers, who did not look back at me. I'd told him *not* to say anything. Did he openly disobey my schemes now? The King continued: 'I know that Rabbie and his lady are the schemers behind this whole nefarious fucking *plan*!'

All feline, Villiers slinked towards the side of the royal chair. Quietly, he laid his hand on his lover's shoulder. I saw the smallest movement of the King towards his touch. Still Villiers did not look me in the eye, though.

'So,' the King began, 'what are ye thinking we do, *Beicon*? Who is gunna care about that snidey horror, Overbury, *eh*?'

I spoke slowly and very gravely – all the while, furious with Villiers for disobeying me. 'Yes, sire, it matters, because I have already heard the story from several sources. The murderers left their inky prints everywhere. This story is going to come out, and if it is also revealed that you knew about it, or even if you are just implicated by association because Overbury's murderers live, unpunished, at court, it will be bad for you. On the street in London.' I paused. 'For your international reputation.'

The King blanched. 'I am very well regarded across the Continent! Every cunt there thinks I am fucking *tip-top*!'

'Quite so, sire. But this way, we can be the ones to reveal the crime and the ones to prosecute and punish. This way, we will control the story rather than catching up with it, when it eventually breaks.' I took a short pause before adding: 'Which it will.'

The King raised his fingers to his lips, his eyes round. 'Ye can kill the small fishies, nae fucker will care about that. It will provide a nice bit of Sunday entertainment for the mob,' he said chillingly. 'But what about Rabbie and his wee girl?'

'We can arrange a prosecution. Edward Coke can be the face of it. You are king, so you can pardon or banish them, if you wish. They could retire to the countryside. I know you used to love my Lord of Somerset well. You can let him slip away from court, if that is what you wish.'

I sensed some tiny movement – some straightening of the back – from Villiers. The royal face twitched. 'I am nae like my old Uncle Henry who cuts off the heads of those he didnae love no more. If we can let Rabbie slip away into obscurity, maybe that is the best way yet.'

Villiers' hand moved on the King's shoulder, who looked to it, then raised his own hand to catch it. 'I am a very *modern* man, *Beicon*. A very *liberal* man.' *Ugh*, I thought. He had taken the words I use about myself and thrown them back at me. He pulled Villiers' fingers to his wine-crusted lips and kissed them; *ugh* again. 'What do ye think, my wee boy?'

Villiers stood there in his nightgown, his hair ruffled with sleep – or sex – a knowing, dishevelled angel.

'I think we should kill them.'

He said it so calmly, it took me a moment to register that he had said it at all. I looked at him, in gathering disbelief. 'What?' I whispered, forgetting that the King was right there.

Villiers' eyes flickered on mine. 'Bacon,' he said slowly. 'I think that we should kill the Carrs. That would be the best thing to do.'

Now, I am not a shockable man. The only thing that ever shocks me is the depth of men's stupidity. But in that moment, I could feel my jaw slacken. Villiers kneeled down at the King's side. I saw how their fingers remained entwined.

'I think, Daddy, that my Lord of Somerset and the Lady too have committed a very great sin for which they should be punished. I think the *moral* thing to do is to punish them as murderers are punished within the law. And it will make us all –' his eyes flashed to mine again '– feel safe if they are gone. And you will appear to be a king who is a champion for justice, for even if Overbury was loathsome, should he have died like that? By means of poison? After all, aren't we all afraid of poison?'

This was a masterstroke of control. Kings are terrified of poison. It is their deepest fear, that one day, someone will slip a phial into their goblet. Catherine de Medici, the appalling old Queen of France, put poison in gifts to old friends, inside books, even the linings of gloves. Yes, Villiers' invocation of poison was masterful. (I ought to have been impressed.) He was whispering to the very deepest royal terror: *there are poisoners at work, they are close, very close, you will be next, sire.*

The King stuck a finger in the air. 'Ach, no! Poison? How ye are right, wee Georgie! Ach, ye are the sweetest, kindest of boys!' He drew a long breath. '*Beicon!* The Carrs must face the full might of the law.' Then his eyes popped as round as pennies. 'We should kill those *evil* bastards!'

And all the while, Villiers was staring straight at me.

*

In the next hours, I roiled with anger. In my head, I practised great speeches I would give him, in which I warned and berated, in which I told him to listen to me, in which I told him the truth of what I felt, and then again, how I denied it.

That evening, there was to be a feast to mark the granting of a new colonial venture in America. As this was Windsor, it was not large – by court standards – and the atmosphere was informal, which was another way to say even more drunken than usual. Whilst milling through the crowd, saying good evening to those who liked or loathed me, my eyes searched angrily for Villiers.

I should have been pleased with the other guests. Howards were there, although not in great number, and neither the Suffolks nor the Somersets were present. Carr was said to be sulking in London, because he had wanted the King to go to Theobalds, where his tantrums got a bigger audience. Plus Windsor was so cold and grim. I should have been pleased, but I was furious.

Very quickly, everyone seemed cross-eyed with wine and brandy, although I had hardly touched a drop. I found a servant and asked where Villiers was, only to be told that he was not coming to the feast. He felt unwell and had asked the King to excuse him. I knew then that he was avoiding me, but I would not be put off. I went up to the Royal Bedchamber in search of him.

The corridors of Windsor were empty and dark; most people were down at the banquet. Here and there, I found servants sitting around, chatting, playing dice or wolfing down scraps between shifts, turning idly towards me as I passed. Finally, I arrived at the door to the Royal Bedchamber and knocked.

'It's Bacon,' I called. No one responded. 'Francis Bacon!'

The door pulled back. It was Villiers who opened it. That meant no servants. 'Good evening, *Francis Bacon*,' he said. 'You'd better come in.'

He stepped back to let me enter; he was indeed alone. There, at the far end, was the royal bed, raised on a dais above the level of the room's windowsills, its curtains pinned back. Elsewhere, the room was largely empty apart from small tables and chairs, and the truckle beds on which the men of the Bedchamber slept – all save for Villiers, of course, who slept with the King every night: he was now England's true queen.

I looked at him. He was only half-dressed, a creamy-white silk shirt unbuttoned down his chest and hanging loose from his britches, his hair wilder than I had seen it for a long time, his feet bare, not even in stockings. Of course I desired him; *of course I did*. There was supper on a trolley near the royal bed with cold roasted game, candied fruit, bread and wine, accompanied by two crystal glasses, one of them half-filled. He had been drinking but he was not drunk. Perhaps, in the whole castle, only he and I were sober. He closed the door behind me and turned the key.

'You do not even have a servant with you,' I said.

'You're angry with me.' I turned to look at him. 'I do understand, Francis.'

'Bacon.'

He shook his head. 'Francis. You are always Francis to me, truly.'

I looked again at the trolley. 'Whose is the second glass?'

He stared at me a moment. 'Yours. Shall we sit?'

'How did you know I'd come?'

'Oh, Francis. I knew.'

Did he mean to mock me? 'Why do you want to kill the Carrs? I do not think it's necessary. I would never have guessed you would want so harsh a measure.'

He looked down to the floor, not evasively but rather sadly. I could see in him, in all that he was now, the new and adored thing at the heart of a castle, the same person he had been before, at Apethorpe and Gorhambury. Suddenly that anxiousness he sometimes showed returned.

'I am frightened,' he said. 'Carr has not fallen. I am frightened that things can turn against me. Against us. I do not trust that everything is going to be all right. How can anyone trust in that? I trusted you, told you that I loved you, and you turned me away.'

It struck at me that he should say that. His eyes were wet, and he wiped at them with the back of his hands, to show that he was not weeping when clearly he was.

'Villiers...'

'Georgie!' he cried. 'You could call me Georgie! Call me by my name for once! I am not just someone you met in passing! I am the person who loved you! The only person! And you call me Villiers – like I am your servant!'

His emotion was enveloping me, like a snake around my body, twisting and twisting. I wanted him to calm down, but he began gabbling about what the future held if Carr did not vanish. And then he spoke about how he had loved me and wanted to stay at Gorhambury. He felt like he had to protect himself, he said.

'From whom?' I asked.

'From you!'

'*What?*'

'From you, who has brought me to the edge of my own *death*!'

I let what he said hang in the air. It was a brutal thing to say, unfair.

'Did you mean it?' I asked. I could see that he did not understand. 'When you said that you were in love with me?'

He looked back at me with a small, sad smile.

'That day at Greenwich, you broke my heart.' He shook his head, a mist of emotion surrounding him. 'It was the day I realised that you would never love me.'

I had hurt him so deeply. I had done things to him that I should not have, and they had drawn him to a place that he did not deserve. 'So I expect now you hate me, then?' I said.

He grew very still. 'No, Francis, I am in love with you.'

I felt the muscles in my back connecting, disconnecting, releasing. I felt the tension in my forearms and wrists release and let go. I had to remember who I was – who I had been before... all this. 'I am not going to kill the Carrs,' I said coldly.

'Is *that* your response to what I have just said?'

He moved towards me, I thought, to kiss me, but he did not. He held his face close to mine, his mouth close, parted lips. 'Was I just this plan to you? Was I only this plan?' He was almost imperceptibly shaking his head as he spoke. 'Was that all we had, a plan?'

'I never understood how someone like you could love someone like me. You are so beautiful. I—'

My voice fell away. We were gazing at each other, alone, it felt, not just in that room, or that castle, or even this kingdom – but across the whole universe; two lovers. I knew I had brought him into this world, and I knew the stress it brought him. I wanted to protect him. I understood why he wanted to kill the Carrs – why he felt that it was among the rules of this place. I wanted him to feel safe.

It was I who reached forwards, I who kissed him. I could taste the wine, sweet and fragrant, on his lips. I heard the happy giggle in his throat as he kissed me back, starting to open his mouth wider to mine. I pushed him down on the bed, and soon we were kissing deeply. He started to peel away his clothes. 'I love you, Georgie,' I heard myself saying. 'I love you.'

I love you. The unsayable, the unthinkable words: here, admitted. How did it feel when those words left my mouth for the first time in my life? Frightening. Intoxicating. Dangerous. As I said them, I heard the soft sigh in his throat, felt him push his weight against mine, there of all places. 'We cannot, not here, someone might come,' I said, starting to pull away from him, but he pulled me right back.

'Fuck me, Francis,' he said again, opening his lips against mine.

'We can't, not here—'

'The door is locked... Fuck me... Please... Fuck me, so that I know... I just need to know...'

'Know what?'

He breathed in and out; I felt it in my own mouth. 'That it was real,' he whispered – and I was lost.

Afterwards, we lay together on the King's bed. My arm was over his body, my cock still half-hard against his thigh. We breathed in a rhythm. He rolled towards me, onto his back, so that I lay, slouched, over his body. He began to speak.

'Do you think that if the King died, we could leave court and go to Gorhambury and live there for ever?'

'The country husband and wife?' I said.

'I think about it every day.' I heard the sadness in his voice. I would have given anything to make it go away. 'I wish we could go back. Do you think it's impossible?'

'I do not know what's possible any more,' I said, thinking I was being honest. This did not seem to comfort him.

'I wish you knew.'

'I will always protect you,' I said, which was hardly a reply.

'Because of the plan...'

'No!' I cried. 'Because I love you.'

He turned towards me fully so that we were face to face. 'What?' he whispered. The words he had so longed for were now with us. There was a light in his eyes, and he began to smile – not knowingly, but shyly, happily, very happily.

'I do not want to kill the Carrs, but we have to,' he said. 'It's the only way to be safe.' His determination startled me. 'It's the only way,' he repeated. I blinked, and he smiled.

'All right,' I said, and even as I said it, I knew I was doing the wrong thing. But sometimes for love, people will do the wrong thing. And they will do a lot more besides.

ON THE SUBJECT OF THE
MEANING OF A YELLOW RUFF
COLLAR ON A COLD WINTER'S
MORNING

First, the men at the Tower were taken. We did it under cover of dark, so that people could not see. With pistols pointing at their wives' faces, held by men who wore black scarves over their mouths and noses, Elwes and Weston were spirited away in the dead of night, into the Tower they had once guarded. How the other prisoners must have gawped through their cell-door grilles to see them coming in as prisoners not custodians. Did Elwes and Weston smell their own deaths? The game turns again.

At daybreak, the major players were struck. First, Mrs Turner was arrested just after dawn in her nightdress, barefoot but – reports said – unsurprised. She said nothing, admitted nothing, went silently towards her fate. Boxes of poisons were found in her private safe. There was Spanish fly, famous as an aphrodisiac when given in small doses, but with the quantities she had, easily fatal; mercury sublimate; an empty metal phial that smelled faintly of garlic, which is how arsenic smells when it is gently warmed, to add to a cake when it is baked. More spectacularly, a letter was found, addressed to Gervase Elwes. It was from Frances Carr, with instructions on when to give Overbury the sweets and when more would arrive. This was the first good, strong piece of evidence. It was not clear whether Mrs Turner had kept the letter and never shown it to Elwes in case she ever needed to blackmail Frances. Therein is the truth of friendship in power: you always need a bit of leverage.

In the morning, the Somersets were arrested, too. Carr was taken to the Tower, kicking and screaming, demanding to see the King. 'Does he know?' Carr kept yelling, in increasingly frantic disbelief. 'Does he know? Does he *know*?' Because Frances was heavily pregnant, she was kept under house arrest in their apartment at Whitehall. No one was allowed in to see her without my express permission. Her father, Suffolk, came several times and was always turned away. He wrote excoriating letters to remind me who the fuck he was. It was such icy delight to me to ignore every single word. Not answering the letters was important. Soon, I heard that some of the minor Howards had left London for their country homes. Panic was spreading. Did Suffolk remember when he threatened to stab me? Did he not know?

Faggots can stab back.

*

The next day, I decided I should go to see Frances to question her, as once I had before, in very different circumstances. I walked across the country edges of London towards Whitehall. It is not a long walk, and I hurried towards I do not know what – something closer to the truth, perhaps? As I walked along the Strand, when Whitehall was almost in sight, I passed York House. The King had asked me not that long ago if I had a property in London I would like, to suit my station better than my rooms at Gray's Inn. Suddenly, I thought of what Villiers had asked: after all this, what would we do? Who would we be? Might we live together here, at York House, as husband and wife? It was a fantasy, of course – but an exquisite one.

At the Somersets' apartment, a gentleman usher led me on silent feet to the receiving room. Frances was sitting awaiting me. She rose as I appeared, her eyes red with tears. The usher announced me, but she shooed him away. 'I know who it is!' she snipped at him, and he withdrew. She was wearing a pretty and clearly expensive lilac-grey gown – loose over her full belly – with a white lace cap. Significantly her ruff was white and rather simple: she was disassociating herself from Mrs Turner already. (But she'd need to be cleverer than that.) When she saw me, her lip trembled for a moment. She must have known I was at least *in part* the architect of her woes. Gazing up at me with her huge blue eyes swimming with tears, she whispered: 'Oh, Bacon. How good to see a friend.'

A friend? I wondered whether she was being sarcastic or strategic. There was nothing to lose in letting me think that she believed it. I might take pity on her, decide to help her.

'When does the baby come?' I asked.

'Another six weeks or so, the midwife says.' She paused. 'Do you think they will wait to hang me until after the child is born?'

'Who says they are going to hang you, Lady Frances?'

She put her hand to her neck. 'Or will they cut off my head?' She blinked heavily. A single tear ran down her cheek. A second did not follow it. 'My cousins were beheaded.' She meant Anne Boleyn and Catherine Howard. 'And my grandfather and great-grandfather.' This was the Earl of Surrey and the Duke of Norfolk, executed for treason under King Henry and his daughter, the old Queen: a father and son killed by a father and daughter. She laughed sadly. 'Beheading is an occupational hazard of being a Howard, I believe.'

Her joke was grimly funny. I actually felt sympathy for her momentarily. Then I remembered how she'd let poison slowly burn out Overbury's stomach lining.

'Lady Frances,' I began, 'if you tell me the truth, I will intercede with the King. He is minded not to kill you, I think, maybe even to issue a pardon for you.' Her eyes widened with surprise. But I confess: I needed the girl white with fear. 'Frances, may I speak frankly and not offend you?' She said yes, hesitantly. Aristocrats like to choose for themselves when they are offended. 'The King loved your husband a long time. The Earl – Robert – was a very precious thing in his life. If only Robert would understand how to use that high value in the King's heart, he can save himself – and you.'

She thought for a moment. Her hands were rubbing her belly instinctively. 'What would you recommend, Bacon?'

I sighed to pretend that I had not yet given it any serious thought. But of course I had.

'I would confess to *knowing* about the plan. There is a good deal of evidence against you that you *knew*.' In truth, there was only a little – the letter to Elwes, Tower gossip, not much else – Mrs Turner's poisons incriminated only her – but Frances was no lawyer. I would exploit her vulnerability, like holding a piece of bread before a frightened animal, coaxing her out of her hidey-hole. 'If I were you, I would throw myself at the mercy of the King. Confess all, say that you were led astray, say that you were bewitched – the King will like that – and that Mrs Turner and her allies, who are already as good as dead, were the real perpetrators.' None of this seemed to offend her: she seemed fine with sending her friend to her death. 'But there is something else you must do. It is very important.' Was I pushing it? Did I have a reason why it was so very important? What I was about to ask was important to me: it would ruin Carr. Everyone else could whistle: it was Carr I needed to bring down. Might she turn against her husband at the last moment to save her own neck, as she had with Mrs Turner? I smiled at her. 'You must say that Robert knew of the murder plot.'

She let out a great gush of air from her lungs; reflexive disgust. 'No, never!'

'Did he not?' She said nothing. 'Did he not, Frances? Or did *you* not?' She did not reply. Now I could conjure fear. 'Every day you deny the truth, you alienate the King even more. Did you forget something about your cousins, Frances, about Anne Boleyn and Catherine Howard? They did not die alone, you know. Perfectly innocent men died with them, hanged, drawn and quartered, with made-up nonsense about lovers and conspirators. If you refuse to help, you condemn your husband to such a fate.'

I saw her physically gulp. 'They would not dare do that to an earl of England!'

'Not to a Howard perhaps,' I said, throwing her a small bone to win her around. 'But if Coke rules that you murdered Overbury because he was going to reveal that you and Robert were lovers' – at this, her eyes grew very wide – finally, a tell! – 'your divorce becomes null because you were not a virgin. It would mean you never married Robert, because you were never divorced. Then logic follows that, legally, Robert was never made Earl of Somerset as a wedding present because your wedding was never real, and the King will annul and revoke everything, and –' I pointed at her swollen belly '– and your baby will be his bastard child. Robert Carr, a plain commoner, will then have not only murdered but deceived the King several times, and will be charged as a traitor as well as a murderer. What is the punishment for traitors in England?' I was marshalling all my skills as an orator now, straight out of classical Rome. She did not reply. '*What*, Frances, is the punishment for traitors in England?'

'Hanging, drawing and quartering,' she whispered softly.

'Just like what happened to those around your cousins.'

'Yes, Bacon,' in the iciest whisper.

'Think for a moment, Frances, about your Robert being hanged by the neck, revived, carefully cut down and kept alive as they scoop out his guts, and all the while, they make you sit and watch it, before they chop him up, still just about alive, and you can smell his innards and blood on the air, and hear his final dying screams. Do you want that?' She was silent and still. '*Do you want that?*' My voice had risen artfully into a shout but now fell back into a near-whisper. 'And you, Frances, will be the mother of a traitor's bastard. Who in London would ever receive you again, Howard or not? You will have worked so hard to rid yourself of Essex, and for what, Frances?' Another shout: '*For what?*'

I knew that she was terribly, irrevocably afraid. Then something changed. 'I will confess my own crimes, Bacon,' she murmured. 'But that's all. I will not incriminate my husband. You can hang me if you wish, but you will hang me alone.'

I admired her – not quite bravery – her spine. She was cut off from her parents, from her husband. I had used my intelligence and my experience as a lawyer to force her into seeing what to do. But still she knew her value. She knew where that Howard spine was and what it was for.

'You will do all this for love, Frances?' I asked.

She looked at me as if I were mad. 'I would do a lot more than this.'

'Do you think that he would do the same for you?'

She looked up at me and proudly, magnificently lifted her chin. 'No, Bacon. I do not think he would. But that does not mean I won't do it for him.' She glared at me, thinking I did not understand. But the truth was, of course, I understood perfectly.

To my surprise, Meautys was waiting for me as I left Whitehall. He had word that Coke was interrogating Mrs Turner. 'So?' I asked. He had heard the interrogation had, as he discreetly put it, 'taken a turn for the worse'. We hailed a row-boat to take us to the Tower. Two long-armed boys sped us downriver and through the Traitors' Gate, where so many people of fame and notoriety had come to die. From there, we hurried into the Tower courtyard, past the elegant, ragged prisoners, who lived here as if they were really exquisite parrots merely waiting for their cage doors to be opened.

We went up into the Wakefield tower, where Coke kept those he was interrogating. Here, facing the river, terrifying screams could go largely unheard, save by those inside the Tower itself. It is always good, men like Coke feel, for frightened prisoners to hear others' screams. As we climbed the steps and approached the top cell, the Tower rats scurried along the stone walls. Continuing through the dank, unlit corridor, I could hear, in approaching volume, Coke yelling. 'Confess!' Silence. 'Confess everything!' The sound of a slap. Silence. 'Did Lord and Lady Somerset order you to murder Thomas Overbury?' Some kind of murmuring followed. I felt afraid. I turned to look at Meautys. I had never told him about my days witnessing torture under the old Queen: Irishmen so drugged by punches that they lost the ability to form coherent sentences; young Catholic mothers whose fingers had all been broken so that they could not sign their own confessions, told (lies) that their young children were elsewhere, limbs snapping on the rack, readily renouncing their Father-in-Rome. I was never the torturer, only the clerk or the observer, but still, the images and sounds haunt me. I thumped at the cell door. The small shuttered window slammed back, and a guard's eye appeared.

'It's Francis Bacon,' I said.

Through the aperture I could hear Coke groan. 'What does *he* want?' Another groan. 'Let him in.'

The door pulled back. I walked into the windowless cell. The air was warm, not from the two lamps – oiled

248

rags wrapped around wood stakes and set aflame – but from the exertion of punches and kicks. I saw a crumpled female form in the centre of the room. Mrs Turner was sitting on a chair that looked like it had been pushed to the ground so many times it was about to splinter. Her arms were tied behind its back. Alerted not to my presence but just to some rearrangement of bodies in the cell, she looked up with eyes that were swollen and purple. Her lower lip was split and bloodied. Her hair had been roughly shorn – not for cleanliness, but to terrorise her. They would have held her down, stood their feet on her body, and as she lay rigid in fear, they would have scalped her with a rough scissors. I recognised it: the salty, sour smell of blood in the air.

'Coke!' I yelled. 'Coke, this is enough. You are done.'

Coke sniffed. 'God's work is never done!'

'*God's* work? You think this is God's work?'

He flashed his eyes towards another person – a priest in the Church of England, I realised – who glared at me with disgust. I was drowning in disgust!

'I am Attorney-General of England, Coke! I order that this interrogation stop. No more torture is to be used against this person.'

'Torture is perfectly legal!' the priest declared, beginning to quote Exodus in justification. Mrs Turner lifted her head. A weird, whistling groan came out of her and did something to the air that made the hair on my neck prickle.

'Oh, Mister Bacon,' she said – only just audible through her butchered lips. 'You never liked my country ways. Your friends here...' She sighed, and a horrible, fluttering laugh cracked in her throat, stopping on the knife-edge of a guttural sob. 'Your friends here...'

These were not my friends. Do not associate them with me. 'Meautys!' I cried. 'Help me get her up.' We released her from her binds and lifted her to her feet. She could walk, but she was weak.

'You are interfering with my interrogation, Bacon!' Coke protested. I ignored him. Meautys and I managed to get her out of the cell and down to the warden's parlour, where two gaolers were shocked to see us, catching them in the illicit act of smoking a pipe.

'You two,' I said. 'Go outside and smoke that thing. I won't tell anyone I saw you do it, if you leave me here fifteen minutes.' They obliged only too willingly, afraid that I might lose them their jobs.

Left alone, we got Mrs Turner to a chair and Meautys poured her a glass of wine – there is no safe water at the Tower. She sipped at the glass.

'Drink,' I said. 'It will take the edge off your pain.'

She took a gulp and began to revive but her words were not of thanks. 'Mister Bacon, you are going to kill me. But now you worry about whether Mister Coke sprained my wrist.' Her laughter was dark and sharp. Even now, she mocked me.

'Drink some more, Mrs Turner,' I said, but she waved the glass away.

I indicated to Meautys to wait outside. When he was gone, I pulled a chair out for myself. Mrs Turner and I sat there in silence for a few minutes. I heard how heavy and laboured her breathing had become. This is what happens to the tortured. As the adrenaline of the moment passes, the victim becomes aware of how hurt they have

250

been. Terror recedes and is replaced by a more sinister exhaustion.

Eventually she looked up at me. 'Why did you stop him? You are on his side.'

I grunted. 'Coke is an animal. He is not the same manner of man as me.'

She laughed in precisely the same way as when I had said we were both outsiders at her house on Cheapside. 'You're a moron,' she hissed.

'I beg pardon?'

'You're a moron!' she yelled, lurching forwards in her chair so fast it seemed she might topple out of it. 'I always thought you were the stupidest person I ever met.'

I have been called many things in my life. A faggot. A sodomite. A slug. A social climber. A conniver. A grubby little clerk of no human worth. But never a moron.

'If you want me to help you—'

'I do not want you to help me, Mister Bacon. I am not going to salve your conscience, and don't you try to salve mine. You have already decided to kill me. Why pretend that you have not?'

'You are the murderer!' I cried.

'Then hang me, Mister Bacon. Murder me in return.' She spat on the floor, and looked at the pink trails of blood in the spit. 'Then we will be equal. Both of us will have killed, and both of us will be damned.'

'I am obeying the law.'

'Good for fucking you!' she yelled. 'Moron.'

I had come to save her but she refused my salvation; it was no salvation at all. After all, we both knew she was going to die regardless. It was I who was playing a game then, and she refused to pretend that I was not.

'Mrs Turner,' I whispered, but she did not look at me again.

'Leave me alone, Bacon. Let me die.'

*

That night, I was at home at Gray's Inn. I felt so grim after meeting Mrs Turner that I was happy to hide there, to pour myself into the release of work. I crouched over my desk, scribbling notes on a case for which a bribe of a silver locket had been sent. (What? Did you think all my other work had miraculously stopped?) The petitioner hoped his 'little gift' would help me see the rightness of his case. I sighed and looked up, remembering my supper. I picked up a slice of cold ham and put it in my mouth. There was a knock at the door. A servant appeared.

'You have a visitor, sir.' Then he added in a whisper: 'Master Villiers, sir.'

Our affair had continued but it was so hard for us to find time, or a place, to meet. But his coming to my home at night was dangerous; foolish, even. I stood up, just as Villiers walked in, resplendent in a purple and gold suit, with solid gold buttons, and a black hat with a saffron-dyed African-bird feather. Our eyes connected, and I felt the flicker of a smile on my face, and saw it mirrored on his. I told the servant that he could go. The man disappeared and the door closed. Villiers took off his hat.

'What are you doing here?' I asked.

'I just wanted to see you.'

A gladness filled my chest. He moved towards me, coming close. I felt his presence buzzing, hot, against the surface of my body. He did not kiss me, but I let his fingers touch my hand, run up my arm and settle on my chest. His eyes were sparkling. He seemed happy.

'What about the King?'

Villiers sighed. 'He was drunk by seven o'clock and asleep and drooling by ten.' He raised his eyebrows. 'My arse has a night off.' He laughed grimly.

'So you brought it here, did you, to get what it wants?'

I thought he'd find that funny, but he did not. He looked at me for a few seconds.

'Do you know what I want to do, Francis?' he said. 'I only have an hour, perhaps. I will have to get back because his bladder will wake him up before morning. He will start screeching for me to talk to him while he takes a piss.' Villiers said this in a matter-of-fact way but I felt sad for him. 'What I would like to do is take my clothes off, get into bed, and lie down with the man I love. I do not want to fuck. I just want to feel his skin next to mine, his breath on my shoulder, the thud of his heart in his chest.'

'And his hard-on poking you in the back?' I joked. (I shouldn't have joked.)

He looked at me completely seriously. 'Yes, I would *love* to feel that.'

'I might try to fuck you.'

'Good,' he said. 'I am not going to let you.'

He turned and put the latch on the door. We began to take off our clothes, watching each other as we did so. Like serpents shedding skins, we were revealed in new, fresh forms. By the time we were naked, both our cocks were erect. We walked towards the bed, and at the last moment, he asked me to blow out the candle on my desk. We got into bed and lay there, him with his back to me.

'Put your arm around me,' he said, as though it were a kind of sensual game, in which instructions are given and then – erotically – obeyed. 'Pull me against your body.'

'You will feel my erection.'

'I know,' he said. I pulled him closer. 'Put your lips against my shoulder but do not kiss me, just breathe against my skin.' I did as he asked. 'Now... tell me that you are my husband.'

'I am your husband,' I said.

He sighed contentedly. 'Say it again.'

'I am your husband.'

'Good,' he said. 'I made you love me.'

'What?'

'I made you love me. You did not want to. You did not believe you could. But I showed you.'

'Showed me what?'

'That you could love someone. And that someone could love you.'

Truly, I think this was the nicest thing anyone said to me in my whole life. I kissed his shoulder and drew him even closer to my body.

'I love you,' I said, and I heard the happiness in his sigh. He turned slightly as if to look at me, though he could not quite, in that position. But I knew that he was smiling.

'You are a good man,' he said. 'I know it's hard for you, what we are doing now, but I just wanted to say it to you, Francis. You are a good man.'

We lay like that for a long time and did not speak any further. There was no need to. Outside, I heard the servants finishing tasks and withdrawing to their beds. Now and then, I moved the position of my arm around him, hugging him tighter to my body. He drew himself closer and closer to me with each movement, until it seemed like every inch of his skin was touching every inch of mine. After what seemed like forever and, simultaneously, no time at all, he said: 'I shall have to go soon.'

I pulled him closer to me than even before, so as not to let him slip away. Not again. 'No,' I protested. 'Stay.'

He laughed a little, happy to hear my objection. 'I have to. The King will be stirring.'

I felt the snap of jealousy. I did not want him to go back to another, I wanted him to fall asleep like this, in my arms, and wake to my kisses. I wanted to be the one to fuck him as the first sunlight crept under the shutters. But I knew that it was impossible.

'Don't let him fuck you tonight,' I said instead, as if that were some kind of oath.

'He will not be able to,' Villiers laughed.

'Or in the morning either.'

He turned and looked at me, with such nakedness, and kissed me. I put my mouth to his ear. 'A country husband and wife,' I said. He giggled a little, and moved his face to mine so that we started kissing again. I pulled him round so that he was lying on top of me, his weight nothing against mine, our mouths open, our fingers interlaced. Then he broke away and shook his head.

'I have to go,' he said.

After he was gone, I lay awake in bed till daybreak, staring out at the night as it occupied my room. I was thinking of him, and then thinking how he had slowly occupied me. When had I started to think of him all the time? When had I stopped being the person who had so seriously, so avowedly, kept love in abeyance all my life?

I tried to think of how he had been able to seduce me so; no, I don't mean sexually, I mean in the marrow in my bones, the blood in my veins, in my teeth, and lungs and belly. He had appeared, this beautiful young man, and taken me over. Every part of me should have been on high alert, I knew it – of course I knew it – but instead I was surrendering to it. What wouldn't I do for him now? This was a serious question. *What* wouldn't I? I wanted him to feel safe. I wanted to make him happy. Suddenly, it seemed so very important to make him happy, at almost any cost.

*

Weston and Elwes were convicted and sentenced to hang. At his trial, Gervase Elwes, a man talented enough to run the Tower, claimed in the dock that he had not realised that poisoning Overbury was wrong. He'd obeyed his betters' orders, but now that I pointed it out in court, he pitifully admitted that, yes, it must be wrong to poison a man to death.

Mrs Turner's trial was a grim spectacle, its conclusion foregone. Meautys told me that in his blistering condemnation of Mrs Turner, Coke had made a curious condition of her execution. He ordered that she wear her famous bright yellow ruff collar to the scaffold. I did not understand why.

The Carrs were quickly arraigned for procuring and consenting to the murder of Overbury, and as accessories after the fact. Frances's trial went very smoothly. She sat before the court, sweetly confessing her crimes, looking for all the world like the unblameable princess who could not be sent to her death. Sometimes during her testimony, she held her newborn daughter, whom she had named Anne – outrageously – in the Queen's honour. Unfortunately, 'Anne' was also Mrs Turner's name, so that did not go down well with the London mob. Assiduously, and infuriatingly, she denied that her husband was complicit in the murder. She looked at the lords who had come to court – many of whom knew her from childhood – and said she was terribly sorry; she alone had been led astray by 'vulgar types'. The lords nodded sympathetically as if to say: well, who hasn't?

Carr's trial was not nearly so easy – for him. I provided evidence for the following: that he lied about his intimacy with the staff of the Tower during Overbury's incarceration; that his protestations that Overbury had been his best friend obscured that they had fallen out over his relationship with the Countess; that, despite his claims, Carr had never interceded with the King over Overbury's incarceration; and further, that he had written to Overbury several times, convincing him he was about to be released when he had no cause to do so; and all the while, his wife and her demonic accomplices were painting sweet tarts with arsenic and sending them to his 'best friend'. Had he not then burned many – undoubtedly incriminating (because why else burn them?) – letters on the matter? And what of a letter that had been found sent to him from Overbury in prison that he used to show their continued good relationship? The dates had been clearly altered to make it look like it had been sent much later than it had. Without a confession, I knew that the Crown case rested on having a great deal of evidence, no matter how circumstantial. So, frankly, I supplied it.

Carr seemed bewildered that this was what lawyers do: find evidence, build cases, create impressions, to get the results we want. His defence of himself was woeful. He said he could not remember everything of which he had been accused. (Which can be a clever thing to say – *I cannot be expected to remember ALL THIS* – but in his befuddled hands was pathetic.) He stated that he had sent tarts to his friend in prison, but he had never poisoned them. But they were poisoned, I said, and your wife has acknowledged it.

'Then who poisoned them?' I asked. This was a trap into which he fell easily. If his wife had said that, then it must be she who poisoned them, he reasoned. Ladies in the gallery shouted, 'For shame, sir! For shame!' After twelve hours standing in the dock – I did not allow a chair to be brought to him – don't protest, the law court is a theatre and these people were murderers – Carr collapsed forwards and grabbed the front of the dock, shaking his head. 'Do you have nothing more to say, *Mister* Carr?' Coke yelled, ostentatiously forgetting the man's ennoblement.

Judgement came, Coke raged and called the Carrs to the dock to stand together. They made a pretty pair, though heavily debased. Coke pulled the black silk over the top of his head and banged the gavel and began his well-practised speech: 'My Lord of Somerset, Countess, I hereby sentence you to death.' There were loud gasps around the court and, after they faded, much furious discussion. *Whatever next for England?*

After the two were sent down, I went downstairs to the cells to sign off the warrants. There, in a corridor, I saw Robert Carr held by two guards. Frances was nowhere to be seen. The last I saw of her, she seemed on the point of collapse. Would she meet her cousins' fate after all? Carr looked tired, exhausted from the trial. But in seeing me, something seemed to revive in him. I knew what spurred him back to life: it was hatred.

'They say that you are in love with George Villiers, Bacon,' he yelled, in front of everyone, as when Suffolk had called me a faggot outside his palace. 'They say that it shines out of you whenever you are around him.' The guards shot cruelly amused looks at each other, the sort the Normal Man does in the moment of the humiliation of the faggot – or a woman. 'They say that Villiers knows that you are in love with him, that he uses it against you, to exploit and manipulate you. He never loved you. He never even liked you, not truly. He just – like me with the King – saw a powerful old fool he could use to rise from obscurity in double-quick time.' He cocked his head to one side and pouted a little, looking up at me. 'Do you think that might be true?'

Unbelievably, embarrassingly, there were tears in my eyes. 'No, I do not think that's true,' I whispered. 'I do not think any of it's true.'

'No,' he said, cut through with sarcasm. 'No, I am sure he just loved you for your old, ugly, flabby self. And there is one more thing, Bacon, you have to know, now that I have nothing left to lie about, now that your connivance has succeeded in killing me.'

What? I wondered. *What else could there be to admit?*

'I did not harm Overbury. I know he was awful and had a big mouth, but he *was* my friend. I knew nothing about it. Maybe my wife did. Frances is a force of nature, for good and ill. But I swear, I knew nothing. If Coke kills me, it is because you allowed it, Bacon, just like you did your old friend, Essex. If I hang, it is because you did not do enough to save an innocent person from the scaffold. And you will nae save poor Rabbie – whose arse you once would have given your left lung to fuck – because you are too busy trying your damnedest to get inside Villiers' hole!'

His eyes were glittering with the hatred he had always wanted me to feel. Then he started laughing wildly in the manner of those who now have nothing left to lose. I hurried away – away from my guilt, away from his accusations, away from the guards' unvoiced contempt for the sodomite, and so, in all three, from my shame.

*

I do not know why I felt the need to go and see Mrs Turner's execution. I just... I don't know, I needed to see it, as if it was my duty to see it through to its conclusion. I asked Jonson if he would go with me. He said, 'Oh, no, thanks, Porkchop,' so I asked him again in a different way, if he did not *mind* coming with me. He did not complain then. I picked him up in my carriage and we rode out together, west to Tyburn.

We rode in silence, for neither one of us relished what we were about to see. I find the public fascination with going to see beheadings and burnings revolting, that it is viewed as entertainment is barbaric. It was only as we cleared the clumps of woodland between the open scrub on either side of the Oxford-Street and the farmsteads at the bottom of the Edgware-Road, that we saw how many people had come. Eventually a priest, the hangman and Mrs Turner shuffled on to the main scaffold and the mood of the crowd shifted. She wore the huge ruff collar as instructed, a most intensely glowing yellow. Only then did I notice the sheer proportion of the crowd also wearing yellow collars. I did not think this an act of irony or sarcasm or support – people did not even realise what they had done. It was merely a fashion, and fashions pass. Jonson said he would not leave the coach, so alone, I pushed my way until I was forty or fifty feet away from the scaffold and did not think I could get any closer.

The priest said a prayer to which no one listened. The good Christians of London were too busy yelling names – *bitch! whore! bawd!* Mrs Turner began to make her death speech, her face still swollen by Coke's fists. Suddenly, with her blackened eyes and bruised jaw, I saw the true meaning of him insisting she wear the yellow ruff collar. Coke meant to humiliate her: her fame and her rise and her wealth had – outwardly, at least – been predicated on her monopoly on saffron starch powder. That spirit of quest, Coke intended to shame publicly. He wanted the world to see the manifold ways a woman like her deserved to die.

'My good people,' she began, more hesitantly than I expected. I half-thought she might begin: 'Assembled idiots.' She took a breath which became a tearful sigh, but she did not weep. It is important not to weep on the scaffold; London hates cry-babies. 'I come here to die for a sin for which I have been found guilty. I pray that God will forgive me, for I am truly sorry of what I have done—' This provoked open laughter in the crowd, and someone shouted, 'Tell that to Mister Overbury, *slut*!'

The shouting unsettled her and Mrs Turner, famous for her confidence in life – a life now over – hovered between fear and performance. 'I will tell you this, then,' she said. 'I have one more thing to say. I rue the day I ever met Lady Frances Howard. I rue ever knowing her, for knowing her has brought me to this very pass!' Hearing her ire, a hush fell on the crowd. She gathered herself. Like Henry VIII's wives knew, it is bad form to criticise your destroyer on the scaffold. 'That is all I shall say on that matter,' she added, more quietly, 'I shall say nothing more on that.' But then she did precisely that: 'My love and help for them has just served to bring me a dog's death!'

At this, her voice seemed to fail. She was done with life. She was done with the Carrs, with Edward Coke, and probably with me, too. A man rushed to the front of the scaffold, with a look of great peace on his face. I thought he might say something consoling or poetic, or something philosophical that might make all of London think. 'Fuck you!' he yelled instead, and threw a clod of earth at her face. It pelted off her forehead, dislodged the cap covering her head, revealing her shorn hair below. A woman near the front of the crowd tore off her own yellow collar. 'Fuck you!' she also cried. 'And fuck your stupid, fucking ridiculous collars too!'

At once, all around, people started pulling off their yellow ruffs. Discarded, they looked like golden swans fallen from the sky, lying dead on the ground. The priest began to say the Lord's Prayer, while the hangman placed the noose around Mrs Turner's neck. She went to say something else, but the scaffold door dropped, whilst the prayer was still being said. She fell fast, her neck tugging with an almighty jolt, her body making the most awful slamming sound as it dropped, her legs kicking wildly for a few seconds. I turned away, if I am honest, because I was afraid I might puke. My eyes scanned for my coach, and I saw Jonson in its window, not looking at the scaffold but straight at me.

He and I went to the George in Southwark to raise a glass to – whom? – a murderer who openly held me in contempt? Our ale was brought, but we did not touch it for a long time.

'What's wrong with you, Porkchop?' my friend asked eventually. 'Isn't this what you wanted?' I shot a sharp, ironic look at him. He knew that this was not my way. 'Look, maybe this is not your first choice...' *Ugh*, I went. Jonson arched his eyebrow. 'It is not the first time you've grubbed around. You understand this world, you know what is necessary to survive.'

'But this is not necessary to survive, Jonson. Killing Robert Carr is not necessary. I know that he is finished, the scandal is too great. He will never be allowed back and the King will put him out of his mind. There is no need to kill the Carrs.'

'All right, Porkchop. Then why are you doing it?' I looked at him for a long time. The longer I looked, the more he became drawn into my stare, until he said: 'Are you going to tell me, or do I have to throttle it out of you?'

I let out an exhausted sigh. 'I am in love with George Villiers. I am doing it for him. He asked me to kill the Carrs, and I agreed.'

Jonson's eyes widened. '*What?*'

I told him everything, in a low whisper. I told him about the plan the Queen and I came up with, about the search for the boys, about how I met Villiers by chance at Apethorpe, took him to Gorhambury to train him to meet the King and replace Carr. I told him how an affair had begun between us, against my better judgement, and that Villiers had said he was in love with me. I told him I had ended it – painfully for him, in what I had thought was relief for me – but that we had remained allies. Finally, I told him that I was very much in love with Villiers still, who had asked me to kill Carr; and in asking, the affair had resumed.

At this, he sat back in his seat. 'Oh, for fuck's sake.'

'And he is in love with me.'

'Ha!' Jonson drawled. 'Are you *both* insane? Have you forgotten what kings do to errant brides? Have you forgotten what happened to Anne Boleyn and Catherine Howard's lovers?'

I almost choked. I had asked Frances the very same question. 'Putative lovers,' I corrected in order to deflect, but I made an error.

'Exactly!' he said, blackly triumphant. 'Putative. You are real – I presume, *physical* – lovers?' I nodded. He gave a loud tut of a laugh. 'Are you *fucking insane*, Bacon?' I could not remember the last time he had called me by my real name. There was silence for a moment. My friend's cheek twitched. 'You do not want to kill Carr, do you?'

'It's unnecessary. And I do not even know that he is guilty, not truly.'

Jonson took a sip of ale. 'Is the boy using you?'

'He's not a boy,' I said defensively.

'*Is he using you?*'

'He loves me. I truly do believe that.'

At this, Jonson began to laugh – sarcastically, derisively. 'Porkchop, I have news for you. This is what these boys are like. They enter this world, innocent enough, I am sure. But they learn the power, the value, of their beauty;

they learn the effects of beauty on older men, and they begin to understand what they can get from it. The young have no heart, they are cruel and greedy, and their beauty is a weapon they use to get the things they desire. He is making a fool of you.'

I shook my head. 'He loves me.'

Jonson drew closer to me, elbows on the table, voice kept low. 'If this boy loves you, he will understand what you have done for him, he will be grateful, he will accept your judgements, and then he will tell you that he still loves you. You are going to do something – well, maybe it's not awful to be rid of Robert Carr – but something you seriously suspect is wrong. If not for Villiers, would you do it?'

'It's not as easy as that.'

'*Would you?*'

'No,' I said. 'No, I would not.'

'You want to change the world, Porkchop,' he said. 'You want posterity to remember you well. Well, how will posterity remember you if you are killing an innocent man all because some boy waggled his arse at you?'

'I love him.'

Jonson sighed. 'You say Carr will be finished either way.'

'Yes.'

'If this boy loves you, he will accept that you do what you think is right. If he is using you, he will drop you. But if Villiers *is* using you, once Carr is dead and he is safe, he will drop you anyway. There is only one way to find out whether he truly loves you.' Then he laughed bleakly. 'Or are you so pussy-blind that you do not care to find out?'

'Stop it,' I groaned.

'What, then, for our great moral mind?'

That night, I wrote to the King with my case for leniency for the Carrs, saying I did not believe it was necessary to kill them. The reasons were threefold, I wrote. Firstly, they were not the primary poisoners, whom had been executed already. Secondly, they had confessed, and was not confession without torture significant? (This was only half-true. Frances had confessed, while Carr had dissembled and blamed others. But I knew the King would see what he wanted to see.) Thirdly – and this most shamefully empty of all – I argued that they were aristocrats and their total disgrace would be enough, as if not being invited to a card game by the Countess of Huntington is a whole other level of devastation compared to a noose around an ordinary man's neck. I suggested their death penalties be commuted to life sentences in the Tower. Then, on a separate piece of paper, I added simply that Robert Carr had once loved the King very greatly (*arguable...*) and that I believed posterity would honour the King very highly for showing mercy (*again...*). What finer thing can a man do than forgive the person that they once loved? This, I knew, would appeal to the King's finer feelings about himself.

I sent for Meautys and told him to ride to Theobalds at once, and to give the note to the King when Villiers was not around. He was to extract from the King as best he could a note to confirm that I, as Attorney-General, could register a commutation of the death sentence on the Carrs. I waited up for Meautys to return to Gray's Inn. In the small hours, he arrived with the note. Perhaps you would think I slept well that night in the knowledge I had done the right thing, but I stared up at the ceiling, bone-white in the moonlight falling through my window, watching for some sign that I was a good person again. But I found none. I found nothing at all save a ceiling.

In the morning, I wrote another note, this time to Villiers, asking him to come to London to see me. I wanted to explain. I wanted him to understand. I wanted him to know that we had still succeeded. Several hours later, Meautys returned again. He said Villiers received and read the note and merely said that he had no reply.

*

A strange, tense relief descended on the court. This was not because people were glad that the Carrs had fallen. To think that is to misunderstand power. Someone always wins, and someone always loses. The relief comes from the battle having been fought and won, so now there can be peace – for a while, at least. It is hard to live in a perpetual war. Villiers and I were the victors – the new power – but at the moment of our victory, he refused to see me. I wrote again and again, but never was there any reply. Even if I went to see the King, Villiers was always absent, hiding in another room. I wondered at how angry he must have been, how betrayed he must have felt, but I knew if I could only speak to him, I could explain my actions.

Two weeks after the King commuted the Carrs' sentence, I attended a masque to honour an American princess by the name of Pocahontas, who had come to live in England. It was written by Jonson, entitled *The Vision of Delight*. The masque itself was exquisite: light and atmospheric, aerial in quality, filled with classical figures who seemed to merge with the clever, intricate set design. The King was there with Villiers, dressed in one of his expensive blue silk suits, with a white ruff collar – no, not saffron-yellow, no, of course not, *no one* wore saffron-yellow any more. Everyone was in high spirits. That day, the King had created Villiers the Earl of Buckingham. Already, he was an earl of England but, unlike Carr, there was no Howard princess waiting to be married and needing her suitor to have a title. The King transformed him for his own sake, out of the sheer exhilaration of love.

After the masque finished, I approached the King and bowed to him. Villiers was seated on his right side. I felt my chest tighten but he did not even look at me.

'*Beicon!*' the King cried in his best humour. 'What exquisite days, eh? What marvellous days!' I wondered at him, the man that he used to love beyond reason now locked away in the freezing damp of the Tower. Everything that they had been to each other – no matter how insanely bad it was – was just to be forgotten?

I bowed again. 'Indeed, sir.'

'Do ye see wee Georgie *here*?' he boomed, so loud that people around jumped a little. 'He's an earl now! What do ye think of that?'

I smiled at Villiers. 'It is very well deserved.' I nodded. 'My Lord of Buckingham.'

Villiers finally looked at me and gave a small, beautiful smile. I could not read its intention – cruel or intimate. He let his hand brush the King's, which was gripping the arm of his throne. He had the shakes. The King then cried: '*Beicon!* I have good news for ye! I am going to make you Lord Chancellor of England, what d'ye say to that, eh? I shall give ye York House too.' York House, my own childhood home, but also my own palace on the Strand. The King turned to Villiers. 'D'ye ken it, Georgie?'

'Oh, yes,' Villiers replied. 'It is very beautiful.' He looked directly at me. 'I should have liked it for myself.' I wondered what he meant by that.

Suddenly the King seemed distracted by music coming from down a corridor. Turning, I could see Prince Charles was dancing with some ladies of the court to a tune played on a virginal. Forgetting all about his gout, and his shaking hands, the King jumped up and started hopping foot to foot, clapping his hands like a child in time with the rhythmic thump of the dancers' feet.

Villiers and I were at last alone. I turned to look at him. He breathed out, a faint trace of tears making his eyes sparkle. It moved me intensely.

'Do you remember,' he asked mysteriously, 'when we used to lie together at Gorhambury, after we had been together? Do you remember how it was?'

I let myself be drawn into his game. 'I fucked you every night we were there.'

His eyes fell. His skin was flawlessly clear; it did not bear a single mark or shadow. His lips were full and pink but bore no smile.

'You did not love me enough to want to save me, Francis Bacon. You chose your fine morality over your love for me.'

'No,' I said. 'No, I do not think I did. I just did not want to kill people I did not need to kill. You have to understand, there is no danger. Carr is absolutely finished. You are safe. I have made you safe.'

His eyes lingered on mine. 'The King means to ennoble you soon, you know. And you are Lord Chancellor, and now you have York House again. You have power. Huge power, and soon great wealth. You have everything you wanted. Are you happy?'

The question was brilliantly bitter. 'I'm in love with you,' I said. He said nothing. He remained dazzlingly silent, so I gabbled. 'What about Gorhambury, the country husband and wife? What about all the things we said? Did we not mean them?' He remained silent. 'You have to forgive me. Tell me you forgive me and you love me still.' I felt myself becoming upset – ridiculously, impossibly. 'You *have to* forgive me.'

His mouth pursed a little, at his most unreadable. 'No, *Bacon*,' he said, as cold as river ice. 'I think all of it has to be over. We did what we set out to achieve, and we are friends. Allies. Nothing more.'

'Allies?' I repeated, horrified. 'What about that night you came to Gray's Inn and asked me to hold you and to tell you that I was your husband? You said I was a good man.'

He merely shrugged. 'I was wrong.'

'*Wrong?*'

The music down the corridor grew faster and louder, so no one could hear me losing my cool, saying things I should never say aloud.

His eyes remained on me. 'I have only ever asked you for simple things, Francis, but all you could ever give was your cleverness. That's our problem. I am very straightforward, and you are... clever.' He sighed. 'Sometimes I think that's all you are.'

I thought of what Jonson said about these boys. 'Have you used me?'

His pale cheeks flushed red with anger. '*I* used *you*?'

What did he mean by that? Suddenly, there was laughter, very close. We both looked up. The King was dancing back towards us, even though I had not noticed the virginal had stopped playing. Like he was the buffoon and not the most powerful man in England, he clapped and hopped and hummed a merry tune.

'Ach, laddies!' he cried. 'What a happy day it is! There can nae be unhappiness in my kingdom no more!' And then he came to a stop, and only momentarily gave Villiers and me a strange look, perhaps sensing us in such connected distress. 'I command it! There can nae be any more unhappiness in England!'

Immediately, the King carried on dancing to the music, off down the corridor, grabbing Villiers' hand so that he followed him like a child, being dragged along by a tide out to sea. And I was left, watching him go, the air sucking out of my lungs. 'I think all of it has to be over,' he had said. The words swooped around me, and I realised there was nothing I could do to get it back.

ON THE SUBJECT OF
A HAPPY ENDING

$\mathcal{A}$ happy ending. Yes, of course I am being ironic.

*

Socrates believed that irony could be used to expose the fallacies of the world. So let me begin like this: and so it began, our great, shared victory, our unparalleled success, our happy ending. None of this is untrue. We *had* succeeded – politically, financially, in every way. The Carrs were destroyed, the Howards disgraced. In the years that followed, our – my – success was dazzling.

In 1617, when the King travelled with Villiers to Scotland, he made me Regent of England. I became rich, and I used my money to buy property and refurbish York House.

In 1618, not long before Sir Walter Raleigh finally was hauled to the executioner's block, I was raised to the peerage as Baron Verulam. Villiers, meanwhile, was unassailable, raised from the Earl to Marquis to Duke of Buckingham, far beyond anything Carr achieved.

Money poured in: new revenues, estates, bribes, gifts. Even I, who never once in his life had spent less money than I'd had, began to see my coffers fill; to overflow. (I know! I, Francis Bacon!)

My political victories became personal ones. Shortly after the trials were concluded, when he should have been basking in his new legal fame, Edward Coke got himself into a confrontation with the King over some small aspect of legal authority. The King asked him to cede – not because Coke was legally wrong, but because he was the *king*. Disastrously, Coke refused and was dismissed from all high position. The vain fool went into disgrace.

Everyone said: don't cross Bacon. Look at Coke! Look at Carr! Look at Essex! And once a spy reported that someone said: Villiers had better watch out, too!

*

All of this sounds wonderful to you, I am sure – my dreams come true, my enemies destroyed – so where did the irony lie? That was quite simple. Once upon a time, Villiers had loved me and craved my love in return. He had persuaded me to give in to my feelings for him. But now – because I would not kill the Carrs – he stopped loving me. He never acted – or, as far as I knew, spoke – against me. I kept my spies in the Bedchamber and they never once reported a thing.

Maybe he felt he needed me. Maybe he *did* need me. Maybe some little flicker of emotion for me was still in him, even though when we met, he gazed at me with cool eyes, communicated nothing, and looked away as fast as he could. But he did not need me like I wanted him to need me. Now and then, Jonson would catch me, brooding quietly, in some drunken moment, and say to me: 'Forget him. Fuck him.' That is what friends should do, in those moments, but how little it helps. The heart keeps beating. It's the only thing it can do – that, or stop.

I tried to imagine what Villiers was thinking now, what he had been thinking before – at Gorhambury, and that night when he came and lay in my bed at Gray's Inn. Was he thinking of Gorhambury now, was he thinking of our secret future, was he thinking of those times down by the Ver River, or walking towards Redbourn with the sound of churchbells on the air? Was he thinking of me at all?

I had hurt him, I knew, by being unable to return his love as soon as I could or should have. I hurt him at Greenwich, when I acted out of some cowardly sense of doing the right thing. I will say one more thing, if you can bear it, watching an old fool making himself even more foolish: I remained in love with him while he was no longer in love with me. That is a cruel thing, even if cruelty is not intended. He had moved on, off into his future. And I was free to move off into mine.

Shall I tell you an upside of all this, something that perhaps you will enjoy? In the middle of all this, I began to write – furiously, productively, across projects and topics. Books of which I had been dreaming for years suddenly began to form into near-finished shapes. *How marvellous!* you might cry. *A book! Who doesn't love a book?* Let me tell you this, then. I would burn every page I wrote to have him back.

Happy endings do not preclude death, of course. Death is the only real truth of life. I remember when Jonson told me Shakespeare had died, back in 1616, only just after the Carrs had fallen. He had never recovered from the loss of the Globe, and had more or less retired from London. He went back to the wife he had spent the last twenty years avoiding and the provincial obscurity his writing had helped him escape. When Jonson told me how he had died – of a fever, in his nameless little town – I was sad for him. I shall not sit here and tell you that I ever liked Shakespeare. That would be a lie, and I am not in the business of deceiving you. But in truth, after everything I've said, I knew what kind of writer he was.

On the day of his funeral, his name should have blazed in the skies across London. Instead, some men who understood nothing of literature, of theatre, of culture, threw clods of earth at his coffin in some miserable country church.

'Where now is posterity?' I cried to Jonson on the day we and some others went to get drunk at the George to commemorate him.

My friend shrugged. 'I think he died happy. With small things, and the love of his family.'

I crowed with sophisticated disbelief, but in my heart, Jonson's words struck hard. Might I have been happy with such simple things?

But that was back in 1616, before my meteoric rise. In 1619, three years later, another death hit closer.

*

The Queen's health had continued to decline in recent times, until she could barely walk and even gave up interest in her architectural ventures. I wrote to Lady Grace Mildmay, asking if she would prepare some good herbs and, being the wonder she is, she did much, but little seemed to work. Gradually, it became clear that the Queen was dying. She just seemed done with life.

The Queen's ladies remained very loyal right to the end, which was neither fast nor painless, and I determined to be a good friend to her. Despite being busy, I visited her whenever I could, to bring her interesting things to read, or news from her native Denmark, which pleased her a great deal. I spared her the worst news from Germany, where her daughter Elizabeth's husband had disastrously been elected King of Bohemia, only to be ejected by the invading Austrians. The young couple now wandered Europe penniless, sending the King endless letters asking for money. She would not know this from the King himself, who only visited his wife three times in the last six months of her life.

Villiers did not come once to see the woman who had so taken him under her wing, whose emotion about her dead son I now saw he had exploited. It surprised me that he could be quite so cold, when to me, at first, he had seemed so compassionate and kind. Which was the artifice: that initial goodness, or the new cruelty? Is it inevitable that all George Villiers eventually become Robert Carrs, and had Carr once been as sweet as that lad of twenty-one I met at Apethorpe, and I had just forgotten? (No, I cannot bring myself to go that far.)

Maybe Villiers was merely using us all. But I have enough awareness to understand that Villiers could say the same of us. I knew that around this time, the King had a much greater project in mind: he wanted to find a wife for Villiers. She was to be a great beauty, and a great heiress and well-connected, and truly cultured, and... and... Whenever I saw the King, he talked excitedly about it, and as he prattled on, I thought how Villiers had drifted off into this glorious future, a future he once said he wanted to share with me.

*

One Saturday in the March of that year, I was at York House. I was working – writing – yes, *writing* – yes, the *Novum Organum*! – when a rider came from Hampton Court. The man, wearing the livery of the Queen's household, was shown up to my office and handed me a note. All it said, in cipher, was:

COME NOW, IF YOU COME AT ALL.

It is more than an hour's ride from Westminster to Hampton Court, where the Queen had been moved in the last phase of her illness. I flew there, like a crow through the air. Coming through the dense woodland that leads west of London to the great hunting parks at Richmond and Bushy, there was a hush all around. Old King Henry's red-brick palace had that stillness of a house awaiting a death. I had hardly dressed lavishly, throwing on only a dark suit and my dun-brown hat, and charging up the stairs I caught a glimpse of myself in a small round mirror: a misshapen country gent. My dun-brown hat was more expensive now, but still, I looked old and tired. It was a long time since a man had touched me. I did not want it any more. I blinked and shook my head. How stupid I was! How solipsistic!

Sweating from the fast ride, I was led straight away to the Queen's chamber. The room was soft with candlelight, all the curtains drawn. The Queen was lying in a large bed with white silk sheets and hangings, the courtly colour of death. Here and there some ladies of the household were busy preparing balms, taking away a kerchief, bringing fresh water. Others sat in gentle waves of tears; some had been with the Queen for twenty years. Prince Charles sat beside his mother, and next to him, all in black, a Catholic priest. It had long been rumoured that the Queen had secretly converted but she had never given any clue to me. The priest was saying a prayer in Latin – I could not hear which – and Prince Charles was reading from a Bible, in English. As I walked into the room, everyone stopped what they were doing – prayer fell away at sight of me, dressed in black and breathless. The ladies, who knew me of old, seemed pleased to see me; the prince and the priest did not.

The Queen was dressed in white, too. Her hair was no longer a great frizz of blonde, but short and colourless, flecked with grey, covered with a lace cap. Her famous blonde hair had been a wig all along, I realised now. If she had looked ill for months, now she was almost a cadaver.

'Oh, Bacon,' she murmured, seeing me, her voice so quiet – nothing like the resounding boom it used to be – and raw with physical pain. 'Bacon, how kind of you to come.'

I bowed. 'How could I not, madam?'

'Oh,' she went, 'it's easy enough when one's usefulness is over. That is a fact of our life. I do not forget how you have never stopped being my friend.' I smiled at her. She turned to her son. 'Charles, my heart, will you give me a few minutes with Bacon?' He nodded and left. 'Monsignor,' she said to the priest, who looked more reluctant to leave. When finally we were alone, the Queen bade me sit. We gazed at each for a few moments, each of us wearing a half-smile. 'It is the end, Bacon,' she said eventually then laughed a little. 'For me, not for you.'

I suddenly felt very moved. I was not sure what to say. Ours is a life filled with death. Half of all babies born will not live to be adults, and half of those who survive will not live past forty, killed by starvation, disease, childbirth or the violence of their neighbours. Plagues come and fill graveyards in days. It is wrong to pretend we do not know death is a certainty for all of us. I did not pretend now. 'Madam, I... I just had to come and see you.'

'Oh, I am glad you have.' Her eyes lit up a little. 'I have not always been well loved in my life. It is wonderful now to know that there are those who do love me, and that they are here. I wish I could see my Elizabeth one last time, but I cannot.' She shrugged. 'But I have my ladies here. My son. And you have come. Have you seen the King lately?'

'Now and then,' I lied. 'I am sure he would come—'

She lifted a hand, as far as she could. 'Do not,' she said. 'You and I both know that he is lying on top of Georgie somewhere, not giving me a single thought.' Perhaps I should have denied this, but again, I did not. What would have been the point except to insult her intelligence?

I smiled at her. 'His Majesty did not know what a person he had at his side.'

She shrugged once more. 'Bacon, he and I were forced together by fate. We were princes. We do not get to choose our spouses. I was fifteen years old. Fifteen – it seems so young.' She chuckled, but it made her cough. 'When I think of the spouses of the monarchs of England and Scotland, I have not done too badly. Henry VIII killed and divorced his wives. The King's own father, Darnley, was blown up. His mother – well, we all know what happened to her. All that happened to me was that the whole world knew my husband loved someone – *anyone* – more than me. I go to my death untouched by any man who loved me, or even truly desired me. No man ever looked at me with eyes that wanted to consume every pound of me. I have never had what any girl strolling along Threadneedle Street has had. Mine has been the emptiest of lives, and I, one of the most famous women in Europe.' She sighed and turned her head to one side. 'They say that you do not love, Bacon. That you have kept it from your life. Love never came to me, but you made a choice to keep it away. Has it made you happy?'

I thought of Villiers with a crushing intensity. *Yes, I have loved!* I wanted to yell. I have loved, much too late, much too fearfully, and now it has left me here, like this, a broken thing. Love is like the alarum bell clanging in my head, deafening, shutting out all other sounds. That is why I work all the time. That is why I write so much. That is why I am so... unhappy. I would have given any-thing – *everything* – for that pretend future we shared: a country-gentry husband and wife, happy together in quiet lives. But I do not have it.

I understood now what my tragedy was. I had come to want love much too late, and when it came, I did not have the experience to recognise it and to keep hold of it. Maybe I could have accepted Villiers' love straight off and found a different boy for the King, or maybe I could have been kinder to him and tended his love carefully, even if his body was in the royal bed. Maybe this. Maybe that. Does any of it matter now? An easy question and a heartless one. I have pursued power and intellect, and fame and posterity. Much too late, I have realised that I should have pursued love. Power, I once said, made men happy. Writing, people think, makes men happy. But what would have made me happy – truly happy – is love. Love saves us. Posterity does not. Posterity only remembers us when we are already dead and it is too late. Love remembers us when we are alive.

*

The Queen died that night; I stayed right until the end. She was still only forty-four; she seemed so exhausted by her life. On the day of her funeral, which the King and Villiers did not attend, it rained all morning. To my surprise, huge numbers of Londoners assembled to watch her funeral cortège, with all the ladies of the court walking slowly through the rain yet seeming never to get wet. They remained defiant in their exquisiteness, as if to honour a woman so ill-treated in life, and so honour all women ill-treated. In England, where women are nothing – or, worse still, nothing until they become turbulently, tumultuously *something*, like Frances Carr or Mrs Turner – the ladies of the court came to show their force that day. Unbidden – but undoubtedly planned – they, as one, began to sing a hymn, so purely that people listened as if the air itself was singing.

> O sacred Head, what glory,
> What bliss till now was Thine!
> Yet, though despised and gory,
> I joy to call thee mine.

I hoped that my loneliness could be remedied in the old way, even though it was many months since I had been out on the prowl. In the place of love, I had always used desire, and desire had served me well. Now it returned to me. The night after the funeral, I walked along the river to the woodland just past Mill Bank that runs down as far as the farms at Pimlico. Here among the trees, male bodies moved in the purplish light of night-time. Men walked towards you, like will-o-the-wisps, appearing from nowhere, staring at you. But these men were not ghosts, not death's-heads, not memento mori haunting the trees. They were real people, driven by want and need, and maybe even hope that *somehow*, as I had with Villiers, they might make a true connection. I had not – I am ashamed to say – realised before that these men were every bit as real as me, that they were not just bodies, not just – forgive me – holes. They came at night to fuck and be fucked, and they did it in order to survive a life that fate, or faith, or plain old hate, had turned against them. They will never have what you have, what you take unthinkingly for granted. They will never have love. All they have is sex, and so they crave and hunt it, in the absolute absence of that love. That is their tragedy, and it is mine.

I went right down to the river's edge, where the trees were thick. There I fucked a young man with red hair and a beautiful face, who just about, if I narrowed my eyes in the dark, might have been Villiers. He lay on his back with his legs in the air and moaned, 'Fuck me, fuck me.' But as he said it, all I could think of was Villiers, that this man was not Villiers, not even if I closed my eyes. And then the man was no longer a man: he was a ghost after all. 'Fuck me, fuck me,' he kept on saying, 'put your seed inside me.' But I stopped, pulled out of the man, kneeled there, in the darkness, hearing him questioning me, then shouting and accusing. The night was all around me as I sat back on my haunches, lifting the back of my hand to my mouth. The man was getting up, calling me a cunt. *Call me what you like*, I was thinking. *I won't say it's not true.* And then I stood up, pathetically pulling up my britches. No one ever told me that the loneliest moments of life are after love, not before.

*

My writing continued feverishly. I amended the works I had already published: *The Wisdom of the Ancients* and prepared another edition of my *Essays*. I began two histories of the natural world: *The History of Life And Death*, an encyclopaedia I had planned to describe life itself and methods of extending it; and a second scientific work, *The History of Winds*. I made notes for my utopia fiction *New Atlantis*, and readied myself to start substantial work on it, when time allowed.

Almost to my own amazement, in 1620, I finally completed my *Novum Organum*. The book laid out my new system for science, and a new method of scientific experiment and discovery, and voiced my radical rejection of Aristotle. The nature of future scientific experiment to find properly tested innovation (for medicine, technology, transportation, whatever, on and on) was outlined. A repository of both existing and this new knowledge would be created, establishing them as objective, demonstrable and scientific *fact*. Knowledge was not its own, interesting end point. Instead, these findings could be put to the service of every man and woman in the world. Science would change people's lives, from the highest to the lowest. A modern world, I knew, was being announced; a world that would not be the same as the one that went before.

The book was published to great acclaim and immediately widely read. I wrote it in Latin, so that copies were shipped straight away to the Continent, and soon letters arrived from the thinkers of our age to congratulate and dispute. Some people told me that I had changed the world, that Europe could not go backwards now, only forwards. Others said I was spitting on the reputation of the Ancient Greek masters. When I read that, I smirked to myself: it was time someone spat in Aristotle's smug face. I was only glad it was me.

There was to be a formal presentation of the book to the King at Theobalds. At first, the word from the Royal Bedchamber was that the King wanted this to take place in front of the full court, to be a celebration of the elevation of English intellectual thought to the very pinnacle of the world. 'That will show them Italian *cunts*!' he had declared. On the day of the ceremony, dressed in my best clothes, I rode from York House to Theobalds in a carriage with copies of the book. But when I arrived

at the King's country palace, instead of full court ceremonial, I found a hunting day. The King – or someone
firing a gun who had not corrected the King's claim to
have done it himself – had shot a deer. The poor dead
creature lay slumped in the middle of a wooded glade.
There was no ceremonial, just a gaggle of courtiers in
hunting clothes. No one seemed even to be expecting me.

Suddenly uncertain, I walked towards the scene – a
servant at my side carrying the copy of my work I was
to present. All I could see was the King on his knees,
inspecting the shot in the side of the beast's belly. I could
not see Villiers anywhere. Over the body of the animal,
the King's face was alive with pleasure, his smile wide. As
I came closer to him, he looked up at me and cried:
'*Beicon!* Look what a prize I have shot down.'

The animal hung over a slight mound in the earth. It
was not breathing any more, but it was not long dead
either. The foul smell of intestines filled the air, warm
steam rising from the innards of the animal.

'What a fine specimen,' I said, bowing, but feeling
sickened. Still, Villiers did not appear. 'Is my Lord of
Buckingham not here?'

'Oh, no,' he cried. 'He does nae like hunting too much.
He's like ye, eh, *Beicon*, a pure wee dafty when it comes
to a bit of blood, eh?' Then the King's face troubled. 'Why
are ye all dressed up, eh, *Beicon*?'

'Today is the presentation of my new work.' I did not
add: *have you forgotten, you idiot?* The King looked at
the servant holding the copy of the *Novum Organum*.

'Is that your wee book, *Beicon*, eh?' I groaned inside.
The King grinned in his childlike way. 'Come on, then,
gi's it here.' And no sooner had he finished speaking, that

he plunged his hands inside the belly of the deer and pulled out the animal's large, red heart. Blood ran down the King's arm as he held the heart aloft. 'Ach!' he cried. 'I think I can feel it still beating!' The servant held back. Did the King mean to take my new work with blood all over his hands? 'Come on, then!' he cried, his hunter's humour now tinged with impatience, 'pass the bloody thing over, eh? Gi's a look, man.' He let the deer's fat, wet heart splat to the ground.

The King started to get to his feet, and menservants rushed over to help him, as his gout and stiffness was now very bad. I started to feel a low panic. All my years of planning, my hopes of some grand ceremonial, and now he was to receive my book like this, on a hunting ground, with a dead animal at his feet. The servant approached him, head bowed, and unwrapped the book from the cloth. The King took the book and flicked through the pages, which his fingers splattered with blood. 'Ach, aye,' he said, as he pretended to understand what he was reading. When he could not be bothered any more, and the purple-red smear of the deer's heart's mess all over my new work, he handed the book back to the servant.

'Did I ever tell ye, *Beicon*, that I wrote a book,' the King began, clicking his fingers for wine to be brought. 'Ach, aye, it was called *Basilikon Doron*, which means in Greek, a *royal* gift. Do ye speak Greek, *Beicon*?'

I looked at my life's greatest work smeared with blood, tossed aside. Of course, there were many copies of it. It was only my vanity that felt threatened. I am the cleverest man on this stupid fucking island, but in England – and probably Scotland too – such cleverness is worthless. The King was asking me questions about *his* book, a ridiculous pile of shit published twenty years before. But I was not listening. I was looking at my book, my singular declaration of the modern world, with his disgusting, bloody fingerprints all over it.

I truly hate you, I was thinking. *I truly fucking hate you. You are a fucking moron, and in a second, I will have to listen to you again, and answer your stupid fucking questions. But just in this moment, I want to stand here – if only for a few seconds – and concentrate on how you have taken what is mine, and how much I hate you for it.* Of course, I was no longer thinking about my book.

'*Beicon!*' the King shrieked. My jet-black reverie cleared. 'Are ye nae listening to me? I was asking ye if you admired the second part of my book, where I advised that kings must act with goodness, fairness and fucking *tolerance*!'

I straightened myself. The game plays on. I bowed a little and said: 'Oh, of course, sir. The whole world admires you.'

At this, the King took a big gulp of wine, looked very pleased, then belched hot white breath out onto the cool country air.

ON THE SUBJECT OF ALL
MY ENEMIES

*P*ower now brought me many things, including, several years after the Carrs had fallen, at last a proper title. In the New Year of 1621, in reward for my service, I was made Viscount St Albans, meaning I was finally an aristocrat. At my investiture, the ermine cloak was draped around my shoulders and the pearl coronet of a viscountcy placed on my head. The King declared my new title. Around me stood the earls of England, most of them scowling with disdain to see me lifted into their number. Villiers looked on, smiling but noncommittal. We had found a kind of peace. I would not quite say we were friends now, but I would not say we were not either. Is this how old lovers always get?

Power also brought me money, enough to push forward and complete the refurbishment of York House: increasing the size of the windows that faced out over the Thames to fill the rooms with light – very fashionable – and give dramatic river views, and beyond that the green fields of Lambeth. Still there was work and I was glad of it. I will confess I still lived in the shadow of the love I had lost, and all the other loves a man of my age should have had. I grieved one and so the others too. Now and then, I wondered if he had in fact used me, but the thought did not linger long. How could I complain? Our plan had succeeded gloriously. Remember: I was the one who had endlessly gone on about that plan. So again: how could I complain?

One morning in the spring, I spent hours going through new legal cases at York House, into which I had moved. I was crouched over my desk for hours, my back and neck stiff with reading, amending and annotating various papers that had been left for me to check and approve. I needed to rest my eyes, so I looked back up at the river. The sun had come out. It was beautiful. I was broken out of my reverie by a knock at the door, and Meautys appeared with more papers, workaday, everyday stuff. I went through them: draft legislation, complaints about the King's proroguing of Parliament, a counter-proposal to a request for money to supply to the Princess Elizabeth and her beleaguered husband in Germany. I made comments, crossed out paragraphs I thought were too risky, or open to misinterpretation. Then I came to a note, which I read without too much thought. The Member of Parliament for Liskeard, in Cornwall, wanted to raise an inquiry about corruption at court.

I asked Meautys what this was about – for whom was this Member, quite unknown to me, gunning? The inquiry was looking into a cousin of Villiers, he said, a tomfool named Sir Giles Mompesson. He was not a close relative, so there was no huge threat. At worst, it might be a bit embarrassing. Sir Giles was an idiot of the first order, and as such both fearsomely greedy and utterly stupid. He had used Villiers' influence to gain a monopoly, which had not existed before, over the granting of licences to taverns. Justices of the Peace had previously operated this work, but now the monopoly was formed and granted as part of a wider giveaway to the Villiers family. Mompesson, realising that innkeepers are not parliamentary clerks and do not keep their businesses in strict order, began to fine heavily all and any lack of compliance, of which there was plenty. Innkeepers were up in arms, hundreds of complaints were being made. Mompesson had taken a money-making opportunity, and turned it into an outrageous violation. (Honestly, you cannot save people from themselves!)

'Well, if a man deserves to fall, it is Mompesson,' I said to Meautys, who looked at me airily without comment. 'All right, good. Find out who the Member for Liskeard is. We can warn our friend –' this meant Villiers '– if need be. We have to understand what this Member's real motivation is.' Meautys nodded and off he went, to dig further. I thought of Villiers briefly and – to my surprise – quite happily, then returned to the papers. I always like to look for signs that I am not as damaged as I was before.

In the morning, Meautys returned. We sat on a long bench, side by side, in the pleasant little garden that runs down from the back of York House to the riverbank. It was lushly green with thick spring grass and a thicket of small hawthorn trees that were sharply, heavily white in bloom.

'What do you have for me?' I asked. He said nothing for a moment. I felt my brow crinkle. 'Well?' I said more urgently, sensing the significance of his silence.

'You asked me to find out who the Member for Liskeard was.'

I did not understand why he was so grave. 'Yes.'

He took a breath. 'It is Edward Coke.'

A-ha, went my brain. Since his fall, I thought he had gone quiet, but I was too busy to keep up with the detail of parliamentary life. Meautys explained that Edward Coke – who, to my best knowledge, had never even been to Cornwall – had become the Member for Liskeard at the last election.

'What does he hope to do? Who cares if Guy Mompesson ends up paying a fine or giving up a monopoly?'

'Mompesson is only the prelude to the real investigation, Coke's real object.'

'Into whom does he want an investigation?'

'You.'

A-ha, my brain repeated, more brutally now. The game is revealed, first in its true nature, and second in its sheer, circular spite.

'Bacon, he has begun with an investigation into the collection of bribes in your years in public office.'

I laughed in genuine disbelief. Do you remember when I told you that ours is a world of bribes? When I said that I would prefer not to take them, but if I did so in England, the claimant would protest that I was not being fair? But remember too when I said that I was the most honest of judges precisely because I love the law, precisely because I do not let the bribes sway me.

Now I was all cold contempt. 'Does he look into his own collection of bribes when he was a judge?' I heard my own snarling anger. So now Coke came for me; I should have guessed. *Let him come*, I thought, fists up. *Let him fucking come; I have* nothing *to hide.*

'There are existing complaints against you,' Meautys said.

Now, this did surprise me. 'From whom?'

'From people who bribed you, in whose favour you did not find.'

Once more: do you see it? Do you see the trick in English justice? People complain not that I found unfairly, but because their bribe did not work! 'And did Edward Coke go and find these complainants themselves, or did he just get lucky and bump into them in the street and extract from them some old gossip?'

Then Meautys said very gravely: 'It has progressed a good deal beyond gossip.' He handed me a scroll that bore the seal of the House of Lords. I broke the wax and read:

TO THE VISCOUNT ST ALBANS, SIR FRANCIS BACON

YOU ARE SUMMONED TO A PANEL OF YOUR PEERS
TO ANSWER CHARGES AGAINST YOU THIS THURSDAY,
NINE IN THE MORNING. FAILURE TO ATTEND MAY
LEAD TO YOUR EXPULSION FROM THE HOUSE AND A
CAUSE FOR PROSECUTION.

It was signed, the Earl of Southampton. Only then did I fully understand the trap. This was a much wider plot than Coke merely trying to settle a score. I did not even know if Coke was the originator of the plot, or whether it was Southampton, or Suffolk, or even the Carrs, whom I had ever so morally left alive in the Tower, free to connive if not to walk the streets. I had fought so hard, and so long, to get to this position. How stupid I had been to think that they would allow me simply to thrive. A long time ago, before the plan, before Villiers, I knew that they wanted to kill me because they would have to, because they had never controlled me. They still did not, and so why would anything be different now?

Had success, had money and power made me blind? A whirr of thoughts blew through me. How long had the plot been going on? How had both Meautys and I missed it until it had got so late? Who else was in on it? Meautys? Villiers? No, of course not: I had to keep calm. Remaining calm is the first, the most important, rule of power. I had to remember who I was, and how hard I could fight – how often I had won, as well as lost. I told Meautys to find out the specifics of the charges brought against me: who had accused me, what had been the elements on which the accusation rested. Over the years, I had been given so many gifts – yes, of course bribes, though none ever requested by me – but I had never allowed it to cloud my judgement.

Meautys was back with me before noon with details of the first complaints. One was by a man named Edward Egerton. Oh, God, I knew this fool. He was suing half the names in England, an inveterate case-bringer. Every judge knows such men, who use the law to settle the most minor grudge, and what a bane they are. They are always the same, when bringing a case egregiously, self-servingly, they have to believe that they are fighting some epic battle for morality. Anyone who does not help them, or find for them, is cast into the role of evildoer and the world becomes a great conspiracy of evildoers. I had forwarded a few of his cases and passed on some of the others. He had sent me small amounts of money on occasion – and more regularly, letters of bright outrage that I had not been persuaded to find for him.

Another complainant was a man named Christopher Awbrey. I could not even remember who he was. He claimed he had forwarded a hundred pounds to me to have his suit settled quickly and I had then attended to it. I tried to think. I could not recall it at all. There has been so much work over the years, how can one remember everything? Meautys then said very gravely: 'There are a good deal more complaints.' I was shocked by this. There was a sudden, awful pressure on my skull, pressing down on my brain. I thought again about who was in on the plot, and something truly awful occurred to me.

For three days, I had been asking to see the King, but he had not sent for me. He was only at Whitehall, not even out at Theobalds. In the past, I could have just turned up unannounced but in recent times, I always sent word I was coming. I understood that this gave Villiers time to slip away if he wished not to see me. But now that I was asking, and the King was not responding, it seemed impossible that I should just turn up. Before, he would have been happy to see me within the hour. Now there was silence. My breathing grew short. Was it possible that the King was in on the plot? Was it possible that he knew the trap that was being set?

I had to see him. *I had to.* If I saw him, I knew he would save me. I knew he was easily swayed, but if he saw me, surely he would remember how loyal I had been to him. He would not be able to deny it – no one had worked harder, had been more loyal. That would surely count for something. (Would it not?)

'Are you all right, Bacon?' Meautys asked in his emotionless way.

I leapt to my feet. '*What do you think?*' The pressure on my skull had a simple, thrumming phrase running through it: *Can your intelligence save you now, Bacon? Can your intelligence save you now?* 'I have to go,' I snarled. 'I have to go and see the King.'

The next thing I remember, I was running along the Strand towards Whitehall. I remember the street was full of bodies, unusually for Westminster, yet the river seemed so silver and still. Was something happening? Did the whole world know what I did not, that the game was about to change again? Still I ran. I am not young now – far from it. The exertion made me perspire, the muscles in my body screamed. Sweat ran down my back, under the compress of my jacket, and down my forehead.

The palace was before me, and I stopped at Scotland Yard. It was here, before the King inherited the English throne, that his Scottish ambassadors came to pay court to the old Queen. Two countries, forever divided, now united. Scotland Yard remained, a shiver from our disunited past, a time when I was just plotting and rising. But can the past come back and overwhelm the future? Now *I* was falling. I staggered into the grand courtyard of the palace, wide and filled with the tricksy, mercurial light that follows the river. The ground was covered with a golden sand and, across the courtyard, the great doors of the palace were open, people washing in and out: servants, secretaries, aristocrats. I saw in my mind's eye, the Queen, Villiers and I standing on the other side, on the wide staircase, awaiting the arrival of the King, that day when our plan came together, and our victory came to us.

Everything about the future had seemed so assured. Now it was in tatters.

A guard of nine soldiers in feathered caps stood in a line before the doors, as they always did, and all with their left arm outstretched, holding pikes. As I approached them, I saw the captain, on the far right, shift on his feet. We knew each other, had a friendly relationship. I expected him to greet me, but instead he puffed out his chest and cried in a loud, clear voice: 'Enemy approaching! He shall not pass!'

I stopped in my tracks. *Enemy?* Then one by one, the eight other guards made the same puff-out motion and began to yell: 'Enemy approaching! He shall not pass! Enemy approaching! He shall not pass! Enemy approaching! He shall not pass! Enemy approaching! He shall not pass!'

Enemy? Enemy? Breathless, I stood before them, understanding what this meant. They were not going to attack me. I was not that sort of enemy. No: the King had forbidden me to come into his presence. And so I understood the truth. Villiers had said that day of the masque for the American princess: it has to be over, and now it truly was.

I blinked in that strange, riverside daylight. Then slowly, the great doors of the palace pulled shut, ceremonially excluding me from the royal presence. The nine guards and I stood in our strange, mute opposition. I turned away, the pressure on my skull a banging drum now, and with each blow, it felt like I would collapse to the ground: *no, no, no, no, no*...

I started to turn in a circle, my feet soft against the courtyard sand. For the first time in so long, I did not know *what to do*. I: who always knew what to do. I remembered that day when Villiers first came to

Gorhambury and I hid in a high window to watch him. The cabbage white butterfly danced on the other side of the windowpane; I tried to touch it, through the glass. Now I looked up. My eyes ran madly along the lines of windows, searching for a sign of him but there was none. Let me throw myself now against the glass. Let me see now if he was hiding, watching me, our positions entirely reversed. I was turning around and around, and then I started to shout: 'Villiers! Villiers! Villiers!'

People in the courtyard were staring. Perhaps they thought me mad. Perhaps I *was* mad. Or perhaps they thought I would soon be dead, and as on the day that they – I – had hanged Mrs Turner, they would come to jeer and clap. I kept turning and turning, shouting: 'Villiers! Villiers! Villiers!'

But he did not show himself. He did not even come to look. But I knew he was there. I could feel, in my bones, that he was there, watching me fall.

*

It was high spring, the day of my hearing. London's chestnut trees were aflame with cones of white blooms and the air was itchy and green with pollen. It is no distance from York House to the House of Lords, an easy walk I would make most days when I had work to do in Whitehall or Westminster. But that day I did not walk. I did not want London's greedy eyes upon me, in the moment of my possible degradation. Yet all I could think of was, why does he not write to me? Is he afraid? Is he protecting himself? Perhaps he thinks he is protecting me, that to have him so obviously in my corner would threaten me.

Perhaps he is saying to the King, you have to save him, you have to stop Southampton. I wondered at this last possibility. Perhaps he thinks that if I knew he was helping me, I would not resist being clever with some enemy of mine, and reveal the game, or at the least not fight as hard as I might. Perhaps he loves me. Perhaps, perhaps, perhaps. Those who are falling, those who once lived in the world of certainty, become refugees in the world of perhaps.

The medieval manor-house building, in which the House of Lords had been housed for hundreds of years, awaited me. As my carriage rolled up to its entrance, tens of lords were entering. As I got out, they – various earls and marquises, barons and viscounts, like me – watched my arrival. None of them jeered and none of them wished me well. They were waiting to see what happened, waiting to commit until they knew how the game would play out.

When I reached the stateroom, it was full with the lords of England. I took a deep breath as I entered, seeing scenes I had, of course, seen before in trials and hearings – but then, I had been the lawyer, not the accused. There was a brief pause in the excited chatter at my entrance, a curious, seasick kind of hush, and then a busy resumption of muttering and cruel laughter. At one end of the room was a dais with a long table, at which no one sat. Meautys had been unable to ascertain who was on the final panel. They had kept the information closed. The King – and thus Villiers – could influence the panel. If there was no Southampton and no Suffolk, it perhaps suggested they would quietly help me, and perhaps that was why they were not seeing me. (Perhaps, perhaps, the world of perhaps...)

There was a seat in the centre of the room where I was to sit. Today I was an inverted star in the firmament, the bright and brilliant thing that was here to be traduced. I walked towards the chair, holding my breath, taking my time. Sitting down, I could feel the eyes of the earls of England on me. I let their eyes run over me, and determined to hold on to what was mine: my trust in my own intelligence. I lifted my chin and nodded confidently to those I knew. Some nodded back, but only out of English politeness. They were being too careful to communicate support.

I became aware of a presence near me. I turned. It was Southampton, that long line of a man, that shadow of the Devil. He did not nod, but only stared as he had the night the Globe burned down. If he was sitting next to me, then he was not on the panel. 'My Lord,' I murmured, nodding so serenely it was almost sarcastic.

'Do you remember how you once conspired to put me in gaol, Bacon?' he spat. He did not call me by my title. He did not lower himself. 'Now I am going to do it to you.'

I gave a very shallow nod. 'I was just serving the Crown, my Lord, as well you know. If anyone put you in gaol, it was the late Lord of Essex. I did nothing.'

'*Nothing?*' Southampton roared, loud enough for people around us to turn and look. 'I know that you are a canker in the flesh of this country, and men like you – ugly, effeminate little scribes, bookish scholars – have no business running England.'

'Then who should?' I asked, obviously to provoke him into some stupid answer about himself. I know that in another situation, he might have reared up, made some threat, but he stilled himself in the presence of his peers.

'You look unwell, Bacon,' he spat. 'I hope that you make it through the trial.'

'Bacon will live to plot another day,' I said, looking away from the Earl and up at the dais.

Southampton brought his mouth close to my ear: 'Will he, Bacon? *Will he?*'

I blinked once, heavily, feeling fear, but hoping I did not show it. A door opened at the side of the room, and the panel of lords began to troop in – those who would judge me. Southampton settled back into his seat, but from the corner of my eye, I could see him staring at me.

The hearing began with a description of the charges. There were twenty-seven cases in all to be considered – *twenty-seven!* – and they went through them one by one, asking me to respond, when I had been given no chance to prepare. It was a roll call of political artifice: a collection not of crimes but of *anything* my enemies could unearth.

'Can you tell us about the alleged bribe from Mister Egerton, Lord St Albans?'

That was easy to knock away. 'Egerton is a courtroom belligerent. He uses the courtroom as other men use food, daily and greedily. He needs it. He has more cases on the go at any one moment than any person can count.' There was some friendly laughter in the room. 'He sends bribes. I do not act upon them. There is not a judge in London who has not received a gift from him. Call any judge in the city right now. They will confirm that.' I looked at Southampton. 'Save perhaps the Member for Liskeard.' There was a rustle around the room. People must have known that the Member for Liskeard was Edward Coke. I had named aloud the bringer of this artifice, implied that I understood the game. It was not me who had blinked first.

'In the case of Hodie versus Hodie, you were sent a dozen golden buttons?'

I felt encouraged so I laughed ostentatiously. 'Do you truly propose the Lord Chancellor of England is to be bribed for the price of a dozen buttons? I cannot help what people send me. Again, judges get sent things all the time.' I wanted to repeat this fact; I wanted to expose its truth and so the lie of the basis for this process.

'What about one hundred pounds from Sir John Trevor?'

'A New Year's gift.'

'Sir Edward Shute sent you a number of wall hangings.'

'Sir Edward is my good friend. He likes me to have nice things.' There was genuine, good-humoured laughter now.

'A diamond ring from Sir George Reynell?'

'I have no memory of such a ring,' I said with a bored sigh. (Do you remember when Carr said the same in his trial? Well, *this* is how you feign ignorance in court.) 'Does Sir George have a letter of thanks from me? Any evidence of its existence?' I paused. 'Perhaps an invoice.' Now bright, partisan laughter.

There were more than twenty further accusations and I tried my best to bat each one away. Birthday gift, New Year's gift, payment for legal advice. Often, I genuinely had no memory of the thing – or even the case – and had to think on the fly, to make up an explanation. Sometimes, the name belonged to someone I would have considered friendly, and it was a shock to hear them accusing me. On and on it went. A hostile panel member asked me,

witheringly, how come there were so many serious accusations when all my answers were so banal.

'Ha!' I went, as if I mocked the idea that he thought
he had delivered some *coup de grâce*. 'Because, sirs, we
all know that the cases are weak. They seem thin because
they *are* thin. This is all an artifice to bring me into disgrace, you know it and I know it. I am probably the most
honest lawyer in the kingdom.'

English gasps everywhere – *how dare someone say the
truth!* – but I did not fear it. I was cracking the lacquer
that surrounded this artifice, and I knew that I was winning now.

'The truth of the matter is this, my lords. My answers
are banal because the allegations are banal, and we all
know it. We know that Edward Coke has concocted an
inquiry against me, and we all of us sit here and pretend
that he has not. Let the record show that I am saying to
the panel the truth of the matter. In England, judges are
sent bribes. When a case comes before a judge, the plaintiff
will send me a letter outlining his position, along with a
bribe. Name anything you like: your dozen buttons, your
unseen diamond rings, your hundred pounds. He hopes
to sway the judge. And here is the truth of the matter:
most judges are swayable. Why not investigate Mister
Coke and see how many times he found for the person
who sent him the biggest bribe?'

Quick whispering in the court, the lacquer splitting
open. 'And now, my lords – gentlemen – I invite you to
examine my decision history, every single case I have ever
sat. You will find no pattern of finding in favour due to
the size of bribe, or even the existence of a bribe, for

sometimes – occasionally – a person will send none, perhaps because he has nothing to give, and yet still I find in his favour. Why? Because his case is good. There is no other reason, *save* reason. I am a lawyer who loves the law. Every one of you might have views on my morality, my politics, my service to the King – but not one of you thinks I am truly a crooked lawyer. I may end up sitting in hell next to the Devil himself, but even he would not be able to find a case in which I have not acted honourably and fairly.'

Someone cried, 'Hear, hear.'

'Ruthlessly, sometimes against my own best interests, I find fairly. I ask you again, go examine my judgements – every single one. If you can find a single case where my hand was swayed by bribery, I will sign any document you wish, admit any crime you wish. But I know that you cannot. The truth is this. Every single one of these names you throw at me now would not have a single word to say against me if I had found simply in their favour. The fact they complain is not because of the bribe he – unbidden – sent me, but because the bribe did not sway me. Find me guilty if you wish, gentlemen, I cannot know if you have already made up your minds. Or if *certain* lords in this realm –' I did not go as far as to look at Southampton now '– wish to persuade you how to find. But I know this, I can face God. I can face my King, and say, I have been an honest man and I have served my country as well as I can.'

I finished speaking with a tired thump of a sigh. There was a small silence; one could almost hear the air moving around the chamber. And then, from somewhere, I heard a pair of hands clapping, and then another, and another. I looked around. Men were beginning to stand up. Others were stamping their feet. Now I felt my body relax. I let myself smile a little, began to nod to those who applauded me. Was it possible that English fairness, our supposed native justice, would find me after all; I, who had found so much in it?

The panel called a close for the day. As I left the House, to my surprise, lords approached me and said I had spoken well, or that it was a bad business, or that I had shown England the stuff of which I was made. I felt hopeful. More than hopeful. Thanking those who spoke to me, I walked down into the Old Palace Yard, where my carriage had waited all day. My heart was thumping in my chest. I leant forwards, not sure if I might faint, breathing hard. Somewhere in the distance I heard a water-seller's cry: 'Clean water from a safe well! A farthing a gulp!' Nothing would have been finer, more cleansing in that moment. I stood up, to call the water-seller, but as I did so, a grey blur passed in front of me. I felt an immediate coldness run through me. I knew at once the buzzard of a man staring back at me: Edward Coke.

'Bacon,' he said. 'I am told you did well at the panel.'

'What did you expect? You know I am a good lawyer. I can defend myself.'

He sniffed and looked to one side. 'And I, Bacon, can prosecute.' He looked back at me, held my eyes for a moment. 'But my prosecution today does not go so well.'

'It is not *your* prosecution,' I said, feeling how parched my mouth remained. 'I am a lord of this realm being tried by my peers.'

He nodded, taking the put-down that I had a title and he did not. 'Do you think the King would protect you from a corruption inquiry?'

'You use an indefinite article,' I replied. My tongue was sticking – glued – to the roof of my mouth. 'This inquiry feels very definite to me.'

He smiled. 'But *do you* think the King would protect you in a corruption inquiry?'

A lawyer knows better than to answer hypotheticals. 'It is not for me to say what our monarch *would* do. All I know is that His Majesty knows my loyal service. I hope that has some value to him.' I paused. 'But I believe he dislikes you, Coke. That is why he pushed you out when you did not know when to keep your mouth shut.'

Coke's eyes flared, even as his grin remained plastered to his face. There was something so indubitably evil about him in that moment, it actually frightened me. 'Then tell me this, Bacon. Do you think that the King would protect you in a sodomy scandal?'

I froze. I watched him staring at me, his grin now turned into a hate-filled smirk. I knew that he had already worked out the answer. I am a sodomite, so is the King. Yes, yes, the King wrote books about the perils of the sin. People lie all the time: it is their most natural instinct. But Coke had been in as many interrogations as me, more perhaps. Where I use quiet solicitations, he breaks wrists. I think of Gervase Elwes, the keeper of the Tower, who did not realise it was wrong to let the Carrs poison Overbury until it was pointed out to him. That is the truth of men's moral depth. No wonder that the least moral men of all become very religious. It provides them cover.

'Do you not think,' Coke was saying, 'that if there was a sodomy inquiry at court, the King might want to see very swift action against the criminals concerned?'

Coke stroked his long beard. There was the most uncon-
scionable look of smugness about him. 'I wonder whom
he might arrest. My Lord of Buckingham perhaps, who
people agree was your catamite before he was the King's.'

Did people think that? Carr had said it after his trial.
But I had never otherwise heard whisper about the two
of us. I held my nerve. Again, I did not know what people
did or did not agree, but I did know that a lawyer likes
to fish in order to find evidence.

'Well,' I said, 'why don't you ask the King his views on
such an accusation? Maybe you could ask him in the
presence of George Villiers? I am sure it would make for
a very interesting conversation.'

Then Coke burst into sweet, bird-like laughter. 'But,
Bacon, I was speaking to my Lord of Buckingham only
the other day.'

Hearing that, I flinched with fear. 'I did not think you
were friends.'

'Oh, we are more than friends. Did you not hear?
Buckingham's brother, John, is to marry my daughter.'

I felt a crack in my chest. 'What...?'

I sensed that Coke knew he had me. Furrowing his
brow, he feigned a moment of realisation. 'I *think* that
means that Villiers and I will soon be family.' I felt my
chest tear open, my knees weaken, my bones crunch.
Villiers had betrayed me. But it was about to get worse.
Coke smiled horribly. 'And so I suppose you do not know
the other news? My Lord of Buckingham is to marry too.'

'To whom?' I asked in a dread way.

Coke paused, enjoying the moment. 'To Lady Katherine
Manners.'

'The Earl of Rutland's daughter?'

Lady Manners was a very great heiress, and no doubt that was part of her appeal. But that was not what horrified me. Her mother was the sister of the Countess of Suffolk. Lady Katherine was the first cousin of Frances Carr. *Villiers was about to marry a Howard*. The game had changed again, but this time, I was the one who had been outplayed. The whole damned trick was revealed. Villiers did not need me any more. I had outlived my usefulness to him, but a Howard bride would be endlessly useful. There is no friendship in power, I had once said to him, to mean that we should be friends. But he'd only remembered the first part.

I felt the tears welling in my eyes; I blinked them away. Coke drew himself very close to me, spitting his words so that I felt them on my face. 'The faggot has abandoned you, Bacon. He has revealed the moral worth of all of your kind, every single filthy one of you.' He gave a low, brutish laugh as he pulled away from me and began to speak loudly and officiously. 'Tomorrow, whatever the outcome of this panel, I will moot a sodomy investigation to the court. I will name you as the first person to be investigated, but say that there are others. How fast do you think the Howards and the King will act against you to stop the investigation spreading towards your *erstwhile* catamite? The news will be very popular in the streets. "Good Judge Coke!" the ordinary common idiot will bellow as they tear any suspected sodomites from their homes and gut them in the street. "Good Judge Coke, Faggot Judge Bacon," they will shout. I already have the men who are instructed to begin the riot that will fill the streets. Hearing of this, the King, on Villiers' advice, will move quickly to quash it by surrendering some... low-hanging fruit.' He laughed viciously. 'And aren't you the lowest *fruit* of all, Bacon?'

I thought I had seen the trap, but I had not. 'What evidence do you have?' I asked weakly.

He looked incredulous. '*Evidence?* What evidence do I need? I am not you with your fine philosophical views, Bacon. I can send covert guards down to the riverside at midnight and round up every faggot whore they'd find there. I will pluck out their ribs one by one and plunge them down their bloodied throats until they beg for mercy and confess to whatever I wish. Or I will go to your staff at Gorhambury and threaten their daughters and wives with heresy or witch-craft charges until they agree to speak against you. They have all colluded in your sins, one way or the other, by action or omission, so they all deserve whatever they get. I do not care. I will burn them all. And as they gasp their last breaths, they will cry, "Bacon! Bacon! It was all Francis Bacon!"

'Once your name is out there, who knows what will follow? If you are lucky, you will go to the Tower.' A shiver ran down my spine. 'If you are not, they will send you to a scaffold. And if you are very unlucky, a mob will come to York House, storm the doors, tie your hands and drag you like an animal through the streets. Francis Bacon, who rose so high and judged so fair, they will pelt you with rotten fruit, and clods of earth, and stones from the road perhaps, and they will run you up to the Covent Garden orchards and hang you from a high branch. And when your neck goes *snap!*' – he yelled that single word, and just for a second, I heard Mrs Turner's body slam through the scaffold trapdoor – 'I wonder what posterity will remember on the subject of Francis Bacon... Philosopher. Politician. Scientist. Sodomite.'

'What do you want?' I asked quietly.

'Confess to these corruption charges. Do not fight then any further. Give me my victory. Go off to your ignomini-ous future, utterly ruined. Give me my revenge so that can begin my return. Take your chances with the King Maybe he will pardon you. Maybe he will not. I do no care. With you gone, I can make my return work. With you gone, I am the best lawyer in the land.' *Ugh*... 'If you take my offer, my worst enemy is *metaphorically* dead. I you do not, Bacon, you can be *literally* dead, and you books will be banned, and your name, and your work erased from posterity.' A small yet emphatic pause. 'So Bacon... which do you prefer?'

*

Apparently, there was much gossip and confusion as to why, after my brilliant defence of myself at the panel hearing, I should go home, write to the King and confess everything. Meautys told me it was quite the mystery. There had been talk that the King would end the corrup-tion inquiry quickly, that he would overcome whatever plot was afoot and save his good old *Beicon*! Some people said that I had looked ill that day in the court and that was why I had confessed. Some said that there was some other, obscure reason; that there must be some secret, deeper plot. *Who knows how Bacon's wicked brilliance works?*

I confessed to all the charges of financial corruption, offering my resignation from all my offices of State. The letter was forwarded to the Lords and then to the King. That night, a group of earls appeared outside York House, drunk, I think, shouting. I went to my window – hiding myself, like a pathetic little mouse – and watched them in the Westminster moonlight. One of them, a tall man, all long limbs and a voice hoarse with beer and hatred, was yelling: 'Bacon! Once you are in gaol, we will find a way to get you! Remember Overbury, Bacon? Remember what happened to him? Overbury was safe in the Tower but died all the same.' Cruel laughter and me hiding myself at a window again. 'Remember the Earl of Essex, you *cunt*, remember what you did to him?' I did not see the men's faces, but I did not need to. 'Now it's finally time for you to get yours!'

In the early morning, after a sleepless night, there was more commotion outside York House. I found my servants pulling a paper down that had been nailed to the front door. They did not want to show it to me, but I insisted they hand it over. I looked at the paper and, in an educated person's hand, the words were written:

WITHIN THIS STY, A HOG DOTH LIE
THAT MUST BE HANGED FOR SODOMIE

*

On the day of sentencing, Meautys arrived at York House with the judgement. I had already sent word that I would not be attending the panel in person. It was not required that I should, and perhaps everyone would be grateful that I did not. The two of us were silent a moment, me sitting in my office overlooking the river, Meautys at my side. I took a breath. 'Read it,' I said. My secretary looked down at the paper scroll he was holding. He unwrapped it, drew it long between two hands. He paused a moment, a heavy, heartfelt sigh, then began:

'Firstly, that the Lord Viscount St Albans, Lord Chancellor of England, shall undergo a fine of forty thousand pounds.' I trembled to hear it. My wealth was great now, but such an amount would ruin me. 'Secondly, that he shall forever be denied any office, post or employment in the State or Commonwealth. Thirdly, that he shall never sit in Parliament, nor come within one mile of the court or London.' I thought I might be sick. 'And lastly—' Meautys' voice faltered and I heard the containment of tears. From Meautys, who had never shown emotion once in all these years! 'Lastly—' Again, his voice failed.

'Say it, Meautys,' I said, the words rasping my throat.

'Lastly, he shall be imprisoned in the Tower for the rest of his life, at the King's pleasure.'

I had to sit down. I had not expected that, not the Tower, not for life. I tried to gather my thoughts, but my head was swirling. I felt if I stood back up, I might collapse. I did not deserve this. This, which had been my greatest fear, the thing that haunted me most: to vanish into the Tower.

No, I tell you again: I did not deserve this...

ON THE SUBJECT OF
FRANCIS BACON

*E*ndlessly, I was thinking: *What did I do wrong? How did I fall?* I knew that at the core of my destruction was my break with Villiers, but did I do so much that was wrong that he could turn against me so? Could he have done nothing more to save me? Or did he not even try? I tried to think back to all the times we were together, just the two of us. I searched those occasions – the words, the promises, the talk of the future, even the kisses, my cock sliding inside his body, the soft look of happiness on his face, how sweet it all was, how revelatory. I just did not believe he had felt nothing for me. Perhaps he had turned against me. Perhaps he felt he had no other choice. Perhaps there were threats. Here I am, again, then: another refugee adrift in this world of perhaps. None of it mattered now. I lay in the damp darkness of my cell, as Overbury had once, left to my bitter reflections.

So I decided to give myself over to hating him. Even if Coke was threatening to blackmail him, he should have come to me. He should have trusted more in me than in their threats. Did he not see how he had put himself at risk? Now he was alone in the lions' den, and I, the only person who could truly be trusted to protect him, was here.

No, I did not feel sorry for him. I hated him now. But in the long, lonely hours in my cell, I dreamt of him too. I fell asleep and I dreamt of him – the hazy, unknowable figure he had been at Gorhambury; that first day we kissed down by the Ver River; happy and playful walking along the ancient paths between the wheat fields; beneath me, together, in a window, me inside him in the moonlight. Had those things been real? I dreamt of him saying mysterious things to me – philosophical things, intriguing things, loving things. What had been real and what false? It seemed impossible to discern. I dreamt of him in the moments when he was most vulnerable – the boy afraid, the innocent thrown into a vicious game, terrified of his own death, asking for my protection. When I awoke, for the first moments, I thought softly of him, before I became aware of where I was. And always my cock was hard. How stupid men are.

I wrote to Villiers, saying: 'You have nothing to fear. Release me.' (No reply.) In total, I wrote five – or was it six? – letters to Villiers from the Tower. (No replies.) I heard rumours, via Meautys, who came loyally, of a plot to strip me of my titles, my estates, properties, even my books. They wanted to denude me of everything. I wondered at the legal process they might use, but I accepted that they did not need a process. I was a prisoner in the Tower of London and a friendless one at that. I felt a deeper chill. What process had they used against Overbury? Cakes and jellies.

Good old Jonson visited me regularly. He tried to bring me only good news, but I could easily winkle things out of him. He could not save himself from my interrogations. Under my careful questioning, he revealed that Villiers had already married Katherine Manners, in a wedding attended by many Howards, including the Earl and Countess of Suffolk, who had returned to favour. On the day, Villiers had brightly said he had no opposition to the release of the Carrs, Jonson told me. This astonished me, but I suppose the game plays on. Who knows what deal he cut with Suffolk? I cannot pretend to be amazed that people in power do amoral, heartless things. What on earth do I expect them to do – feed soup to orphans, holding a golden spoon to their lips?

But at night, I lay on my stone bed, staring into space and I did not sleep much. In the Tower, the rats rustle beneath your bed and if you sleep too soundly, they come into the warmth of your covers, and so you wake with rats in bed with you. If you scream, the guards come and tell you to shut up. Those same guards once bowed to you, but now, like those at Whitehall that day, are instructed to imprison you. These are the small, unexpected signifiers of what it means to fall so absolutely.

Shall I tell you how in the Tower, with no other work to do, nothing to fill my life that had always been so full, I had time to write? Will you fold your bookish hands and say, 'Oh! That's nice!' whilst I languish in a cell for the rest of my life? Will you say, 'Now you have all this time to do some proper work!' whilst down the corridor, a woman on the rack screams the names of Jesuit priests she is now only too desperate to betray? Then fuck you.

Time has to be filled with writing because otherwise, terrors fill it instead. I was desperately afraid of torture. Do you think it could not come to me? Then let me break the truth to you: it can come to anyone who enters this place.

Meautys sent more and more paper to my cell, ink for my quill. I worked on my *History of Life and Death*, my encyclopaedia of scientific knowledge. I wrote my utopia fiction, *New Atlantis*, years after that night when Jonson and dead Shakespeare had mocked me as a poor storyteller. In it, I told of a new dream world in which fairness, reason and liberalism would reign unchallenged, and scientist-philosopher-kings would rule benignly and with love. And when I pandered and wrote a dedication to His Majesty the King, I scratched it out and put the manuscript away, ashamed of myself. It was all I could do not to burn it on a fire. Save, of course, there was no fire, and so I shivered with it next to me in my damp cell.

At night, I often could not sleep for fear of what would come next – Coke's sodomy accusation, torture, death – and I felt my unburned writings near me. Do you want me to tell you they offered me great comfort? They did not. I have grown to hate my own work. I should have spent my life searching for love, not posterity. I should have recognised it when it came and treasured it. I did not. All my work does now is mock my failings. Mrs Turner called me a moron, and I was shocked. I should only have been shocked that no one called me it before. I am the cleverest man in England, and its biggest moron too.

*

About four weeks into my incarceration, Jonson came to visit me. He had already been twice, as much as he was allowed. It was not like I had a bevy of friends queuing up along the river to see me. There was no sort of sunshine that day, the kind the London sky loves to torture its inhabitants with: a cold, grey gauze utterly bereft of joy. As we walked around the courtyard, we kept our coats buttoned up. Jonson would have been happy to hear me speak ill of Villiers but I did not want to that day. I spent enough time thinking about him. Jonson started telling me about a masque he was writing, named *The Gypsies Metamorphosed*. He talked about how innovative the masque was going to be, how it was going to change masque-writing. It would be the story of gypsies transformed by goodness into Englishmen. This made me laugh, and I asked what was innovative about Englishmen praising themselves. He laughed too, and as he did so, his eyes flitted to the other side of the courtyard.

'Isn't that...?' he began. I looked too.

There was a dark-haired woman across the courtyard. I recognised her voice before her features. 'Anne, darling girl, do not fuss around with that cat. It is a foul prison puss and clearly it has the mange.' As her face clarified, I saw her sadder, older: Frances Carr, with her young daughter. The girl was exquisitely pretty, with tumbling blonde curls, the very image of her father. Then Frances's head turned, with the puzzled air of one who realises that they are being watched. When she saw me, her eyes widened with surprise. I bowed to her, and instinctually Jonson and I walked over. As we approached, her look of, well, more shock than surprise did not fade.

'Mister Bacon,' she said. She did not call me by my title.

'Lady Frances.' I smiled at the little girl who looked at me cautiously, as children do when strangers approach and evidently know their lady mother. 'Good day,' I said to her, as she nestled into her mother's long, full skirts.

'This is Anne. Say good day, Anne, to Mister Bacon.' The girl sweetly curtseyed and said it. Frances patted the child's head, who looked up at her mother. 'Anne, sweet, go and play for a moment. I wish to speak to Mister Bacon. He is an old –' her beautiful eyes flashed uncertainly at me '– an old friend.' The child ran off.

'How are you, Frances?' I asked.

She looked back at me and smiled, relenting from her earlier frisson. She sighed. 'I heard of your fall. A very great scandal, they say.' She shrugged, laughed. 'Like you are the only corrupt man in England.'

I said nothing of that. 'How fares your husband?'

She continued to look at me in that blank way. 'He and I... are separated now.' Her eyes became alert – first to me and then to Jonson who stood slightly behind me. She looked to one side for a moment. There were tears in her eyes. 'But I suspect you knew that, Bacon.'

In fact, I did not and it gave me no pleasure. Carr ate hearts like most of us eat apples. Now he had eaten hers. I thought of that pretty, confident, determined young woman with whom I had strolled in a pear orchard, how she had toyed with the white pear flowers as she tried to charm me. It was not that many years before, but both of us seemed so transformed by time and hurt.

I looked at Jonson and he nodded and took a few steps away.

When he was gone, I said, 'I think a great deal of Mrs Turner, do you?'

'No,' she hissed. Her anger surprised and then intrigued me.

'You never see those yellow ruff collars in London any more,' I said, persisting in picking at what made her annoyed. 'People have turned against them. I always admired her for how she transformed her life from nothing to something, no matter the sins that brought about her destruction.'

'Ha!' Frances went, mercilessly. 'The woman destroyed herself. She destroyed herself and she destroyed Robert and me too.'

Now I felt annoyance; self-serving, I know! 'How did she destroy *you*?'

'Because it was she who introduced us to that world of poisons!'

'That does not mean you had to go and apply the poisons! You were perfectly capable of saying no, Frances. What you did, you did for love, and that is the truth of the matter.'

Her eyes were round with anger, her cheeks still red. 'You know nothing!' she spat – actual spittle sprayed from her lips. Then she said it again, more quietly: 'Nothing, Bacon.'

'I know that killing one's enemies is wrong.'

She laughed so brightly it almost became a shriek. 'Do you, Bacon, then why do *you* do it?'

I felt revulsion towards her. I remembered how my outsiderness had been used against me. She had done the same with Mrs Turner, letting her hang whilst she lived on.

'You are the worst sort of person, Frances. You are nothing save what your fate has given you, and yet you behave as if you are the wronged party. I admired you when first

I knew you, when you were seeking your divorce. You asked me once why should you not pursue your happiness. I thought you were right: it was a very modern thing to say, but now I see you are just a cauldron of selfishness. You have nothing *like* a heart beating in your chest.'

She seemed quite stopped. I doubt anyone had ever spoken to her that way, not even Edward Coke on the day of her trial. Then a smile appeared on her lips.

'If I die tomorrow, Bacon,' she almost whispered, 'I die a Howard, and that means I die better than you. There is nothing a dog like you could say to me that could even touch me, that could penetrate my skin. You claim to love modern things, Bacon. I will let you flatter yourself that you and I are the same, but we are not. This is England, and it shall remain so. People like me will decide what matters – not you. You are nothing, Bacon. Even if I die in this place, I will be immortalised in history books. People will gasp at me and my story, when you –' she cast her hand across the courtyard '– you wrote some silly books once that will have meant nothing. *You* will have meant nothing.'

How briskly she turned and marched across the court-yard, towards her little daughter, who had been alerted by her mother's sudden shouting.

Jonson strolled back towards me. 'So, you managed to upset her, then?'

I sighed. 'I think we probably upset each other.'

'*Quid pro quo*, Porkchop,' he said. I was not looking at him directly but could feel his gaze on me. I called the guard and said I was ready to return to my cell. Just at that moment, another guard – a more senior one – appeared and called over the first guard to confer with him. The two of them muttered together, now and then taking glances at me. A deep and vicious dread gripped at me then, burning down through my flesh, filling me with terror. Was this it? Had Southampton or Coke or – Villiers – come up with a device to effect my destruction?

The more senior guard called over to me, in a bright and agreeable voice: 'Lord St Albans!' Prisoners are always called by their name: *Bacon!* 'Lord St Albans, return to your cell and prepare your things. The King has granted his pleasure. You are to be released.'

A wave of hope – no, joy – swept across me. I turned back to look at Jonson. 'Do you think…?'

He shook his head, his wide grin half happy, half confused at my sudden change of fortune. 'What?'

'Do you think this is *his* doing?' Jonson was gazing at me. And then I said that magical name: 'Villiers.'

'Oh, no,' Jonson said. 'No, Porkchop, no.'

*

My release came with many conditions. I was to be banished to a country village named Fulham, far from London. I was still forbidden to enter the city or approach the King. I was housed by Sir John Vaughan, a man I should have regarded with suspicion because he had connections to the late Earl of Essex, but who in fact treated me with great kindness. He gave me a bedchamber and a second room in which to write. From my writing room, I composed letters as well as books. I wrote first to the King (which was allowed) and then to Villiers. To the King I wrote: 'Let me live to serve you, or else life is but the shadow of death,' and to Villiers a note merely saying thank you. I had no evidence that it was he who had saved me from the Tower, but I could not think who else it could be.

More news emerged in the next days. There were rumours that the Carrs would eventually be released but not yet, and Villiers was now fully allied to the Howards – there was not a paper's width between them, by all accounts. (Perhaps, then, this had been a last chance to save me.) The King had taken to declaring that this was the *happiest* kingdom in the world, in which all sides were reconciled, and old enmities forgotten. But where in that happy kingdom did I exist? The King would forget I ever existed. But I was not angry; I know what princes are – heartless, monstrous things. We exist in their world only from one blink to the next.

At Fulham, I worked on my revised version of *The Essays* and then a work of history. My *History of the Reign of Henry VII* was designed as a new kind of historical work, in which two eras – or monarchs – might be compared to examine how power and kingship operate. With whom did I compare the great Tudor Welshman? Why, with a 'great' Scotsman, of course, his great-great grandson, our own king. (I toadied before, and so I can toady again.) I wrote to Villiers once more, this time to tell him of the book I was writing, to tell him I was well and happy and hopeful, and that whenever he was ready, I would see him again. Then, finally, I got a reply. He agreed to see me the next day at noon in Hyde Park. I was beside myself with joy. I knew now that he would reveal to me his plan for how I would be saved and returned – perhaps to court, perhaps to him.

That evening, I stared up into the darkness of the chamber Sir John had given me, at the ceiling which was softly indigo in moonlight. I was going to see him again and we would walk into some woodland at Hyde Park. He would say he had always loved me, he had never stopped loving me, and he had come to save me. I wondered if we would end up fucking. But I did not truly care about fucking – I just wanted to see him.

In the morning, I told Sir John I was going out for a ride in the carriage. He reminded me I could not go to London or near the person of the King. I laughed and told him not to worry, I was hardly going to turn up at court, demanding an audience. (Although it was still not so long since I had run to Whitehall and done just that. But now everything was so different.) I told him all that was behind me now. He laughed indulgently, I knew, at the fallen man.

It was an overcast sort of day, warm enough but with a white-grey haze blocking the sun. I arrived at ten minutes before noon. I waited for ten minutes, then twenty, then thirty. Villiers was a young man of fashion and fame, so of course he was late. But when I had been waiting forty minutes, at half past twelve, I began to wonder if perhaps he had changed his mind. I felt my skin becoming hot with worry. And then, three-quarters of an hour late, I saw a large blue carriage approach us. It was not identifiably Villiers' yet I knew, deep in my hollowed heart, that it was him. It was like I could sense his presence, like it communicated itself to me through the air.

The carriage trundled right up to mine, and when our windows were parallel, I saw him looking out at me. He was gazing at me, not quite smiling, but rather studying me in his hazy way. He got out of the carriage, and I followed suit. The two of us stood, facing each other, watching each other. The world seemed completely silent for a moment, a different kind of silence; a true stillness existing between two people, perhaps.

'I am happy to see you,' I said.

He kept gazing at me, but I could not read his expression. 'Shall we walk?' he asked. He pointed down towards a small clutch of trees that fell away below us. To reach it, one had to descend a rippling slope, covered with thick, unkempt country grass. 'Down there?'

I was guessing he wanted more privacy, away from the carriage drivers. He was dressed fairly simply, in one of his blue silk suits – the fabric was exquisite but elegantly restrained. The colour of his ruff collar was a bluish pearl grey. It was the new fashion, the next saffron-yellow. He carried a wide-brimmed fawn hat with him, decorated with the latest thing, a purple-green Indian peacock feather, a signifier of someone very, very rich. We began to walk, and his expensive pale blue shoes – the heels ivory, enamelled over wood – quickly became muddied. No doubt he could afford just to throw them away, and buy a new pair – a new pair every day!

A westerly wind raced across Hyde Park, down the Thames river valley. The wild open country beyond Hyde Park was scented sweet on the breeze, hawthorns and sycamores, water in the ground and meadow flowers. It was coming close to midsummer now, almost two months since my fall. How dizzying it had all been, such a turning of a circle. And here I was, back again, at the foot of the mountain, but at least alive – and looking up.

'You look very handsome,' I said to him as we walked. He turned to me with the hint of a smile, but his eyes fell away.

'I thought you would look a hundred years old.'

I exhaled sharply, happily, at his cheek. 'How old do I look, then?'

He sniffed. 'Eighty-five.'

I burst into laughter, remembering how funny he was, and how at Apethorpe and Gorhambury I had been surprised by his humour and irreverence. We came close to the clump of trees I had seen from further up the hill. We had been walking several minutes. The conversation had been sparse. Eventually, he pulled something from inside his jacket.

'Look,' he said, 'I have a letter from the King.'

Ah, I thought, now the plan will be revealed, in which I would be given a route back to power. Stay at Gorhambury for a year, let everything die down. Write some marvellous book that all of London acclaims, until you are applauded back to power. A new secretaryship – a wholly new role – that the King could create at will. Then, after however long, I would come back, and he and I would resume our love.

The letter was not in an envelope, but was a scroll, the wax stamped with the royal seal. It was in the form of a proclamation. I did not understand the lawyerish formality. He handed it to me and I opened it.

There was nothing much to it at first. The King apologised to his loyal servant but there was not much he could do. The basic judgements of the panel were to stand: I was not to return to power, I was not to return to the King's person. I looked up at Villiers, whose eyes were on me, hard and unreadable. I felt the first pang of doubt.

I read on. The King could mitigate one thing, it said. He would write off my fine, but there was a condition. I was to sign the lease of York House over to the Duke of Buckingham – to Villiers – and then, after so doing, I was never to write to him again. I could not return to London, but I could live outside in some country village like Highgate or Hampstead, not too far away, where I could receive friends.

I was gripping the scroll in my hands, still scanning the dreadful words. Dazed, I could not think of a sensible thing to say. 'You want York House?' was my best attempt. 'Why?'

'I said I liked it.' His voice was matter-of-fact, rather heartless, truth be told. 'Now I want it. I think I am owed it.'

'*Owed* it?' I cried. On what basis was he owed what I had worked so hard for, what I had dreamt so long about?

'And I want you to leave me alone, to stop bothering me.'

'*Bothering* you?' A gust of wind blew across Hyde Park. It was so hard in my eyes that I blinked, and there were tears on my lashes. 'We were in love,' I said. 'It was you who said we were.'

Villiers took a step towards me. Our bodies – our faces – were very close. In another universe, I could have thought he was going to kiss me, were it not for the words that I had just heard.

'You are ridiculous,' he spat.

I understood nothing of what he was saying. 'What?' It was like we were each talking alien languages.

'You heard me,' he said, just as diamond-hard. 'You are ridiculous, and most of all, you are ridiculous because you cannot see the world as it truly is. You see it as you want to, to flatter your own, vain self. You owe me that house because of everything you did to me. I have come to take my due. I want my due...'

'*What?*' I repeated, not understanding what he even meant, but this only made him angrier.

'You pose as the moral man, the liberal man, the *modern* man, but I see nothing in you that is any different to Suffolk, to Southampton, to Coke. Oh, you do not torture, Francis Bacon? How fine for you – but you see no issue in using the evidence gained from others' torturing. How moral.'

I still did not understand. I had been talking of love, and now he attacked my morality. Why? How can one talk honestly of love and be attacked for one's morality? I turned from him but he grabbed my shoulder and yanked me around. I almost toppled, he grabbed me so forcefully. From where did his violence come? Still I had no clue.

'You stand at the edge of the world to which you aspire, for which you plot, to enrich and empower yourself. You tut and wag your finger, and say, "Oh, why can you not be as fine as me?" then watch the bloodied bodies pulled from the Wakefield Tower. You leave your spies to be murdered, go and stand at the scaffold of those who you have tricked to their death, and cry, "Oh, isn't the world unfair?" I despise you, Bacon. I despise you.'

Despise? It felt like my chest, my lungs, were pushing upwards at my throat, choking me, killing me.

'I went to see Robert Carr,' he said.

It surprised me. 'At the Tower?'

'Yes.'

'When I was there – you went to see him when I was there?'

He laughed cruelly, as if I was so pathetic, so solipsistic. 'He told me all about you, how you pursued and bothered him, how he was hardly seventeen years old and you came at him with offers and seductions—'

'No, that's a lie!'

'He said how you badgered him to let you fuck him. He did not want to, how you disgusted him, but he was afraid of what you would do to him, this powerless boy from Scotland, in London only a few months. How in the end, he had to say no so brutally to drive you away, and that he used to lie awake at night, wondering what vengeance a powerful man like you might wreak on him.'

'No, no, that's not true! He was horrible to me, cruel, years afterwards—'

'Because he hated you so much for what you had done to him! And look at me, I wish I had been as strong as Carr and resisted you, but this is the world men like you create for boys like me, these are the choices you give pretty boys, beautiful women, any woman, in fact – two choices: this world, or oblivion. And even if we choose oblivion, the threat remains that you will destroy us out of sheer vanity and malice.'

'But you were so ready to kill the Carrs.'

'Because that was what you made me think this world was. I played the game I thought I was supposed to. I have learned well, Bacon, for it is you who took my face and forced it up against the grubbiness of your world. And when I asked you to kill the Carrs, remember, you said yes, and why? Because of my arse. You almost killed people because of my arse. Sift that through your morality.'

He stopped talking. I was astonished by his words. I recognised nothing about how he described me.

'I...' My voice faltered. I did not know what to say. I was afraid of the truth, the truth which seemed reluctant to come out. 'I met you and everything changed. I fell in love with you, and you gave me an intensity of happiness that I thought I had been so... so clever to exclude from my life. But you showed me the value of love. You showed me how it could transform... a .person.' He was listening to me speak. 'When you lay in my arms at Gorhambury and dreamt of quiet country lives together, I thought that – I do not know—' I felt emotion welling up in me and I wanted to push it away, but it came at me, in great crashing waves. 'I knew that we were in love.'

He was gazing at me. *Are you mad?*

I could not believe how hard – how vicious, and how dishonest – he was being. 'Don't say things now just to hurt me.'

'Hurt *you*? Do you think that boys like me, who look like me, crave the attention of old men like you, who come into our lives and whisper of what you can give us as long as we slip down our britches and let you fuck us?'

His words were like a knife cutting into my flesh. 'You do not have to do it!' I yelled.

'Yes, we do!' he yelled right back. 'We have to play the game that *you* constructed.'

'Why?'

'Because we cannot tell what we'll lose if we do not! And because this is the world you have given us. You did not tell us that any other existed. You said that the first time, that if I did not want to kiss you, you would give me ten pounds and never hold it against me. And that was what I was worth, in that moment, my whole

333

future: ten pounds. I did not know whether I could even trust or believe you. You could have been lying.' He laughed blackly to himself. 'Do you remember when you told me about the maid you gave five guineas to let herself be fingered to protect Frances Carr, in her virginity test? You thought you were so clever. It never occurred to you who that girl was, and whether she truly wanted those five guineas. You simply made a joke about how she got her five guineas and opened a shop on Old Jewry. "She was happy." Who are you to decide if such girls are happy? Or young men like me, on whom old fools like you and the King prey?'

'*Prey?*' We were in love!'

'Love?' he cried. 'Can you truly believe that I could have loved you? That day, down by the river, when we went for a walk, and you confessed you desired me, and I kissed you, I was terrified. Terrified of doing it, of not doing it. Your whole value for me was based on my being able to seduce old men. So I went along with it all, because I thought I had no choice, even though you *revolted* me—'

'No!'

'Well, I do not have to be afraid of you any more, Bacon. You pose as the outsider, but you were as *inside* as they come. You call yourself an outsider so that you can have permission to take what you want, use up who you want, be as hypocritical and amoral as you want, and then flatter yourself that you are unlike those you despise because you are The Outsider.' Now he was raging, ranting, cruel, cold. 'Fuck you, Francis Bacon! Fuck you! I hate you! And I always hated you, and I am glad now that you are excised from my life!'

My head felt heavy; I felt dazed by his words. I staggered away from him, my hands reaching out for a small tree to steady myself. The bark was so rough it almost cut the palms of my hands. I fell forwards, letting my forehead touch the bark. Its hard, cracking edges were painful where there was no flesh between the skin of my forehead and the bone of my skull.

'When did you decide to act against me?' I said.

Ugh, he went – out loud, *ugh*, just like that! 'Oh, your vanity remains, Francis Bacon. You think it was me who turned against you, but it was you who turned against me.'

I looked at him, standing a short distance from my shoulder. 'I do not understand.'

'Ha!' he went cruelly. 'The cleverest man in England does not understand – when it serves him well to act stupid. You turned against me when you saw a pretty boy you thought you could exploit. You turned against me when you seduced me and saw me as nothing but a plaything—'

'*You* seduced *me*!'

'I was twenty, and you were a grown man! An *old* man! You turned against me because you were the one with all the power, and you knew you could use it against me, if not to harm me, then to direct me and coerce me!' He took a step towards me.

'Did none of it mean anything to you? Was it all just a... just a *game*?'

In that moment, seeing the anger in his eyes, the power in his youthful form, I felt fear, but then something changed. His anger seemed to abate, vanish into nothing. Just a haze of sadness remained. 'Francis, at Gorhambury, I did not lie.'

'What?'

'The things I said at Gorhambury were true. I was afraid, I felt so lost in this frightening new world into which you led me. I thought, if I make myself love this man, he will protect me. If we can love each other, I can be safe with him. And you were the most remarkable person I had ever met, and you looked at me and saw something in me. You, with all your intelligence and brilliance, saw something in *me*. You cannot know how beguiling that is, to some country boy.' *Beguiling*, that word; that word I thought might never apply to me. 'Anything you said or warned me about, about age, or fate, or the future, I did not care. I was alive with the possibility that someone like you, so intelligent and insightful, would even deign to look at me.'

I felt such hope in that moment. Maybe things could repair, revive. But then his back straightened; his face grew cold and severe. 'But then that day, at Greenwich, when you so breezily released me, I realised that you were the one with the power, the one who had the power all along. I realised that in falling in love with you, I was deceiving myself, just as you had deceived me. I knew I was nothing to you, not truly, just some stupid and pretty boy, nothing more. The game was *yours*, Francis Bacon, not mine. You invented the game, and I was just a pawn you played with in it. Later, at court, you only wanted me back because someone else wanted me much more. Knowing that, I saw definitively that you cannot love. Because you are too poisoned by your desire to control things, even how I felt about you. You just wanted to possess me once again because you wanted to know that you could control me. That you could control love.'

'No,' I whispered. I could not hear another word. I did not want to hear his truth, *this* truth. I wanted to hear my own, in my own head. I am the cleverest man in England. In posterity – the only place that *truly* matters – they will call me the inventor of the modern world. I will live in my truth, not *his*.

I started running away from him, back up the slope we had just descended. At first he did not move, his contempt was too great. Then he began shouting: 'Bacon, come back!'

I ran, stumbling up to the brow of the ridge, to where our carriages still waited. The wind was fluttering around my body. I did not know what to do. Get in the carriage, return to Fulham, pretend that this had never happened? I could not. I just could not. I saw in the distance, the city: London. Desperate, maddening, awful, life-saving London, the only place in the world where sinners can be safe: I wanted to be there then. I wanted to walk in her streets – if only one last time. I wanted her to throw her arms around me and say: you are alive, Francis Bacon, how we missed you, now you live to plot... (Oh, you know the fucking rest.)

I was running down a rough path along which Sunday carriages paraded. Only dimly I became aware that Villiers had started to run behind me too. 'Francis, stop! Stop, Francis! Come back!' Now he called me Francis – why, to manipulate me into obeying him? Confused, heart-broken, I came to a stop, breathing hard. I wanted to turn back and face him, in hopes... In stupid hopes...

The wind kept fluttering, attacking me, mocking me. I understood then, that I was at an end: the end of all that I had ever been and had hoped I could be. I never would be a better, greater, man now. I would hide away hole myself up, protect myself from any kind of hurt or harm. But what kind of life is that? Life – love – is risk and to cauterise yourself from love is to stop living. But again, that is your tragedy, Francis Bacon, the wind whispered. You were always hiding from love, and from life, Francis Bacon. You sought posterity because you could not bear the risk – and joys – of being alive. But in the end, inevitably, love came to you, and look, it has killed you.

Still I ran, turning downhill, stumbling but managing to stay upright. Villiers, so much younger than me, was quickly at my side. He threw out his right arm to barge me over. I kept my balance and shoved back at him. I am bigger than him, and my weight easily knocked him over. I heard him crash to the ground, the crunching of his body as it fell hard. I kept running and soon I had got to the edge of St James's, where the city is throwing up new streets, a suburb for the rich just outside Westminster.

There in the distance I saw the royal guard – four or five men – standing with pikes and feathered caps. I stopped, not knowing quite what to do. They looked at me with the sort of quizzical face that suggested that they knew they were supposed to do something, that they vaguely remembered seeing me before, back in the days when I still existed in this world. (Only two months ago!) Then I heard Villiers' voice: 'Men, I am His Grace, the Duke of Buckingham!' At this, they straightened up sharp-ish. They *knew* they'd seen him somewhere before! 'This is the infamous enemy of England, Francis Bacon! He is forbidden to come near the person of the King and to enter London! Stop him! Protect your country and your king! Stop the traitor Francis Bacon!'

Traitor? *Traitor?* The guards rushed at me. I felt their mass envelop me, a fast, looming shadow, a blackness swamping my form. I felt their fists and their feet slamming into me, the storm of blows coming down on me, as I heard them shouting:

'Traitor!'

'Thief!'

'Faggot!'

'Fool!'

Did they say the words or was it just my shame inventing them? Their violence shocked me, made me go still. Make no mistake: I felt every single punch and kick, until my body was reduced to nothing but a ball that children bash around in the street, hollering and cheering as they kick it and score goals. But as I lay there, hammered by blows, my world unravelling, everything I thought I might be exposed as a lie, I thought of only one thing: that night in Gray's Inn, when we lay together naked, not fucking, just holding each other, knowing that we were in love, knowing I was a good man still.

Was what he said true? I did not know how it *could* be true. (But why would he lie? To protect himself? To hurt me?) It was as if the entire world had spoken one way, and then, just like that, it started to speak in another. And in that different way, it said that I was not a good man, but an evil one. (How could that be?) I had thought that I would write history, but now history would be written *about* me, and not necessarily as I had imagined.

Eventually the beating stopped. The blackness parted, and the shadow bodies of the guard stood in a circle around me, so that the spare, white daylight could fall through. I blinked at the sudden illumination. At the edge of the dark circle of men appeared Villiers. The wind was blowing his reddish hair around. His hazel-green eyes were just about visible. And he was smiling – his beautiful smile just the same as his vengeful, hate-filled one, I could see now. The smile belonged not to me, but to him. I had misunderstood all along.

I could taste salty, warm blood in my mouth, running down from my nose. I gazed up at my Villiers, that most beautiful boy in the world, who taught me how to love. I wanted him to see that I am a good man, I am a moral man, I am a liberal man, and I am a man who loves and deserves to be loved. But his eyes – those miraculous eyes – were filled with hatred and contempt.

And *still* I did not understand how that could be for me.

AFTERWORD

Bacon died in 1626, five years after his fall from power, without ever returning to favour. In his will, he left Gorhambury to his secretary, Meautys, who lived there until the end of his life. The King had finally drunk himself to death the year before Bacon died. His son, Prince Charles, also favoured Villiers, although only as a friend, but Villiers was stabbed to death at the age of thirty-five by a disaffected soldier. Prince Charles – as Charles I – was beheaded during the English Civil War. Robert and Frances Carr were released from prison shortly after Bacon's fall but were banished from high society and did not reconcile. Following Bacon's release, Edward Coke returned to favour and power and lived happily to a great age, dying at home in his country estate aged eighty-two.

During the seventeenth century, Bacon's work became more and more influential, although his revolutionary ideas proved controversial. By the eighteenth century, Voltaire was calling Bacon the 'father' of the new world of reason and science. In the nineteenth century, the historian William

Hepworth Dixon wrote: 'Bacon's influence in the modern world is so great that every man who rides in a train, sends a telegram, follows a steam plough, sits in an easy chair, crosses the Channel or the Atlantic, eats a good dinner, enjoys a beautiful garden, or undergoes a painless surgical operation, owes him something.'